Praise for the Garrett Sinclair series

"If you are looking for a good night's sleep, leave this one on the nightstand."
>—Jack Carr, #1 *New York Times* bestselling author of *Savage Son,* on *Chasing the Lion*

"Tata just keeps getting better and better, slowly but surely cementing his future as a thriller master."
>—Steve Berry, #1 *New York Times* bestselling author of the Cotton Malone series

"Tony Tata has written a white-knuckle read that I dare you to put down."
>—Joel C. Rosenberg, #1 *New York Times* bestselling author of *The Last Jihad* and *The Jerusalem Assassin,* on *Chasing the Lion*

"Full of energy and snapping with action, *Chasing the Lion* is Tony Tata at his best."
>—Marc Cameron, *New York Times* bestselling author

"General Tony Tata uses his experience to give us a glimpse into the fascinating world of military intrigue with a real human touch."
>—James O. Born, #1 *New York Times* bestselling author

"*Chasing the Lion* is a red-hot thriller as timely as tomorrow's headlines."
>—Stephen Coonts, *New York Times* bestselling author

BY A. J. TATA

TOTAL EMPIRE

A. J. TATA

ST. MARTIN'S PAPERBACKS

This is a work of fiction. All of the characters, organizations, and events portrayed in this novel are either products of the author's imagination or are used fictitiously.

Published in the United States by St. Martin's Paperbacks, an imprint of St. Martin's Publishing Group

TOTAL EMPIRE

Copyright © 2023 by A. J. Tata.
Excerpt from *The Phalanx Code* copyright © 2023 by A. J. Tata.

All rights reserved.

For information, address St. Martin's Publishing Group, 120 Broadway, New York, NY 10271.

www.stmartins.com

Library of Congress Catalog Card Number: 2022035465

ISBN: 978-1-250-84587-0

Our books may be purchased in bulk for promotional, educational, or business use. Please contact your local bookseller or the Macmillan Corporate and Premium Sales Department at 1-800-221-7945, ext. 5442, or by email at MacmillanSpecialMarkets@macmillan.com.

Printed in the United States of America

St. Martin's Press hardcover edition published 2023
St. Martin's Paperbacks edition / January 2024

10 9 8 7 6 5 4 3 2 1

In memory of my parents, Bob and Jerri Tata, who in 2021 reunited on their sixty-sixth wedding anniversary

The children of those who die in war; the highest authority is specially entrusted with the duty of watching over them above all other citizens.

—PLATO

Empty chairs at empty tables
Now my friends are dead and gone.
—"EMPTY CHAIRS AT EMPTY TABLES,"
LES MISÉRABLES

IF I HAD KNOWN Dr. Zoey Morgan was going to disappear in the Sahara Desert, I would have done everything differently.

But there was no way to know my command sergeant major's daughter, who happened to be my goddaughter, who years ago babysat my kids, and who had been all but a daughter to Melissa and me, would act so impulsively in one of the most dangerous places on earth.

The Sahara reinvents itself every twenty thousand years, a perpetual rotation from lush tropical jungle to barren arid desert and back. Oceans and lakes aplenty in one version; bone-dry and windswept sand dunes in another. In either format, the Sahara has hosted and consumed expeditions, tourists, traders, nomads, armies, and entire species. The Sahara today is the largest hot desert in the world, filled with pit vipers and scorpions to attack you from the baked desert floor and an unrelenting sun that suffocates you from above.

Less than two weeks before Zoey disappeared there, her father, Command Sergeant Major Sylvester "Sly" Morgan, and I were in the Sahara at the direction of the president of the United States. We were leading a subunit of the Joint Special Operations Command called Task Force Dagger. President Kim Campbell had tasked us with rescuing a kidnapped American missionary, who also happened to be a large donor to her campaign. Sly was the ground mission commander of the operation.

To add a layer of intrigue to our mission, we were operating near an obscure terrain feature called the Eye of Africa. It was a twenty-six-kilometer-wide series of three perfectly concentric circles that some postulated were formed by tectonic plate shifts and others claimed were the remnants of Atlantis, as described by Plato in his writings.

Typically, I led these types of missions. This night, however, my chain of command had convinced me against my strongest inclinations to instead fly in the command-and-control aircraft, an MH-60 Pave Hawk helicopter, piloted by the quite capable Lieutenant Colonel Sally McCool.

"Jumpers away," Master Sergeant Randy Van Dreeves said into his headset. We were seated in the cargo section of the Beast, our special operations helicopter that was outfitted with satellite communications and visual displays. We watched the jumpers glide silently through the air toward their target. The Beast's blades chattered against the night sky. Cool air swept through the cramped cargo bay.

Van Dreeves was a talkative California surfer with shaggy blond hair and a lean face. Next to him was Master Sergeant Joe Hobart, a quiet, reserved man with brown hair and the remnants of youth acne scarring. These two men were my most trusted operatives.

The hostage we were rescuing, known as a "Jackpot" in military parlance, was Clark Stockton, a successful rancher in Oklahoma who had been instructing

Senegalese livestock farmers when an unnamed kidnap-for-ransom group had snatched him from Senegal. Americans were high-dollar merchandise in this part of Africa, and unfortunately, Stockton had fallen prey to the grifters a few weeks ago. They had even used his Land Rover as the getaway car when theirs failed at the scene.

The French had wisely placed GPS trackers on Stockton's vehicle in Senegal upon his arrival and had noticed once the kidnappers went to ground that the GPS overlapped with the location of a French ex-pat mercenary turned treasure hunter named Henri Sanson. The French Special Forces conducted a raid on the outskirts of Chinguetti, Mauritania, in pursuit of Stockton and also to reach out and touch Sanson to see if there was a threat to his expedition.

As good as the commandos were, however, they missed Stockton *and* Sanson, but found a farmers' almanac that Stockton was famous in agricultural circles for maintaining, confirming to us that Stockton had been near Chinguetti. As we prepared to rescue Stockton, the French had shared the GPS information and the almanac with us. We traced the vehicle to a different location north and east of Chinguetti and Ouadane that consisted of steep ravines and sharp inclines, a rocky wasteland in the oven-baked Sahara.

The Eye of Africa.

As McCool banked the helicopter, I studied the ruggedized monitor and watched my team assemble in the desert after landing. They moved swiftly over the next hour on a northeast azimuth.

"Dagger Six, Dagger Seven," Command Sergeant Major Morgan said.

Sly was my senior enlisted advisor and had jumped

into the objective area with my team. While we had departed from Dakhla, Sly and the rest of the Dagger assault force departed from Spain to conduct a high-altitude, high-opening-jump offset from the objective area.

"Red zone, over," Sly said. *Red zone* was the code for the ground team reaching the outskirts of the target area directly prior to actions on the objective.

"Roger, Charlie Mike," I replied. *Charlie Mike* stood for "continue the mission."

"Wilco, out."

My men, represented by thermally induced human-shaped black figures on the screen, moved across the rocky wasteland toward the cave mouth near our objective. As one team positioned themselves to provide supporting fire from an outcropping, the other team continued toward the target. The helicopter vibrated as it banked, and McCool came over the intercom saying, "Apologies, sir, we've got a little chop up here from some wind shear."

"Roger that," I replied, focused on the gunfire I was now seeing on the screen. McCool was one of my most trusted friends and soldiers. She was a sharp-witted and talented pilot who had been on my team intermittently for over a decade.

Enemy gunfire, while always possible, was not expected and could only mean a compromise at some point in the mission. The ten soldiers in the supporting position suddenly began shooting into the ridges overlooking the cave mouth as my assault team scattered under withering fire from above. Our intelligence had postulated a few sleepy guards at this time of night, and the belief was that we could get inside the cave to retrieve Stockton if he was there.

A few men had rolled onto their backs and were

shooting upward, at which point I said to my team, "Drones."

"Not expected," Hobart said.

"I'm having the satellite pan out to see if we can get a visual," Van Dreeves said.

"Roger," I replied.

"Dagger Six, this is Dagger Seven. We're taking heavy fire from the ridgeline above the objective and two, possibly three, bogies, over."

"Roger. Recommendation?"

"Charlie Mike," Sly said.

"Roger, Charlie Mike," I replied. "We've got a B-2 bomber circling at high altitude and two A-10s in race-track with us that can be there in two minutes. If you need supporting fires, say the word. Also have casualty evacuation on standby."

"Roger, out."

Not being on the ground as the plan began to unravel gnawed at me not because I didn't trust Sly, which I did completely, but because I felt helpless in the helicopter. I was a passenger, not a participant. And while I understood that my years of combat experience were better applied in the relatively unfettered climate of the Beast where I had full situational awareness, than in the mêlée on the ground where my scope of understanding was largely confined to my immediate geographic area, it didn't make me feel any better.

The scene on the monitor showed the situation on the ground dissolving into bedlam, too, worsening the boiling in my gut.

"Boss," Van Dreeves said.

I looked up at him across from me, his eyes staring at his monitor.

"Roger?"

"We've got two armed drones and one reconnaissance

drone in the area. All VTOL and using pop-up technique." *VTOL* stood for "vertical takeoff and landing." These were hover drones that flew like helicopters as opposed to fixed-wing that flew like airplanes.

This wasn't good news. The enemy was highly sophisticated. Their communications and network discipline were matched by their tactical creativity. Small drones were nearly impossible to defeat on the battlefield, their most common method of neutralization a result of having expended all their ammunition. They gave off little to no traceable signature, negating the effectiveness of our high-tech systems.

"Casualties!" Sly shouted, bypassing the radio procedure of using call signs. I recognized his voice, and that was all I needed to order the Osprey medical evacuation aircraft into the objective area.

"Five minutes. Mark the landing point. Coming in with Apache escort," I directed.

"Roger that!" Sly responded. His high-pitched, barked words came through the radio with the *tap tap tap* of machine-gun fire an accent to his shouts.

Soon, two Apache gunships buzzed onto the screen, pumping 30 mm ammunition from its M230 chain gun into the ridgeline above the objective.

"What is that?" Van Dreeves asked, pointing at the edge of the screen. Our command-and-control software suite included an air traffic control program that identified air-breathing aircraft and missiles. Hobart played with the satellite imagery picture by twisting some dials and spreading the screen with his fingers.

"Something behind the ridge," Hobart said. "Looks like a fixed-wing aircraft."

We had identified a flat road behind the objective area that we intended to use as our extraction point for the Osprey tilt-rotor aircraft to recover our team.

The captors had given no indication of being anything other than a well-disciplined group of thugs who detained Western citizens in exchange for big ransom paydays.

What we now realized we were facing was a high-functioning military team akin to Al Qaeda or ISIS with drones, fixed-wing airplanes, and complex tactics.

"Get AWACS to track that plane," I said. The aircraft touched down briefly, then took off and banked to the north, eventually leaving our field of view.

"Roger," Van Dreeves replied.

On the monitor, an explosion appeared as a blossoming black mass. One of the Apache helicopters had been hit on a run-in to the target.

"Aircraft down," Sly said over the radio. *Destroyed* was probably a better term. There appeared to be little remaining from the state-of-the-art helicopter. We were at a tipping point. Our losses were rising. The enemy was better prepared than we had expected. Our advantage of stealth and surprise had evaporated. We had not accomplished the mission. We had multiple casualties, and we still had the entire force on the ground in a hornet's nest of a firefight.

Did we continue to fight or cut our losses and recover to our staging base?

"Cools, break racetrack and reposition closer to the objective," I said. My instinct made no real tactical sense other than my tactile desire to be able to influence the operation and my refusal to quit. My gut, though, was telling me that we might need extra aircraft to provide supporting fires and/or evacuate personnel.

The medical evacuation Osprey had turned around during its landing sequence as the destroyed Apache had been providing covering fire, and now the essential life-saving support to our wounded was forced away.

"Second Apache going bingo on gas, boss," Hobart said.

The problem with doing operations far from established logistics bases was the extended lines of communication ultimately resulted in less time on station to support the operation. Our rehearsals had estimated no more than five minutes on the objective. The Apaches had burned fuel on the flight in from refueling at a remote runway ninety miles west and then on the racetrack as the operation developed.

"Launch the backup attack aircraft," I directed.

Hobart radioed the aviation commander at our classified forward operating base and said, "Launch. Objective hot."

"Roger. Blades turning. Takeoff in less than one minute," the commander said.

Ninety miles away at two hundred miles per hour meant the two quick reaction force Apache helicopters would be on station in twenty minutes, maybe less knowing their brethren were in a dogfight.

The tipping point loomed large in my mind. Was I pouring more resources into a black hole, feeding my elite teams into an irreversible maw of death and destruction, or would more firepower win the day?

"Status of the fixed-wing bogey?" I asked.

"HQ saying no pursuit authorized," Van Dreeves said. "They might be about to tell us to pull the plug."

"They can't," I said, but I knew they could.

My first glimmer of hope came from Sly, who radioed, "Assault team on the objective. Have relocated with them. Enemy drones destroyed."

"Roger," I replied.

The monitor showed four of my team at the mouth of the cave with maybe ten pouring inside. Incessant gunfire popped as Sly keyed his radio mike. I assumed the soldiers at the front of the objective were Sly, his radio operator, and his two-man security detail. He would want to be outside to be able to talk to me with a direct line of communications uninterrupted by however deep the cave tunneled into the hillside.

As time passed, concern began to grow in my gut. We trained and rehearsed these missions to the point that we knew what should be happening when. From the point of entering the cave to the team emerging from it should have been less than two minutes.

My fears were confirmed when the satellite imagery showed a small group of insurgents counterattacking from the backside of the mountaintop. They were on top of Sly and his three men in now what looked like hand-to-hand combat before we could even alert them.

Helpless, I watched with dread as the scene played out on the monitor. Two insurgents were up and moving, recognizable because they weren't wearing any distinguishable equipment such as rucksacks or radios. In their wake were three motionless bodies.

"Dagger Seven, this is Six, over."

No response.

"Dagger Seven, this is Six, over."

Nothing.

The two attackers were dragging a body into the cave. I continued to call. Still nothing, and I knew it was a hopeless drill. Another couple of minutes passed when the assault team came running out, dragging either one of our wounded or the hostage.

Then, over the central command radio net, came the words, "Jackpot, over." The sender of the message was Master Sergeant Josh Wright, the leader of the assault team and second in command on the ground.

With the American hostage in hand, I focused on Sly and his team.

"Roger. Status of Seven?"

"Negative contact, over."

"Seven and team compromised fifty meters to your west," I said.

The video from the drone feed showed my men move quickly to where Sly and his team had been. They huddled around, some facing outward looking for enemy, while others looked inward, inspecting the damage.

Awaiting their report, I said to Hobart, "Status of recovery aircraft?"

"Just launched them at Jackpot. They're fifty minutes out. Walk to the pickup zone is forty minutes," he replied.

"Not if we don't have Sly and his team," I said. I pressed my radio microphone's push-to-talk button and said, "Status of objective?"

"Enemy neutralized. Maybe a couple of squirters out the back," Wright said. "But . . . three KIA," he said. "Plus, an Apache crew down."

A *squirter* was someone who escaped from the objective area, usually by running. The airplane that had landed might have picked up whoever had fled out of the backside of the complex.

"Roger. Status of Seven?" I asked Wright.

"Negative contact," he replied, which meant Sly might still be alive. Maybe a new hostage for the enemy. If so, it was a tough trade, but one I would accept right now if it would keep him alive.

Then to Hobart, I said, "Divert the pickup to the objective area."

Then to McCool, I said, "Cools, take us as close as you can get to the objective."

Hobart and Van Dreeves snapped their heads up. We were in Mauritania on a highly sensitive and classified mission to recover a hostage. The standard protocol was to exfiltrate to an offset site because the commotion at the objective area was undoubtedly setting off radars, satellites, and other intelligence apparatus that would alert the Russians, Chinese, Moroccans, Mauritanians, and any terrorist groups such as ISIS and Al Qaeda. Piling into the objective area significantly increased risk to the mission and personnel.

But still, my longest and best friend, my command sergeant major, was on the ground in the cave.

"Suit up, men," I said. "We're going in."

2

McCOOL LANDED THE BEAST on the flattest surface she could find. The helicopter teetered gently as all three wheels made purchase with the shale beneath us.

"We have twenty minutes of station time, General," she said.

"If we're not back, leave without us and go refuel," I said.

"Not leaving you, sir," McCool shot back.

"That's an order, Sally," I said. "But since medevac isn't here yet, you can take the wounded back if it's not here before you have to pop smoke."

There was a long pause before she said, "Yes, sir."

Hobart, Van Dreeves, and I ducked as we ran beneath the whipping blades into the cool February night air of the desert. We stopped about twenty meters away as McCool lifted the Beast into an orbit to make herself less of a target. It was a cloudless night, and the shouts of my men could be heard echoing through the wadis and spires of this mountainous landscape.

My two-man security detail, Corporal Zion Black and Sergeant John Wang, joined us. Black was a large man, having played college football at the University of Georgia. Laudably, he had chosen to serve his country in Special Forces before accepting the professional contract he had been offered by the Green Bay Packers. Wang was a heavyweight mixed martial arts and wrestling expert who was a California state wrestling champion. Having grown up on Coronado Island, he'd pursued a career with the Navy SEALs but instead wound up in Marine Force Recon. I chose both men to be on my security team for this mission. They looked like a couple of college dive bar bouncers.

Hobart led us into the objective. My men were hidden behind rocks the size of cars. The landscape was barren of any vegetation and looked a lot like the Mojave Desert, where we trained frequently. Wadis cut paths through the terrain, hillocks rose high into the air, and I could see why this had been a tough nut for my men to crack. It was a defender's dream and an attacker's nightmare.

We reached the mouth of the cave, where Wright had set up a medical triage location. Three men were covered in body bags while four were being treated for wounds by the team medic.

"Any status on Sly?" I asked Wright.

"Negative, sir."

"Anyone go back in there?"

"We're ready to go back in. I wanted to stabilize the wounded first. The rest of the men are over there." He pointed to a large boulder near the cave mouth, where four men were kneeling, shining flashlights into the ground.

Wright and I joined them. Hobart and Van Dreeves were already there. Wang and Black followed.

"The cave has three forks about a hundred meters in," Wright said, kneeling in the middle of his team. "We found Jackpot in the middle one and cleared that, then came back out ready to exfil."

"We saw two insurgents dragging one body into the cave. It had to be Sly," I said.

The men looked up at me. Their faces were unrecognizable in the moonless night, but I recognized their voices as they did mine.

"We must have missed them on the way out, which means they took one of the other routes."

"Of the two options, any idea which one they took?"

"No idea. We didn't know he was missing until we got out here with Jackpot," Wright said.

In the distance, I heard the Osprey medical evacuation aircraft approaching.

"Josh, secure the site, handle the medevac of your troops, and Hobart, Van Dreeves, and I will go into the cave looking for Sly."

"Roger that, sir, but I think you need a bigger force in there, and reinforcements could be on the way. This could be the Alamo in an hour."

"Understand. Give me another team for the other tunnel and one to defend against counterattack from the middle."

"Ready in one minute," Wright said.

Hobart, Van Dreeves, and I charged our M4 carbines and checked our equipment before stepping into the dark cave mouth. Wang and Black followed as rear security. We were dressed in digitized fatigues, lightweight tan boots, Kevlar helmets cut around the ear, CamelBaks, and sand-colored outer tactical vests carrying ammunition, first aid kits, and knives. We turned on the infrared lights of our night vision goggles, which were only visible to those wearing similar devices and would help us maintain some element of localized tactical surprise. Five minutes had passed since we had first touched down. With each passing second, the chances of finding Sly alive waned.

"Alpha team in tunnel one, Bravo team defending tunnel two," Wright said. "You're Dagger team and in tunnel three."

His clarification was for the sake of communications as we improvised to confront this new development in the plan. The old saw about no plan surviving contact with the enemy wasn't entirely true. Planning typically forced you to think through multiple eventualities and resource accordingly to minimize risk. We had a forward arming and fueling base, multiple redundancies in aircraft, and a quick reaction force in Dakhla all because we had mapped out what might go wrong.

There was no contingency, however, where we envisioned one of our personnel becoming a hostage, much less that hostage being my command sergeant major.

Hobart, Van Dreeves, and I snaked our way through the cave. It widened, narrowed, and curved until finally opening to the north side of the mountain where radar had shown the Sherpa airplane had landed briefly. The faint buzzing indicated it was still in orbit or on the ground, perhaps evacuating the insurgents.

The starlit night created enough ambient light for us to see four men standing above one kneeling person maybe one hundred meters away on a plateau. A few muzzle flashes coincided with the sharp ping of lead sparking off the cave mouth walls on either side of us. We took up positions where we were able to focus our Integrated Visual Augmentation System, or IVAS, and see the horror unfold.

Sly was a large man, having spent the last thirty years of his life either in the gym or on combat missions. It was obvious to me that he was the man kneeling with his hands tied behind his back. He was flanked by two armed thugs wearing headscarves and robes. A third man was standing to his side, holding a large sword. A fourth man was on the phone or radio behind the third man.

I sighted my M4 carbine and prepared to fire, when mortar rounds began exploding around the cave mouth where we had taken up firing positions. I squeezed the trigger too many times to remember as the cloud of sand, dirt, and rocks smothered us.

Through the haze, I saw the sword rise and fall before another volley of mortar fire enveloped us.

3

AS I LED THE charge to where Sly lay dead by the executioner's sword, the Sherpa buzzed into the night.

I looked skyward briefly, searching for God and wondering if he was there. The firmament was pricked with a million angry stars. The cool morning air would soon evaporate into stifling heat propelled by harsh winds when the sun rose. My command sergeant major was gone, and we weren't outfitted or authorized to sustain combat operations on the ground for more than twenty-four hours. I sucked in rapid breaths, stifling the emotions swirling in my mind and heart. I thought immediately of Zoey Morgan, Sly's daughter, and the impossible task of telling her this horrible news.

"Boss," Hobart said. He stood there in his combat gear, his IVAS cocked atop his helmet.

I nodded. "Roger. Let's get Sly and exfil. Do we have anything that can track that plane? Drone? JSTARS?" The Joint Surveillance Target Attack Radar System, or JSTARS, often provided additional situational awareness to our missions, but like everything else, the extra time on target had multiplied the logistical issues.

"I've asked," Hobart said. "No transponder. Flying

low to the ground. Not seeing it. Too much ground clut-
ter. Breaking station in five minutes. The usual bullshit."

I looked at Hobart, too overwhelmed to fight the inertia that weighed on every single mission. Shaking my
head, I nodded and walked toward the cave mouth.

Wright and his team retrieved a body bag and secured
Sly's remains. By now, the medical evacuation Osprey
and those that were designated as exfiltration aircraft
had landed on the opposite side of the mountain.

"All wounded and KIA loaded," Hobart said.

I was numb as we picked our way back through the
cave. Arriving at the pickup zone, Van Dreeves called
for McCool to land, which she did after the three Osprey departed. We boarded and remained silent on the
long flight back to Dakhla, Morocco. I stared into the
black night, only getting my own haggard image in return in the plexiglass windows. I wondered how this
could have happened and of course blamed myself for
not being on the ground. After some time, the sloping
desert gave way to water as we approached Dakhla.

We landed and moved into a warehouse on a remote
section of the airfield. As we debarked, I immediately
walked into the makeshift communications suite and
called the Special Operations commander, four-star
general Bill Luckey.

Luckey was known throughout the ranks as a career
climber but nonetheless had been promoted repeatedly,
much to the amazement of many of his peers. It never
surprised me, however, because the military is no different from any other bureaucracy. Those who could
keep one eye on the path forward and the other eye on
covering their tracks always fared the best. I preferred
commanding down, as it were, instead of up. I always
remained more concerned about the men and women
I led than those who led me or my next career move. I

had always believed that if you focused on your troops, the rest would take care of itself, and you would wind up where you could best serve.

Still, this was going to be a challenging call. In one sense, we had succeeded. We retrieved the American hostage. However, I couldn't look at this mission as anything other than a failure. Four of my men were dead, plus two Apache pilots, with several wounded, which reminded me of the perpetual debate between mission and men. Which was more important? I had always striven to balance both and had, until now, believed that it was possible to do just that.

The cost of this mission did not justify its result. Sly and his command team would be regaled as heroes, to the extent we publicized any of this and I was reminded of the saying of one of my former operators, a Croatan soldier named Chayton "Jake" Mahegan, who, whenever we had a KIA casualty, said, "Better to die a hero than grow old."

I wanted nothing more than for all my teammates to be heroes *and* grow old so that they could enjoy the liberties they helped secure. But a soldier's life often resulted in denial of that privilege.

As I pressed the video conference feature, Hobart and Van Dreeves exited the room so that I could have some privacy with my commander.

The screen jumped to life, and I saw the hard angles that were Bill Luckey's face. He maintained a daily workout regimen that kept him in peak physical condition. An Army Ranger and Green Beret, Luckey had commanded at every level from platoon to corps. Now he led the prestigious Special Operations Command headquartered at MacDill Air Force Base in Tampa, Florida. In the background of his video was a lacquered mahogany bookcase with trophies and trinkets from his career, a green bottle of sparkling water glistening with sweat, and a paperback novel split open facedown.

"Garrett," he said.

"Sir," I replied.

After a long pause, he said, "Well?"

"Six dead, including my command sergeant major and two Apache pilots," I said. Followed quickly by, "And Jackpot secured."

"I needed to hear it from you. My team monitoring the radios heard the shit show."

"Roger."

"Anything else before I call the chairman?"

The chairman was marine general Lucius Rolfing, the chairman of the Joint Chiefs of Staff, who reported to the president as the senior military advisor.

"I haven't had a chance to talk to Zoey Morgan, the sergeant major's daughter, yet, or the other families. If we can keep this under wraps until then, I would appreciate it."

"No promises. The bad guys get a vote here. Haven't seen anything yet, but given the enormity of this colossal fuckup, I'd take advantage of it if I were them." He took a sip of his Pellegrino and smacked his lips.

I couldn't help but detect a twinge of satisfaction in his voice. My demise would be one less competitor for future plum assignments and retirement board seats, according to his worldview.

"Sir, when I get back, I'll submit my resignation," I said. I surprised myself with the statement, but it made sense. I had criticized the advancement of generals who had overseen major strategic and tactical blunders, so it was logical that I would hold myself to the same standard.

"It might not wait that long. I'll let you know how my call with the chairman goes, if necessary."

He clicked off the video conference. I hung my head and put my face in my hands. My remorse centered on the six soldiers I had lost in combat and not remotely anything to do with my career or the call with Luckey. I knew that I had fought the good fight and only stayed in the picture to continue to lead the men and women I loved. I pictured Dr. Zoey Morgan, the tall, beautiful, athletic, and intelligent daughter of Sly. This news might completely break her.

To get in front of any leak, I used my personal cell phone to call Zoey. She answered on the second ring. Because it was morning here in Dakhla, it was past midnight her time.

"No," she whispered, knowing that I would only call this late in an emergency. Her voice was hoarse. I had woken her.

"Zoey—"

"Is he alive, General?"

"Zoey—"

"Goddamn it! No!"

I stared at the cinder block wall, wanting to blast through it and free myself of the guilt and responsibility that was crushing me right now.

"I've got him. He died in combat."

A minute of sobs passed before she spoke. "At least you've got him." Another minute. A tear streaked down my face. How much more could we all take? Thirty-plus years of combat. The loss. The grief. Shattered families. Broken friends. An ungrateful political class.

"Goddamn it. I knew this was going to happen!" I let her sob for another minute until she finally spoke. "When you called. I knew it."

"I'm sorry, Zoey. He was my best friend, but he was your father. He was the best."

As a doctor, she understood the finality of death, and

as a devout Baptist, she believed in God's hand in all that happened.

After a long pause, she said, "He died for a reason. I may have it."

I said nothing and waited for her to continue.

She recovered control of her voice and said, "I want to see you the minute you're back. I have something to show you. Can I send it to you?"

I nodded as if she were standing in front of me. "Okay. Use the secure Dagger server. Send it whenever you can. Our comms suite is up."

I stepped into the hangar where my men were cleaning weapons, checking helicopter engines, repacking gear, and doing what they always did—prepare for the next mission. The six body bags lined along the wall were a reminder of today's failure.

On the opposite side from my fallen soldiers was Stockton. He looked sullen, as if he knew the cost to rescue him. I walked across the concrete floor to where Hobart and Van Dreeves were speaking with him. Stockton was seated, his long legs and arms overwhelming the small gray chair with a fold-down tabletop as if it were taken from a fifth-grade classroom. He had hawkish eyes, an angular nose, and a wild white beard that matched his thick, unkempt hair. No doubt he was leaner than when he had entered Senegal on his education mission several months ago.

I motioned for Hobart and Van Dreeves to join me away from Stockton. They stood and walked toward me. I put my hand on Hobart's shoulder and said, "I notified the chairman and Zoey."

"Jesus," Hobart said, running a hand through his hair. He pulled away and turned around. Van Dreeves slid his arm around his longtime combat buddy. Hobart rubbed a hand across his eyes. We were all still running on adrenaline, still in execute mode, fumes being the only fuel.

I gave them a few minutes to recover, then walked toward Stockton.

"Mr. Stockton," I said. "Welcome home." I shook his hand, which was every bit as strong as I expected from, I guessed, years of roping, branding, and riding. "I'm General Garrett Sinclair, commander of the mission."

"Heavy price your men paid, General," he said. His gray eyes bored into me as I nodded. He then watched Hobart and Van Dreeves hug each other for a moment. It was all I could do to hold everything inside. The personal loss was staggering. The echoes of death ricocheted throughout my force, touching them all deeply.

"It's what we do," I replied. "Not going to lie, though, this was a tough one."

"Not sure I'm worth it, but I'll do everything I can to honor their sacrifice," he said, nodding at the six body bags.

"That's all we can ask," I said. "That and any information you might have on your captors. I don't think we're done with them."

Hobart and Van Dreeves returned to join us, taking seats across from Stockton.

"Was going over that with these two gentlemen. Mostly locals from Mauritania and Senegal. They thought they'd get a couple million for me. I speak some of the Senegalese dialects, as well as fluent Spanish, Portuguese, and French. They moved me at least once a day, sometimes two or three times. Usually did it at night. Most of the time, I had a burlap sack over my head and earmuffs on, but I still caught bits and pieces."

"Anything interesting?" I asked.

"One man spoke native French, not the derivatives you get . . ." He looked around the hangar and shrugged. "I just realized I have no idea where the hell I am."

"That's not important," I said.

"Well, I guess as long as I'm with you guys, that's true."

"You're with us. For operational reasons, we can't disclose where you are, but official channels are going to notify your family once we make sure all our assets are safely out of the strike zone."

He swallowed some water from a plastic bottle and nodded.

"My family. Jesus," he said. A tear cut a path down his face. The dossier showed he had a wife of thirty-eight years, five children from thirty-six to twenty-four, two boys and three girls, all involved in his ranching business in some respect. "Just glad Emily wasn't here with me."

I needed to nudge him back to the debrief.

"Us, too. It's important that we get your memories fresh before other emotions come to bear, Mr. Stockton," I said.

He nodded. "I understand." Then, "I'd say there were three things I remember that might be relevant to you guys. First, as I was saying, there was one man who spoke perfect French. It was his native language, no doubt about it.

"Second, I heard them say *pièces d'or* several times. That's French for 'gold coins.' I never let on that I understood what they were saying, but there was a French contingent and a Senegalese contingent. They both discussed gold, like buried treasure stuff."

I looked at Hobart, who was making notes, and Van Dreeves, who was recording this conversation on his MacBook and typing simultaneously.

"Okay, a Frenchman and gold coins," I said. "What else?"

"I never understood this last part, but there was some sense of urgency to their gold-finding mission because they were worried about the Chinese."

"The Chinese?" I asked.

"Yes, *chinois*. And *socle chinois*. A base of some sort. We've all heard about them sniffing up and down the coast looking for a port like they've done in Djibouti, where they've built a full-blown navy base with aircraft carriers and everything—"

He stopped talking and looked around the room.

"What am I talking about? You guys know more about this than I do."

"Maybe, maybe not," I said. "Your information is helpful and important."

He nodded again and continued, "The French guy seemed to have some insight on the Chinese. I personally know that Equatorial Guinea is looking at a deal with the Chinese, so hearing they might be involved in Mauritania surprised me. I only heard him twice, once in two different locations. We stayed tightly packed to minimize footprint, I presume. He traveled in a prop airplane, like a Casa or a Sherpa, something like that."

"An airplane?"

"Yes. I heard it twice," Stockton said. "I've got two Mooneys back home. Wasn't a Mooney. Sounded like a Sherpa when I heard it. But could have been a Casa."

"Hear anything tonight?" I asked.

"Didn't hear much in that cave until your boys came running in."

"Last question," I began. "Did you overhear the name of this Frenchman?"

Stockton took another sip of his water and nodded. His hard, flat eyes leveled on me when he said, "*Le bourreau.*"

The executioner.

4

WHEN WE WERE DONE with Stockton, Van Dreeves was spending an inordinate amount of time on the phone coordinating our return trip.

"What's up with the logistics?" I asked Van Dreeves.

We required three full C-17 sorties to return all our people and equipment back to Fort Bragg and other places in the continental United States. My command team with the Beast and our command pod alone consumed an entire aircraft. Add in six transfer cases for our casualties and we had issues.

"SecState and SecDef just left today from Dakhla, where they did some ribbon-cutting bullshit with a bunch of tech CEOs," Van Dreeves said. "Chewing up airspace and resources. One of our planes got diverted to haul a couple of their limos. I told them we had some casualties, and they basically said, 'Tough shit.'"

No surprises there. Priorities. "Okay, leave some of our equipment here with a couple of guards. We have to get moving."

We decided to leave two of our communications base station contractors to guard the remaining gear, an enviable task here on the Dakhla Peninsula with its pristine beaches.

After getting the snafu sorted out, we departed on our standard C-17 with our dedicated crew that maintained all the appropriate clearances to see our faces, our helicopter, and our command-and-control pod. Somewhere over the Atlantic, Van Dreeves stepped into the command suite and reached into the printer that had been spitting documents into the tray.

"From Zoey on DaggerServe. Told me not to look at it. She wanted me to print it out for you," he said. DaggerServe was our internal encrypted server that operated on the private satellite we leased.

Van Dreeves handed me the stack of papers, which I began poring over about the time General Luckey's executive officer, a Navy SEAL captain, called me on behalf of his boss.

"General, you need to come to the Pentagon ASAP. The boss is here explaining the shit show. Needs you to fill in the gaps," Captain Lars Lufkin said. On the video screen, his head was the size of a bowling ball. His black hair was long by any military standard, reaching down to the ripped muscles in his neck.

"We're headed to Bragg first, Lars. Then I'll switch up and get up there," I replied.

His eyes narrowed, and with a furrowed forehead, he replied, "I think I was pretty clear in my first comment."

Lufkin was one of those officers that wore his boss's rank on his sleeve. Plus, Luckey had probably tipped my fate to him, which would also account for his smugness.

"And I was clear in my response," I said. I touched the End button on the screen as his face turned red and neck veins bulged, the image disappearing like a magic trick.

I took a deep breath, realizing that my career was most likely approaching the end, and that was okay. I could serve in other ways no matter how much I would miss these men and women with whom I labored.

Hobart, Van Dreeves, and McCool entered the pod and occupied their three seats around a small drop-down table. Hobart closed the door behind him, and we were in a secure container in the middle of the floor of the large C-17 Globemaster aircraft.

"If you hear anything to the contrary, we're continuing on to Fort Bragg, where everyone will get reset for future operations," I said.

"Why would we hear anything different?" McCool asked. She was bone-tired from flying the Beast well beyond her authorized crew rest minimums. Her green eyes were bloodshot marbles, and her blond hair was knotted in a ratty ponytail. Her small, upturned nose still had the indentations over the bridge from wearing her night vision goggles.

"There's some effort to have me come to D.C. immediately," I said. "But I want to get everyone to Bragg, and then I'll head up. It's an extra two hours, max, before I get up there."

"It's optics, not timing," McCool said. "We can drop you and then head to Bragg." She was nothing if not protective.

"The only optics I'm concerned about are our goggles and weapon sights," I said. "We've got six dead bodies on this plane. Nothing is more important. Understand?"

They nodded, perhaps surprised by my terse response. We were all operating on frayed nerves.

"Now, I've looked at the stuff Zoey sent. Forget you saw it for now. What do we have on Sly's killer?"

"Didn't look at Zoey's stuff, boss," Van Dreeves said.

"What stuff?" Hobart snapped.

"She wanted me to look at some of Sly's files. I'll brief you guys when I'm done."

Hobart looked at me and then at Van Dreeves, who shrugged.

Van Dreeves typed a password into the keyboard, and the monitor we had built into the frame of the command pod jumped to life with the image of a large man with wavy black hair and brown eyes. He was wearing a khaki explorer's outfit with long pants and a long-sleeve shirt rolled up on his ropey forearms. The man looked like a movie star or professional athlete. He was standing in front of a caravan of camels that were carrying an assortment of equipment. The sky was clear blue interrupted only by the ascending tan sand dunes in the background.

"This is Henri Sanson. He is the French aristocrat that is leading a dig party to the middle of this terrain," Van Dreeves said.

The monitor showed the same feature we had been close to. From its satellite image, it looked like the eye of a hurricane or even just an eye, complete with a dark ridge above serving as the eyebrow.

"This is the Eye of Africa," Van Dreeves said. "Like we discussed prior to the mission, the dimensions are almost exactly those of how Plato described Atlantis. Twenty-six kilometers wide; three concentric rings; large rectangular structure in the middle, which some are saying was Poseidon's Temple, and so on."

"Who cares if this was Atlantis or not?" I asked. I was familiar with the concept of the underwater city that had been the story line of so much science fiction but didn't see the relevance here.

"Whether it is or isn't Atlantis isn't as important as the fact that Sanson believes it might be, and if he believes it might be, then he's motivated to find the gold that is rumored to be there."

"The gold coins Stockton mentioned," Hobart said absently.

"What else do we have on Sanson?" I asked.

"Not much," Van Dreeves said. "He's somewhat of an enigma in French society, but there's this. *Sanson* is the name of the French family that were the executioners. It was a lineage thing, handed down through generations. Instead of working in a coal mine, you mastered a blade and cut off heads."

"*Le bourreau,*" I said in French. "The executioner. That's him."

I remembered Sly and the blade and the mortars and the shrapnel.

"Do we have any way to track him?" I asked.

"Not in that plane, if it's his. Our intel is marginal. The Sahara is the size of the United States, maybe bigger. We're talking about an area the size of Texas where we would be looking," Van Dreeves responded.

"He's got a caravan out there doing an archeological dig in a fifteen-square-mile area. He has to have some footprint and logistics," I snapped.

"Boss," Van Dreeves interrupted.

"I'm not finished. And we know the general location of where he's looking. His technique, it seems, might be to let the caravan move to the dig site, excavate, and, if they find something, he lands in the airplane to check it out. Can't be that hard to find, can it?"

I was fuming. Rarely, if ever, had I spoken to my inner circle this harshly.

"Roger that."

"What about what Zoey sent? Why don't you want to talk about it?" Hobart asked, eyes boring into mine. He was pushing back on me about Zoey, and I knew why.

"I'm reviewing it. Could be something. But it's very preliminary."

"Four heads are better than one and all that," McCool said.

"Not yet," I said. And that settled it for the moment.

They left the command pod, and I stayed inside alone with my thoughts. I reflected on Sly's three-plus decades of service to the nation until our plane began its descent to Pope Field next to Fort Bragg in North Carolina. I stepped from the pod. Saw the Beast with its feathered blades and beyond that the six transfer cases anchored to the floor. My team was sleeping in the red strap seats. As we landed, I could see Sly's daughter, Zoey, waiting at the JSOC hangar, arms folded, shivering in the biting winds sweeping across the deserted airfield.

"Jesus," Hobart said, looking away.

The back ramp lowered with a hydraulic hiss. The team let me lead the way onto the runway and held back as I approached Zoey, who was stoic.

"General," she said.

"I'm so sorry," I said, hugging her. She wrapped her arms around me. Holding me tightly, sobbing into my shoulder.

"What have you done?" she muttered into my Gore-Tex coat.

"Nothing compared to what I intend to do," I said.

Zoey's embrace was strong. She pushed away and stared at me with copper eyes.

"I want in on whatever you're doing."

"I don't think that's wise," I replied.

"He was onto something big," she said.

"Maybe," I said. "I saw what you sent."

"I found more in his safe. Check this out," she said. "It's worse. It's a geometry thing."

She slipped a flash drive into my hand. I looked at it and dropped it into my pocket.

A movement caught her eye across the airfield. She looked over my shoulder and nodded. "Is that him?"

Six Humvees approached the back of the C-17, one for each soldier. The transfer cases would be transported to mortuary affairs and prepared for onward movement to their final resting place.

"Yes," I said. "And the others."

My team assembled at the ramp of the aircraft. Zoey and I joined them. Hobart stood to the right of Zoey, with me on her left. We saluted. Zoey held her hand over her heart. I could feel her shaking, softly crying. I troubled with keeping my own emotions in check. Six soldiers entered the aircraft and reappeared with flag-draped silver transfer cases six times. They carefully loaded each one into the back of a separate Humvee. We stood in formation until the last Humvee disappeared from the apron, on its way to mortuary affairs.

I had done ramp ceremonies hundreds of times. Each one ripped my soul from me, leaving a barren wasteland of brittle emotions skittering around like tumbleweeds. We spent some time hugging one another before I returned to Zoey.

"I have to head to D.C. Not sure I'll have a job when I get back. But I'll text you. I want to discuss this stuff your dad was working on," I said.

Zoey wiped her eyes and nodded. "Look at the flash drive on your flight."

"I will," I said.

"I'm getting mine on this, General," Zoey said. Her teeth were clenched. Eyes boring holes in me. Her anger surfacing.

"Again, I advise against doing anything before we talk."

"No promises."

I nodded and walked to the King Air C-12 that had both of its turboprops spinning.

I was already worried about Zoey, but the fire in her eyes hinted at a pending reckless abandon, like wild horses pushing at a corral.

5

WANG AND BLACK TRANSITIONED with me to the small aircraft we used for shorter flights.

It was late afternoon, and we would be getting to the Pentagon about 5:00 p.m. with no sleep for the last seventy-two hours. Appropriately, the sky was slate gray and dark, the sun blocked by layers of clouds we were flying through.

Wang retrieved a MacBook from his rucksack, and I powered it up to review the flash drive Zoey had given me. As I scanned, I couldn't believe everything I was seeing, but Sly had done a good job of aggregating and synthesizing the information he gathered.

After reviewing Zoey's info and Van Dreeves's intelligence dump on Sanson and synthesizing my own thoughts, I typed up a note to the president and included it in the drive. I rearranged some items and deleted a few so that the hard-hitting information would be apparent immediately. I saved the pictures and notes on the MacBook hard drive and then typed a few words in the encrypted flash drive.

It's a geometry thing.

Then I handwrote a missive on a plain white sheet of printer paper. I folded the note and stuffed it in the cargo pocket of my uniform. Ejected the flash drive and asked Wang for a piece of duct tape, which he gave me. I slid both in my other pocket and watched as we flew low over the Potomac River, finally exiting the clouds that had rocked us in the air. Upon landing, a driver and vehicle from the Pentagon Protection Agency picked us up from Reagan National Airport and dropped us at the River Entrance of the Pentagon.

Arriving in Luckey's outer E-Ring office, I nodded at his receptionist, who stared at me blankly until Lars Lufkin emerged from his office and approached me with his standard Navy SEAL swagger. His large forehead and long hair made him look more like a television actor trying to play a SEAL than someone who lived the code of that special breed of warriors.

"General, the boss has been waiting for you for two hours. He's not happy," he said. Lufkin noticed Wang and Black standing behind me and took a step back.

"Save it. I just off-loaded six bodies at Pope," I said.

He turned on his heel and stuck his head in Luckey's office and a moment later said, "You can go in now."

I stepped inside the office and closed the door. Luckey was nowhere to be seen. I assumed he was in the small bathroom in the back of his office. A large mahogany desk was centered in the expansive room. An American flag stood next to the Special Operations Command flag behind his chair, which was tucked neatly into the opening beneath the top. The novel was still on the desk, and the Pellegrino was in a wooden designer trash can. While I had never employed the "make them wait" tactic, I understood it was a technique to demonstrate superiority and power. Instead, I just saw insecurity and weakness.

On the walls were dozens of pictures and trinkets that military officers collect over years of service. His Silver

Star from the October 2001 Objective Rhino jump into Kabul International Airport was prominently displayed. He had been the Ranger company commander in charge of the assault force. The September 2021 *Washington Post* article dubbing him "the American Warlord" was plastered in the center, framed with triple matting. Offset from the article was a blowup of the picture *The Post* had used. His face was clearly visible beneath sunglasses propped on his head. He wore the standard tan-and-olive combat uniform and outer tactical vest filled with ammunition, radio handset, and medical pouch. He was staring at the camera as if posing for the shot with thousands of frantic Afghans in the background, crushing against Abbey Gate like a mosh pit presses against the concert stage. His blue eyes, blond mohawk, and clenched jaw gave him a movie star image. Between him and the Afghan mob stood a gaggle of civilians, some U.S., and others perhaps from allied nations.

Luckey had been the general in charge of saving the botched retrograde operations in Afghanistan. He had swooped in as a two-star general in command of one of our elite units and stopped the bleeding.

Two years younger than I, Luckey had pole-vaulted to four-star general based upon his perceived performance in that mission. Save a president, make a career. I had spoken with President Campbell briefly about Luckey when she had asked, and I had simply replied, "He did a good job." Which was true.

"That article was something, wasn't it, General?"

I turned around to face Secretary of Defense Angela Blankenship. She was dressed in a sharp black wool blazer and skirt with a white blouse and a string of pearls midway down her neck. Her hair was perfectly coiffed, blown, and freeze-dried in place. She held a pair of glasses in her right hand and a phone in her left. She had entered through the side door from a connecting conference room. Two members of her security detail hovered in a small, dark corridor. She had just been in Dakhla, and now here she was ambushing me.

"Madam Secretary," I said.

"It could have been you, you know?"

I said nothing.

"The article. The fame. The promotion. The command. It was all yours for the taking. But you went rogue. And now you're going rogue again with this Africa nonsense."

"You ordered me on that mission, ma'am," I said.

"I ordered your *team* to do that mission," she replied. "I would have hoped you led from a more appropriate place like your Fort Bragg headquarters or maybe Rota, Spain, or I'd even give you Dakhla, Morocco. But on the objective? Seems you're a few stars beyond your comfort zone."

I said nothing.

"Now you've gotten your command sergeant major killed with your reckless example," she said. "If it weren't for the inspector general investigation on you, I would ask for your dismissal right now, but I believe it's worth the effort to see your actions thoroughly examined."

To be dressed down like this by someone who had sacrificed exactly zero for her country wasn't sitting well with me. If Zoey's flash drive of her father's notes was accurate, Blankenship had enriched herself through her government connections. My anger must have flashed across my face, because the two thugs a few feet away stepped closer to her.

I said nothing.

Anyone who thought generals and sergeants major didn't fight from the front lines didn't understand combat. "Patton at the crossroads" was the epitome of senior leadership placing themselves at the critical point in battle where General George Patton moved to the decisive point of the fight—the lack of command and control at a critical junction where confusion was sapping the momentum of the attack—and personally took charge directing traffic during the World War II breakout. "Jumping Jim" Gavin, the Eighty-Second Airborne Division commander in World War II, made all four combat jumps into Sicily and Salerno, Italy, to Normandy, France, and lastly Nijmegen, Holland. For every jump, Gavin transitioned from individual paratrooper to teaming with a few privates and sergeants who had landed on either side of him, to leading dozens of men against the enemy, often under direct fire.

These men, and others, were my role models for leadership. Air-conditioned offices were for the perfumed princes who believed that longevity in service accorded to them a measure of safety for which their troops were not eligible, a well-practiced "let them eat cake" attitude that had ossified into somehow being acceptable up and down the ranks.

It didn't surprise me that Blankenship had no understanding of either this ethos or the charges she was appointed to lead.

"Aren't you going to say anything in your defense?" she snapped, flustered. She dropped her glasses and bent over to pick them up. Had she not been a woman, I might have played soccer with her head, but my chivalrous streak precluded even considering the option.

"I haven't heard a question, ma'am," I said. "Just some random accusations and opinions proffered by someone who doesn't know me well and who just got back from Dakhla herself. I believe it was you who had strongly recommended Sergeant Major Morgan lead this mission and not me."

She smiled a thin, pressed-lip grimace. Her eyes got distant. She said, "I know you well enough. Whatever suggestion I might have given General Luckey was to nudge you into the proper command role. And my travel schedule is of no concern to you."

"Surely the secretary of defense has more important things to do than dress down some three-star general. Is there something you needed from me?"

"I actually thought I'd come in here and meet you to try to understand . . . and now I do," she said.

"Understand what?" I asked.

"Understand how someone could so breezily toss everything aside and destroy their career. Flame out at three stars, provided you can keep any of them," she said.

"I just do my best every day," I replied.

"You think your sugar momma in the White House will keep protecting you? Not for long."

With that, she turned on her heel, stumbled into the chair to her right, and stepped quickly into the dark hallway with her bodyguards. My "sugar momma" was President Kim Campbell, who had been college roommates with my wife. Before Melissa died, my relationship with Campbell had been good. Now, not so much.

Seconds later, Luckey emerged from the bathroom wiping his hands. He held out a fist for a bump as had become the norm with COVID protocols. I responded in kind and nodded.

"Civilians," he said with a big smile. "Can't live with them. Can't live without them."

"What the hell, sir?" I asked.

"She was the reason we were trying to get you to fly back here sooner. Wanted to bust your balls in person."

"She's going to have to do more than that," I said.

"Be careful what you wish for, partner," he replied.

He stared at the newspaper article framed on the wall and pointed at it. His eyes sparkled. Jaw flexed. Hint of a smile on his lips. He poked a finger at the picture.

"Made my career right there. Probably what she's talking about. Save a few politicians, they owe you. They don't give a fuck about anything else, my friend."

"That was a ballsy move, I have to admit," I said. "But I'm sure you do care, right?" There was a hint of sarcasm in my voice. "Given the risks you took."

"I do, but I'm not going to beat around the bush here, Garrett," Luckey said. "People are calling for your head. Only reason SecDef didn't is she can't because of the IG thing. Plus she's worried about POTUS."

"Sly Morgan was decapitated. Executed. You told me Blankenship wanted him on the mission, not me. What the hell is going on?"

"Decapitated?"

"Someone cut his head off with a sword as we were trying to rescue him," I said. The words were hard to say, their utterance making the memory reappear fresh, as if the incident was reoccurring in real time.

He worked his jaw a few times, the muscles flexing. He often did this when he was processing information. "How does that change the outcome other than making it look worse for you?"

"The outcome is the same. I'm curious why Blankenship wanted Sly boots on the ground there and not me," I said.

After a moment, he said, "She has an issue with guys like us leading from the front. Thinks it's too risky to have someone like you captured with all the intel you have. Thinks they'll torture you and so on."

"Makes no sense," I said.

"And don't even think about going back there. Revenge is never a good option. I saw Hobart put in a request for a C-17."

"We left some stuff there, that's all. Blankenship and her minions chewed up the fleet with her Dakhla Accords," I said.

"Okay, but that doesn't involve you," he said.

"Don't bust my balls, too, Bill. Just trust me for a change."

"Trust you? You just got your sergeant major killed and you're asking me to trust you? You've made the entire team look bad here, Sinclair. The last thing you should be asking anyone for is more rope."

"Three-plus decades of faithful service don't place any credits in the bank?" I asked.

"I just asked the SecDef for more time for you. My ass is on the line. So, no, not when it comes to my career," he said. I was surprised by the honesty, even if it was unintentional. "Your career. The careers of your men," he continued, attempting to recover.

"There are a lot of things more important than careers, sir," I said.

After a moment, he said, "I'm not authorizing you another mission in Africa."

I nodded, reached into my pocket, retrieved the folded piece of paper, and handed it to Luckey.

"Well, then, here you go," I said.

He opened it, took a few seconds to scan it, raised his eyebrows when he looked up, and said, "You're kidding, right? Can't unring this bell."

"I'm sure," I said.

"I can't approve this," he said. "You're the subject of an active inspector general investigation. You just came off a failed mission where your sergeant major was killed. How can you even pretend to do this now? You heard the SecDef."

"It's just what needs to be done. You don't need to approve it. The president knows about it and supports it."

That was always the ultimate hole card. Does the leader of the free world know your plan and support you? If so, no careerist general officer would get in your way. I wasn't sure how much support I would get from Campbell, if any, but those that knew about my close relationship with the president would ultimately defer to her.

Luckey folded the paper and stuffed it in his coat pocket. As I was preparing to leave, a diminutive man with John Lennon glasses and a bald pate entered the office.

Willard Ringley was the Department of Defense inspector general. He investigated, among other things, alleged misconduct of senior officers. He had legions of lawyers and colonels who turned people's lives inside out based upon sometimes true, sometimes untrue, and sometimes directed allegations. Part overseer and part weaponized operative, Ringley managed the optics of the department.

"Will wanted to have a word with you before you left," Luckey said. He continued, "I've got to go brief the chairman on this, so you guys can use my office."

I watched Luckey walk out of the office with Lufkin hustling by his side and couldn't remember the last time I had been so thoroughly ambushed.

"General," Ringley said.

"Inspector," I said.

"Will is fine. Or Mr. Ringley. No one actually calls me *Inspector*."

I nodded.

"I have to ask you some questions, and so I've got Colonel Janice Mixton here to record your answers."

"Shouldn't we be at GTMO?" I quipped. An ambush by the secretary of defense and the inspector general wasn't something I saw coming.

"You mean Leavenworth. GTMO is for foreign nationals," he said. He had a small, round face and wore circular glasses that looked like Venn diagrams trying to overlap inside the larger oval of his facade.

A colonel walked in and sat down and set a small tape recorder on the conference room table.

"You may be wondering why we're here and whether you're entitled to a lawyer, which you're not. The inspector general uses an extralegal means of finding evidence, and our standard is the preponderance of the evidence, not beyond a reasonable doubt. Whereas in a civilian trial I would classify the standard at nearly ninety-nine percent proof, our bar is much lower, around fifty-one percent with me being the judge and jury."

I said nothing. Mixton clicked on the digital recording device.

"General Garrett Sinclair III, I am Inspector General Willard Ringley, and we are in General Luckey's satellite command suite in the Pentagon with Colonel Janice Mixton present for asking and answering specific questions related to allegations regarding your involvement in the death of former secretary of state Kyle Estes, misappropriation of government resources—to wit, an MH-60 helicopter for your private use—and potential collusion with enemy forces including Ben David, Mossad double agent, and Quds Force commander Dariush Parizad. Colonel, can you swear the general in, please?"

Mixton stood up and raised her right hand, giving me an opportunity to stand up, as well.

"General, please raise your right hand and repeat after me—"

I smiled at them both and said, "No, thank you." I did an about-face and unintentionally opened the door directly into Lufkin's face, which sprayed blood everywhere. He had been looking through the peephole the Pentagon senior leader offices typically had to allow military aides to see when their boss might be off the phone or available for their next appointment. Lufkin was holding his bleeding nose and lunged toward me when Wang throat punched him, causing him to double over, gasping for air. Black pulled him by his hair and tossed him into Luckey's office and shut the door. I continued walking while I presumed Black and Wang were serving as my detachment left in contact, providing space to evade the ambush.

Tack one more charge to the list. Assault?

I navigated the byzantine paths of the Pentagon, passing identical-looking men and women in uniform as I had on my earlier walk. I walked out of the Pentagon with Black and Wang scrambling to catch up and perhaps find the Pentagon carpool vehicle that had delivered me here. I kept walking, though, until I got to Arlington National Cemetery, where I stood in the middle of Section 60, the area reserved for those who had served in Iraq, Afghanistan, and Syria. White tombstones stood in formation like a precision military outfit, which, I guessed, they were. I saw the names of many men and women with whom I had served.

I didn't fight the emotions in me and let them flow. In the waning moments of a lifetime of service, I spent a few minutes thanking the men and women that had paid the ultimate sacrifice. Death was the currency of combat. How many did we bring home alive? How many dead? The arbitrage was always the metric that seemed to assuage the guilt. The gray sky, browning grass, and barren trees were an amorphous backdrop to the simple headstones, like the missions these men led, often ill-defined and obscure.

So much sacrifice for such measured gains. Whether the dead laying before me were worth the cost, I didn't know. It wasn't for me to judge. All a man can do is his best. As Melissa had often told me: *Good wins*. But standing among these headstones and thinking of her and Sly's too-early departures, I wasn't so sure anymore.

Maybe nobody wins.

Looking at the tombstones facing Washington, D.C., and the Pentagon, I thought about the juxtaposition. Here lay the dead of countless wars started and mismanaged by often incompetent elected officials and unaccountable appointees. It was as if these men and women were prisoners, their tombstones a constant reminder not to the political elites that snickered at the sacrifice but to those who served; that this was our ultimate destination. The elites would always be in the marbled buildings while cold headstones awaited us on the wrong side of the river.

I reconciled that the decisions I penned on the paper and handed to Luckey were necessary. I had commanded a mission that, while successful, had also failed. It was an odd happenstance that having my best friend killed in combat on a mission I was commanding would occur toward the end of my career. Depending on how my next steps unfolded, I would be proud to go with Sly. A careerist general, a lifelong government bureaucrat, and an opportunist political appointee were a hat trick of fools that only accentuated the decisions confronting me.

I reached into my pocket and knelt in front of a specific headstone. I placed my hand on the back and made sure the clear duct tape held the small device in place near the ground. While I was still alone, I retrieved my presidential burner and snapped a photo of the name on the stone. Then I texted:

Pay respects

Wang and Black had caught up with me by now and pulled up in the Suburban.

Pocketing the phone, I turned around and stared at the Washington Monument poking into the sky like a giant middle finger.

About right, I thought. The political elites' message to all of us.

6

FIVE FUNERALS, A HUNDRED ignored phone calls, and a week later, I and over two hundred soldiers and friends weathered the biting February winds that were hawking over the North Carolina Sandhills at Sly's funeral, the last of the dead from the Stockton mission.

Several years ago, my deceased wife, Melissa, and I had purchased a four-acre piece of land in Vass, North Carolina. The large lake to our east was the one-minute reference point for jumpmasters who hung outside of the air force airplanes with their bodies fighting the 140-knot winds to ensure the jumpers were ready to exit the airplane on the correct drop zone during training jumps.

We had cordoned off one acre of that land and registered it as a cemetery. Melissa and I knew for sure that we wanted to be next to each other for eternity, and we wanted our soldiers and their families to have that option, as well. Melissa had discussed the idea with some of the spouses, and the conversation carried over into the single unit members who wanted to be part of the conversation. So far, thirty-seven soldiers and their families had secured sites. All I required was an affidavit from the soldier and their loved ones, and the designation had to be mentioned in their will.

I had buried Melissa there, and now Sly had joined her. That gave me some modicum of peace to know that they were together. I had fond memories of Melissa and Sly conversing over coffee while Zoey, Brad, and Reagan would play in the family room. I visualized their spirits above me in the sky comforting one another, watching us, loving us.

Melissa's headstone was at the very top of the hill. We had a single plaque above our grave sites that listed our names and dates, mine obviously with just my birth date, and Melissa's showing her dates of birth and death. Beneath the dates was Melissa's guiding maxim, reflected in its simple inscription:

Good Wins

I had reserved two plats for Brad and Reagan, but they were still of that age where death was an abstract notion and not something to be considered just yet, any thoughts thereof otherwise manifesting mortality as a reality they were unprepared to consider.

Sly had commanded a large gathering at his funeral, including many military luminaries who passed through to pay respects and be seen. Oddly, Luckey and the inspector general never showed. I guessed they had given me a few days to mourn Sly, and they would soon be after me with the military police in tow.

Most of the well-wishers had already filtered down to the house, where we had catered food and drinks so that everyone could celebrate the amazing life of a great American hero. My daughter, Reagan, and son, Brad, had come down from Virginia to support Zoey as much as they did to support me. Both Sly and Zoey were family to them. Zoey had become an integral member of our family after her mother's death. Through all of that, she mentored Brad and Reagan as she babysat and cheered them on in sports.

"It's not fair, Dad," Reagan said to me through tears before storming down the hill to the house. Brad was standing alone on the side yard talking on the phone. He was still dealing with trauma related to Quds Force commander Dariush Parizad kidnapping him and strapping a suicide vest onto his body as an insurance policy. It was a miracle that we both survived that incident. Now Sly's death. It was as if the world were turning faster on its axis, aging us all beyond our means. The nation expects its servicemen and -women to execute missions in the common defense, but few understand the full measure of the sacrifice. My kids, my best friend, my goddaughter, my team, my team's families were emotionally shredded right now.

I watched Reagan storm off the hill, long auburn hair just like her mother's flowing over her black wool coat. I was the only one remaining at the top, the scent of pine trees carrying with the blustery wind. Beneath the dark gray sky, the Fort Bragg drop zones were visible to the south, the golf course and lake to the east, and Southern Pines to the west. Forest shrouded the hilltop to the north, and I liked it that way. A black wooden fence separated our land from the trees where long, bony branches scratched at the sky, arms pleading to the heavens, shouting unanswerable questions.

A hundred meters to the south was our two-story farmhouse. It had all the modern conveniences of a new home, which it essentially was, and a basement, where I had constructed a classified command center.

As the sun was setting over Southern Pines, the moment I dreaded most unfolded before my eyes.

She walked in long paces up the subtle grade from the house to the black wrought iron gate that safeguarded the cemetery. Her long legs took measured strides to ensure she maintained balance in her heels along the gravel path. Large copper eyes watched me as her broad shoulders beneath the black wool coat swung with athletic purpose.

After I returned to Fort Bragg from the Pentagon last week, Zoey had been waiting on me, as promised. We went to Sly's house, which she still called home. At first, she had been stoic, but eventually, the veneer cracked again, and the wellspring of deep emotions she held for her father had bubbled up until she got them under control to review with me what she thought she had discovered in her dad's files.

"I think he had a bad feeling about the Stockton mission. He left the files I gave you plus this," she had said. She pointed to a manila folder with some papers and an orange external flash drive. We reviewed the information, which I thought was a good distraction for both of us. The intelligence Sly had assembled was a bombshell if it could be proven. But it was difficult to process because Zoey kept breaking down emotionally.

Today, she seemed more measured, though the finality of it all was obviously weighing on her. At the V of her neck hung a necklace her father had given her with our unit insignia done in diamonds, a glittering lightning bolt against a shield. Her hair was brushed straight back with a slight part on the left side, ending around her shoulders. Her cocoa skin shone in the amber light of the setting sun. A manicured hand with red polish on her fingernails held a blue Solo cup filled with something strong, I hoped. A new gold-and-black memorial bracelet with her father's name on it slid up her wrist as she tilted the cup into her mouth. The scar beneath her left eye looked like a two-inch hash mark.

"General," she said.

I nodded. "Zoey."

She looked away. Her eyes were moist.

"I told myself I wasn't going to lose it today. Dad would want me to be strong." Mist escaped her trembling lips, carried away by the swift breeze.

"You are strong, Zoey. He's proud of you."

She looked at the freshly tilled orange dirt. The backhoe had finished filling the grave about thirty minutes ago.

Sly's headstone read:

Better to die a warrior than grow old.

"Jake's motto," she said. Then after a beat, "He's down there, you know. He came."

She was speaking of Jake Mahegan, a former operator of mine who had left the team and remained available in contract status when we needed him.

"I saw him," I said. "Looks too tanned."

"Well, he is Croatan," she said, offering a smile that faded too quickly.

"So? Where are you on the scale?" I asked.

"I'm not okay yet, but I will be," she said. "Duke has given me a couple of weeks off from the insanity."

Among many other things, Zoey was an emergency room surgeon at Duke University Hospital in Durham, North Carolina, about an hour up the road from the farm.

"How can I help?"

"Give me time, General. I'm going to spend some of it going through his stuff at our . . . his house and figure things out. With Mom gone years ago and me being an only child, I need to sort some things out."

"You've got all of us, which I know is no replacement for your father, but you grew up with us, Zoey."

"I know, I know." She nodded, took a sip of whatever she was drinking, grimaced, and then looked toward the gathering in the backyard. She folded her arms across her stomach, warming herself against the biting winds and the cold darkness of grief.

Hobart, Van Dreeves, and Mahegan were talking, listening to each other, glancing up at us, and no doubt scheming something.

"You bringing Jake back?"

"The right question is, does Jake want back in?"

"Joe said, 'Maybe,'" she said.

When she mentioned Joe Hobart, her eyes had a hint of an extra spark even under the circumstances.

"Maybe," I said.

She looked back at her father's grave and then a bit to the right of his headstone.

"I wanted to ask, General—"

"I've already done it, Zoey. It's yours if you want it."

She stepped forward and hugged me, her body heaving a few times, wet tears falling onto my neck. She had been of Brad and Reagan's school of thought regarding thinking about the grave sites and where she wanted to spend eternity. The wars today, though, brought mortality to our children too soon.

"Thank you," she said. "I just want to be with him."

"In due time," I said. "You've got a world to save, girl. Just don't go rogue on me again."

She stepped back and smiled, her face a disaster zone of tears and makeup, though she never looked more beautiful, completely bare in her grief, her soul laid out for all to see.

"No promises there," she said. I shook my head and looked away when she asked, "Have you given any thought to what we discussed at Dad's? Everything I've given you?"

"I have," I said.

"And?"

I thought about the maps Sly had created. The significant players he had documented as being involved. His reams of notes. The mathematical calculations he had made. Sly's due diligence had uncovered something that was unbelievable but at the same time entirely possible. What to do with the information was the dilemma.

"I think what we discussed may be appropriate, Zoey, but let's talk more later. I'm exhausted right now. First Melissa. Now your dad. Afghanistan. COVID. The world is spiraling. If we have a chance to stop it from spinning away from us, we should."

She nodded and pursed her lips. "I agree and understand."

"I hope you do, because things are going to get complicated from here on out."

"Like I said, it's a—"

"—geometry thing."

She nodded, perhaps realizing that I understood the totality of the intel. A long moment passed between us. There was an unspoken bond, but the silence was more than that. It was an acknowledgment of commitments to each other and to our country.

"Can I call you?"

"I think being your godfather gives you special privileges," I said, smiling. "You know I'll stop the world, Zoey. Anytime, anyplace. Just don't make me come looking for you like last time."

She looked away again, her eyes suddenly distant.

"No promises there, either," she said, preparing to walk back to the house.

"And, Zoey," I said. She stopped and looked over her shoulder, staring at me with expectant eyes. "Take care of Joe."

At first, she squinted with a practiced look of feigned curiosity, and then her eyes grew wide.

"Did he—" She pointed at her father's grave.

"Yes. He was proud that you and Joe finally decided to be together, but we've all been disappointed that you haven't come out in public yet."

She put her hand to her mouth. "Oh my God. How did he know?"

"He has two eyes, Zoey. I knew. He knew."

"Anyone else?"

"I think it's on the *Welcome to Fort Bragg* sign, but other than that, not sure."

"Stop it." She pushed at me playfully, then brought her hands to her face, realizing the joy a daughter could have brought a father through her own simple happiness in finding love. "Why didn't we tell him?" She sobbed for a moment, wiping at tears, looking away, a million images most likely running through her mind.

"We were gone a lot, Zoey. He was happy for both of you. He approves."

For the last year, Zoey and Joe had been secreting around North Carolina, mostly in Durham away from the prying eyes of her father and Joe's teammates. Hobart was naturally a quiet man, so he didn't have to put up much of an act.

"He knew," she whispered to herself. A mournful smile formed on her lips.

"So just take care of each other. I don't want any more of this." I waved my hand at the headstones. I lost Melissa, and Zoey lost Sly. We were kindred spirits in that regard, though I wasn't sure who felt more alone in the world now.

"You're in the wrong business, then, General. All sorts of 'this' is going to happen and has been happening," she said. "It's what you do. And if you men didn't do *this,* who would? Some man-bun-wearing soy boy worried about his latte not being hot enough?"

I managed a smile. This was the Zoey that I had known for all thirty-two years of her already amazing life.

"Be careful, Zoey. Now, get back down to everyone who wants to hug you. We'll talk tomorrow."

She looked away, paused for a long moment, then nodded and said, "Sure. Tomorrow."

Though I should have seen it in her eyes, I had no idea that Zoey would be gone tomorrow.

7

TWO DAYS AFTER SLY'S funeral, Hobart notified me that Zoey was missing, maybe dead.

Zoey was no ordinary child of my best friend. Nor was she just my goddaughter. She also was on another government agency's short list of deep-cover operatives. Her doctor credentials provided the perfect legend for penetration into difficult networks. We, JSOC, had not activated her, though, and today, I was reminded of the time we had saved her life in Afghanistan.

She had previously leveraged this government affiliation to take a three-month leave of absence from Duke University to help Afghan women and children evacuate in the weeks before the surprise withdrawal and rapid Taliban takeover of Afghanistan.

OVER THE YEARS, Zoey and I had long discussions about Harriet Tubman's Underground Railroad network. We lived in North Carolina, which famously was a hub for the perilous migration of former slaves, Zoey's and Sly's ancestors, to freedom. Little did I realize she would put that study to use in Afghanistan to shockingly good effect, evacuating over five hundred women and children before being captured by the Taliban.

Unbeknownst to either Sly or me at the time, in July 2021, Zoey flew from Raleigh to Qatar, where she presented her medical credentials, which got her on a flight to Kabul. From there, she used her charm and intellect to network with local Afghans to begin setting up Route Tubman, as she had dubbed it.

Route Tubman was a network of people, caves, trails, and tunnels she used to move women and children to qalats, adobe homes, and hide them beneath the floorboards or in the hidden walls before secreting them to Hamid Karzai International Airport using a variety of alleys and back roads.

As the Taliban were rounding up women for subjugation, Zoey became a target. Some enterprising bureaucrats in the State Department had put her name on a list of Americans needing evacuation. This list was issued to the Taliban in the naive hope that they might help with the evacuation.

Shortly thereafter, she was chased down by a group of Taliban fighters in pickup trucks, searching from door to door. Route Tubman had been revealed, and the nefarious terrorist forces in Afghanistan went into overdrive to shut it down . . . and find Zoey.

She had done all of this without mentioning it to her father, me, or Hobart. So, as we had separately received our mission to flow my Special Forces teams into a remote airfield we had previously constructed in the middle of the country, we had no idea that she had established this network or that she was on the run from the Taliban.

Shortly upon arrival a week before the tragic attacks at Kabul International Airport that killed thirteen marines and a navy corpsman, one of my teams alerted me that intelligence was indicating celebration of capturing an American doctor and that a medical assistance team had been taken hostage in Paktia Province, normally a hotbed of terrorist activity astride the Pakistan border. Home to the infamous Haqqani network, Paktia ran diagonally from the south side of the Tora Bora mountains in the north to Gardez in the south and was a major smuggling thoroughfare from Parachinar, Pakistan, into the center of Afghanistan.

These types of rescue missions fell squarely in the JSOC protocols of responsibility, and as I was instructing Josh Wright and his team to prepare for a search and rescue mission, Sly came racing into the tactical command post to alert me to a text he had received from Zoey.

She was the captured doctor.

While she was my goddaughter, she also was in the Department of Defense medical database as a member of Doctors Without Borders, which made it not only my personal responsibility to retrieve Zoey but my professional responsibility, as well. I didn't imagine that Zoey's altruism ran deep; rather, her inclusion in an esteemed international agency gave her much-desired creditability globally and the perfect legend for missions within another governmental agency.

I compartmentalized my emotions and focused on this mission by pulling together Hobart, Van Dreeves, and Josh Wright's team to conduct an immediate rescue effort. We ran a trace on the GPS coordinates of the phone and saw that she was in the Shah-i-Kot Valley, a place with which we were all very familiar from Operation Anaconda, the first major conventional fight in Afghanistan in the early winter months of 2002 after Bin Laden had already escaped from Tora Bora some fifty miles away. The valley was a high mountain redoubt surrounded by massive peaks, such as Takur Ghar, that dominated the terrain.

Night had fallen, and we flew on the bench seats of MH-6 Little Bird helicopters that alighted on the rocky, sloping terrain like dragonflies on grass blades. I was always amazed at the skill, bravery, and talent of our Nightstalker pilots of the famed Task Force 160th Special Operations Aviation Regiment. They shot through narrow defiles with precision and always delivered us on target. This time was no exception as we disembarked and scrambled to protected positions, hunkering down until the helicopters were away. Traversing the rocky terrain, we approached the GPS location of Zoey's iPhone, halting about a hundred meters away from where the beacon was blinking. We scanned, not seeing anything until Van Dreeves, using an infrared spotter's scope, said, "Phone. Rock pile."

"Look for snipers," I said.

"Got two on the ridge at two o'clock," Hobart said. "Baited ambush."

"Keep looking," I directed.

Based upon the disposition of the snipers, we surmised the hostages to be on the backside of the ridge. Our Predator drone piped a video feed that showed a huddled group of women and children surrounded by men with headscarves and AK-47s. To our knowledge, we were undetected.

Our IVAS night vision systems painted a clear picture, and I thought I could see Zoey on the drone video feed. She appeared to be arguing with one of the Taliban fighters who was significantly bigger than the others.

"See that?" I said to Hobart, who was also looking at the streaming video download feed on the handheld satellite device.

"That's her," he said.

"Mother of God," Sly whispered. I put my hand on

his arm, a signal of both support and restraint. One wrong move and she could wind up dead.

The man Zoey was debating had a swagger about him that I had never seen before in any of these Taliban fighters we had been confronting for years. The way he stood in the group, arms crossed over his clean and pressed tunic, red sash across his flat stomach, large saber hanging to his right side, and AK-47 situated to his left, was uniquely distinct from the ragged Taliban fighters around him. With his perfectly coiffed turban, he looked like a European trying to fit into the Pashtun culture, a modern-day Lawrence of Arabia.

"Biggest threat?" I asked.

"Two guys arguing on the other side of the group. They've got their rifles in their hands and look like they might get trigger-happy."

I could imagine the discussion revolved around executing all the women, including Zoey, or keeping them as hostages for ransom. These were unacceptable options. While our political leaders might be removed and aloof from the scene on the ground, it was our responsibility to compensate for their lack of understanding or concern. Soldiers fight for the men and women on their left and right, not for the people who occupy offices back in the United States.

"Randy?" I asked Van Dreeves, who was studying the images on the video feed.

"There's six of them, not including the snipers. Joe gets two. I can get two. But the key is if these two snipers are in comms with the six on the back of the ridge. We kill them with no comms, we can get close enough to do damage. If we miss the snipers and they radio to the group behind the ridge, everyone there could be dead."

Van Dreeves's words were not intended to anger Sly,

but I felt him tense up at the cold analysis delivered by one of our best warriors.

"Roger that. Don't miss," I said. "Josh, let us know when your team is in position to kill the enemy behind the ridge. Once you're there, Joe and Randy will take their shots."

Hobart and Van Dreeves repositioned behind their weapons, took a minute to get the clicks and mils right while Josh Wright and his five men backed off our hide position and circled around the ridge to get behind the snipers without being detected.

"Got to tell you, boss, I'm freaking out right now," Sly whispered.

"Me, too, Sly. Me, too."

The twenty-minute wait felt like hours. Sweat trickled down my back as I thought of Zoey, Brad, and Reagan playing together at Fort Bragg, in Fayetteville, at summer camps on the coast in Wilmington or the Outer Banks. Zoey had babysat both of my children dozens of times, and after her mother, Sly's wife, died, my wife, Melissa, had become a surrogate mother to Zoey.

"Ready," Wright whispered over the radio.

"Go," I said to Hobart and Van Dreeves. Two ratcheting whispers sang into the valley. Watching through my IVAS, I saw one enemy sniper drop on top of his weapon, and the second was crawling toward a small rucksack. Van Dreeves put a bullet in his head.

"Moving to you," I said to Wright and his team.

"No change in status," Wright replied.

It took us nearly thirty minutes to join Wright, and fortunately, there had been no communications between the now-dead snipers and the force they were protecting. Though the scene we came upon had changed dramatically.

The large man with the red sash and saber slapped

Zoey, who was dressed in tactical clothing, cargo pants, polypro shirt, outer tactical vest, and combat boots. The only item paying homage to local customs was her hijab, which the man had snatched from her head and shook it in her face.

"American spy!" he shouted in her face.

His accent was European, but it was difficult to tell from which country fifty meters away.

"Plan?" I asked Wright.

"Randy and Joe kill the two at either end. That leaves the guy with Zoey and one staring at the group of women."

"Who's got the red sash?" I asked.

"I do," Sly said.

"And I've got the guard with the group," Wright said.

"Execute," I said.

The silenced weapons made sufficient ratcheting noises to echo through the narrow valley, and as Sly was preparing to pull his trigger, Red Sash snatched Zoey and began backing up, holding a knife to her throat.

"Zoey!" Sly shouted, lowering his weapon.

They were backing toward a cave mouth, just one of many here in the Shah-i-Kot.

"Any shot?" I asked my men.

"No shot," they said back in unison.

"Let's move," I said.

We picked our way quickly through the rocks with Wright and his team ensuring the Taliban fighters were dead and securing the women and children, huddling amid muffled cries for help. Hobart, Van Dreeves, and I ran toward the cave, dodging random gunfire, which meant Red Sash had either let go of Zoey or the knife, or both.

Our first steps into the cave were met with heavy gunfire, and I wondered if there was a backup force in here. The IVAS gave me a view of Zoey lying on the rocky floor and Red Sash behind a machine gun, using Zoey's body as firing support.

There was literally no shot at Red Sash, who was surprisingly agile. His machine gun either jammed or ran out of ammunition as the echoes ringing loudly through the cavern faded. We dove headlong into the cave mouth and raced toward Zoey, who was whispering, "Help me."

I chased the giant through the winding tunnel until I didn't see him anymore. As I turned, a baseball bat hit my chest, though it was a 9 mm piece of lead caught by my body armor. Stumbling back, I lifted my pistol and fired blindly to suppress any further shots. I had gotten lucky once and wasn't counting on a second time.

The man mumbled something unintelligible and fled deeper into the tunnel as I tackled him. A knife swiped in front of my eyes, the turbulence washing over my cheeks. I had my knife out and was flailing when I heard shots fired at the front of the cave. The man's fist caught me on my chin and rocked me backed into the wall. I stumbled as he adroitly fled through an open hatch that led to the ground above. He started pumping pistol shots randomly into the opening, denying my pursuit.

I shuffled back to the front, where Wright, Van Dreeves, and Hobart were assembled with their troops. Van Dreeves was finishing a patch job on Zoey's left shoulder and cheek.

"Gonna be all right, baby," Sly was whispering to his daughter. "Gonna be all right."

"Counterattack force," Wright said. "Killed them. Called for extraction. Zoey's lost some blood."

Sly and I lifted Zoey when we heard the whipping blades of the Apache gunships that were escorting the Chinook helicopter. Rockets screamed from the

Apache's pods, the Chinook landed, the women and children boarded. Sly and I had Zoey's arms around our shoulders as we flanked her and helped her limp to the back ramp before my operators funneled into the aircraft.

The loadmaster snapped the ramp shut, and like that, we were airborne.

Sitting next to Zoey, I looked at her eyes, weak and vacant, and wondered if we could keep her with us. A deep gash angled beneath her left eye, oozing blood.

Sly was staring at his daughter, tears streaming down his face, mouth contorted, whispering, "Hang in there, baby. Hang in there, baby. Hang in there, baby."

An Afghan woman got up from her seat and stumbled forward toward us. My defenses went up, but the woman knelt in front of Zoey and rested her head on Zoey's leg. Another woman rose and joined her. Then a little girl. And another. And soon the entire contingent of women Zoey had saved that night were surrounding her in supplication, praying for all the gods to save this angel.

I looked away and stared at my men who were, in a rare moment of introspection, simply watching the women lift Zoey up with their hopes and prayers.

AND SO, I had a strong sense of déjà vu when Hobart said to me today, "Sir, Zoey is missing in Africa."

8

IT TOOK THE RIDE back to our headquarters on Fort Bragg for me to recognize how far gone I was.

Loss can come at you incrementally and erode your faith like water on a stone, or it can hit you like a wrecking ball you don't see coming.

Or it can be both, like a one-two punch, and I imagine in retrospect that was what happened to me. Unfortunately, I didn't fully appreciate the impact on my decision-making. I had to move quickly if I was going to do what needed to be done as much for my own soul as for Zoey and our nation. I simply couldn't handle another deep personal loss *or* another setback in our national security. We all knew soldiers who had lost half of their squads in combat and the resultant suicide rates that skyrocketed, no matter how much (or little) the country tried to help.

Standing in my spartan office in JSOC headquarters, I was staring at the map of Africa hanging on my wall when Hobart walked in.

"Got a Global Hawk over the target area," he said. "There's an update on her location."

"Where is she?" I asked.

My office had a large-screen monitor where a map of the world spun when Hobart pressed a button. There was a blinking red dot maybe twenty miles from Chinguetti, which was nearly three hundred miles from the coast. The way the map was situated on the monitor, Chinguetti appeared to be just south of a major terrain feature that looked exactly like an almond-shaped eye, complete with a circular iris in the middle and a dark eyebrow above.

"Looks like the same terrain feature," I said.

"The Eye of Africa thing. We were on the southern rim of that," Hobart said, pointing to what basically looked like the bottom of the Eye. "It's maybe sixteen miles across."

"Looks man-made," I said absently. During the Stockton mission, I hadn't paid much attention to the broader terrain feature other than its tactical implications for my team.

Hobart shrugged. "Guess I need to read Plato again."

"Anything relevant from the ISR?" I asked.

"Nothing yet, but we should be able to see Zoey as long as her GPS is working," Hobart said.

"Any allies in the area?"

"The French are in Senegal," Hobart said.

"Yeah, but I asked about allies," I quipped.

Hobart's upper lip twitched, the closest he ever came to smiling, but he knew we had little to smile about.

"Who else knows she's missing?" I asked.

"No one. Duke gave her a couple of weeks, so they're not tracking her," he said.

Just then, Van Dreeves came barreling into the office.

"Boss, you should have shared this with us sooner. I mean, holy shit," Van Dreeves said.

"You've got it now. We'll talk on the airplane."

"What's that?" Hobart asked.

"The external drive Zoey gave the boss," Van Dreeves said.

Hobart snapped his head toward me. "When?" he asked.

"When I got back from the Pentagon. Two days ago."

"Neither of you said anything," he said. Hobart swiveled his head from me to his lifelong friend, Van Dreeves.

"I'm saying it now," I said.

Even though they were displeased with me, I wasn't worried about our bond. Not too long ago, I had dragged Van Dreeves from a cell where Iranian Quds Force commander Dariush Parizad had placed him directly before a bomb had destroyed the remote building as part of a chemical weapons plot against the United States. Both Van Dreeves and Hobart had saved my ass too many times to count, and now it seemed I'd had the opportunity to return the favor. Even Hobart, rarely not in control of himself, had needed evacuation after a near miss from the deadly chemical weapons.

"Roger that, but this external drive has some wild shit on it from his recce missions there. Lots on China nukes, the Dakhla Accords, blackmail, the Eye of Africa, and crazy geometric drawings, like Galileo kind of stuff. And completely, seemingly unrelated, there are several pictures of bags of gold coins with several dig sites in the desert looking for the gold."

I felt the presidential burner phone buzz in my cargo pocket. Instead of engaging in conversation, I grabbed my gear and began walking out the door.

"Grab your shit. Sally and the team are loaded. We need to move now before our airplane gets canceled."

"Boss—"

"I said, 'Move.' Let's go."

Once we were on the airplane, it taxied quickly and was airborne as we huddled in the command pod.

"When I talked to Zoey the night Sly died, she thought he might have been killed for a reason. He had information that he had gathered from his previous trips to Dakhla and gave it to Zoey in case the mission went bad for him or all of us," I said. I owed them an explanation and was just now able to process everything without emotion clouding my judgment. I had read Sly's summary, which included communications intercepts from the Dakhla Accords discussions that vaguely referenced Chinese nuclear weapons.

Van Dreeves, McCool, and Hobart remained silent as I talked. They were seated in their respective positions around the small, rectangular drop-down table.

"Boss, WTF," Van Dreeves said. "You've been on our asses. We all want the same thing."

"Randy, I know you like to talk, and I always let you, but I'll give you your turn in a minute. First, this has nothing to do with trust. I trusted you, Randy, to print out everything from Zoey last week and then to review the external drive she gave me."

I looked each of them in the eyes. They understood.

"Second, Zoey may be missing, or she may be operating on her own, expecting us to follow. I truly don't know and would tell you if I did."

"Wait, what?" Hobart interrupted.

"I said exactly what I meant, Joe."

He stared at me hard, face flush, eyes shooting ninja stars.

"Third, I moved fast because the president tried to call me, which most likely means she got my message. I gave her some of this information because it implicates senior members of the military and her cabinet."

All three of them looked down and shook their heads.

They didn't like politicians or direct political influence on our missions, but there was no other way to proceed.

"Last, when I saw Zoey, she said to me, 'It's all about the geometry.' In Sly's files were drawings of the Eye of Africa, with graphs and lines reaching into the atmosphere. Either it's an Indiana Jones kind of thing, where the sun shines through a diamond and opens a vault, or it's some type of strategic weapon. I need to know what kind of calculations he's got going on in those files."

I stopped talking. Locked eyes with each of them. Returned their hard stares. Tough love.

Van Dreeves nodded.

"I'd add a fifth. Gold."

"Gold?" I asked.

"Yes. He's got reams of notes about gold finds in the Eye of Africa. Supports our debrief with Stockton. Little sacks of gold stacked in a dark tunnel," Van Dreeves said.

He clicked on the track pad of his MacBook, and the pod's monitor jumped to life at the opposite end of the table. He pointed at a series of photographs of brown leather bags cut open with oddly shaped coins spilling out. He clicked again, and a menu of information appeared.

"This is the EXIF data. Exchangeable image file. Shows date, time, and location."

"A little over two months ago," I said. "A day after Sly and his team made contact when conducting recon."

"Roger that. Might not have been a random thing," I said.

"Location?" Hobart asked.

"Ouadane, Mauritania," Van Dreeves said. "The Eye of Africa." He pointed at the image on the monitor.

"Same location as Zoey and close to where our guys

were killed. Looks like a moonscape," Hobart said. "Everything keeps coming back to the Eye of Africa."

He was right. What was it about the terrain feature that looked like a hurricane on the map that had so much activity surrounding it?

It's all about the geometry. Zoey's words circled in the back of my mind like a hawk searching for prey.

"So the gold is hidden in the crater. Where did it come from?" I asked.

"The coins aren't perfectly round," Van Dreeves said, pointing at the screen. He dragged the cursor and expanded the picture of one of the coins, which had edges that looked like a third grader had tried to draw a circle freehand. The coins had small nicks in the bevel and what only could be seen as hieroglyphics on either side.

"Egyptian?" I asked.

"All I could find is this image," Van Dreeves said. He pulled up a picture from the internet that showed a similar-looking coin called an Egyptian stater.

"How did an Egyptian coin get to Mauritania?" Hobart asked.

"Maybe Timbuktu," I said.

I had read about the lost treasures of Timbuktu, a major trading post along the Niger River on the southwesternmost edge of the Sahara. It was a key pivot point for merchants, travelers, explorers, safaris, and expeditions. With the Sahara to the north and tropical sub-Saharan Africa just to the south, it was like Denver in the early North America days, a stopping-off point before traversing treacherous terrain and a redoubt in which to settle after attempting and failing. Business opportunities sprouted from the intersection of needs. Water for the parched, food for the hungry, stores of both for the wanderers, and shelter from the incessant heat.

"Is there a nexus between the Dakhla thing and the

gold? There's millions of dollars of gold in that tunnel, and people looking for it," Van Dreeves said. I looked at Hobart, whose face was drawn with worry. "And then there's all this other stuff Sly gathered that seems to bear no relation."

"Maybe there's no connection," I said. "Seems to pale in comparison to the rest of the information. Like it's a distraction."

"Why would Sly have this in the file, then? There are probably a million unrelated things he didn't include. This was deliberate," Van Dreeves said.

"He did say he had more work to do. Maybe it was understanding the connection between the two. Add in nukes, China, and blackmail, and I can see why he was struggling with pulling it all together."

"This stuff about nukes, though, is crazier," Van Dreeves said. "Just makes no sense."

"I saw that," I said, leveling with them.

They paused and looked at me.

"This is what Zoey's doing?" Hobart asked. His voice was clipped, tight, restraining anger with me.

I nodded. "Maybe."

"Why her?"

"The medical thing gives her cover," I said. "But she got in front of me on this. I honestly didn't know she was going to leave so soon."

"So you guys were plotting without us?" Van Dreeves asked, hurt.

"No. We were having discussions."

"Sir, you know Zoey well enough to know that she's going to find a green light in anything you tell her!" Hobart said.

It was the most emotion I had seen from him in the three decades of operating with him. Van Dreeves looked at him with big eyes.

"I agree. I should have seen that coming," I said.

"We've got to find her," Hobart said, settling his voice.

"We will," I replied. "Now let me call the president."

I was focused. We needed momentum, and we were starting to achieve some.

"Before you call the president," Van Dreeves said, "this picture is interesting." He showed a digital image of seven people standing on the balcony of a castle overlooking the ocean. Secretary of Defense Angela Blankenship and Secretary of State Bryn McHenry were flanking Chinese general Liang and the CEOs of two of the largest Big Tech companies in the world. Behind them were French defense minister Albert Gambeau on one side, and an armed, bearded man wearing sunglasses on the other.

"Saw that," I said. "We know who the VIPs are, but how about the guy in the beard?"

Van Dreeves zoomed in. "Look closer."

Then it hit me.

The bodyguard was Sanson, the executioner. He was the link that Sly was pursuing. Sanson was the connective tissue between the gold and the Dakhla Accords, but what did that mean? And how did it relate to Chinese activity at the Eye of Africa?

Which led me to believe that Sanson's execution of Sly might have some personal connection and might not be some random act. I recalled a conversation with Luckey prior to the mission when he told me to "Sit this one out and let Morgan lead the team."

Had someone fed Sly into the executioner's blade? Had he known too much?

"Sanson," I whispered. "*Le bourreau.*"

9

WHEN PRESIDENT CAMPBELL HAD given me the phone to use for communications with her, she'd said at the time, "I've got so many layers of bullshit between me and reality, I never know what the truth is anymore. Call me if you need to tell me anything or even if it's just to talk about Melissa . . . especially if it's to talk about her."

While I doubted anyone could miss Melissa as much as I did, Kim Campbell could be a close second—that is, if she didn't play a role in Melissa's death. I still had reservations about what could have been a career-ending incident for Campbell that occurred in college and which only Melissa had known about. I'd had reasonable suspicion that Campbell had been involved in Melissa's "cancer" until I realized that her killer was another person I'd known. But still, the doubt lingered, and I would never fully trust her.

I had used the phone exactly four times in the two years I'd had it, two of those in extremis, requiring her intervention, and most recently at the cemetery. I excused my team from the command pod in the airborne C-17, checked the classified presidential calendar, saw that she was finishing a meeting with the leadership of the International Association of Bridge, Structural, Ornamental and Reinforcing Iron Workers Union in the Oval Office and had fifteen minutes before she was to go to the briefing room and take questions from the press.

I retrieved the presidential burner, which I kept in my uniform cargo pocket, and took a chance calling her. She answered on the second ring.

"Garrett, why did you hang up on me?"

"Technically, I sent it to voice mail," I said.

"Right," she scoffed. "What have you done with this piece of paper? You can't do that. Especially after I visited Arlington."

"Nothing to worry about presently, ma'am. I'm still good."

She paused, understanding my cryptic response.

"But, Garrett, you can't do this," she said as if she had a say in the matter. Well, actually, she did. With the inspector general investigation, she could dial up or down the heat on me however she wished. "I have big plans for you."

"That's what worries me," I said.

"More to the point. I stopped by Arlington the other day and paid a visit to one of your Rangers, a Sergeant Laxalt," she said. "I do that sometimes to pay my respects. It helps ground me when confronting big decisions, national security or not. It was bitterly cold, but I feel such peace there. And knowing that I've got you to execute missions both large and small in the name of preserving our freedoms reassures me," she said.

"I'm glad you had a meaningful visit," I said.

"Which made me concerned about what you presented to General Luckey. I need you on the team even if it's a curtain call. Even if it's to find your friend's daughter," she said.

"I understand." This was her way of giving me the Campbell two-step. She took a step to open the door to the mission I was quietly pursuing while I took a step through the door without any specific reference to what she was partially authorizing. For anyone recording or listening to this call, and voice programs existed that might rapidly find our conversation in the spectrum, the takeaway would be her displeasure with the document I had handed to Luckey and some generic caveats about a "curtain call."

What was unspoken was that members of her administration were conspiring with the Chinese to ease the United States into a power-sharing agreement in Africa and were going to blackmail her into complying if she didn't agree.

That was Sly's conclusion based upon the intercepts he had recorded. We were still mining the details but had enough to get into action. That information alone wasn't sufficient to light the fuse on a breakneck mission to Africa, but him finding reference to five nuclear weapons in the Eye of Africa was. We didn't know if these were intercontinental ballistic missiles on transports or what their purposes might be.

But we were going to find out.

"And so, when the chairman called me today, it gave me a good excuse to reach out and try to understand what you're doing. While I don't openly support it, there's really nothing I can do to stop you."

Green light. If this conversation ever came to light, she could reasonably argue that she was saying there was nothing she could do to stop me from doing what I indicated in the letter that I had delivered to Luckey. My clear interpretation, though, was that she was not going to prevent me from getting to Africa to discover what could be a grave threat to the country and, if true, stop it.

She continued by completely changing the subject.

"Plus, these ironworkers I just met with gave me a hard hat, making me think of the time I visited Bragg and you gave me a helmet to wear in the helicopter."

"Glad you're keeping safe, Madam President," I said.

"Did you know that since I signed the Keep American Jobs Act, steel production has increased ten percent here in the United States?"

"I think everyone's tracking that," I said.

She paused. "Wait. You're busting my balls?"

"I don't believe that's actually possible, ma'am."

"I've got a press conference in ten minutes, and I'd rather pull a fishhook through my forehead."

"Have a good press conference, ma'am," I said.

"Is there such a thing?"

"I imagine not."

"Garrett . . ."

"Yes, ma'am."

"We've been friends since we were teenagers. Life has gotten . . . challenging. But the friendship remains through everything. Always."

I wasn't so sure about that. She might have been reaching for *my* approval in a moment of self-doubt or reflection.

When I didn't respond, she continued, "This is the first time we've talked without you mentioning Melissa. Are we good?"

I paused for a long time, to the point that I wasn't sure how much time had passed. Images of my beautiful wife danced in my mind, auburn hair flowing across her shoulders. Her quick smile and quicker wit. Green eyes that bored through my soul and hooked me from the first meeting in our church in Fayetteville, North Carolina, as teenagers. Raising our two children, Brad and Reagan, both now young adults struggling to make it in this troubled world. Her whispering in my ear one night when I was home from West Point on leave for Christmas and she was home from Meredith College. She had been upset, distraught. I didn't push her but also let her know I was ready to listen if she needed me, which she did. Finally, the night before I returned to the frozen tundra of the military academy, she whispered into my ear, "Kim did something terrible. She killed another student. Kept pouring this girl alcohol at a party." Then she pulled away and refused to talk about it ever again.

"You should report it to the police," I had said.

"Someone already did," she replied. And she'd left it at that. The investigation was sealed. After heavy Meredith College interference, the police ruled the death as accidental alcohol poisoning. Kim's name was listed as simply another girl at the party. The record was later erased from all the databases, including that of the Raleigh Police Department.

Years later, when Campbell announced her candidacy for governor of North Carolina, Kim had come to Melissa and talked about working on her candidacy and seeking plum promotions for me. Holding my hand in our quaint Fort Bragg quarters, Melissa had said, "Kim, I know what I saw. You can't bribe me. Now please leave."

Campbell had departed, ruffled, and no doubt concerned about Melissa's defiance. Melissa had broken down crying into my shoulder that night, saying, "There was an investigation. The matter was resolved. It remains resolved."

She never uttered a word to anyone except me, but

there was no way for the aspiring governor and presidential candidate to know that she would remain quiet. Five years later, Melissa was dead, and I wasn't exactly sure what, if any, role Campbell played in her death.

"Garrett?" The president's voice brought me back to the moment.

"Melissa loved Zoey, Kim. She would want me to do this," I said.

Campbell was silent, perhaps nodding and looking wistfully out the Oval Office windows, wondering if I still doubted whether she was involved in Melissa's death—or, for that matter, how much I knew. I would never know the truth, and I might never reconcile that concept with my conscience.

I was a warrior, and I really didn't care much anymore about anything but the people I loved, which included my kids, my troops, and their families.

"Be safe, Garrett, I've got to run," she said ambiguously. Either she lost track of the real purpose of the call—going around my chain of command for her approval for me to find Zoey and perhaps more—or she intentionally left her response open to interpretation.

Be safe.

If we were hugely successful, she could claim credit. If we failed, she could deny involvement. More importantly, we had created the plausible story that would provide her an out. The truth was far more dangerous. She was a seasoned politician, and I hung up without saying goodbye. She was probably already gone and didn't notice.

Roger that.

10

PRIOR TO THE "ALEXA Files" being made famous by *The Washington Post,* Van Dreeves had figured out a way to hack through the presidential burner and tap into the network in the Oval Office with the help of an enterprising White House communications sergeant who had been eager to join JSOC.

President Campbell had placed an encrypted Amazon Web Services Alexa home assistant video and audio recording base station, disguised as a Remington horse statue, with networked cameras dotted elsewhere in the Oval Office, Situation Room, and Air Force One. The statue in the Oval Office sat in the middle of the coffee table in between the two sofas. Van Dreeves's hack was no different from tapping into a Ring home security camera. For all its protections, the White House was extremely vulnerable to intruders as the Solar Winds and other penetrations had demonstrated. A modern version of Nixon's tape-recording system.

After she hung up the phone with me, my team transitioned back into the command suite in time to watch and listen as General Luckey, Secretary of Defense Angela Blankenship, and the chairman of the Joint Chiefs of Staff, General Lucius Rolfing, all streamed into the Oval Office.

Campbell said, "What can I do you for, ladies and gentlemen?"

"General Sinclair gave me this, ma'am," Luckey said, the paper crinkling as it passed hands.

Campbell looked at the document briefly and asked, "Seen it. What do you make of it?"

"He's lost it, and he might be trying to negate the IG investigation," Secretary of Defense Blankenship said. She was midfifties, black hair streaked with gray, conservative pantsuits, and a stern face with small eyes. She looked severe at times, as if the world were burning right in front of her every day all day. Her nose was angular and looked larger than it really was, juxtaposed against her eyes. She had been a Washington, D.C., denizen most of her life, rotating between academia, consulting gigs, and the Department of Defense, depending on which party was in power. The common denominators were access, power, and money.

"Define 'lost it,' AB," Campbell said.

"He's lost his wife. He most likely killed the last secretary of state, and now he's gotten six soldiers killed in random action in Mauritania."

"How was that random? It was approved by me and recommended by you," Campbell said.

"I think what the secretary is saying—" General Luckey interrupted.

"I'm quite capable of speaking for myself, General," Blankenship snapped. "What's a general doing on a hostage rescue mission? What was he doing facing up against Parizad before that? He should be a major, not a three-star general, if that's what he wants to do, and I told him to his face."

"So, in your view, generals should be in offices while

their troops are in the trenches duking it out? And my understanding is that you're the one who ordered him *not* to lead the Stockton mission."

"There's a place for everyone," Blankenship said. "And certainly, a general shouldn't be mixing it up with the troops."

Campbell turned to Luckey and asked, "Tell me, General, when you snuck out of Karzai airport during the withdrawal and cut that deal with the Taliban that saved scores of American citizens, what rank were you?"

"Ma'am, I was a two-star general," Luckey said.

"Why didn't you send a major out to do that, though?" she quickly added.

After a pause, Luckey said, "Sometimes leadership at the decisive point can make a difference . . . make *the* difference."

"Kind of like you did in Objective Rhino when you were the ground commander as a captain, right? Or did you have some supervision?" Campbell asked.

Luckey nodded. "Yes, ma'am. The Ranger regimental commander and his staff jumped into the objective, as did the battalion commander and his staff, not to manage me and my one hundred and fifty Rangers but to manage the significant strategic implications."

"I see. So, AB, the inspector general is investigating the allegations that Sinclair killed the secretary of state, who, mind you, was working with Iranian Quds Force commander Parizad and, accordingly, had committed treason. Three of his coconspirators are in pretrial confinement in Leavenworth right now on charges of sedition and treason. I believe you were on the Capitol steps on inauguration morning when Sinclair jumped from a helicopter and stopped a drone with chemical weapons from spraying us, right?"

Pause, then, a muted, "Yes, but as you said, they're all allegations. Innocent until proven guilty. There's some traction out there that Sinclair, being the spy that he actually is, orchestrated the entire thing and hung everyone else out to dry."

"So, whatever your personal animus against General Sinclair might be, he is to be given all due consideration," Campbell said.

"I have no animus with the general," Blankenship said. "I'm looking at this strictly from a Defense Department point of view. I have it on good information that the dead sergeant major's daughter is over there seeking revenge and that Sinclair wants to go chase her down. I don't recommend authorizing a fishing expedition to go find his friend's daughter, especially in the same location as the Stockton recovery. The place will be crawling with bad guys. Help me out here, Generals." She turned to Luckey and Rolfing.

"The 'dead sergeant major' has a name. It's Sylvester Morgan. And his daughter is Dr. Zoey Morgan," Campbell said.

"Yes, I'm sorry, I should have said that," Blankenship said. "Generals?"

"She's right, Madam President. This is tough terrain. Easily defendable. Whatever you say about Sinclair, and he is one of our best, I have noticed a change in his decision-making since Melissa's death. He's disobeyed several orders to comply with the inspector general. I'm out of rope to give him. He's different," Luckey said.

"Wouldn't you be? I suggest you find more rope," Campbell said.

"Yes, but I would recognize my own limitations if the change clouded my judgment," Luckey said.

"Would you now?" Campbell asked, a rising pitch in her voice, perhaps a chuckle.

"Yes, ma'am," he replied.

"Is there any reason we need to be in Western Sahara or Morocco's Southern Province or whatever they're calling it these days?"

"No reason for risky missions," Luckey said. "Unless we want to add to the death toll."

Blankenship added, "The only possible reason to be anywhere on the west coast of Africa is that China is looking for a base there, like they've done with Djibouti. They're looking at Equatorial Guinea, Nigeria, and, to some extent, Mauritania. The question is, do they want to be tucked in the Gulf of Guinea, or do they want to be farther west along the open coast—i.e., Mauritania? Secretary McHenry and I signed the Dakhla Accords last week, which includes China—already a major presence on the continent, by the way—in the decision-making process. Gives us all transparency, not unlike the Treaty on Open Skies with Russia. They see us; we see them. It's all good, but to satisfy our curiosity about this activity, I'll call Defense Minister Albert Gambeau, my counterpart in France, who was instrumental in establishing the accords."

"We don't need to worry about China," a male voice said. It was her chief of staff, Wilson Jordan IV. Most called him by his nickname, "Quad," a nod to his IV suffix and the fact that he dominated all four corners of the basketball court as a high school and collegiate athlete. He was young with dreads hanging loosely on his shoulders. His royal-blue suit was perfectly tailored around his lean frame. Tall and athletic, Jordan had run for Congress at twenty-seven years old, won his southeast Raleigh district, and abandoned that when Campbell asked him to serve as her chief of staff. Jordan had spent his two years in Congress focused on social issues, and Campbell had hired him because of his domestic policy strength and generally good reputation in Congress.

"Why not, Quad?" Campbell asked.

"Not relevant to this mission. Their economy is about to implode. Why would they be pursuing global hegemony?"

"What is our intelligence-collection capability in those regions?" Campbell asked, ignoring the academic statement.

"We have embassies with defense attachés in each country, and that's about it," Blankenship said.

"There's no real pressing national security interest in Mauritania, ma'am, other than rescuing Stockton, which was a long shot but which we accomplished," Luckey said. "We have one last load of equipment to withdraw from Morocco based on the Stockton raid. My staff tells me that Sinclair's team has put in the requests to fly on that C-17 with their helicopter. I can shut it down or let it go."

A long pause ensued until Campbell said, "I'm not going to micromanage your business."

"So, on rescuing Dr. Zoey Morgan . . . ," Luckey had started, but then a door opened, and a new voice entered the conversation: "Ma'am, the Chinese have a large flotilla off the coast of Morocco, reports of activity in the Sahara in Mauritania, and two rockets have launched from western China. We need to do a pop-up principals meeting right now. The Moroccans are asking for our assistance under our existing defense agreement with them while NORAD is tracking the rockets, which seem to be going into space."

"That's ridiculous," Blankenship said. "The Dakhla Accords cover this, and we checked the Sahara thing. There's a large expedition looking at the Eye of Africa for historical artifacts. The rockets are satellites to support their space mission. This is not an emergency. China has declared their intent to fish in international waters, and we don't care about a French treasure hunter."

"Who said anything about the French?" Campbell asked.

"That's what the intel shows," Blankenship replied.

"Well, I for one would like to hear what they have to say," Campbell said. "Can all of you join me in the Situation Room immediately?"

The Oval Office emptied out as if a vacuum cleaner had pulled them through the door. As Campbell moved out of the camera range, her voice was a faint whisper speaking to a nameless staffer.

"Keep their cell phones, and don't let them talk to their aides." Then the door shut, followed by silence.

"THAT'S SOME WILD shit," Van Dreeves said. The plane rocked as it powered toward the first of its in-flight refuel operations. "By today's hybrid work standards, we were in the Oval Office. So many morons."

"Nobody breathes a word of this, or I'll just have more IG allegations," I said.

"Yeah, um, boss, what are we going to do about all of that IG stuff?" Van Dreeves asked.

"I'm handling it," I said.

11

IN RETROSPECT, CAMPBELL MIGHT have been savvy enough to give me a head start while covering her flank. She was ever the politician who tried to also remain a friend. Perhaps some flicker of conscience burned intermittently in the back of her mind. Doubtful for any politician, but one could hope.

The brief, off-topic discussion about my mental stability and recovering our equipment in Dakhla was exactly the cover I needed. No doubt that Luckey was going to shut me down, but by then, we should already be on the ground in Morocco. President Campbell had done what she needed to do, whether intentionally or not, to at least allow us to get underway. There was enough activity to make my trip there seem beneath me yet well within the norm of what, in their minds, a slightly unhinged general might do.

What they weren't considering was that one of the second-order impacts of a weakened foreign policy was that China and Russia immediately flexed their muscles. Russia moved two hundred thousand troops to the Ukraine border. China intensified its focus to snag land on the west coast of Africa to envelop the United States from the east and place pressure on NATO from the south. I knew less about the Dakhla Accords that Blankenship mentioned, but if she and McHenry were involved, I suspected it had more to do with furthering their longtime business interests than anything that enhanced U.S. national security. Perhaps they would get a piece of the port profits if China was pursuing a deep-sea naval base off the Mauritanian coast.

Regardless, if the information gleaned from Sly's reconnaissance efforts was accurate, then we had little time to spare.

While the Chinese situation in Morocco was unfolding, I was reviewing the dossier we had on Henri Jacques Sanson, who never seemed to have escaped his nefarious family heritage.

It was true that his family had taken up finer pursuits since the French Revolution had tapped the metallurgic expertise of his forefathers. Most notably, his great-great-grandfather Charles-Henri Sanson had lopped off the head of Louis XVI along with nearly three thousand other French compatriots.

Sanson was a monster who had been co-opted by the French intelligence agency DGSE to perform their dirtiest missions. Executions had been his family legacy, and Defense Minister Gambeau put Sanson's carnal inclinations to good use over the past decade. French Ministry of Justice officials were constantly privately battling the DGSE and the Ministry of Defense to hold Sanson to account for multiple murders, mostly beheadings, to no avail yet. Part of the reason Gambeau chose Sanson for his Mauritanian gambit was to spirit him out of the country to avoid the mounting investigations.

As Malik, Sanson's Moroccan *khabir,* or caravan leader, later relayed the story, Sanson was worse than anyone could have envisioned.

This night as we flew to Dakhla, Sanson was in

Mauritania, sharpening his family sword on a grinding wheel he was pumping with his left foot, sparks flying off the metal blade in orange and yellow bursts. It was a one-meter-long saber, forged razor sharp on either side with a slight outward bevel in the middle.

Sanson stood before two of Stockton's kidnappers. They were the remainders of the cell that had been decimated by the raid into l'Oeil d'Afrique, the Eye of Africa. The men were on their knees, heads bowed, hands tied behind their backs. He flipped his saber in his hands, twirling it like a golfer spins a golf club.

Pacing back and forth a quarter mile away from the dig site where he hoped to find Poseidon's treasure, Sanson waxed eloquent at his own genius.

"Your men did well," he said. "You brought me Sergeant Major Morgan. Thank you for that. But you should have killed him in Dakhla when I first told you. Your incompetence forced me to deal with the situation."

"Please, Sanson," one of the men muttered. "The Americans were very good."

"You were supposed to be better," Sanson said. "Your incompetence forced me to play a high-level chip I preferred to keep in my pocket for the time being."

"You wanted Morgan. We brought you Morgan." Both men were sobbing uncontrollably.

"You can kidnap someone and kill an entire Senegalese family, but you weep before my blade?" Sanson scoffed. "Be a man."

"Sanson, please. We did what you asked."

"Yes. You did, but I can't take the risk." Then to Malik, he said, "Film this."

Malik reluctantly lifted his phone and began recording.

Sanson squared up to the first of the two, raised the

sword above the man's head, and swung it down with a professional efficiency that would have made his fore-bearers proud. The head rolled onto the ground at Malik's feet. He turned and vomited. Sanson repositioned himself and repeated the process for the second man.

He rotated to Malik, who was wiping his mouth with a shirtsleeve. Eyes wide, mouth trembling, fearing he was next to meet the sharpened tool. Not that he had done anything to warrant having his head severed, but the bloodlust in Sanson's eyes told of an unquenched thirst. Blood spatter dotted Sanson's face like freckles. Teeth bared against pink lips. His white cotton shirt was unbuttoned to the waist, showing ropey muscles, flexing and preening with each beat of his heart.

Instead of lifting the sword, he spoke.

"*S'en débarrasser d'eux,*" Sanson said. *Dispose of them.*

Malik skittered across the rocks, glad to be out of the arc of the blade, and began the unwelcome task of bagging the remains.

Sanson's satellite phone rang. The executioner retrieved it and placed it on speakerphone as he sat on a rock watching over Malik's handiwork, answering, "*Oui?*"

"There has been a development," Albert Gambeau, the French defense minister, said.

"What is this development?" Sanson asked.

"The daughter of the dead command sergeant major is looking for you," Gambeau said.

"That's not possible," Sanson replied. "The only person that knew about Dakhla is now dead. That was the point of the entire plan. There's no one who knows where I am, what I am looking for, or what the larger plan is. What makes you believe this?"

"Yes, it's true. A Polisario constabulary reported that her car broke down near Chinguetti. She's got maps and pictures of you. The local militia is holding her," Gambeau said.

"Why would she have pictures of me?"

"Exactly my point," Gambeau replied.

"Very well. She shall meet the same fate as her father," Sanson said.

"Use your head," Gambeau said. "If she knows what her father knew, she'll destroy all of us and the plan with your Asian friends."

Malik stole a glance at Sanson, a frisson of fear running through him. As far as Malik knew, they were on a complex Chinese-funded mission to find the center of what Sanson believed to be Plato's Atlantis and the gold it supposedly held.

Sanson had already discovered barrels of Egyptian gold coins, probably worth millions, and was ferrying the find via his airplane to the new port city of Dakhla that was bustling with ships, wealthy tourists, banks, and souks. It was a perfect place to launder their treasure and pay off their Chinese investors.

"*Oui*. Always careful," Sanson said. He walked away from the bonfire that was crackling behind him. Stepping onto a rock ledge, he peered into the valley below, layers of black cascading away from him, the first edges of morning with a gray meniscus seeping through the horizon. The sweet scent of burning acacia and eucalyptus limbs wafted through the air. The camels sounded off with their morning roars, perhaps a male in rut among the crew.

Malik disposed of the bodies in previously dug graves and returned to Sanson's location overlooking the caravan.

Malik was an athletic man with brown Moroccan

skin and bloodshot eyes that peered from beneath tired lids. His khaki pants and shirt were stained. His face was smeared with black streaks of blood. He was bone-tired, having been on the expedition for the last two months, tending to Sanson's *every* need. Not tonight, he hoped. Sometimes Sanson wanted to talk, and sometimes he wanted rough sex with the girls and sometimes with him. What would it be tonight? The job paid well enough, but this all-encompassing servant role was beyond what he had thought he was signing up for. A washed-up cricket player, Malik was now a practiced tour guide and caravan leader, though he had never had a client such as Sanson who crossed the boundary so quickly from professional to personal and sucked him into his evil world of murder, treasure, sex, and betrayal.

"Quelle est ma raison d'être?" What is my reason for being?

Malik didn't respond to what he considered a rhetorical question from Sanson but was glad that he seemed to be in a talking mood. Maybe the kill had sated his primal desires. Unpredictable, Sanson sometimes spoke with him like he was a childhood friend with whom he had shared a lifetime of secrets. Other times, he chastened Malik like the servant he was. Tonight, he waxed philosophical about the mission.

"This gold is only money. Gambeau and his plans are only temporary," he said. "The Eye of Africa, though, is of unprecedented historical import."

Malik washed the blood off his hands in a bowl of water that he had placed by the fire.

"Why should I be using my creative intellect to entice the Americans to rescue an American citizen? The kidnap was easy. Leaving behind Stockton's journal was almost too obvious. Allowing for the tracker to be placed on a truck was the perfect baited ambush. The hard part was ensuring Sergeant Major Morgan would be on the mission. There was no guarantee."

"You're a genius, Sanson," Malik said, figuring placation was better than severance.

"True. True, Malik, but *this* mission is much larger than either of us. Gambeau and his Chinese gambit is temporary. The money is necessary, but the geopolitical winds will shift in another twenty years. True, they are paying me, and that is how we afford this enterprise. These fools we just disposed of were a risk to my eventual purpose. It is *my* higher calling to find the center of the Eye and search for Poseidon's Temple. Finding the tablet inscribed with the names Evenor, Leucippe, and Cleito next to Poseidon's, that is the treasure. And the tablets with the names of Poseidon's five sets of twins. His family tree. Once we find that, Malik, we will know for sure we are amid Poseidon's Temple in Atlantis. It will replace the Rosetta stone in historical import. I will be eternally famous. Instead of being *le bourreau,* like my ancestors, I will be the one who found the temple. I will live forever."

"Yes, Sanson," Malik whispered. "Forever."

"No amount of *chinoise francs* can replace that!"

Malik had found that Sanson didn't really want a conversation; rather, he sought affirmation of his monologue. At one moment he was a brute, the next a feigned scholar. Enough of a sociopath to want to be known forever for *something,* Sanson had concluded that unearthing the Eye of Africa and proving its existence as Atlantis would bind him forever in the annals of history. If he could prove that Plato had been right about Atlantis being in the middle of the Mauritanian desert, that would possibly earn him the Vautrin Lud Prize, the Nobel Prize of geography, and certainly qualify for a Wikipedia page that lived in eternity. He would proudly ascend the stage at the International Geography Festival in Saint-Dié-des-Vosges to accept the award. For centuries, elementary school students would be researching his name as the one who had discovered the fabled city—the man who made reality out of science fiction. Lesser men were remembered for lesser deeds.

But his soliloquy laid out the chain of events quite clearly. Gambeau had retained him to oversee the Dakhla Accords security and the Chinese actions in the region. Sanson convinced the Chinese general he could double any investment, which he then used to pay for his pursuit of the riches and fame he believed resided within the Eye of Africa. Any threat to the overarching mission, Sergeant Major Morgan included, had to be extinguished. Malik had researched Poseidon's Temple. The tablet Sanson referenced was fabled to have been four small pieces of granite that served as the cornerstones of the temple. Poseidon had his children's names etched into each corner, one for each cardinal direction, signaling the ever-expanding trajectories of his empire.

Sanson spat in disgust the name that could disrupt it all. The fame. The wealth. Living to infinity.

"Zoey Morgan."

Malik looked up at Sanson, his face reflecting orange and black in the crackling fire, a theater mask.

"Who, Sanson?"

Sanson looked at him. "I must get her tomorrow morning. I will go to Chinguetti and bring her here. Then I will learn what she knows." He stood; his large frame silhouetted against the black sky. He was a giant. He walked back into his tent some fifty meters away.

Malik sat by the fire and thought about the name.

American. Female.

He retrieved his satellite smartphone and searched the internet, finding the picture of a beautiful Black woman smiling with a graduation cap and gown, holding her degree. Next to her was a man who looked a lot like the man they had killed.

The man whose wrists he had bound and held until he filmed Sanson severing his head.

12

ON THE FLIGHT TO Dakhla, we reviewed the intelligence on Sanson and the Eye of Africa. I didn't care if the people who inhabited the terrain feature where Zoey was located were half-god and half-human, as Plato theorized, or nomads stopping at an oasis, I would fight to the death to save the daughter of my fallen comrade and pursue Sly's intelligence leads.

One of the maxims I had lived by was to leave no soldier behind. My peers in the Pentagon who forsook that solemn duty during and after the Afghanistan withdrawal demonstrated their allegiance to themselves more than to their troops and their families. Given today's political environment, there was no upside in any of them resigning, though that was exactly the point. You either stood with those with whom you served or you didn't. Loyalty isn't a situational convenience. It's an imperative to serving.

Which was why I didn't even give the national command authority the opportunity to tell me no on my plan to find Zoey and pursue associated missions. I was certain they would do the bureaucratic slow roll as they had done, and were still doing, with other hostages still being held captive. The politicians tweeted and used hashtags to make bold pronouncements about our commitment to our citizens, when in fact actions—*our actions*—always spoke louder than their words.

My dilemma was that while SOCOM had approved the C-17 flight to recover the last of our equipment in Dakhla left over from the Stockton raid, I had no express authorizations to take the Beast or my team into Mauritania. Contrary to popular opinion, the U.S. military could not simply go wherever it chose. We needed the authorities to do so, granted by the leadership of the country in which we intended to operate. Certainly, the president could invoke Article II authority to put the military wherever she chose, but it was a last resort, and I didn't expect that type of support from President Campbell, friend or not, and definitely not from her cabinet.

I had ordered a mission that was not sanctioned by SOCOM or the chairman of the Joint Chiefs but one for which I had seduced the president into half-baked support, leveraging my friendship with her to bypass the system. My priority was to not leave Zoey or any associated concerns to the decision-making inertia of the federal government, but I also wasn't naive. My actions were the ultimate form of "beg forgiveness, as opposed to requesting permission." Sure, Van Dreeves and Hobart had submitted all the usual requests for the C-17 from U.S. Transportation Command and SOCOM, and it was their network of master sergeants and sergeants major that greased the skids until some generals signed the missions and it was just another line item in a secretary of defense orders book mostly overlooked by the too-busy brass. Our mission to recover the remaining equipment was technically approved, but anything beyond loading up the gear and coming home was not.

The president's tepid support of my extended mission

would only last twelve hours or so; enough time to get me a decent head start. By so doing, though, I endangered my team, their careers, and their families, forcing me to confront the perpetual dilemma of "men or mission." The mission, though, if we were right, more than qualified for the risks we were taking and the jeopardy in which I was placing my team.

As we were landing, the sun was rising over the Sea of Dakhla and the golden sands of the Sahara six miles farther east. The sunlight lifting above the water and terrain was an illusion of sorts. It painted a beautiful morning sky with orange and golden streaks across the pristine waters separating the Dakhla Peninsula from the African continent mainland. The image was an imposter, though, a charlatan that tricked you into thinking it had your best interests in mind with its alluring pastels. The problem was God never turned down the daytime heat on the Saharan stove, and as day progressed, the sun continued to rage, baking, and suffocating everything. We would have to carefully plan our operations for nighttime execution with solid exfil plans to reset and rest during the day until we were successful.

No matter how illusory the mainland appeared, the peninsula looked peaceful in its remoteness. I thought of Sly Morgan's missions here in support of gathering intelligence during the meetings for the Dakhla Accords. The reports we studied on the flight and previously were voluminous and, like all intelligence, inconclusive. His imagery, like the one of Sanson, Gambeau, and the others at a castle, were snapshots in time. They did, however, piece together what was happening. Why were Secretary of State McHenry and Secretary of Defense Blankenship spending so much time here with a delegation from China and France? What was to be gained in this remote part of the world that warranted the investment of so much time from such high-level political appointees? Did Sanson's mission in the Sahara hold the key?

Our plane pulled into the same hangar we had used for the exfiltration of Stockton two weeks ago. As we were deplaning from the cargo ramp in the rear, one of the pilots of the C-17 came down the steps and asked to speak to me. We walked toward a corner of the hangar where pallets were stacked with our equipment set for return. McCool and her team rolled the Beast off the back ramp. Then a couple of forklifts fired up and began filling the back of the C-17. Even the air force special operations logisticians were pros.

Lieutenant Colonel Jeremy West was an air force special operations pilot who could fly every operational airframe in the air force inventory and several in the army's. A modern-day Chuck Yeager, West had flown us on cargo missions and rotary insertion and extraction missions. He was a good friend and a force to be reckoned with. Tall and muscular, West was an imposing figure in his flight uniform. We huddled in the corner of the hangar as the engines whined on their spin down. He leveled his blue eyes on me and smiled.

"General, I got a call about two-thirds of the way here that we were to turn around and come back to Bragg, or if we were committed because of fuel, to land, load, and reposition in Rota. Know anything about that?"

"First I'm hearing," I said.

"Our missions, like yours, are compartmented, but I would like to know how far you want me to put my neck on the chopping block here. We left here with SOCOM and TRANSCOM approval for a simple equipment haul-back. I already told them I didn't have the fuel to get back, which was true, and that I would reposition to

Rota as soon as we got refueled and loaded, which they have now ordered me to do."

"I think that's what you should do," I said.

"The funny thing is they asked me to, as the air mission commander, pull rank on you and not let you off the aircraft."

"Seems you failed at that."

He smiled. "And now that you're off the aircraft, you outrank me, and I have no authority over you. So I'm respectfully requesting you to get back on the aircraft."

"Request denied," I said.

"As I figured it might be."

"You can report that we disobeyed you and went rogue."

"Well, that probably won't be necessary, though they are going to have some questions about why I allowed you to off-load—or onload, for that matter—your Black Hawk helicopter."

I retrieved my officer's Beretta pistol from my hip holster and held it low, pointed at the cement flooring, trigger finger along the rail.

"You can now say that I drew my weapon and demanded that you allow me to off-load my helicopter."

He nodded and smiled again. "I only like dancing with my wife, General, but here we are."

I holstered my weapon. "Jeremy, how many missions have we done together?"

"Arkansas public schools don't teach math that high," he said.

"Right. Since you pulled that stunt in Afghanistan, I'm guessing you understand my mission here."

"I wouldn't claim to know your mission, but if it involves recovering an American citizen related to Sly, I want in."

The dance had not been about covering his ass but about wanting in on the mission.

West continued, "I can just tell them I had a loose cotter pin and had to land here and then my crew chief busted a hexagonal flange and found an inoperable jackscrew gyro, and before we knew it, the army assholes had done their thing and I couldn't put the genie back in the bottle or use some other fancy phrase that will make them nod like they understand."

I replied, "I understand that hexagonal flanges are hard to get and that jackscrew gyros are mission essential, not to mention anything of the import of cotter pins. If we didn't have those operating at peak performance, the plane could go down. The military wouldn't worry so much about the soldiers and airmen as they would about losing a three-hundred-million-dollar airplane, all because of a ten-dollar hexagonal flange, a twenty-dollar jackscrew gyro, and a five-cent cotter pin."

"I can order more fictional hexagonal flanges and jackscrew gyros, General. That's not the issue. People are the issue, as they always are. Getting serious for the moment, after the trauma I've seen my men and women go through the last year or two, we have to do everything we can to help *our* people. We broke a solemn fucking bond to our men and women in uniform. Only guys like you and me can restore that."

West had disobeyed orders as a helicopter pilot in Afghanistan by pulling out twenty U.S. citizens and Afghan Special Forces who had been protecting them after the August 31 deadline. He had flown in from Tajikistan as the Taliban were overrunning Panjshir Valley and plucked everyone he could to safety. West was that special breed of warrior who always seemed to be on the same objective as the rest of us when the gunfire started.

"Still keeps me up at night," I said. "Watching our people get their throats cut."

He nodded.

"Best course of action is to reposition to Rota, as I've been directed, order some hexagonal flanges and jackscrew gyros in the twenty-four hours of crew rest we are authorized, and you probably need to ferry that helicopter around, making sure you've got all of your equipment. If you're back in twenty-four hours, call me, and I'll reroute to get you here and take the ass chewing when I'm back," he said, holding his cell phone. "If you're not back in twenty-four hours, I'm going to fly this bitch back to Bragg and be on the first flight here from Raleigh. If you're still here, good. If not, I'll try to find you."

"That's a deal on the first part. On the second part, if we're not back, we'll be long gone, Jeremy. You've got a family to take care of," I said.

"I love my wife of twenty-five years and my four snot-nosed kids, but this here is every bit as much family to me," he said, waving his hand around the hangar with the team busy doing all the things he was supposed to prevent them from doing.

"You got it. If we're here, we're here. If not, be safe trying to find us."

"That's all I can ask for. Got some leave coming up, anyway. But if you don't mind me saying, this is one hell of a big risk you're taking. Only the chairman or that dipshit Luckey would call down and try to cancel this mission. So, while this part is okay, getting the gear and going back, what you're doing is unauthorized. Not that I give a shit about authority, but you gotta know they're going to cut your satellite feeds, comms, GPS, everything. You'll have no intel, no support."

"Yes. On the upside, sort of eliminates the eight-thousand-mile screwdriver," I said. I had thought about those concerns. They were huge issues, but not insurmountable.

"I wouldn't be too sure about that, General. Never underestimate a politician's ability to fuck you over no matter where you are in the world."

I nodded in general agreement.

"And I don't need to tell you this, but your people—Hobart, Van Dreeves, McCool—they'd follow you through the raging fires of hell."

His point was one I had spent the better part of the flight thinking about. Like West, they all had hopes and dreams, something to live for beyond combat or whatever trouble I was about to get them into. Van Dreeves and McCool had rekindled their relationship. Wang and Black both had significant others. Chief Warrant Officer Jorge Suarez, McCool's new copilot who had maxed out Nightstalker selection, was married with two children. Hobart had Zoey, we hoped. And there was me, with my children, Brad and Reagan, already responsible adults. Our love was strong, for sure, but could they survive without me? Most likely. The real question was, would they prefer me as a whole person who lived my values authentically or someone who had given away a part of myself to continue to move up the ladder of "success"?

We all knew the answer to that.

I was reminded of that Janis Joplin refrain, *Freedom's just another word for nothing left to lose . . .*

I was at that point of having nothing left to lose, but my team deserved a fair discussion about the mission, and I was going to give them one.

"You need to reposition to Rota, correct?"

"I could risk staying here, but it's a risk for my crew, too, and they're not as frisky as your team. My preference would be to push our crew rest window and reposition to Rota. You and I both know that there's no such thing as hexagonal flanges or jackscrew gyros, but it sounds good to the brass."

"Give me forty-five minutes. Anyone on my team not showing up is choosing to stay. I won't show up, so have a safe trip back, Jeremy. I hope not to see you again for a while," I said.

"For a while," he said, looking away and then at me. We did the warrior hand-to-forearm clasp and bumped shoulders.

As McCool and her crew were finishing spreading the blades on the Beast with the help of Wang and Black, I summoned Hobart and Van Dreeves.

"Team meeting as soon as Sally is done with her checklist and has the Beast tied down."

They alerted the team, and fifteen minutes later, we were in the same spartan office bay where we had spoken with Stockton and recovered from the mission two weeks ago.

Hobart, Van Dreeves, McCool, Wang, Black, and Suarez gathered in front of me, none of them choosing to sit down, most likely expecting to sprint out of the room and pursue actionable intelligence on Zoey's location.

I studied my team, each member with a river of experiences we collectively shared, save Suarez, who had maxed out in Nightstalker selection. They stared at me expectantly.

"Team, we've had a good run-up until two weeks ago. I made some mistakes that I should have foreseen. The last couple of years have been tough. The veteran community is shattered, not to mention those of us who remain on active duty. There comes a point in time where I must ask myself if I can continue to serve a government that abandoned our people and our allies in a combat zone. For a while, I thought I could do more from within the system than from outside and had concluded until two weeks ago that staying inside was the proper course of action.

"But now I have a decision to make because I'm concerned our government will not authorize us to begin active search and rescue operations for Zoey and to then conduct subsequent operations. We have until this point been mostly between the guardrails. Joe and Randy have all the approvals for our flight here. We got a wink and a nod from the air force to include the Beast because there was the potential that some ammunition and gear might need to be transported from the ammunition bunkers twenty miles away. But the brass is onto us—rather, they're onto me. They've requested we reposition with the C-17 to Rota, Spain. Also, you need to know that I am the subject of an active inspector general investigation into the incidents surrounding the secretary of state's demise during the Parizad incident."

"Don't say it, boss," Hobart said. He had no idea what I was about to say, but I understood his comment. The less they knew, the better. They could go on this mission believing they were following lawful orders. Even though he was angry at me for allowing Zoey her head start, he was able to rise above his emotions and see the bigger picture.

I nodded at Hobart and said, "Joe, I understand. What I will say is that Jeremy is standing by in the C-17 to ferry anyone who wants to leave back to Rota, where he will remain overnight before heading back to Bragg. I'm expendable. All of you have full lives to live. There is risk to this mission beyond the immediate tactical danger we will be putting ourselves in. There will be fallout. I will, as always, attempt to shield you from that, but given that I'm most likely reaching tracer burnout in my career, I don't want any of you to step forward if you're uncertain in any way about what the risks are. I've always said that personal motivations are either the least or most pure with no in-between. My motivation is to find Zoey, avenge Sly's murder, and to see if he was right about what he believed he discovered. It may not be a national command authority priority; in fact, I'm pretty sure it's not. If Sly was right, though, there could be nothing of higher import. Zoey's already taken the risk, and I'm going to find her. And after what we've been through together, all of us, I would rather pursue this mission without sanction than put a fist through the wall at Fort Bragg, frustrated that I didn't."

They stared at me for a full minute, speechless, their collective dumbstruck countenance watching me not in an astonished way but in a *what-are-you-fucking-kidding-me* way. A *how-could-you-even-consider-we-wouldn't-stick-with-you* way.

Then McCool took charge of her team. She picked up her aviator kit bag that contained her weapons, night vision goggles, and other necessary gear and stepped forward toward me and turned around.

"I'm with the general," she said. "Don't even have to think about it."

Hobart and Van Dreeves did the same, turning around to stare at Wang, Black, and Suarez. Wang and Black didn't hesitate, stepping forward and turning around to face Suarez, who maintained a stern, set jaw. He stared back at the entire team, most likely feeling somewhat intimidated by the situation in which I had unfairly placed him.

He broke into a broad grin and said, "My *mamacita* has huge *cojones* . . . but not bigger than mine."

He stepped forward and turned around. Jeremy West

stood in the doorway, saying, "I'm guessing I've got zero pax for backfill."

"Roger that," McCool said.

With that, my team had chosen an undeniable career-ending move. I had placed them in this position and would absorb as much of the blowback as possible, but whatever blame was to come was entirely mine. The question many operators had been struggling with since Afghanistan was, which is more important: *My career or my commitment to my team?* The nation broke faith with our citizens and our partners that had helped us for two decades, leaving those of us who had spent multiple tours in this fight to ponder the misalignment of our nation's values from our solemn, unbreakable, leave-no-person-behind commitment. There was no reconciling that issue. Our national policy had been to abandon American citizens and our allies in Afghanistan in direct contravention of our warrior code and ethos. There was already a stark dissonance between the 3 percent of the population who served and the country's political leadership. Now much of the veteran community was adrift, convinced their sacrifices were worthless.

To us, finding Zoey was not some theoretical drill; it was a moral imperative. Not to mention the larger issues at stake that Sly's research and intelligence operation had uncovered.

In our corner of the U.S. military, we collectively saw that finding and securing Zoey would in some small way begin to tilt the balance of our ethos to never abandon a fallen comrade back toward fulfilment of that solemn pledge. Our one step would lead to other steps. We expected no praise for our effort. In fact, we expected punishment would be the likely outcome.

West climbed back into the C-17, closed the ramp,

and was pushed out by the aviation tug before spooling up his engines and screaming down the runway. Left in the echoing silence was a team that had chosen loyalty to each other over their next career move, an uncommon occurrence in today's military, but a union borne of our shared sacrifice and the mounting conditions that indicated our country and perhaps world was in peril.

Proud and focused, I now wonder how each of their lives might have played out differently had I not put them in such an untenable situation.

13

FULLY COMMITTED AND WITH pretense out of the way, we huddled in the conference room at the metal table and discussed our options.

Our DaggerFind software ran on an internal virtual private network, VPN, that the technology geniuses in the Pentagon would take a day or two to figure out and shut down. We had outsourced the development and hosting of this satellite-based location platform to a private company with all the proper top-secret clearances. We contracted for a low-earth-orbit satellite that housed all our classified data, which so far had worked perfectly to our knowledge.

Van Dreeves pointed at the monitor in the conference room toward the Eye of Africa terrain feature.

"Zoey's just north of Chinguetti," he said. "In between Chinguetti and Ouadane. Or at least that's where the watch and phone are, though both are on their last legs. Watch is showing nine percent battery, and the phone had fourteen percent. I'm sure the heat isn't helping anything, either."

"Can you plot the history of her movements?" I asked.

"Sure, give me a few minutes," Van Dreeves said.

Then Hobart looked up and said, "I've got a message from Farouk."

"Go ahead," I said.

Hobart's friend Farouk Ahmed was a renowned Moroccan Special Forces sniper. He and Hobart had attended sniper training in the United States, Morocco, France, and Belgium and had won all the requisite badges and awards that are winnable in the sniper community, which is relatively small.

"Turns out he's here in Dakhla with his unit doing some security patrols," Hobart said.

"Still on our team?" I asked.

"Wouldn't be talking to him if he wasn't, boss," Hobart said.

"Can he come in for a face-to-face?"

"Be here in thirty minutes."

"Don't read him onto the full mission. Just the pursuit of Sanson," I said.

They nodded in understanding, if not agreement.

By then, Van Dreeves had the plot of Zoey's movements from Rabat. He said, "She must have landed from the United States and followed Route N12 along the Draa River, passing through the lower Atlas Mountains, hitting Tiznet along the coast and then Smara before crossing into Mauritania. She followed N1 down to Atar, which is about forty to forty-five miles from Chinguetti, where we did the Stockton mission." Then, "Looks like she got stuck here," he said, pointing at an icon that indicated she'd stopped moving.

"Or she went to ground to plan," I said.

"She's definitely bait there. Sanson has most likely bought off the locals," Hobart said.

"Wait a minute," McCool said. "She's not in captivity yet?"

"We're not sure," I said. "She hit DaggerFind, which we are presuming that she would only do in extremis."

"We've hung out some," McCool said. "She's got a wild streak. Very unpredictable, I would say. Enough of a wild streak to call in reinforcements as opposed to asking for help."

It didn't surprise me that McCool had gone there so quickly, but it still was unnerving. Intelligence was only crystal clear in hindsight, and analysis always involved speculating on enemy intent, which was an imprecise science. Either Zoey was our advance party to kill or capture Sanson and exploit gained intelligence, or she was held captive already.

"Does it matter?" Hobart asked. The defensive tone in his voice persisted.

"No," I said. "We have to find her either way. But now you can see the ambiguity in the mission and why we had that conversation a few minutes ago."

Hobart's phone buzzed. He walked to the door and let Farouk in. He was dressed in a Moroccan Special Forces black uniform, a balaclava pulled down around his neck, an Ops-Core high-cut helmet tucked under his arm, and PGM Ultima Ratio sniper rifle slung across his back. He was dark skinned from birth and reddened from the sun. His black hair was thick and wavy, matching his trimmed beard. He had copper eyes that were two cold stones set deep in their sockets.

"General, this is Sergeant Farouk Ahmed, the best sniper in the Moroccan army, if not the world. He worked with Sly during the Dakhla Accords mission."

"Farouk," I said, reaching out my hand. He shook it with a firm grip. I motioned for him to sit down, and he took a minute to disassemble his equipment so that he would fit in the chair. The PGM was spotless.

Its Picatinny rail was filled with a flashlight and night vision laser.

"Joe tells me you are looking for Sanson," he said without preamble.

"Yes," I said.

"Sly was a good man. I want in on anything going after Sanson. He's been running caravans out of Ouadane. We have humint inside the town and inside his caravan. They believe that l'Oeil d'Afrique is Atlantis or some such nonsense."

"I'm told they found gold," I said.

"Yes. The French army found some near Chinguetti, too, but that doesn't mean Poseidon's Temple is around the corner. Trading routes from Timbuktu and Oualata go right past there. When Timbuktu was burning, there were reports of the merchants moving north to hide mostly books, but the gold, too. Because it was a trade hub, it became a banking center. People today forget that commerce has gone on as long as we've been on earth in one form or another."

"So, either way, Sanson is motivated to find more gold, and if he's lucky, he finds some dishes or something from ten thousand years ago that show signs of civilization," Van Dreeves said.

"Something like that, but it's not that simple. Whale bones have been found near Ouadane. Seashells are everywhere in that part of the desert. Plato's hypothesis was that the ocean was there directly up against the Richat Structure, which is the formal name of the terrain feature," Farouk said.

"So now you're arguing against yourself, Farouk," Hobart said.

"No, Joe. I am saying that a narcissistic criminal like Sanson could easily believe that his rightful place in history is to discover Atlantis."

"And therefore, he will be determined to continue his mission, if that's all there is to it," I said.

"Exactly, General. And what happened with Sly is tragic. My sources tell me that they had an altercation in Dakhla a couple of months ago," Farouk said.

"Sly and Sanson?"

"Yes. Sanson had reverse engineered some of the intercepts that Sly had acquired. Followed him. That's why Stockton was kidnapped. To bait your team into a trap," Farouk said.

We all sat in stunned silence. My mind was racing. If that was true, how could Sanson guarantee that Sly would be boots on the ground? He couldn't unless he had a connection inside the U.S. military.

Luckey? Rolfing? Blankenship? Luckey had expressly ordered me not to be on the mission. Was that at the urging of Blankenship or Rolfing?

"Jesus," I said. "What evidence do you have of this?"

"Americans are not the only ones that can intercept intelligence. We have sources and methods, General. Just as you are not reading me into the entire scope of your mission, I cannot reveal everything I know. But know this: Stockton was a baited ambush. None of you were supposed to survive."

"Why didn't you tell us sooner?"

"Intelligence has latency. Information must be assessed and analyzed. Sometimes it only works in hindsight. I looked at everything we had after your mission and rearranged a few pieces of information, and there it was. Sanson calling a well-known group of kidnap-for-ransom thugs in western Mauritania and coordinating the abduction. That was followed by another call to a burner phone in America telling the recipient to keep you, General, off the mission and send in Sly."

"This is crazy," Van Dreeves said.

"As crazy as it is, it is true."

"Who else knows what you just told us?" I asked.

"My general, General Atouk, a good man, and my two teammates, Samir and Lokmane. They have experience with Sanson and can confirm this."

"We're keeping this to a minimum right now but will keep them in mind. I'm sure we'll need the help sometime." Then to Hobart, "Joe, what do you think?"

"It changes nothing. Zoey's out there, and we have to find her," he replied. "She's the key."

"I agree." Then to Farouk, I asked, "What's up with Sanson's airplane?"

"He's got a Sherpa that can land anywhere that has two hundred meters of flat road. He braves the caravan site on occasion but typically flies out when the caravan is relocating. He used to come here to Dakhla and keep the Sherpa in a hangar next door. Because we are onto him, he's been using other airfields, primarily one down in Nouadhibou, about three hundred and fifty kilometers south of here. There's a Mauritanian military base close by. He buys them off, and they give him safe passage. He's been spotted meeting with French, Chinese, and U.S. officials."

"What don't you know?" McCool asked. Her eyes were flint. No smile on her lips. Suspicious, maybe.

"Lots of stuff, ma'am, but the king has tasked my team with tracking the Polisario uprising, gathering intel, and reporting back. A couple of years ago, we annexed the Western Sahara, which we now call our Southern Province, which is where we are. All this development you see is at risk. We are trying to replicate what you have in California or Florida with lucrative resorts that attract tourists. Any terrorism or rebel activity to disrupt this effort is the king's highest priority," Farouk said.

"The king?" McCool quipped.

"Sally, Farouk used to be the king's bodyguard. This makes sense," Hobart said.

"I also just met him five minutes ago, so cut me some slack, Joe. He just told us Sergeant Major Morgan was a targeted killing. Are we next? Is Zoey bait?"

Everyone was on edge. We were a tight-knit team, and allowing a newcomer immediate access, while necessary, was unusual. McCool was protective of me specifically and of the team in general.

"I understand Colonel McCool's concerns. I am a new face to her and the rest of you. Joe, you have known me for years. We have shot together and broken bread. I am here to help if you need it. Anytime Joe asks for something, he gets it from me. He has done the same for me."

"Good enough, Sally?"

She nodded and said, "Though Hobart's kind of sketchy, so I don't know."

Hobart coughed something that sounded like *Fuck you* into his hand, and Van Dreeves laughed.

"Who's your source in Sanson's caravan?" McCool asked.

"Again, not telling anyone that. Not revealing my sources," he said. "And it's best that you don't know until you need to. My information is reliable."

I took control of the conversation again and said, "So between Farouk's intel, Zoey's phone and watch, which will die any second, but both of which we can track passively, we have something to formulate a plan around."

"Chips?" Farouk asked.

"Yes. Homemade within JSOC," Van Dreeves said.

He nodded and said, "Those should keep working." Then he turned to me and offered, "I have some leave coming up if you need a guide."

"I'll take that under advisement with the team, but I'm inclined to say yes," I said.

"I'm good with it if everyone else is," McCool said. Van Dreeves and Hobart gave thumbs-ups, also.

"Okay, so you're in. It's 0900 hours local. What's your recommendation on rescue mission? Daylight or nighttime?" I said.

"Nighttime is always better simply because of the heat, but given the pressing matter of the situation, I'd recommend as soon as we review the intel and have discussed a plan," Farouk said.

"What size force does Sanson have?" I asked.

"He's got a caravan of about twenty camel handlers, tent pitchers, and archeologists. It's a basic caravan team out of Marrakech. He has two personal security guys that are always within orbit, but I'm told they can be lax. They're big guys. They're French who have some affiliation with the Polisario. They worked in Brahim Ghali's security detail for a while as contractors. Cut from the French military and went into the private mercenary business."

"Ghali?"

"The leader of the Polisario Front. They are amped up about Morocco seizing control of the Western Sahara. They've been creating problems, trying to get somebody's attention, but it's pretty low-level stuff. Though we have some indications that they have new weapons, perhaps U.S. surplus equipment from Afghanistan. Humvees, rifles, night vision goggles."

"The goggles could be a problem. What's Sanson's connectivity with the Polisario? Just the guards, or is there something more formal?"

"There's nothing much formal about the Polisario other than a loose political and military structure. They would like to attack to reclaim the Southern Province, but they lack the organizational capacity to do so."

"So not much security with Sanson or threat from the Polisario," Van Dreeves said.

"The twenty or so with Sanson have weapons and can defend, but they're not a professional security team. Not since your team killed most of them. He may be rebuilding, but we've seen no sign of that."

"Have they found anything on their digs besides gold?" I asked.

"They have staked out multiple locations in l'Oeil d'Afrique. They've found gold in two of the tunnels or caves. If you go by the Atlantis theory, they're tunnels. If you go by the nature theory, they're caves. The Chinese have been sniffing around there."

Since Farouk had some basic knowledge of the Chinese aspect of our intelligence, I said, "We can discuss the Chinese part next. We know it's connected, but we need to find Zoey first. Back to Sanson. Do you know where on this map he is now?"

"The caravan moves. The only known fixed point is their resupply run in Chinguetti here." Farouk pointed at the map to the small town southwest of the Eye of Africa. "The caravan master is a Moroccan named Malik. He is a professional guide. Not political. Just a merchant, so he could help us if we interdict a supply run. They have good communications, though, and Sanson will be gone if any part of his network is disrupted. If he's gone, Zoey's gone. If we don't find Zoey, perhaps we don't figure out the rest."

After pausing, Farouk continued by tracing a long finger around the circular terrain feature. "Here is the Eye, with the concentric rings that make some believe this was Plato's Atlantis. The eyebrow is up here, and the caravan has been all over these locations. Their gold finds have been on the western edge, along the trading routes, and their digs happen wherever Sanson believes Poseidon's Temple must be buried near the middle."

Farouk walked us around the image with practiced ease as if he were about to perform several sniper shots on each location he mentioned. He spoke with the professional efficiency of someone who studied terrain for a living, which all good soldiers must do.

"Why hasn't someone nailed him down?" McCool said.

"The Sahara is large. The Eye of Africa is large, also. Morocco doesn't have the aerial reconnaissance assets that your country does, and I'm guessing that you don't have access to those, either. The information I have is at least a day or two old by the time I receive it."

Farouk's comment made me believe that he had a contact in Chinguetti where the resupply occurred for the caravan.

"I agree. Sanson is skilled. He's managing an entire caravan, finding gold, moving around in an airplane, and is connected in France, maybe Morocco, and maybe China," I said.

"The French part I'm not sure about. I know the king is interested in his archeological pursuits from a strictly historical perspective, but I am not aware of anyone in Morocco who directly supports him," Farouk said. "The meetings in Dakhla have been highly irregular, forced upon us by your country and France, quite frankly. As a result of that meeting, anything Morocco, the United States, France, or the Mauritanians do in this region gets shared with the Chinese and supposedly vice versa, but that much is doubtful. The Dakhla Accords. Your tech CEOs were there, too. All double top-secret kind of stuff. Thought it was Bilderberg for a few days."

Hobart said, "What if the dig thing is all bullshit? What if it's a ruse for something else?"

"A magician's trick?" Van Dreeves said. "Like, look over here while I do the real thing here?" He wiggled both hands in the air, spread apart, to demonstrate his point.

"Maybe that's why he moves around so much," Mc-Cool said.

Farouk was silent, pensive. He was pondering the thought, which was a good one. What kind of ruse would you need in the desert to make someone look in one direction so that they didn't see what was happening in the other direction? The Sahara was vast. The Eye of Africa was an enormous structure within a massive, indistinct piece of land the size of the United States. What would they be hiding if anything at all?

While everyone was pondering Hobart's insight, two chimes sounded with successive *ding-ding* alerts, putting a stop to the conversation. We stared at the map displayed on the monitor and watched as the icon marked *Watch* moved fractionally north and the icon marked *Phone* moved slightly south.

"Her watch and phone decoupled," Van Dreeves said. "I wrote the program to alert if they were ever spaced more than thirty feet apart."

"Could she be recharging her watch or phone?" Hobart asked.

"There's no indicator showing that either device is actually active or has power. We're just tracking chips right now. So, I don't believe so," Van Dreeves said.

"She either lost something or has been robbed," Mc-Cool said.

"Or kidnapped," Hobart said.

"This is it," I said. "It's go time."

As we were moving to the helicopter, the presidential burner in my pocket buzzed. I continued pacing to my chariot and answered the freshly charged phone.

"Yes, ma'am?"

"You're *way* outside your lane, Garrett."

"Yes, ma'am," I replied. I pressed End and stuffed the phone in my pocket. Was that a warning? An admonishment? A heads-up? A confirmation? Venting?

Regardless of interpretation, we *were* completely outside of our lane.

14

WE HAD GONE OVER the plan several times. Refined it and looked at branches and sequels to the main course of action. As always, actionable intelligence would be the main driver, feeding decision points as they arose.

We still didn't fully comprehend how the Eye of Africa factored into the equation. We understood there was a railroad that fed from the coast to central Mauritania near the Eye. We also knew that Sanson was operating around that structure with a light footprint, but a signature nonetheless.

McCool and team had secured two external stores support system fuel tanks on either side of the MH-60 that increased the range from just over 400 miles to around 1,100 miles.

Chinguetti was 320 miles to the east. Ouadane was another 60 miles from there. With hover time and searching, we were going to be pressing up against the limits of the airframe if we wanted to make it back to Dakhla.

"There are three small airfields in the area. I figured we could have Farouk talk to them if we get in a bind," McCool said. The helicopter lifted from the airfield, heavy, laden with five full fuel tanks, which included the internal tank. We were a flying bomb. A few stray bullets into any of the tanks would create a spectacular explosion, sending us all packing well before we might have hoped.

"That might not work out the way you want," Farouk said. "Morocco just annexed the Western Sahara. We're not super popular with the Mauritanian rebels. But I can try."

We were seated in the cargo area of my command helicopter, wearing headsets and watching the drone feed that Van Dreeves had piping into the helicopter communications suite. Hobart and Van Dreeves were facing me with their backs to the cockpit while Farouk and I were next to each other on the rear bench seat. Black and Wang were in their respective crew hatches, manning machine guns and wearing their space-age crew helmets. Suarez was in his copilot seat, hands on his knees while McCool had the controls. The air smelled faintly of jet fuel. The cloudless sky promised that by the time we got to the Eye of Africa, the temperature would be well over one hundred degrees Fahrenheit. The gates of hell.

"Understand," McCool said. Her voice vibrated with the shudder of the helicopter blades whipping at 250 rpm.

"Maybe we'll get lucky with some that don't support the rebels," Farouk said.

"Maybe. Anyway, we have these two rally points if we all get separated. The one here on the right we'll call the Mole because that's what it looks like on the map. It's just above the eyebrow on the Eye of Africa. The other is here, to the left by about five miles. We'll call that the Freckle because that's as creative as I could get."

"The Mole and the Freckle. Got it," Van Dreeves said. He smiled from across the table we had between us. Hobart remained focused on the map.

"Boss is super creative," McCool said.

"Drone has movement," Van Dreeves said, focusing our attention on the monitor, which showed two men escorting a Black woman, whom we assumed was Zoey, along a road. Others were watching. Her hands were tied behind her back. Some uniformed men stood at the entrance to a building, most likely a constabulary or police headquarters.

"That's her," Hobart said.

"Can you have them zoom in?" I asked. I wasn't as sure as Hobart. The odds were that it was Zoey, but the grainy image was from above, perhaps capturing three buildings on either side of a dirt road and showing maybe ten people, including the onlookers.

"Roger," Van Dreeves said, and then the screen went blank. "Reaper, this is Beast control," Van Dreeves said.

"Beast control, this is Reaper, negative comms going forward."

"They're shutting us down," I said. The simmering pilot light of rage began to grow inside me. At least the operator had the dignity to let us know he was disconnecting, as opposed to simply doing it and leaving us to wonder.

"Still a go, boss?" McCool asked.

"Still a go," I replied. But we were blind. We had no intelligence, surveillance, or reconnaissance capabilities. "Randy, pull up the DaggerFind."

Two dots blinked on the screen, one green and one blue.

"Blue is the phone, and green is the watch," Van Dreeves said. "Like I said, both are dead, but we're tracking chips."

The Beast rocked with turbulence. The winds off the desert floor collided with the ocean breeze as we crossed the shoreline. Sand crept from the waterline as far as the eye could see, as if Western Sahara was one giant beach. Only a few black and brown boulders added any perspective to the terrain. A small town slid beneath us to our starboard side, a smattering of adobe huts crisscrossed by dirt roads.

"Where is she in relation to those two dots?" I asked.

"Working that now. Didn't have time to geo-locate the feed, but I did screenshot the image," Van Dreeves said. After a minute of silence, Van Dreeves hit a button, and an image appeared on the screen.

"She's got her watch on, boss," he said.

"Okay, so where's the phone?" I asked.

"There's a building here. That's where it probably is," Van Dreeves said.

"Okay, we're following the watch," I said.

"Roger that," McCool said as she nosed the Pave Hawk forward, reaching maximum speed of just over two hundred miles per hour. At this rate, we would be in Chinguetti in an hour and a half. Zoey could be anywhere by then.

Under my breath, I cursed the president, Luckey, and anyone else involved with shutting down our strategic video feed. But what was I to expect? I was fortunate to have my team and our helicopter, who had not only followed me into what very well might be the burning gates of hell, the Eye of Africa, but had breezily tossed their careers aside.

Unsanctioned and unsupported, we pressed ahead in near silence until we approached Chinguetti.

"Where's the green dot?" I asked.

"Not far from the blue dot now," Van Dreeves said.

"Okay, let's put down on the north side of town and

work from building to building," I said. "Randy and I will move on the north side, and Joe and Farouk will move on the south side of the road. Mission is to secure amcit Zoey Morgan and return her to safety."

"Roger that," they said in unison.

"Cools, you reposition to a protected space," I said.

"Roger that. Will find my safe space," she said, the corner of her lip turning upward. She was cool under fire if nothing else.

As the Beast clawed at the hot desert air, we did a map drill on the table between us.

"Boss, there's high ground here to the north," Van Dreeves said. "Joe will move along the ridge, and I'll stay on this trail behind the buildings at the base of the ridge. It's better if we split the two snipers."

His finger moved along a black feature just above the village on the satellite image.

"You and Farouk will be on the south side. When we encounter locals, Farouk, you're our go-to guy. The boss is already sporting a beard, so he can go local with the best of them. Speaks French, too."

By now, I had two days of growth on my face. My beard always grew fast, and it would only take a day or two in the sun to help my face blend better with those of the local population. What didn't blend were our outer tactical vests, digitized combat uniforms, and weapons. I carried an M4 snapped to the front of my body armor and my Beretta pistol on my right hip. A Blackhawk knife was attached by Velcro to my vest just above my first aid kit and ammunition pouches. I carried a mix of 5.56 mm and 9 mm ammunition. We used the CamelBak systems, filled with three quarts of water each, save Hobart, who carried a HAWG with nearly a gallon. Van Dreeves was the team medic and carried a mission-tailored first aid kit.

"Why don't we put Farouk on the ridge with Randy, and I can go in with you," Hobart said.

"I'd rather have whatever local knowledge we can have at the point of inflection here, which seems to be the hands-on rescue op and not a lifesaving sniper shot," I said. "Besides, he's only the world's best sniper."

A little levity sometimes goes a long way.

"Second best," Hobart said.

"The general is a smart man," Farouk said. "A great instinct for talent."

The tension eased for a moment, each of us understanding that what we were doing was not only for Zoey's sake but to honor Sly's memory and certainly what he would want us to be doing. Hobart wanted to be the first to see and secure Zoey. I wanted to separate his emotion from the task at hand.

McCool touched down lightly, and we poured from the Pave Hawk. She was maybe on the ground for three seconds. In the wake of her departure was deafening silence slowly attenuated by the recovery of our hearing to the point we were whispering commands and on the move.

Farouk found a wadi into which I followed him, allowing us to remain covered and concealed from the village. We were maybe a mile away, using the offset landing zone and terrain masking to maintain as much stealth as possible. As we narrowed the distance, camels barked and men shouted, sounding like the normal regimen of business in a small African village. Languages spoken seemed to be Arabic, French, and some local African dialect I didn't recognize.

"Overwatch established," Van Dreeves whispered into my earbud. I tapped Farouk and gave him a thumbs-up, so we pressed ahead. "Eyes on the crowd in front of the constabulary."

A small adobe hut was to the south of the road that led from Chinguetti to Ouadane, the path to the center of the Richat Structure that was the Eye of Africa.

"There," Farouk said.

A man carrying an AK-47 and guiding a train of three camels tethered by ropes was walking east, out of town, and would pass us in another minute. We kept our profile low, hugging the side of the wadi, which was an apparent refuse dump for the villagers. The sun was well into the hottest part of the day at after 4:00 p.m. local, and the stench from the trash and human waste was revolting. The smell of dead animals was pungently mixed with that of feces and urine. There was little wind to whisk away the odor.

"Bogey approaching airfield," McCool said into our earpieces.

"Sherpa?" I whispered.

"Roger," she said.

We were maybe four hundred meters from our target, which was the police station. The airfield was another half mile from the police station on the opposite side of the village.

"I've got visual on a Sherpa aircraft similar to the other night coming in for hot landing," McCool said.

"I see Zoey," Hobart barked. "They've put her in a car headed to the airfield. Tan Renault. Looks twenty years old."

We started running along the wadi, but our efforts were useless against the speed of the vehicle. Maybe the helicopter had tripped a sensor that had signaled the airplane to land, or perhaps it was already planned. Regardless, the vehicle was as Hobart described: an old sunbaked, tan Renault riding low on its axles.

There was no opportunity to use our weapons against the car to stop it. Shooting out the tires could work if we didn't have the risk of a stray round harming Zoey. When bullets hit roads or vehicles, the ricochets were unpredictable, no matter how excellent the shooter. The two machine guns on the Beast were too imprecise for the surgery we were attempting here. McCool could interdict the airplane, but she and her steed were our only way out of here.

"Shot on the airplane?" Hobart asked. "Vehicle arriving airfield."

The real predicament was that if we took hostile action and missed, didn't kill the king, as they say, then the retribution against Zoey could be fierce and swift.

"Scope whoever is on the plane. Pilot, passengers, et cetera. Worst case, we follow it," I said. Keeping stand-off and following the aircraft could create the same situation of shooting and missing. But we had no good alternative. We finally reached the edge of the airfield, baking in the heat as the Renault swiftly turned onto the tarmac and parked next to the Sherpa. The pilot slid open a side door, and they dumped Zoey in like a sack of cargo, closed the door, and then buzzed along the runway before lifting off.

"Sally, can you track this thing?" I asked.

"Roger. But we have an issue. If I come and pick you up, that will take fifteen minutes, and we blow our cover. By then, I'll lose the airplane. My air-to-air radar only goes out twenty miles. That thing flies two hundred miles per hour, and in fifteen minutes, it will be out of range. Plus, I've got fuel issues depending on where the airplane goes."

This was a moment where the cessation of U.S. government support hurt the most. I could have used drones to track the airplane, or satellites or AWACS or JSTARS, all airplanes that tracked aerial and/or ground movement.

One of the basic rules of Ranger School was to never split your patrol beyond line of sight. If I ordered McCool to pursue the airplane, I would not only be splitting the patrol but also potentially stranding her and us. Mechanical issues were prevalent in desert operations, and while I had full confidence in her team, there would be no help coming from Uncle Sam.

But still, we had to try.

"Where are the green and blue dots right now?" I asked.

"Watch is moving. Phone is at the constabulary," Van Dreeves said.

"Sally, follow the Sherpa for thirty minutes and then return. Try to get an azimuth on their direction and possible destination. Stay far enough behind that they don't notice you."

"Roger, though Sherpas don't normally have air-to-air radars like ours; there's no telling what this guy has put in the cockpit. Point being, I may not be invisible."

"Do your best. Then come back here to the airfield, and we will secure the fuel pump after investigating the town."

"Roger; see you in a bit," McCool said.

"Status?" I asked over our internal communications.

"Three and Four, up," Hobart said for himself and Van Dreeves, who used the Dagger Three and Dagger Four call signs. Hobart handled operations and Van Dreeves the logistics.

"Up over here, also."

"Break, break, convoy moving from south to north toward Chinguetti," Hobart said.

Farouk and I repositioned to be able to look to the

south and see what Hobart was referencing, but we didn't have the elevation. After ten minutes of repositioning, we finally saw four flatbed trucks heading north. On the backs were shiny black tarps covering large mechanical parts. The tarps were strapped down tightly, professionally done, cinched to the frame of the bed, covering whatever mysterious cargo lay beneath. This wasn't some haphazard nomadic delivery with flapping canvas and loose cargo. The Mercedes-Benz cabs glistened in the dusk, fresh paint winking at the setting sun to the west. Resupplies for Sanson? Construction equipment for an unknown project?

The trucks roared past Chinguetti, passing within a half mile of us, then turned northeast toward Ouadane and the lip of the Eye of Africa.

"Anybody know how to read Mandarin?" Hobart asked. "Because all I'm seeing through my scope is Mercedes-Benz peace signs and Chinese writing."

As the dust plumes created by the vehicles faded to the northeast, the chopping of helicopter blades initially reassured me. But these weren't the Pave Hawk blades, which had a distinctive throttle. These blades sounded choppier, perhaps a different rotation direction, like the Russian Hind or the Hip aircraft, but not quite that, either. I had heard many of those in Afghanistan and other conflict zones.

"Chinese Z-10 spitting thirty mike mike," Van Dreeves said.

The explosions of a 30 mm ammunition round shook the ground like artillery. Because of the high velocity of the guns, hundreds of small explosions turned into a relatively large blast when you put it all together.

Farouk and I leaped back into the wadi we had been traversing, dust, rocks, and shrapnel clawing their way across the scorched desert earth.

Breathing deeply and checking on Farouk, who was wide-eyed but silent, perhaps wondering what the hell he had gotten himself into, I thought about Hobart and Van Dreeves exposed on the ridgeline. They were seasoned soldiers that could take cover from a strafing run. And while I didn't know much about the Z-10 attack helicopter, I did know that it came armed with an air-to-air missile capability.

As soon as my mind processed that information and I prepared to alert McCool and the Beast crew, I heard an explosion over the horizon. An orange fireball billowed upward, black smoke curling inside like a poisonous snake.

I tapped my throat microphone and said, "Beast, Dagger Six, over."

No response.

"Beast, Dagger Six, over." My voice climbed an octave.

No response.

"Damn it, Sally, answer the radio!" I shouted.

For a moment, I heard absolutely nothing except the ringing inside my head.

Then Farouk dove on top of me as machine-gun fire raked our position.

15

PRESIDENT CAMPBELL'S ALEXA COMMUNICATIONS network kicked into gear as she spoke in the White House Situation Room.

"Talk to me about this Chinese flotilla," Campbell said.

"They've been doing this for years. It's not a big deal. The flotilla is about seven hundred fishing vessels. The industry term for it is *distant-water fishing*. We use the euphemism *illegal, unregulated, and unreported* fishing," Secretary of State Bryn McHenry said. McHenry was a tenured professor at Harvard and a business partner of Secretary of Defense Angela Blankenship when she was tapped for the senior diplomat position. She had short gray hair, a snub nose, and designer glasses with red rims. She was a large woman with broad shoulders.

"Thank you, Bryn. Are these fishing vessels a threat to us?"

On the Situation Room screen was a map of the northwest tier of the African continent between Senegal and Morocco, showing the Atlantic Ocean from Cape Verde to the Canary Islands. The interactive map was littered with small white maritime icons indicating the hundreds of fishing vessels that were prowling the fertile waters off the coast of Africa.

"They're not necessarily a threat to us. There's this report, and some seem overly concerned about it, but not me. As you know, Angela and I just signed the Dakhla Accords that reduce tensions with China by increasing transparency in communications with them, especially on the African continent."

"I would say this, Madam President, that Chinese IUU *does* threaten food security not only in Africa but worldwide, but as Bryn has said, it doesn't directly threaten the United States," Secretary of Defense Blankenship said. Her voice strained toward an authoritarian effect but landed somewhere short.

"Does this impact our foreign aid program to the Sahel?" Campbell asked. The Sahel was the important transition zone just south of the Sahara and north of the dense tropics of the African continent.

"Perhaps," McHenry replied. "We have education programs and partnerships with the fishing industry in Morocco, Mauritania, Senegal, Côte d'Ivoire, and a few other countries. Nigeria is the largest consumer of fish, and they buy from the Chinese. It's classic harmless Chinese muscle flexing."

Campbell made a show of yawning and said, "What's the issue, then? This is a diplomatic thing. Does it impact any of our national security vital interests? Our homeland?"

"Well, that's the thing, ma'am," Blankenship said. The secretary of defense was known for listening and joining the conversation when appropriate, a skill set her peers underestimated. "Our imagery intelligence is picking up some unusual activity in this fleet. Some of the ships are larger than the normal distant-water fishing vessels. There have been reports of helicopters flying from these ships. The Moroccan navy has rallied the *Mohammed VI,* its newest French and Italian frigate with enough ammo and missiles to dispense with about a third of the Chinese fleet, should it come to that."

"Why would it come to that? Over some fishing?" Campbell asked.

"Some intelligence analysts think the fishing is a cover for a military operation. Morocco is probably our strongest ally on the continent, and they are sounding the alarm bells," Blankenship continued.

"This is where AB and I differ," McHenry said. "Our State Department analysts believe these helicopters are merely recon for the ships, finding schools of fish using advanced sonar radars. We've inquired with the Chinese, and they sent us these."

McHenry handed Campbell a manila folder with pictures of helicopters with bulbous sonar radars hanging off the fuselages. Earnest-looking pilots peered into the oceans and monitors, presumably vectoring the armada into the most productive waters. The entire operation made sense. Hundreds of distant fishing vessels would need some type of guidance and communications.

"What is the recommendation? Or is this just an education session?" Campbell asked, her voice clipped.

"The Moroccans are formally requesting support under our existing defense agreement," Blankenship said. "And consistent with the new Dakhla Accords."

"Which says what, exactly?"

"We recognized their annexation of the Western Sahara, which they now call the Southern Province, and in turn Morocco, a predominantly Muslim nation, recognized Israel. There are details beyond that, but it's safe to say that Morocco is probably one of our top five non-NATO defense partners. Its strategic location at the mouth of the Mediterranean and western edge of the African continent makes its geopolitical positioning paramount."

"Bryn?" the president said.

"We think defense is overvaluing the Moroccan contribution, and we think their support of Israel undermines our longer-term goals in Palestine," she said.

"Is anyone going to make a recommendation, or are we just going to have an academic discussion about this?"

"As you can see, we are divided on this issue, but I have to side with State on this one," Benito Kidman said. Kidman was the national security advisor. A longtime Brookings Institution policy wonk and son of the former ambassador to England Johnathan Brooks Kidman, Benito was well known in the landed oligarchy of the D.C. elite. Best known for his divergent views from his neocon father and his Telemundo movie star mother, Juanita Kidman, Benito was barely pushing forty years. He wore his black hair long and slicked back Gordon Gekko–style, but without the machismo. Slender and dressed in a white shirt, sleeves rolled up, pin-striped navy suit coat flipped haphazardly over the back of his chair, Hermès tie loose around his neck, and trademark yellow socks, Kidman was attempting to set himself apart from his famous parents. He had served as Campbell's chief of staff when she was governor of North Carolina, and Campbell decided she trusted him more than any of the D.C. denizens vying for the top national security position.

"Meaning what exactly, Benito?" Campbell asked.

"Meaning, we let them lead with diplomacy between China and Morocco. It's a perfect test case for the Dakhla Accords. We have Defense in the conversation certainly, but we don't want to lead with our chin here," he said.

"But we do want to lead," Campbell said. "If China

is up to no good in the Atlantic, wouldn't it be better to flush that out right now?"

"Only if we can do it without creating an international incident," McHenry said.

"Why are we the ones always worried about creating international incidents when we are the most powerful nation on earth?" Campbell asked.

"I think that's precisely why," Kidman said.

Campbell paused for a long moment and then said, "Here's what we'll do. Bryn and AB, both of you fly this week and meet with your counterparts. Do it in Dakhla. Meanwhile, put some assets over this armada and figure out if it's strictly fishing or a Trojan horse of some type. Give me daily updates. And I'd like to know what military assets we have in the area." Her voice was crisp and authoritative.

"Seems like overreach," McHenry said. "We were just there."

"Are you always insubordinate, or are you just dense?" Campbell snapped.

McHenry remained silent, offering only a passing nod as she exited the Situation Room.

"AB, please follow me into the Oval," Campbell said. As they dismissed, Blankenship followed the president into the Oval Office, where it was just the two of them speaking.

"We've got a routine equipment retrieval in Dakhla. Our consulate there reports that the C-17 has loaded the equipment and taken off for Rota," Blankenship said. "Sinclair went on the mission but didn't return with it."

"How well do you know Garrett Sinclair?" Campbell asked.

"Not well at all. I met him for the first time the other day," Blankenship said. "We need to get his Special

Forces numbers more in alignment with our national demographics, but I intend to talk to him about that."

Campbell coughed, or maybe she laughed, and then said, "Why do you think he didn't return?"

"I thought it was odd that he was going on the trip, but I've seen the papers he gave you and General Luckey, so I gave him some latitude."

"No one *gives* Garrett Sinclair latitude. He consumes it, AB. Pretty soon, he'll be taking your longitude. Be careful."

"Yes, ma'am."

"And, AB, I agree with you. This thing is different. China's up to something."

Blankenship stepped back and held her hands up.

"The China thing is a red herring, actually. I like jousting with Bryn. I'm more concerned that the previous administration made a commitment to the Moroccan government that I do not feel is in our best interests. Annexation of Western Sahara was a racist move against the Indigenous people. We're looking at recommending a clawback on that."

"Might be difficult," Campbell said. "Besides, we have bigger issues to tackle than Mauritania and the Sahara."

"Understood," Blankenship said. "By the way, I have the Moroccan military on alert."

"On alert?"

"Yes. Neither you nor I have given any approval for any mission in Morocco or any surrounding nations. If General Sinclair goes rogue, I will need to rein him in. As you just stated, he is a wild card."

"I believe I said that he wasn't routine. I never used the terms *wild card* or *rogue*."

"Yes, of course. I'm also cutting all JSOC access to national assets. I hope you're okay with that."

"As I told General Luckey, I'm not going to meddle in the details of your business," Campbell said.

Blankenship held Campbell's stare until Campbell said, "And, AB, if you want to joust, join the renaissance festival."

16

THE CHINESE VEHICLE CONVOY continued northeast to Ouadane with the protective cover of attack helicopters.

"Dagger Four, Dagger One, any indication of Beast or Zulu?" I asked. Zulu was an unimaginative moniker for Zoey.

For thirty minutes, I hadn't heard from McCool or Suarez, fearing the worst. The airplane that loaded Zoey had departed, and I was left with two equally bad possibilities. McCool had crashed in the Beast or the airplane with Zoey had exploded.

Van Dreeves responded to his Dagger Four call sign in a whisper.

"Negative comms but two bogies inbound, over," he said.

Two tan Chinese cargo trucks hooked a hard left off the road to Ouadane and sped toward Chinguetti. In the village, the trucks stopped at the entrance to the airfield, maybe a quarter mile from our covered position. Because night had fallen, the infantry disembarking from the vehicles were not as careful as they might have otherwise been. They jumped down, mingled, checked their ammunition by slapping their magazines, and tightened straps on their rucksacks.

"Ten per truck. Total of twenty. Mission unknown," Van Dreeves said.

"Roger."

A file of ten soldiers began running along the north side of the runway, which was freshly paved asphalt, while the other troops ran down the south side; every hundred yards or so, a pair of two soldiers stopped and faced outward.

I looked at Farouk and whispered, "Any clue?"

He shrugged and pointed. "Waiting for arrival."

Securing the airfield for an arriving aircraft was the only sensible deduction.

"Large cargo aircraft inbound," Van Dreeves said. A minute later, an unmarked Y-20 Chinese cargo jet touched down at the airfield. It taxied, blowing hot jet wash on us as it turned to the north and pivoted for eventual takeoff. A forklift motored to the dropped ramp, which disgorged several pallets with black tarps tightened around bulky cargo. The forklift loaded the pallets onto the trucks, and the aircraft engines spooled up as the ramp snapped shut. With the airplane taxiing fast along the runway, the Chinese infantry collapsed onto their respective vehicles, which then sped north to Ouadane.

A few villagers stood and watched as the aircraft departed to the west and the vehicles to the northeast. It was a smooth operation and one that hadn't occurred for the first time tonight. I was left to wonder if we were looking at two separate operations: Sanson's folly to find Poseidon's treasure in the Eye of Africa and some unknown Chinese military operation for some unstated purpose. While our goal remained to secure Zoey, and that was truly all that mattered now, tonight's events piqued the strategist in me. Had these reports come from my team without me having seen them firsthand, I wasn't sure I would have placed the necessary import to them as history has shown was warranted. But given what Command Sergeant Major Sly Morgan had left behind for us, it was beginning to make sense.

"Rally point," I said.

"Roger," Van Dreeves replied.

Over the next hour, Farouk and I quietly moved two miles northwest of Chinguetti airfield into a rocky hillside that overlooked the runway and village to the south and provided line of sight to the horizon in the north. A flame still flickered several miles away. McCool and my team? Or Zoey and Sanson?

Soon, Hobart and Van Dreeves appeared and authenticated themselves with two flashes of the infrared light on our IVAS night vision goggles. We huddled in a circle of four, Hobart and I facing inward and Van Dreeves and Farouk facing outward for security.

"Thoughts?" I asked. We whispered in our throat microphones and listened in our earbuds despite our proximity.

"Cannonball express from the south and airlift from the north. No idea what the equipment is, but what the hell is China doing in the middle of Mauritania?" Van Dreeves said.

"Nothing the rest of the world knows about," I said. "But part of our purpose here."

"We need to focus on Zoey," Hobart said.

"Agreed. How does this impact, if at all, finding Zoey?"

"Doesn't," Hobart said. I understood his singular focus. It was the same for the rest of us.

"Need to confirm or deny status of Sally and team," Van Dreeves said as if to emphasize my point.

These missions were intensely personal, and it was my job to make sure we remained as objective as possible while executing.

"Joe, you and Randy recon the crash site and send a sitrep. Looks like four miles or so. Will be approaching daylight by the time you get there. If it is our people, call us forward and we will come. Farouk and I will maintain eyes on the airfield and monitor any traffic heading your way. Change batteries before you run out of juice. Depending on who's in the crash site, we will figure out a way to recover remains and exfil," I said. "If we don't reestablish contact, continue with Sly's mission."

There was a long moment of silence. I knew what they were thinking. We had a detailed plan to follow through on what Sly had uncovered. Zoey was part of that plan, and Hobart was struggling with the dual focus of finding Zoey and pursuing Sly's ultimate goal.

"Roger," they said in unison.

"And, boss," Van Dreeves said. "The tracker took some shrapnel during the gun run from the Chinese. We don't have eyes on Zoey's watch anymore."

I nodded. "Charlie Mike," I said.

After a few minutes of checking their gear and topping off with water, they picked their way to the bottom of the rocky ridge.

Farouk stood and said, "I am going to scout this area. The Freckle is just over there," he said, pointing to the northeast. "And the Mole is much farther to the east."

I nodded, not thrilled with my base camp being split into three factions, but we were in uncharted waters, and any intelligence he could deliver would be welcome. My men were professionals and knew how to call an audible and snatch victory from the jaws of defeat.

After an hour of repositioning to stay awake, a light buzzing noise filled the sky. It was a familiar sound, one that wasn't mistakable for any paratrooper who had waited on the drop zone for the next pass of aircraft.

Adjusting the focus of my IVAS, a formation of three twin-propeller cargo planes was lined up along the road to Ouadane to the north and east. Silhouetted against the faint moonlight were parachutes opening beneath the planes. Either paratroopers or cargo bundles were being dropped. Based on what we had seen earlier, each was as likely as the other.

Supplies needed to survive in the desert were considerable. It was unlikely that Sanson had more airplanes that could deliver supplies to him, but not impossible. Observing that the Chinese had some type of operation ongoing here, it was more likely that the drop was either security personnel or even more equipment for whatever they had planned, or a combination of both.

To add an accent to the events that had been unfolding, nearly a half a mile away, a lone pickup truck with lights out crawled along the goat trail where I had scratched out my observation post high on the north ridge opposite the airfield and village. Unless the driver had similar night vision gear, I was invisible to the naked eye, but it was obvious the vehicle was aimed in my direction. Sighting along my rifle and focusing my IVAS for a longer-range target, I was unable to determine who was in the vehicle, but there were at least two people in the front seat.

We had kitted Farouk with a throat microphone and earbud connected to our communications system and given him the call sign Dagger Ten.

"Dagger Ten, Dagger Six, over," I said.

No response.

"Dagger Ten, Dagger Six, over."

I waited another minute as the truck continued to approach when Van Dreeves's voice cracked in my ear.

"Boss, we found it."

17

SANSON RETURNED TO THE excavation site with his entourage plus one additional captive. Fresh meat, as Malik called the victims of Sanson's bloodlust.

Malik had the team establish base camp on the northwestern rim of the center piece of the Eye. The dig site was two hundred meters to the southeast. Already they had found a tunnel system filled with satchels of gold. Malik was a skeptic of Plato's Atlantis theory, but he had to admit that they were finding some convincing discoveries. Though, the gold was equally rationalized as having been stashed by traders or citizens of Timbuktu fleeing north from invading armies. The Eye was considered a spiritual sanctuary, and many probably believed that their gold would be safe in the remote tunnels or, if not, they had made a sufficient tithe to enter the awaiting heavens. Religions had been built upon less evidence, and Malik knew that the denizens of the Sahara considered the Eye sacred ground. Here he was clawing at something that could possibly be spiritual, connecting him to other worlds or planes of consciousness. He struggled with his role in the caravan.

Sanson's two goons led the captive, who had a burlap

sack covering their head and hands tied behind their back, into Sanson's large tent.

"Refuel the airplane," Sanson directed. "I know this wench."

Malik led one of his camels to the dirt road where the Sherpa had landed. The pilot leaned against the fuselage, smoking a cigarette. Probably not the best move, Malik thought, but who was he to judge? The pilot was a short man with thick, matted hair and bushy eyebrows. His face was wizened from years of squinting through the windscreen into the horizon, most likely. Originally a Moroccan bush pilot accustomed to flying in the Atlas Mountains, the man who called himself Rabout chuckled and said, "A refueling camel?"

"*Oui, c'est practique,*" Malik said with a slight chuckle.

"Sanson *est fou,*" Rabout said, waving his arm across the large encampment. "But if he's finding gold, I want to know."

"We are exploring for Atlantis, Rabout," Malik said. He put the lead of the camel's reins under a rock and then slid the hose into one of the ten gas cans on the camel's saddles. Malik used this fuel primarily for generators, but Sanson had asked him to be prepared to refuel the airplane. It was a simple gravity-feed operation using jet fuel, which burned in the generators just fine.

"We'll need more fuel on your next trip," Malik said.

"No problem."

As he was switching the hose from one can to the next, Malik asked, "Who is the hostage?"

Rabout smiled and said, "How much gold do you have?"

"Like I said, we are just exploring historical sites," Malik said.

"And I'm just carrying passengers."

Touché, Malik thought.

"It's just another body for me to dispose of, I guess," Malik said.

After a moment and the flick of a cigarette, Rabout said, "I wouldn't be so sure of that."

"Has our master changed his ways?" Malik pressed.

"How much gold you got?" Rabout laughed again.

He withdrew the hose and tucked it in the saddle. Looking at Rabout, he said, "Four cans. We're going to need replacement in a day." As he was tightening the saddle for the two-hundred-meter trip back, he leaned over to lift the rock and secure the reins. A few meters away was a black object that looked like a watch.

He leaned over and stepped forward, as if tripping. Pushing against the ground, he scooped the watch up in one hand and the reins in another.

"Be careful there, Malik. We don't want Sanson's blade on either of our necks."

Malik smiled. "It is an occupational hazard we both are going to have to deal with," he said.

"Speak for yourself. I keep flying for him and I'll be retired in a year, hanging out with the hookers in Dakhla."

"Good for you," Malik said. "But we are all expendable."

He turned and led the camel toward the pen and then walked past Sanson's securely shut tent doors. As the Sherpa bumped along the road for takeoff, Malik was certain he heard the lash of a whip and the yelp of a woman from inside the tent.

Crack. Pop.

Nooo!

"What is your name?!" he asked in French.

Malik stood still, watching the shadows move inside the dimly lit tent. The woman was on her knees.

Sanson stood tall above her, reared back, and lashed at her with the bullwhip.

Crack. Pop.

Malik cringed. The female voice whimpered a hoarse sob. "Please," she said.

"Name! American spy!"

Crack. Pop.

"Afghanistan?! Africa?!"

Crack. Pop.

He felt for the woman, whomever she might be. Was it the woman Sanson had mentioned? Zoey Morgan?

When signing on to be the caravan leader, he did not sign up for this. He had brothers and sisters who had daughters, and he respected women. Even before tonight, Sanson's treatment of women was appalling. But now this?

The bodies became intertangled, and he watched to try to determine what was happening when he heard ripping cloth and a plaintive "Nooooo!" from the woman. He turned away and stepped into one of Sanson's two large bodyguards, who said, "It's for the best you do not hear or see this."

Malik returned to his meager shelter and walked into the open face of his tent. To distract himself from the trauma of listening to Sanson abuse the woman in the tent, he studied the watch he had found. He pressed on the watch crown, but there was no response. Sliding his thumb along the back, the smooth metal was cool to the touch.

He wondered if the watch belonged to someone on the airplane or a distant research party that had come and gone. Its band was clean, and the face showed limited signs of wear. He couldn't imagine this watch baking in the Sahara heat for more than a day or two.

No, he concluded, this watch fell off someone who had been on the airplane. If no one asked for it in return, he would keep it, certain he could get a decent price for it back in the souks of Marrakech.

Could it be the woman's?

18

"SEND IT," I SAID to Van Dreeves.

"Chinese attack helicopter crashed and burned. Negative comms with Beast still," Van Dreeves said.

I stood, my spirit lifted just briefly until I realized the pickup truck was closing on my position and I had just made a giant target out of myself. Despite the flicker of worry, though, there was still hope for McCool and her team.

"Roger. Quick intel sweep and return to rally point," I directed. I immediately returned to my covered position among the rocky terrain.

Gunfire echoed in my earpiece as Van Dreeves said, "Roger, taking fire."

On the horizon, tracers etched arcing lines, green against the night sky, some ricocheting at right angles after hitting rock or metal. Was it the paratroopers who dropped a short while ago? A separate land-based Chinese team to recover its downed pilots? A rogue band of nomads seeking to scavenge the debris? Polisario headed to claim victory? Sanson's men to investigate? The Moroccan army pushing across the border to secure the location? Russian private military contractors such

TOTAL EMPIRE   149

as Wagner closing in on the wreckage? I needed information to make decisions.

At that moment, I fully realized the jeopardy in which
I had placed my team.

*Your people . . . will follow you through the raging
fires of hell.*

I may have led them there. While the temperatures
had dropped into the 60s tonight, they would be soar-
ing above 110 degrees in the baking heat of the Sahara soon after sunrise in a few hours. With no support
from our country and limited ability to communicate,
we had staked success on staying together and executing
as we always had—with precision. Instead, we were
confronted with myriad operational turns that disadvan-
taged our team.

I immediately tried to contact McCool, who would
have a better direct line of communications from her
aerial platform. I switched to the dreaded "Any station
on this net" calls trying to raise anyone who might be
listening. Then I tried Farouk, and even he didn't respond.

It was rare that I took counsel of my fears. Perhaps
it was a cumulative build over the past two years of loss
and frustration. Or maybe it was normal that after a career of combat, I would fall deeper into an abyss with
no obvious way out, the towering walls of loss no longer
scalable from unimaginable depths. Regardless of its
origins, the despair I felt at this moment was distinctly
new and unique to me. The people I loved were either
dead or in danger.

And I had put every one of them in that position.

Screeching brakes and a sputtering engine interrupted my self-loathing and fixation on the fireworks
display miles from my position.

I quickly braced against a rock outcropping, which was providing marginal protective cover, and sighted my weapon on the mass stepping from the truck, which had stopped twenty-five meters away. Another person remained still in the passenger side, head down.

My finger began to squeeze the trigger as two infrared flashes appeared from the night vision device of the driver.

He stepped forward and said, "*Mon général.*"

Farouk.

"Farouk," I said. "Why didn't you answer me?"

"I got into a minor debate, and my radio was damaged," he said.

As he approached me, he was bleeding from the left side of his scalp. I could smell the copper scent of blood.

"Who's in the truck?"

"A prisoner," Farouk said. "I think she knows something about what's happening here."

"She?" I said.

Farouk nodded.

"Okay, let's talk to her."

I walked to the truck with Farouk and saw a body lying still in the bed.

"The subject of your disagreement?" I asked.

"Yes. He was not treating her well. They are both from Sanson's caravan, though the man will be of no use."

"Dead?"

"*Comme peut être,*" he said. *As can be.*

I studied the man in the truck bed. Dark skin, long black beard, cut throat, layers of brown and white clothes, tan sandals.

"I got his phone, rifle, and pistol. He was parked on the other side of this ridge and was . . . taking liberties with the young lady in the cab."

We moved to the passenger's side, where Farouk opened the door. He unbuckled a lanky Black woman dressed in a niqab, showing only the woman's large eyes. Farouk guided her to the partial cave where I had my gear stashed and sat her down, back against the wall.

"Have you checked her for explosives?" I asked.

Farouk looked at me and nodded. He wasn't happy with my question, but I had never operated with him before. With either Hobart or Van Dreeves, it would be a given that they would have thoroughly processed the detainee if that was indeed her status.

He began speaking to her in an African dialect I didn't understand. Her voice was a lyrical whisper when she responded. Her eyes remained focused on his, unblinking, perhaps as she pondered a fate worse than the assault she had been spared. Her niqab slid down around her neck as she spoke, and she used her hands to gesticulate with some animation.

After a lengthy conversation, Farouk turned to me and summarized.

"She is a concubine with Sanson. One of the archeologists took her in the truck supposedly to get water and fuel from Chinguetti, but he instead pulled into a valley, where he tried to rape her. That's when I found them and altered the situation."

"Has she seen Zoey?"

"Maybe. First thing I asked her. She's scared. Thinks we are going to give her back to Sanson."

"Maybe?"

"She saw a 'Black woman like her' as she described it."

I looked at the captive. She was covered in filthy clothing, white desert dust clinging to the black abaya covering her entire body. The moonlight cast a pale glow over her face, which had hard angles with high cheekbones, a broad nose, and wide eyes. Despite her dire circumstances, she was a beautiful woman, and I could see her relating to Zoey.

A Black woman like her.

"Can she lead us there?"

"I'll ask, but is there any word on the chips in Zoey's watch or phone?"

"I can't reach Hobart and Van Dreeves, and they've got the tracker, which wasn't working during the last comms we had."

Farouk nodded and turned to the woman again and engaged her in another lengthy conversation, this one more animated.

"She can, but she doesn't want to go back. She says that if Sanson sees her, he will kill her with his sword."

"His sword."

"Yes, evidently he cuts off the heads of his women once he's done with them and those of anyone else he may be displeased with."

"Well, that confirms he's our target, not that we had any doubt. Convince her to lead us there and let her know we will protect her."

After five minutes and more animation, Farouk said, "The best she can do is tell us the route the truck takes to Chinguetti. Once Sanson or someone named Malik knows the truck is missing, they will send the other for them. Usually, it's a daily run either to Ouadane or Chinguetti. She says they are treasure hunting in the Eye of Africa for Poseidon's Temple. They've found gold, and the man she calls Sanson believes greater treasure lies beneath."

"Who's Malik?"

"The caravan master," Farouk said.

"Who normally makes the run? What do they pick up?"

"She said it was typically the guy I just killed, but sometimes Malik did, also. They get generator fuel, sometimes gas for the airplane, and of course food and water. There are sometimes motorcycle escorts if there's a threat."

"So, they're short a guy and a concubine and will be making a run within twenty-four hours, probably with motorcycles. Does she know the exact route?"

After a few minutes of conversation, he turned back to me and said, "Yes. She has made the trip many times because she is from the village, speaks the local dialect, and interprets for them."

I stared into the distance, the tracer light show now only a random line here and there. I touched my throat mike and said, "Dagger Four, status?"

No reply.

"Dagger Three, status?"

"Hobart and Van Dreeves lost comms?" Farouk asked.

"They were in contact," I said.

We locked eyes. He seemed to process that I knew I was left with him for the moment. He nodded at me as if to accept the challenge. I looked at the captive.

Her breathing was raspy and quick. Farouk's eyes were still on me, judging, I presumed. He had killed for us and brought a major intelligence trove to the team. Zoey's life was hanging in the balance with a maniacal French swordsman, and the Chinese military was probing or conducting some operation in the same general area. It wouldn't be long before the three separate entities—our operation, spread out as it may be, the Chinese, and the Frenchman—conflated into one giant clusterfuck unless we could act quickly.

Melissa had always emphasized the importance of family and even more the importance of our team and *their* families. She had knit together a seamless entity, as if we had all been raised together. While McCool, Hobart, Van Dreeves, and Zoey weren't my blood, they were my kin.

The catch-22 that I faced a few days ago was that of knowing Zoey was in peril and having the small window to secure her safety on the back of the already scheduled routine mission to Dakhla versus the sure knowledge that if anything went wrong, there would be little to no support from our country. We were fortunate to have Farouk on the team, and I still had confidence in the abilities of my unit. They were resourceful operators and had overcome greater challenges in the past.

Plus, we had the foundation of a plan.

But to be spread out in the desert amid uncertain perils such as the surprisingly active Chinese ground forces and an aggressive French swordsman who believed they had found Atlantis was a developing challenge that would test the best capabilities of my team in pursuit of confirming or dispelling the intelligence that Sly had uncovered.

Still, the imperative of continuing phase one of the mission—reclaiming Zoey—persisted. The only way out of the ambush, as they say, was through it, and we were indeed in the beaten zone.

"When is the next run?" I asked.

They spoke for a couple of minutes until Farouk looked at me and said, "Tomorrow night at nightfall if they don't come sooner looking for them. They only have one other truck and a couple of motorcycles. Dirt bikes. The rest of the caravan is camels. Maybe thirty or so."

With all of them in danger, perhaps worse, I was thankful for Farouk and his captive waif as a starting point for turning the tide back in our direction. We were a team accustomed to success, which begets more success if handled properly with modesty and humility. While I wasn't overconfident, neither was I giving any more counsel to the gremlins of fear snapping at my ankles. When circumstances don't naturally conform to what you immediately desire, assess and adapt, but more importantly, remain focused on finding solutions. With so much hanging in the balance, it was my responsibility to lead us out of the situation into which I had placed us while still accomplishing as much of the mission as possible. Creative solutions helped fortify my mind against the onslaught of doubt creating a Pickett's Charge against the confidence that still held the high ground in my mind.

I processed for a few minutes of silence, the endless black sky merging with the endless desert at the infinite horizon. I thought about Farouk's comment back in Dakhla when I first met him. Everything went through Sanson. Any change in rhythm and he would be gone. We had no immediate path to their location in the desert, and if more than a day went by without any report from Chinguetti, I was concerned Sanson would pack up again, and we would have no path to Zoey or the rest of the mission.

"I have an idea," I said.

19

WHEN THE SUN ROSE, I still had not heard from McCool or Hobart or Van Dreeves.

It was possible that their radio batteries had died, but Farouk had repaired his own comms gear and we were still able to talk on our throat mikes, which made that possibility less likely than not. Van Dreeves also operated our UHF radios at farther distances, not that we had any allies who might listen to our calls for help. I imagined that General Luckey and the secretary of defense had shut down all support to us and were only happy enough to accelerate my departure, whether from DoD or earth.

But we had human intelligence, which was the hardest of all to secure. Our detainee's name was Amina. She was a teacher in Chinguetti when Sanson's men took her months ago under the threat that her family would suffer the blade if she resisted or fled. As we sought shade in the shallow caves on the north side of the mountain, I engaged Amina via Farouk in conversation, learning the habits and rhythm of the caravan. I thought through the different permutations of what the dead man in the truck must have done daily to make himself useful.

"They speak French, mostly," Farouk said after an exchange with Amina. "The dead man was a researcher, she said, and sometimes laborer who had some status in the caravan, but not much. It's doubtful that Sanson even knew who he was, she said."

"Malik?"

"Yes, of course, Malik knows him, but he was just a worker who took an interest in research, which is why he joined the caravan."

I pulled out my shaving kit and stared in the handheld mirror. My four-day beard was full and black with hints of gray. My face was deeply tanned, bordering on red. I undressed and put on the dead man's clothes, white with a tan vest that I used as a makeshift outer tactical vest. Not a perfect fit, but close enough, and with the looseness of the layers, there would be no second glances. Farouk and I spent the better part of the day immersing me back into the French language I once spoke fluently. By late afternoon, my mind was thinking in French vice English, which was where I needed to be. Amina had a small satchel of henna in her pocket, which she used as eyeliner per Sanson's request and which I used to erase the flecks of gray from my beard.

A half mile away at the bottom of the steep incline where we were positioned, two military trucks passed slowly until they stopped about a mile to our north and unloaded maybe one hundred infantry, who began scratching out fighting positions in the foothills, facing away from us.

Chinese infantrymen.

Farouk looked at me and shook his head. Sometimes doing nothing about an event was the best course of action. So far, their actions seemed unrelated to ours.

I tried to reach McCool, Hobart, and Van Dreeves again to no avail. With no other options remaining and the sun beginning to dip after a long, hot day, we loaded into Farouk's captured truck and made the trek in the opposite direction from the Chinese military over the mountain to Malik's supply route.

Now, with the edge of the day's heat subsiding, the cloudless night allowing the warm air to escape into the heavens, a truck engine sounded over the far hill, climbing and straining, and finally wheezing with relief as it crested and became visible on the downslope. The grind of the diesel engine was accompanied by the chain saw whining of two motorcycles. Amina had mentioned that Malik kept two motorcycles in his caravan. He was expecting trouble. As they approached, I knelt next to Farouk and whispered, "Five seconds."

Farouk nodded and sighted down his rifle. I kept my night vision goggles locked on to the fast-approaching convoy, the familiar green and black shades providing an odd comfort, reminding me of so many missions with my team and their eventual success even when the odds seemed most daunting. Never before, though, had we faced such a lopsided situation. When the chips were down and fate seemed to be pinning you against the wall, my experience and nature compelled me to extreme action . . . opposite of what anyone else might consider. Something so creative and unique that it surprised even me. Like the Israeli tank platoon attacking with spotlights into the teeth of the Syrian offensive, stopping the entire Yom Kippur War and saving Israel.

"Now," I said.

The best sniper in the Moroccan army, perhaps the world, squeezed the trigger, and the near-side motorcycle escort jerked straight up, hands shooting skyward as if he were signaling a touchdown. A second shot sent the opposite escort pinwheeling into the adjacent ravine.

Both BMW HP2 dirt bikes spun on the dusty road, sparked off the aggregate, and flipped over the sheer cliffs bracketing the narrow lane.

The driver of the Mercedes-Benz flat-nose truck looked left and right with frightened eyes. The man riding shotgun stared straight ahead with flat affect. Seconds later, my night vision device was obscured by the vehicle headlights and then by the IED that exploded in front of the truck.

Shrapnel fell upon us like hail, the truck nosed into the air, teetering on its front end for a brief second, then clumsily crunched onto its cab, completing the 180-degree flip onto its roof. A concern had been that the truck would slide into the deep ravines on either side. So far, that had been avoided.

Farouk put a bullet into the gas tank, causing a river of fuel to snake toward us from about thirty meters away. The engine hissed and moaned its final gasps. The driver hung loosely from the cab of the truck; his neck apparently broken. The passenger was motionless, his face resting against the dashboard as if he were napping.

I wasted no time in snapping my carabiner into the rappel rope some twenty meters behind us as we zipped down the face of the cliff, hopping off and receiving one last doubting, frightened look from Amina, who wasn't quite certain what we were doing. Best I could tell, she was still concerned we were going to kill her. My plan, however, was for her to stay with Farouk. If she had been a useful interpreter for Sanson, she could be invaluable to us.

Farouk looked at me and said, "Are you sure?"

"This is the only way," I replied. I slid into the 2014 Renault Duster SUV/pickup truck that Farouk had captured. It smelled of dirt and fried food. The six-cylinder engine fizzled as I powered through the switchbacks wearing my bloodstained tan kaftan and headdress lifted from Farouk's victim.

Luckily, French had been the language I studied at West Point, and my daughter, Reagan, continued that tradition at the University of Virginia. She kept me current by practicing with me, and the practice with Farouk all day had honed my skills.

As I crested the hill, the truck's one winking headlight finally sputtered off, and the Renault's weak beams shone into the cab. The passenger had managed to slide onto the narrow piece of ground next to the truck and was crawling forward, toward me. I navigated the narrow path between the leaking truck and the cliff, the Renault's wheels pushing shale two hundred meters below, before stopping the car.

Exiting the sedan, I stammered in my best shocked French, *"Mon Dieu, que s'est-il passé?"* My God, what happened?

The flat, black eyes looked up at me. Blood oozed down his face, its wellspring a hematoma centered on his forehead.

I knelt before him, reaching out my hand.

"My friend. What happened? You're hurt. I must get you to a hospital."

He had a gash on his forehead, which was bleeding along the left side of his face and running onto his kaftan. Otherwise, he looked banged up but okay.

"Pas d'hôpital," he croaked. *No hospital.*

"Please, I must."

A bullet pinged off the smoking cab. Another shattered the side mirror two feet from my face.

"Weapons?" I asked.

The man moved his arm and pointed toward the disheveled cab as a third shot came so close, I felt the wash when it smacked into the windshield. I snatched the Beretta AR-70, a forty-year-old Italian assault rifle not known for its accuracy, that was lying on the ceiling of the inverted cab and charged the weapon.

Two more shots snapped nearby, and I sprayed in the general direction of the muzzle flashes, but deliberately high. The bleeding man brandished a pistol, and for a moment, I thought he was going to shoot me, but instead he aimed in the same direction as I had and fired several rounds.

"Now," I said, figuring the return fire would provide a window for us to move. I lifted him into a firefighter's carry and dumped him in the hatch of the Renault.

As I spun the wheels against the dirt and gravel road, a giant fireball erupted in my rearview mirror. Putting distance between us and the flame, I noticed my passenger's head swivel from staring out of the hatch window to looking at me.

"Who are you?" he asked.

Farouk and I had spent some time discussing my potential nom de guerre, and ultimately, he chose Abdel el Harim, an obscure Moroccan who excelled at surfing, a sport for which Farouk and Van Dreeves shared a mutual affection.

"I'm just a researcher," I said. "I'm Abdel el Harim. You are?"

He looked at me with weak but discerning eyes.

"Malik," he said and left it at that.

As for me, it was a very American convention to lead with my ersatz profession and was not the last of my mistakes made on this gamble to save Zoey. But I was assured of my path when I saw Zoey's black watch lifeless on his wrist.

20

AROUND MIDNIGHT, THE SECRETARY of defense requested to meet with the president in the Situation Room.

"What's the emergency, AB?" she asked.

Secretary of Defense Blankenship was seated to her right while Secretary of State McHenry was to her left. A few functionaries were scattered along the back row with appropriate furrowed brows feigning deep concern while they looked around fidgeting, unable to check their phones in the secure conference room.

"China is not the problem here, Madam President," McHenry said. She cut off the secretary of defense before she could even speak.

"I think I was speaking to AB, Bryn," Campbell said without removing her eyes from Blankenship.

"Just giving you context," McHenry said.

Campbell turned toward McHenry and said, "I think that is properly called an opinion. Now, AB, what do we know as fact?"

"Ma'am, the Chinese fishing fleet is reported to have launched some helicopters from their decks. These helicopters are armed attack Z-10s very much like our

AH-64 Apaches. They are using refueling stations they've set up at remote airfields."

"To what end?" Campbell asked.

"We're not sure, but there are random reports of Chinese infantry on the ground, also, and some heavy equipment transports."

"Where are we getting this information?" Campbell asked.

"Our defense attaché at the consulate in Dakhla reported seeing the transports and aircraft when he was returning from a visit to the capital, Nouakchott." She pronounced the word *knock-shot*. "He intentionally took N1, the interior road, north to investigate the increased Polisario activity and passed two transports with tarps before two helicopters flew over him at a high rate of speed."

"That consulate is mine," Bryn said. "I didn't know we had an attaché there." The big woman looked over her shoulder and motioned to her lackey, who provided the appropriate nod and look of mutual concern accompanied with a finger gun and scribble on a notepad.

"He's new," Blankenship said. "I'll make sure my undersecretary for intelligence follows up with your team. I'm sure the notifications are somewhere in the system."

"No time for rice bowls," Campbell said. "Is there a threat to U.S. vital interests?"

"That's an emphatic no," McHenry said. "We can't go confrontational with China every time they pop up on the world stage somewhere. We are talking about the heart of the Sahara. Our only concern there is climate change and the fact that the desert is growing faster every year and consuming arable land. Our strategic interests in Africa are climate change, women's rights, and disease prevention."

Campbell spun back toward Blankenship, who said, "From a national defense priorities standpoint, our strategy clearly lists China as our main competitor. Their economy is growing at eight to ten percent. Their military is bigger than ours. Their nuclear arsenal is expanding exponentially. They've practically attacked Taiwan. Zooming out, our strategic priorities for Africa are countering terrorism, ensuring navigation in coastal and blue waters, and building capacity to defend themselves."

"Like we did with Afghanistan?" McHenry quipped.

"That's unnecessary, Bryn," Blankenship said.

"Ladies, we're supposed to be the adults in the room here. Let's act like it," Campbell said. "I'm still wondering why I'm here in the middle of the night."

"Me, too," McHenry said, unable to help herself.

"I thought it was important to let you know that this situation is developing rapidly and that fishing fleet may not be a fishing fleet at all. It could be, as previously discussed, a Trojan horse of sorts with some capabilities to establish a lodgment along the coast of Mauritania or Morocco."

"Again, to what end?" Campbell asked. Her eyes cast downward. The strain of the presidency had given her a few gray hairs mixed in with her blond. Her crow's-feet seemed more accented in the glaring lights of the Situation Room. Still, she was a beautiful woman whose patience, more than her intellect, was being challenged by the carping of her cabinet.

"We believe they may have designs on building a military port on the west coast of Africa, perhaps the Dakhla Peninsula," Blankenship said.

"Seriously?" McHenry chortled.

"Seriously," she replied.

"I'm with Kim here, AB. To what end?" McHenry said.

Campbell snapped a quick look at McHenry at the use of her first name but kept quiet.

"It could be they simply want a port on the west coast to gain geopolitical advantage over the United States. They do believe this is their time for empire. We discussed all of this at the Dakhla Accords signing."

"*Their* time for empire?" Campbell said. "We'd be ceding geopolitical advantage to China how? They're already mobbed up in Panama, Cuba, Venezuela. What's so special about Africa, where, I might add, they already have a significant presence?"

"A strategic navy base on the Dakhla Peninsula would put them a few days away and within nuclear weapons range of our homeland. All these other countries you mention, China uses soft power—money, tech, some military training—to influence their potential partners and leverage against us," Blankenship said.

"Well, that's a good point, AB. So, what's the plan? Want me to call the king of Morocco or whoever is in charge of Mauritania nowadays?"

"Let us handle it first, please. We can start at our level," Blankenship said, gesturing with her hand toward McHenry. "We can call a follow-up to the Dakhla Accords. A check-in on the standards we put in place."

"I agree," McHenry said, seemingly placated. "We leave tomorrow, as you directed."

"Very well, then. Keep me in the loop."

As everyone departed, out of sight of the president, Blankenship snuck a thumbs-up signal to McHenry, who nodded in return. When President Campbell reentered the Oval Office, she retrieved a cell phone from her coat pocket and pressed a button.

Director of National Intelligence Koby Bertrand charged into the Oval Office, interrupting her phone call, and said, "Yesterday's Chinese rocket launch? China has put at least five hypersonic glide vehicles in space, possibly with nuclear weapons."

21

I FELT THE PHONE buzz against my thigh but continued to stare straight ahead at the road as we crested a shallow rise and let the call go through to voice mail. I had some idea of what President Campbell may be calling me about, but with Malik sitting in the passenger seat, I couldn't answer.

The sun was blasting overhead. The Renault air-conditioning system had struggled to keep us cool as we strained and heaved over the mountains. After "saving" Malik, he was determined to continue his mission and had directed me into Chinguetti, where we picked up prearranged supplies from the airfield. I had offered to take him to the small village clinic, but he refused. I glanced a few more times at his wrist and was convinced that he had Zoey's watch.

Was she alive, or was this a trophy?

"We have a doctor," he had said.

I loaded the supplies in the truck and drove through the night and most of the morning until we passed through the village of Ouadane, where we stopped briefly for Malik to go into one of the adobe huts. He came out a few minutes later, still clutching his side. I was waiting at the wheel like an Uber driver. He could have used the restroom or obtained a pistol to try to kill me. I used the time to refuel the truck from one of the many fuel cans stacked in the bed of the pickup.

I also used the time to think. We had a direct path into Sanson's dig site, which potentially was a cover for something else entirely, if Sly was correct. Instead of spending days or weeks looking for the well-dispersed caravan and associated equipment, I was going to be there in a matter of a few days since launching our operation. Given Sly's notes, which suggested that the Chinese had compromised the highest levels of the American government, it was best that we were unsupported without any overhead imagery or signals intelligence.

As we continued to drive, we crested the ridge in front of me now. In the distance, maybe a mile away, there was a camp with tents and a few people milling around. The promised land.

"Pull over," Malik said.

He was staring directly at me. His eyes were flat. His face was drawn tight. He clutched at his rib cage, a reaction to pain or an attempt to grab a weapon he might have obtained in Ouadane.

"*Oui.*"

I turned the steering wheel to guide the truck to the side of the road and brought it to a stop.

"Who are you?" he asked again.

"I told you my name."

"Why do you have one of my trucks?"

This was a problem that Farouk and I had discussed. On one hand, we could have gone to Chinguetti and exchanged it for something Malik wouldn't recognize, which would have exposed us to any of several threats out there. On the other, I risked immediate exposure if he didn't buy my story, at which time I would kill him.

On the off chance that Zoey was not in the camp, I wanted him alive as long as possible.

"I bought it from a man in Chinguetti. He and his wife were flying to Algeria for a new life, and he sold it to me."

He was speechless for a full minute until he said, "What was the man's name?"

"Here is the receipt I have from him," I said. I handed him the truck registration written in French, meaning it was a Moroccan vehicle, with the dead man's henna thumbprint on it, as was the customary form of barter in Mauritania. Farouk had written the man's name beneath it and then used his thumbprint for the recipient's signature under my name. A quick call to one of Farouk's contacts in the Moroccan government had determined that the dead man was an Algerian researcher and hieroglyphics specialist named Hamza al Asman. This was an important detail that we believed might make a difference.

"He flew? With a woman?"

"Yes. I was staying in Chinguetti near the mosque, writing my report and awaiting instructions from the Sorbonne, when I received a directive to try to connect with the expedition at the Richat Structure. I was given the name 'Sanson.'"

He flinched at the mention of Sanson's name. While he didn't say anything, he was probably thinking, *I've lost four men and one woman from the caravan, two of whom have escaped and could potentially talk. Here's a guy who saved me from an ambush and works in the research field. Maybe I can say I've exchanged a few basic laborers for a connection to the Sorbonne.*

At least that was what Farouk and I had discussed as a potential line of reasoning. We had no direct intelligence capability to locate the expedition in the middle of the desert. Airplanes with all the radars in the world rarely find small ships lost at sea. This was no different, and when I had originally scoped out the plan, I had relied on two possible courses of action. One, the chips in Zoey's watch or phone would guide us, or, two, we would leverage U.S. intelligence assets to pinpoint the location prior to being shut down. Neither of those options was available to me presently. We needed someone to guide me to the location, or at least get close enough. I thought about that as Malik was questioning me. I could see the location, which meant I no longer totally needed Malik. I could kill him now and avoid risk of exposure inside the camp prior to finding Zoey. Or I could rely upon his need to save face and introduce me as a new member of the team.

I considered both options as he continued to question me.

"How much did you pay for my truck?" he asked.

"Eighteen thousand dirham," I said. Which was basically $2,000.

"This truck is worth ten times that," he said.

"It was priced for a quick sale. He and the woman were in a hurry." It was important to remind him of the people and equipment he had lost. Our plan banked on his needing, at the very least, additional labor and a plausible story. I kept my answers short, many of which Farouk and I had rehearsed.

His cuts and scrapes had stopped bleeding, but he still needed to see an actual doctor. I could see his mind calculating the costs and benefits of asking me to take him into the camp, adding a new person, and not having his head sliced off by Sanson. I was banking on the probability that Sanson would not be there when I arrived. That I could blend in and start digging or feeding the camels or whatever mundane tasks awaited until I could find Zoey and develop a plan to rescue her. With such a small endeavor as Malik operated, every man counted. There were shifts and timelines to make. Logistics runs to be made like the one we just did. He had a mission to complete, or Sanson would surely kill him.

"Why were you traveling at night?" he asked.

"To avoid the heat."

He nodded and paused, thinking.

"Why were you attacked?" I asked, seizing the initiative of the conversation.

"These roads are dangerous. I travel with guards because we carry valuable supplies. The supplies are a lifeline for us but also useful to others. The Polisario. Others."

"But you had no supplies," I said. "You were going to the town, not coming from the town."

He shifted nervously in his seat. Maybe the pain from broken ribs was kicking in, or maybe this line of questioning made him uncomfortable. He might have thought I was probing at the possibility that he was carrying newly discovered gold for airlift out of the desert. Why else would you have two motorcycle guards escorting you? The Polisario were scavengers and surely knew the terrain better than most. They would know a full supply run from an empty one, but Farouk and I had seen the Polisario and Chinese infantry scuffle recently, and there were plenty of threats in this ungoverned land.

"I'm sure whoever it was assumed there was something valuable in the convoy. It was not the first time we've been attacked."

"I understand. It was good that I came upon you, then," I said. "Before they had time to find you."

He paused and nodded. "Yes. But it was not me they

were after. It was the truck that went over the cliff." He grimaced as he talked as if either there was something in the back of the truck that was valuable, or the simple fact he had lost his resupply capabilities was enough of a pain. I imagined he had budgets under which he had to operate. Sanson most likely tracked costs closely. While the mission might produce a massive payout either in gold or notoriety, or both, he still had to make ends meet until that occurred. Additionally, if Sanson's site was a ruse, as we were out to confirm, any lost equipment would inevitably trace back to the caravan, the only one on the docket as being active in the Richat Structure at the time.

"Still," I said. "You are alive."

"For now," he muttered, which confirmed my suspicion that he was primarily concerned about Sanson and what his reaction might be.

I said, "That's good."

"You're a researcher?" he asked, changing the subject. Which I took as a good sign. His mind had shifted from *Should I believe this man?* to *What can this man do for me?* Or maybe, *Okay, if he turns into any kind of threat, I have weapons at the caravan. No harm. No foul.*

"Yes," I said, not wanting to get too involved in a conversation I couldn't carry.

Even though the more I spoke French, the more it came back to me, I didn't want to push credibility.

"Do you have any proof of this?"

"All my notes on the Richat Structure are in my hotel room in Chinguetti."

"You don't need them now?"

"I did not want to risk losing my work."

It was the weak link in my story. Where was my researcher stuff? Farouk had an iPad in his rucksack, but it was filled with military files. There was no way to create a legend any deeper than we had already improvised. I had no Sorbonne papers. No university pass. Only a decent understanding of French, a beard, and a dark tan.

"What part of the Richat are you studying?" he asked.

"The Sorbonne and the government are interested in any connection between Plato and Atlantis. The dimensions are precise, and the Sahara has evolved."

"The government?"

"Speculation, but I make a few francs if you accept me on the team."

The mention of the government was also a matter of debate between Farouk and me. Ultimately, we decided to make it part of my backstory because Malik would have no way of independently verifying it. Sanson would be a different story. I imagined that he was connected at the highest levels of the French government.

At the end of the day, most people made decisions in their selfish interest. If he was debating whether to save his own ass or protect Sanson from a remote but potential threat—me—he acted as most people would have.

"Drive," he said.

He had weighed the risks to him being down five people—Amina, her assaulter, two motorcycle drivers, and the truck driver. Worse for Malik was that Amina had been the personal concubine for Sanson. Sanson would notice her absence. Malik pocketed the truck registration and grimaced as he clutched his torso.

"You have asked me many questions. Who are you to this caravan?"

"Just do as I tell you to do and you'll be fine," he said. "I'm in charge."

I nodded at him. He stared in the distance, probably devising a story. *Hey, I traded up for this researcher*

from the Sorbonne. Off-loaded some deadwood oxygen
breathers that weren't performing. This is all part of the
routine. How I do business. We were getting stale.

Realizing my reservoir of French was exhausted, I put
the Renault in drive and headed toward the caravan.

22

I TURNED THE VEHICLE into a small tent city, a few with flaps rolled up and cots visible through the shimmering waves of heat bouncing off the desert floor. Malik directed me to the back of what appeared to be the mess tent. I sweated profusely as he had me off-load the supplies and stack them on pallets inside the tent. The musty canvas brought back memories of so many field training exercises performed in tactical operations centers over the years.

Beyond the open front flap of the tent, there was a larger tent that had three women performing various cleaning functions in what appeared to be the Sahara version of glamping—glamorous camping.

One woman shook the sheets of a king-size bed with large pillows. Another worked on a shower with a pull chain behind the room that contained the toilet. Three bureau drawers were open as the third woman ran a feather duster along the inside. Amina was probably the fourth of this crew, and they were all likely from Chinguetti. They appeared to be young, but it was impossible to determine their ages.

None of them were Zoey.

"They're Sanson's," Malik said. "Stop staring. Hamza had the same problem. He was always eyeing the ladies."

Which now made sense to me. Hamza was the man Farouk had killed. It was plausible to Malik that Hamza had eloped with Amina.

"Pardon me," I said. "Shouldn't I get you to the clinic?"

"There's no clinic. Just a doctor. I'm going to see him now. Raoul's cot was in that tent. That's where you stay."

I nodded and then a shadow fell over the opening to the mess hall tent, where a giant of a man now stood.

"This is Josef. He will show you the way," Malik said.

The plywood flooring of the mess tent rumbled when Josef walked toward me.

"Who's this?" Josef asked.

"Abdel el Harim," Malik said. "He's a researcher from the Sorbonne. I picked him up in Chinguetti."

"The others?" Josef asked.

I got the impression that while Malik was in charge, Josef held some sway over him. Judging by his size, he was probably Sanson's bodyguard. Or he was a ditch-digger. His neck muscles bulged out of his tight polypro shirt, which clung to him tightly, revealing washboard abs and not an ounce of fat on his muscled frame.

"We will discuss that after you get him to his bunk," Malik said. Then to me, "We have a 4:00 p.m. meeting here. That's in an hour. Go to your bunk and wait there. You'll get your assignment at the meeting. We go out at dusk to avoid the heat. We've had many dehydration concerns."

Josef walked me to the bunk tent, which had ten cots. All had an assortment of personal belongings, clothes, backpacks, water bottles, and notebooks strewn around them. The sun was baking the area, and it was suffocating inside. Three men in the back were huddled together, talking across from each other on two cots.

"I'll come get you," Josef said. "Stay here."

I received no instructions on which bunk was mine, but I knew that four of them would not be occupied tonight. Every cot, though, was littered with personal belongings. Sleeping bags. Magazines. Water bottles. Backpacks. Shoes. Towels. None were empty. So, I sat in an empty chair next to a collapsible field table in the corner. I thought about Hobart and Van Dreeves, McCool and her team, and Farouk and Amina. Three sets of variables out there all who had missions to perform with little to no support from our country. I had no secret way to communicate with any of them, and I had left my throat microphone with Farouk in case of a search by Malik or his men. The best I could hope for was that Van Dreeves was still alive and had fixed the chip-tracking device to find both Zoey and me. I thought about the legions of expeditions that had entered and never left the Sahara. How this forsaken land consumed every living thing except the sturdiest and most enduring, like the horned vipers and camels that had adapted to the climate. The odds were stacked against us from the very beginning, but what Sly had uncovered was too important for the national security of our country and the world. I considered multiple options and outcomes for the next hour until the three men, who spoke in Arabic, walked past me.

"*Salam alaykum,*" one said.

"*Alaykum salam,*" I replied. And quickly followed up with, "*Allez-vous à la réunion?*"

"*Oui,*" the last man said, nodding.

They ambled into the heat wearing headscarves, white long-sleeve T-shirts, ripstop lightweight cargo pants, and ankle-high desert boots. All of them were fit, muscled, and young. Based on how they were dressed, I guessed they were basic labor, ditchdiggers. Their beards were no longer than mine, and their black hair was matted with sweat. I fit right in.

I stayed in the tent until the last man turned and said, "*Viens avec nous.*" *Come with us.*

The giant had told me to stay put until he came back, but I figured these guys could be helpful.

"*Le grand homme m'a dit de rester,*" I said. *The big man told me to stay.*

The man laughed and said, "*Josef n'est pas responsable.*" *Josef is not in charge.*

I walked with them across the rocky terrain. The desert was at full volume now. Probably 110 degrees. The wind was pushing at the tent flaps as if they were frigate sails. Now that I had changed the language of the dialogue from Arabic to French, one of them asked me what my role was.

"Researcher," I said.

"That's Abdul's job. Are you joining him?"

"As we get closer to discovery, the Sorbonne has asked me to come down."

"The Sorbonne?"

"Yes, the university in Paris," I said.

"I know the Sorbonne," the man laughed. "I attended for two years before graduating from INSAP."

Not knowing what INSAP was but feeling like I should, as I was assuming the identity of a professor in the field of archeology, I said, "Impressive. Which area?"

"My degree is prehistory. Jamal and Omar are archeology."

"All students?" I asked, waving my hand across all of them.

"Yes. We are getting course credit for the dig with

Sanson. No one understood the importance of the Eye of Africa until Google Earth was invented. Astronauts saw it from the sky, but only when the images persisted on the internet did people become curious."

"The Richat Structure is very unique," I said. "Where do you come down on the natural versus man-made debate?"

He stopped and looked at me as we stood outside of the mess tent where I had delivered the supplies. With a big smile, he shrugged and said, "We shall learn. I am Kareem, by the way."

"Abdel," I said, shaking his hand.

"I told you to stay in your tent," Josef the giant said to me, placing his catcher's mitt of a hand on my shoulder.

"These men invited me with them," I replied. "Very friendly team you have here."

Kareem made a joke in Arabic as they looked over their shoulders and continued walking. Either Josef didn't hear the joke or didn't speak much Arabic. His French had a deeper guttural texture to it than others who spoke the language synthetically, such as I, who had learned it from afar.

He stared me in the eyes as I studied him. *Josef* was a French or German name. His light brown hair bordered on blond. He had Nordic features—tall, prominent brow ridge, and blue eyes—which told me he might be from northern France near Lille or even as far east as Strasbourg or Metz or Nancy in the Alsace-Lorraine region. With his size, his descendants might have helped dig the Maginot Line, the famous trenchworks constructed during World War II to block the German blitzkrieg from rushing through the rolling plains of central France.

"Do as I say. You come in here to eat and drink. You

work with the crew. Listen to the briefing," he said. His dialect was Alsatian. When he said *eat,* he used the French word *manger,* but when he said *drink,* he actually said *trinke,* which is the Alsatian version of the German word *drinken* and nothing close to the French word *boire.* He got the best genes of the Germans, the Vikings, and the French, and by extension, I could assume he had at least a two-thirds warrior spirit.

"I have to catch up on the research team's efforts," I said.

"Listen to the briefing."

We stood at the very back of the tent at the farthest edge of the plywood flooring. Josef was one step behind me and to my right as Malik limped to the front. There were twenty metal folding chairs arrayed in four haphazard rows of five. I counted twelve people. The three women who were cleaning Sanson's tent were seated to the front right. The three archeology students were seated next to each other on the middle left. Four were scattered around the remaining chairs in no obvious grouping. Then there were Malik and Josef.

Zoey was not visible.

Which meant she was in custody somewhere. Which meant that there was at least one, most likely two more guarding her.

Discounting the women and the students, which was not a certainty, I would have to contend with the two guards on Zoey, Josef, his likely doppelgänger with Sanson, Malik, and Sanson himself.

Six against one . . . maybe ten to one if the four randomly scattered men were loyal to Sanson.

I've had worse odds. I imagined that the shelf life of my legend would decay quickly once Sanson returned. A couple of quick phone calls and he would be put in touch with the university president and discover that I was not connected to the Sorbonne. The real question was, beyond the women, did Sanson take note of who was on his caravan?

Most caravans were normally larger, but for security reasons, Sanson had evidently trimmed his to mission-essential personnel. And Farouk and I had done some trimming of our own.

Malik spoke in French to his charges. He discussed the resupply that had just come in. Made mention of a resupply trip in two days. Referenced a VIP arrival in the next twenty-four hours, which I took to mean Sanson. Made quick mention of me as a replacement for the Algerian researcher, who was taking some leave before his return. Mentioned that Amina was home in Chinguetti because her mother was sick. Commented about two men named Max and Heinz who were also rotating out of the caravan in normal fashion. Said that Najab was waiting on Amina to bring her back. I assumed Najab was the dead truck driver. After accounting for his missing people, he explained that tonight's mission was to continue the dig on the northeastern corner of what they suspected to be Poseidon's Temple. They had found an underground tunnel, and there was some construction needed for continued exploration.

Max and Heinz must have been the motorcycle guys. Both names were French or German, which reinforced my impression of Josef as a northeastern Frenchman. Max and Heinz, who were dead or dying in the ravine near Chinguetti, were probably friends of Josef's.

Malik spoke with confidence about the changes in personnel as if these types of rotations were frequent and necessary—important, even. If he had any concerns about my appearance inside his base camp, he did not reveal them to the assembled team. I suspected that managing the image for the moment, with Sanson's return imminent, would be better than having chaos reigning when the blade master arrived. Plus, even if he wasn't sure, he had to be careful. If he killed me and I truly was from the Sorbonne, or requested by Sanson, his head would be next. If I was bogus, he could determine that rather quickly with Sanson. Still, he had to play it right. If Sanson was the sadistic monster that he appeared to be, Malik had every right to attempt to establish a normal routine, get his information during Sanson's brief visit, and then deal with me after his departure, if necessary.

Malik broke up the meeting with a clap, the way a football quarterback might break a huddle. Afterward, he strode directly toward me with a disheveled-looking older man in tow. I had seen the man sitting on the front left in front of the students.

"Abdel, this is Mohammed Fahzel, the head of archeology at the university in Rabat. Perhaps you two know each other? It is, after all, a small community."

The man looked at me with a blank stare. I've been judged to be of a few different professions. The most common were soldier, marine, farmer, and truck driver. At six foot two, 195 pounds, and a Ranger high and tight, never have I been mistaken for being an academician.

Perhaps I should have thought of that before establishing "researcher" as my legend. As the professor stared at me in wonderment, the buzz of a single-engine airplane cut against the dusk sky.

23

SANSON'S LANDING THANKFULLY BROKE the awkward moment between me and the Moroccan archeologist but of course heralded a new set of issues to confront. The sun was hanging low in the western sky. I thought about my team again and silently prayed they were continuing their missions and surviving.

Most importantly, I had no opportunity for unguarded freedom of movement yet to search the camp for signs of Zoey's presence. Malik ushered everyone to their posts with a few efficient claps of his hands that sounded like gunshots.

"Let's get going. Move! Move!"

The three students addressed the archeologist as "*Professeure,*" which of course meant that they were a single unit and that my role would most naturally fit in their circle, perhaps decreasing by even more the shelf life of my cover.

I walked with them a few hundred meters down a trail that forked, one going southeast, the other northeast. Both appeared well worn. We veered right onto the southeast trail, switching back and forth downslope until the path leveled out onto a rocky moonscape with strings running along stakes. Beyond the yellow tape was a descending set of stairs that predated the dig site. Built with black and tan rocks that were smoothed by wind or water, the staircase was etched into the side of a wall that led some twenty meters down into a large square that had been hollowed out to maybe the size of a baseball diamond. On the opposite side was a plywood ramp wide enough for a backhoe to creep down as it switched back and forth.

Above it all were generators and lights, like a football stadium. This operation might have been visible from the space station. The only way to operate with any sustained effort here in the Sahara was at night. But still, there was something off about the setup, which I couldn't put my finger on just yet.

The backhoe was being operated by one of the figures in the briefing who didn't appear to be a member of any of the cliques. Another man was using a flashlight to ground guide the machine toward a dark tunnel on the opposite wall. A third was standing at the entrance to the tunnel. In the middle was a woman who was hammering more stakes into the ground and making squares into the larger grid in the deeper hole where I now stood. She had her own set of lights inside the pit, casting a garish yellow beam across the entire expanse, and a doctor's lamp on her forehead.

This was a massive undertaking, especially for such a small operation. Maybe Malik was focused more on execution of the dig than he was worried about security, and therefore, I got an initial pass. I wasn't banking on any breaks, but I wouldn't refuse any, either. When we got to the bottom of the stairwell, the woman looked up, flipped up her doctor's lamp, and waved at the group, motioning to the professor.

"Here is something I think you want to see," she said. Her French was distinctly more Parisian than country.

Her syntax was soft, with smooth transitions between the words, yet with an emphasis on precise pronunciation. I got the impression she was an exacting woman.

I wondered why she had not been in the meeting, and after a minute of watching her speak with Professor Mohammed Fahzel, I knew that she was an impatient individual focused on the primary task at hand, whatever that might be. As they spoke, Fahzel relayed a quick summary of the meeting and she waved her hand in the universal "I don't have time for this bullshit" expression.

Kareem stood next to me and said, "She is brilliant but eccentric."

"Who is she?" I asked.

"Evelyn Champollion. Direct blood descendent of Jean-François Champollion," he whispered. Champollion was renowned for having cracked the hieroglyphics of the Rosetta stone and translating them in the early nineteenth century.

"She's on the wrong side of the continent," I said, pretending I had much deeper knowledge of her ancestor's archeology.

"She has lived in his shadow for so long that she is hoping for a breakthrough with us. We are quite lucky to have her," Kareem said. "Being in Paris, have you met her?"

Every question was a potential land mine. Answer no, and they will think I have no status at the Sorbonne, which would in effect be true. Answer yes, and I'll have an additional slalom of questions to navigate.

"Definitely heard of her, but I imagine that on my salary, we are in different arrondissements," I said. *Different neighborhoods.*

My comment got a laugh from Kareem and his two peers but a scolding look from Evelyn Champollion. She was a beautiful woman, perhaps fifty. She was wearing a large, olive-green Aussie breezer hat, white with sweat stains that climbed the brim like age rings on a tree, each outing depositing a new line of salt. She had blue eyes and light brown hair, and she wore khaki pants beneath a loose, long-sleeve shirt. The sun had already baked this pit, which didn't benefit from the breeze above. I imagined this place was a furnace at high noon and late afternoon, with the only possibility for getting out of the sun being the mouth of the cave, where the one man stood. I had been sweating since my arrival hours ago, and the searing stare of Champollion was no help.

"Who are you?" she asked bluntly.

"Abdel. I'm just here for a day," I said.

"He's from the Sorbonne," Kareem bragged.

"The Sorbonne?" She smiled briefly. As if to already question my ersatz credentials.

"Yes, just a contract researcher," I said.

"For whom?" she asked.

This had been the point of some discussion between Farouk and me. Our going-in assumption had been that this operation was either a cover for something nefarious or that it was purely a gold mission. We had made the classic mistake of underestimating Sanson's belief that the Eye of Africa was Plato's Atlantis and that it could be both a cover and an actual dig. We believed the Plato theory was too far-fetched to be anything beyond a cover story for an operation that had another purpose. But now standing here among the gridded twine and stakes with black buckets of relics scattered throughout this near-vertical hole in the ground, it was obvious that someone was working in earnest to see what, if anything, was down here. Thankfully, Farouk had used his phone to do a quick search of the internet and found a midlevel functionary in the Sorbonne contracting department that supported the Department of Art and Archeology.

"My contracting official is Henri Bousier. I'm sure someone of your stature wouldn't have any dealings with him," I said.

"Oh, but I have," she replied. "Henri has been with the Sorbonne for a long time," she said. "I speak at Professor Marmont's annual conference, and he always makes sure I'm paid in a timely fashion."

This was why the intelligence agencies took months to develop a legend, not hours as we had done. With each new person I met, my alias's shelf life was deteriorating. By my best judgment, it had declined from our anticipated twenty-four hours to maybe nightfall. I needed to run interference for the next several hours until I could locate Zoey.

"Then you know him," I said.

"Yes, but who is your proctor?" she asked.

"Ma'am, if you please, I'm not at liberty to say," I said.

She studied me for a moment. I imagined she was considering several possibilities and certainly nothing a ten-minute phone call couldn't uncover.

"DGSE, I presume. Very well. What you see is what you get," she said, waving her hand across the gaping dig site. "The French are deeply vested here, both politically and financially."

I nodded and said, "Thank you, Evelyn."

She lifted her chin in acknowledgment, her eyes skeptical as if something was not quite settling with her, but she had work to do and had already wasted five minutes on me. Though the hottest part of the day had come and gone, the remnant temperature was sweltering, like an oven turned off that didn't cool down for hours. I visualized the sun setting in the ocean west of Dakhla. Mauritania was some 1,700 miles north of the equator, with the Tropic of Cancer dissecting its upper third, approximately on the same latitude as southern Florida.

She and Mohammed walked toward the cave mouth out of earshot. I followed along with the students, whom I presumed were awaiting instructions. I hadn't slept in two days and had eaten very little. Sweat was soaking my clothes. I took a tug of my water from the tube. That and my boots were the two luxuries I didn't exchange with the dead researcher in the truck.

A voice called out from above. It sounded like Malik. We all stopped walking and looked up. In the twilight, the three figures were silhouetted, backlit by the end-of-evening nautical twilight that remained.

Josef and his doppelgänger were flanking a man nearly equal in stature, a long saber hanging by his left leg.

I recognized him.

Sanson.

24

MALIK POINTED IN MY general direction, but he could have been pointing at anything in the dig site.

In the fading light, there were people milling around digging with shovels, pounding stakes into the dirt with rubber mallets, sweeping dust from artifacts with paintbrushes, and maneuvering a Bobcat mini-excavator into the cave mouth with flashlights.

I turned and came face-to-face with Evelyn Champollion, who was eyeing me curiously.

"Let's take a walk, shall we, Professor?" She tilted the last word upward an octave, almost a question but not quite. Definitely some sort of emphasis.

"Yes, ma'am," I said, forcing a smile.

She led me to the mouth of the cave and took me inside about forty meters. In front of us by another twenty meters was the Bobcat clawing at the bedrock as surgically as possible, which was to say, not very. I found it unusual that heavy equipment was gnawing at what they suspected to be, at least on appearances, a historical dig site potentially filled with priceless artifacts. The actual professor and his three students were continuing to outline the grid in the open area behind us in the stadium lighting. Every time the excavator backed up, it beeped. It had carved a ten-meter-high by ten-meter-wide tunnel into the wall.

"I have been here for two weeks. Our minister of defense, Albert Gambeau—a dear friend, by the way—asked me to come and check the veracity of some of the reported findings," she began.

I nodded and let her continue. The backhoe crew had set up work lights that shone on her face. She seemed to have something she wanted to convey. Her eyes were magnetic. Once I made contact, I couldn't let go. She never blinked. Her lips moved with the typical contortions of the French language, exaggerated baring of teeth and movement of the cheeks. But she did so in a way that was fluid and not distracting.

"Many people don't know what to make of me. Some think I am Parisian aristocracy. Others think I am a garden-variety college professor—no offense *if* that applies. While others believe me to be a spy with the DGSE."

I nodded and said nothing, though I didn't miss the emphasis on *if.*

"And while I could be any or all those things, I am uniquely me. I have a significant command of the history of the artifacts we are finding. I'm a Plato scholar. Very few of us left today, by the way. There's a not-so-secret society called 'the Academy' named after Plato's own academy. I am very comfortable in my own skin, and I have no problem with who I am or my chosen purpose in life, which is to continue to discover every day."

She adjusted her Aussie hat and looked me over with her eyes.

"You, sir, look more like an MI6 spy, DGSE operative, or football player—the European kind, not that dreadful sport in America. A university professor? I don't think so. Tell your handlers that they got this one wrong. Besides, your French is very average. Stilted, even."

I would take average. Even *very* average.

"You're forcing it, but obviously, you understand me, so you're doing fine projecting the proper role. It's not your act at all. It's your persona—or legend, as they say in the spy business. You couldn't pretend to be a college professor, ever."

I remained quiet.

"I'm not going to question you about your role or purpose for being here. We've had a few visitors come and go to both sites. I'm leaving in a couple of days myself. So, what I will tell you is that whatever your goal here is, do not get in my way. If you do, some people bigger than you will find you no matter where you are. And when they do, it won't be pleasant."

"I imagine not," I finally said.

"Good. So, you understand, which is another reason I'm not buying your act."

The backhoe was beeping as it backed up toward us. It had a spotlight shining on the wall the bucket teeth were scraping. Her wide eyes reflected white in the ambient light. There were specks of dirt on her face. She bared her teeth when she put her finger in my chest.

"Do not get in my way. I have a mission. In fact, you're better off at the second location. I don't care if your name is Abdel el Harim, Henri Sanson, or Samuel Wilson, I will not let you get in my way. Do you understand me?"

"I do," I said.

And I did. Perfectly.

"Why are you using heavy equipment at an archeological dig site?" I asked.

"Is that what this is?" she responded.

She walked past me and into the stadium lights of

the larger dig site. The relative coolness of the cavern was an inviting respite from the leftover searing heat. I imagined that the dig team took turns hydrating and cooling off in here. I walked to the edge of the cavern, already supported by four-by-four lumber to reinforce the ceiling, and watched Kareem and his team using paintbrushes to remove dirt from objects.

My conversation with the discerning Champollion was interesting for four reasons.

First, she referenced football, needlessly pointing out that she was not talking about American football.

Second, she mentioned the obscure name Samuel Wilson. Wilson was a meat-packer from New York who supplied barrels of meat to army troops when the War of 1812 was raging. He stamped his barrels with the letters *U.S.,* which the troops affectionately named Uncle Sam.

Not only was she an astute historian, but she also knew, or suspected, I was an American.

And she wasn't, yet, blowing my cover.

Third, her cheeky response regarding this being an archeological dig site convinced me that she was some type of government operative.

And last, her reference of a second dig site could have been a clue to Zoey's location.

Her elaboration about not interfering with her work could only mean one thing—that she was DGSE. It was a hint to do my thing but not to disrupt her doing her thing, whatever that might be. With her double emphasis of the point and stress of what might happen to me if I did get in her way, I suspected that whatever her mission, it was important to someone powerful.

My mission, of course, was finding Zoey and getting safely the hell out of here, among other things. On the surface, this looked and operated like an entirely legitimate archeological dig. But with the Chinese military in the area and Zoey somewhere close by, there was nothing normal about what was happening here in the desert.

The backhoe was making the *beep, beep, beep* until it finally coughed and sputtered to a stop. The ground guide and operator were talking in animated Arabic. I walked past them unnoticed on the opposite side of the backhoe, the only light that of the backhoe's spotlight and the dancing flashlight of the ground guide, whose hands were shaking as he spoke. There was enough light to see that the backhoe had clawed through a wall of sorts, which opened to another passageway. Diesel fumes wafting in the air like an apparition were pulled toward the opening. The air smelled of gas fumes and musty dirt. The engine ticked loudly and whined as it spooled down and cooled.

The bucket at the end of the arm had a full scoop of dirt where previously it had been dumping into a mound behind which I now stood. The backhoe spotlight shone through the hole and into the far side, where trunks were stacked upon one another. There was a commotion at the mouth of the cave to my left. I slid farther behind the mound and against the wall of the cave opposite where the backhoe operator and ground guide were still shouting.

Someone called out, "What is this?" in French.

It was a voice I had not heard today but was distantly familiar. Because I had been staring into the lighted portal between the existing tunnel where I stood and the new chamber unearthed by the backhoe, my night vision was briefly impaired. Three figures stood at the mouth of the cave talking to the two backhoe operators.

"Did the new man come in here?" Josef asked them.

"What new man?" the operator replied.

"The man pretending to be a scholar," a different, familiar voice said. It was a voice I hadn't heard recently but one that brought back a memory of Zoey and Afghanistan. Visions of the man with the red sash standing among Zoey and the women she was rescuing in Paktia Province, Afghanistan, cycled through my mind.

American traitor!

Could the man I had chased through the tunnel in Afghanistan be Sanson? In the heat of that moment and the excitement about returning Zoey to her father, the French accent had seemed less important than ensuring the safe return of the assembled group to our clandestine runway a few miles away. With the Taliban closing in, we had moved swiftly to collapse the team on our makeshift command post and exfiltrate the women, including Zoey, to an intermediate base in Tajikistan.

There was no question now, though, that this voice was the same voice of the man with the large saber. Afghanistan, Chinguetti, and now the Eye of Africa.

Sanson.

The men entered the cave mouth. My eyes had fully adjusted. Sanson was flanked by Josef and his doppelgänger. They approached the two men on the opposite side of the backhoe. The doppelgänger, however, stared at the dirt mound and scanned left and right. Because of the lack of direct lighting, the mound looked smaller than it was. The conversation ensued as sight lines on either side of the mound prevented my movement, but I noticed that the hole in the wall to my right reached ground level and the mound of spilled dirt to my left was at least three feet high. I low crawled until I was astride the new breach and began sliding through it. The Bobcat engine continued ticking loudly as it cooled. Shouts from outside the cave reached inside but were unintelligible.

"There's a man. He claims to be a professor, but he's not. He's somewhere down here in the dig site."

"We have not seen him, but we have a discovery," the operator said, certainly eager to change the topic to prevent an anticipated beheading.

I slid through the fresh gap in the wall, rocks and shale scraping at my torso. I continued to crawl beyond the stacked chests as if I were back in Ranger School. I slid deeper into the freshly discovered tunnel. When I was about forty meters beyond the trunks, the tunnel narrowed, but the diesel fumes continued to waft past me, indicating a potential escape route if I continued.

Flashlights danced behind me as Sanson and team entered the chamber that the operators had unearthed.

"Is this what I think it is?" Sanson asked.

"Gold," Josef said.

I continued to crawl until I noticed a slight change in the pattern of the tunnel ceiling.

Stars.

I had traveled seventy-five meters beyond the trunks as I clawed my way up the shaft. At the top, it was maybe three feet wide, large enough for me to escape. I scratched upward, pushing out of the hole, shaking off any remnant claustrophobia from having my shoulders briefly stuck. I stayed low and took a knee behind a rock. Studying the stars in the sky, brilliantly lit because of the absence of substantive ambient light, I quickly got my cardinal bearings. Looking to the west, I saw the outline of the encampment, which would place the dig site to my left at about a forty-five-degree angle.

Remembering the fork that we had taken to the southeast and Champollion's comment about "the other site,"

I stood and jogged, hunched over as if I were running beneath helicopter blades to keep my profile low and consistent with the horizon. After running maybe two hundred meters, I found a trail, presumably the one that forked northeast from the tent city. Following the trail, I crested a ridge and saw a lone tent with a weak light bleeding from beneath the flaps. The tent was situated in the middle of what looked like another dig site complete with grids and a parked Bobcat. This could be simple shade for the workers, or it could be something else.

I took a full minute to adjust my bearings to the new ecosystem. The random mechanical banging from the dig site a half mile away echoed into the ether. The heat had fully escaped into the cloudless sky, and the cool night air was getting colder. The rocky sand and shale beneath my hands was brittle from the heat. The wind carried the scent of desert thyme that managed to survive in the harsh Saharan environment.

There was no sound from the tent, but a rhythmic metal-on-metal clattering sang in the distance. It reminded me of the Metro in Washington, D.C., as it continued to churn away until it faded into the northern distance.

A train. Less than five miles to the north. I tucked the information in the back of my mind as I quickly moved toward the tent. The flaps were staked down in every direction, forcing me to move to the far side, where a lone figure stood outside smoking a cigarette and looking at a phone. He had a weapon slung across his back in the eternal lazy-guard fashion. He had probably stood guard here countless nights with nothing occurring, which resulted in a complacency that provided opportunity. I picked up a rock and tossed it twenty meters on the opposite side of my location, causing him to look away from me.

I charged and tackled the man, elbowing him in the temple to put him to sleep for a bit. I had seen some good people here as well as some potentially nefarious ones and had no idea where this man was on the scale. No need in killing someone who didn't deserve it, though they all probably knew that if they failed, they would suffer the fate of Sanson's blade.

I took the unconscious man and slid him behind a grouping of large brown boulders. He had a PVS-14 night vision monocular device strapped around his neck. I removed that and lifted his cell phone, pistol, knife, ammunition, flashlight, key ring, and AK-47. Situating those implements on my body where appropriate, I stepped to the tent flap and listened.

A low hum emanated from inside. Stepping through, I swept left and right with the pistol. A swamp cooler was in the corner, the source of the hum. Near the far wall was a ladder protruding from a circular entry.

The throaty sound of a diesel engine roared in the distance, an approaching truck. I used the flashlight to investigate the hole.

Peering up at me was Zoey Morgan, her eyes white with fear and her wrists manacled on opposing walls of the dungeon.

25

"THE CHINESE HAVE LAUNCHED five hypersonic missiles that are loitering in outer space right now waiting to be directed onto targets in the United States and maybe Europe," Koby Bertrand said.

Bertrand was the director of national intelligence and typically pursued a background role in supporting the more forward-facing agencies such as the State and Defense Departments. Tonight, he was lighting up President Campbell's Alexa in the Oval Office. He was bald and wore rimless round spectacles and a gray suit. He had large ears and a slender nose, looking like the academic he was. Previously head of the Georgetown national security studies program, Bertrand had been tapped by Campbell to fight a mostly losing effort to reverse the weaponization of the intelligence agencies.

"Like they did two years ago?" Campbell asked.

"Yes and no," Bertrand said. "These aircraft are like small space shuttles, maybe half the size. Just big enough to fly a nuke, like a cruise missile. Launched on a rocket, released in space, fly like the shuttle, and then reenter the atmosphere to fly to a certain point. The engines, however, use hydrogen and can propel the vessel to five times the speed of sound, making it impossible to detect or interdict. Not a fossil fuel–consuming air breather, which our satellites are trained to detect."

"I thought there were accuracy problems," Blankenship said.

Secretary of Defense Blankenship and Secretary of State McHenry were seated on one sofa with Bertrand and the chairman of the Joint Chiefs, General Lucius Rolfing, on the other. Campbell was seated in a chair at the head and in between the two sofas. A few staffers stood in the background, scribbling notes and nodding at appropriate times, always with furrowed brows of concern.

"There were," Bertrand said. "Tense being important here, which is to say that there may not be any more issues. A couple of years ago, the tests had the payload missing by ten to twenty miles."

McHenry nodded and said, "This was my understanding also. Instead of Washington, D.C., they hit Fairfax, Virginia, for example." She hunched her shoulders and held up her hands, palms up in the "no biggie" pose.

Bertrand nodded and continued, "The Chinese have tested a terminal guidance system that increases the accuracy of delivery."

"So, instead of Fairfax, it's Arlington," McHenry said.

Campbell said, "Now is not the time to minimize this, Bryn."

McHenry looked at Campbell and then sideways at Blankenship. Both women adjusted their positions on the sofa and crossed their arms. Blankenship hung her head and locked eyes with McHenry, shaking her head slowly as Bertrand continued.

"To carry the analogy, though, Madam President, now it is the Lincoln Bedroom and not the Oval Office."

"That's less than twenty yards. I've paced it," Campbell said.

"Yes, I accounted for the margin of error. The more likely result would be your chief of staff's office right there through the wall." Bertrand pointed at the far wall, his uncharacteristic boldness perhaps a signal of the seriousness of the matter.

"You're joking?" Blankenship asked.

"I'm afraid not, AB."

"How have they achieved such accuracy?" Campbell asked. And followed with the equally relevant, "And how have we missed this?"

"I'll go in reverse order. You brought me in to return the focus of the intelligence agencies to actual threats to our national security in an attempt to disentangle us from being used as a political arm."

"That's right," Campbell said.

"I've repurposed many of the task forces that were set up over the last few years from focusing on domestic issues to threats from our adversaries."

"China's *not* an adversary," McHenry said.

Bertrand removed his glasses and looked at the secretary of state with knowing eyes.

"Bryn, I think you should sit this one out and let me finish the briefing. Time is of the essence here. Unless, of course, you'd prefer I not make my point so the president can't act in a timely fashion."

"What are you saying, Koby?" Campbell asked.

"Did you just accuse me of something?" McHenry interrupted.

"Madam President, I suggest we continue this briefing in private if these unprofessional interruptions are going to continue from someone who might not be the most impartial person in the room," Bertrand said, living up to his moniker as a no-nonsense bulldog. Anyone who judged him on his diminutive looks and not on his keen intellect was making a mistake.

"I think Bryn is just surprised," Blankenship said. "She's been working hard at building bridges."

"Sometimes the enemy uses bridges to attack," Bertrand said.

"Both of you, shut it. Koby, continue," Campbell said.

"China has tested a global intermediate nuclear targeting station, what we are calling GLINTS, to take the reentry vehicle and guide it by powerful lasers to the very specific target they are seeking to destroy. Think of how our special operations troops use lasers to guide smart bombs with deadly accuracy onto targets. It's the same principle here, only the laser is guiding a nuclear weapon moving at Mach five to a very precise target without detection. Only recently have we discovered this improved accuracy after I repurposed personnel to focus on China. The hypersonic glide vehicles move so fast that we can't detect them and can only know either from assessing a launch and tracking that launch until we can't track it anymore, or through human intelligence, which is sparse in China. So, we've been relying on the 'dog that didn't bark' theory, meaning, if there was a launch and we can't see the payload deployed in space, typically a satellite, we assume there is a hypersonic missile whipping around the globe with miniaturized fissile material, which allows for maneuverability and accuracy."

"You're scaring me, Koby," Campbell said.

"You should be scared. China's geopolitical positioning allows them to strike or hold hostage the Western world from this unique positioning in Africa. The Cold War has been digitized and modernized. This is a twenty-first-century Cuban Missile Crisis."

"How does Africa help China here? I still don't get it," Campbell said.

"There's one place in Africa that gives China the ability to precisely designate targets in North America, South America, Europe, and the Middle East."

"Where?"

He held up a large diagram of the Eye of Africa on a piece of lightweight gatorboard.

"L'Oeil d'Afrique. The Eye of Africa," Bertrand said. "Within one hundred miles of this terrain feature."

"Why there?"

Bertrand pushed a button, and a simulated GLINTS system in Mauritania fired a laser, which reflected off a satellite mirror in outer space and fired beams down to every major city in the Western Hemisphere.

"It's positioning here is unbelievably perfect," Bertrand said. "They can strike anywhere with nuclear hypersonic glide vehicles with precision."

"But why there, specifically?" Campbell asked.

Bertrand held up a new graphic. On it was an image of the earth suspended in space surrounded by three layers of satellite fields. The map showed lines emanating from China, Djibouti, and the Eye of Africa and terminating into the satellite constellations in the atmosphere.

"Here you have the southwestern Chinese deserts and the Yunnan Missile Guidance Base," Bertrand said, pointing at a region in southwestern China, south of Mongolia. "The directed-energy systems here can only range the high-earth-orbit satellites. The curvature of the earth blocks the beam from getting to the medium- and low-earth-orbit satellites."

A bright line was drawn from the base in China to a satellite symbol deep in space.

"The catch is that the directed-energy systems they

have been testing for many years don't have the power to maintain the beam as it refracts off the satellite mirror for any meaningful control of the glide vehicles re-entering the atmosphere. Same with the medium-earth orbits. We have imagery of them trying this from Yunnan and Djibouti. What does the Eye of Africa give them? The ability to reach a low-earth-orbit satellite without earth interference and the power to refract and control the glide vehicle. That fleet, the helicopters, the infantry. They're all part of this, I can assure you. China can hold hostage the United States and Western Europe from this location. It's genius."

The group remained silent.

"So, there's no defense against this? We'll have to bluff and negotiate our way out of it like Kennedy and Khrushchev?"

"It's worse than that. This is the equivalent of Khrushchev having the nukes assembled and fired up, ready to launch in Cuba. We could appeal to China, but they hold all the cards. We wait and see what happens to the suspected five hypersonics they've got flying now."

"You said, 'five'?"

"Five."

"Suspected targets?" Blankenship asked.

"If you were paying attention, I said we can't know where they are going. With traditional intercontinental ballistic missiles, we track them the entire way, algorithms computing precise parabolic arcs and paths the entire flight. Those computations are used to intercept and destroy incoming nuclear missiles. When something is maneuvering at five times the speed of sound, we have no idea where it is, where it might land, or what the payload might be. It's the perfect weapon."

"The perfect weapon. And we didn't develop it or any defense to it," Campbell said. She looked at McHenry and Blankenship. Both women were fidgeting with their hands. Blankenship stared at her shoes while McHenry fired laser darts at Bertrand.

"How do we even know about it if it is so double top secret?" McHenry asked.

"A few things, Bryn. First, we tracked five launches over the past two weeks. Those launches went up and came down after a noticeable period of invisibility in space. We take that to mean they launched the vessels in space, which we assume are in orbit expending very little energy right now. Our assessment is that the Chinese are either going to launch more missiles into space until they have some number of swarming mass to attack one target such as your Fairfax, Virginia, example, or to have sufficient capability to reenter on separate paths and attack multiple targets, such as Los Angeles, New York City, Chicago, Miami, and, of course, Fairfax. The GLINTS will help them be very precise."

The room was quiet for a minute until Campbell asked, "But where is this GLINTS system?"

"Thanks to our State and Defense Departments, who are treating China as an ally and not an adversary, we, the United States, have helped the Chinese upgrade a rail system in Mauritania that reaches from the coast to the inner Sahara near this terrain feature called the Eye of Africa. This rail system has improved gauge and capacity to haul very heavy equipment. When we were alerted on the significant illegal fishing that has been ongoing off the coast of Mauritania and Morocco, we began layering intelligence capabilities onto the area. We began noticing over the past few days that ships from the Chinese fishing fleet were making port in La Batterie, Mauritania."

Bertrand produced a satellite image of the port

facility on lightweight gatorboard and handed it to Campbell.

"The ships come in here and off-load covered materials, which then get railed to the interior of Mauritania, where they are off-loaded and moved about both aboveground and belowground in the Eye of Africa. Yesterday, we got a satellite over it and saw this."

He handed her another piece of gatorboard that had a satellite shot of the desert.

"Here you've got what looks like an expedition or archeological dig. Next, you've got another bed-down site here. And about a mile away, you've got the train tracks here and a road that connects the bed-down location and the off-load location. All three locations comprise the entire operation of building this giant laser that can grab these hypersonic vessels when they fly through an active laser beam, receive terminal guidance, and accurately strike the target."

"The dig site is a ruse?" Campbell asked.

"Indeed," Bertrand said.

"Wouldn't they need five GLINTS or whatever?" Campbell asked.

"This device here has at least five, if not ten—it's a little hard to tell—lasers that we believe can guide separate vessels. It would be like having five or ten, or pick a number, lawn darts in the air, all of which could be maneuvered electronically to land exactly where you want them to."

"How did we not know about what is happening in Mauritania?" Campbell asked.

"That question might be better directed at Bryn or AB, who have been working overtime to extend olive branches to China, signing deals such as the Dakhla Accords, which allows for Chinese docking and heavy equipment manufacturing in Mauritania."

"Which means they're doing nothing illegal," McHenry said. "I still don't see the issue. There's no way to interpret any malintent here."

"No, Bryn, nothing illegal perhaps, but exceptionally damaging to our national security, don't you think?" Campbell said.

"Like I said, there's no evidence that China is acting with malintent," she responded.

"You mean other than the five missiles flying around in outer space waiting to reenter and the Chinese construction of a laser system in the Sahara to potentially land one on top of our heads?"

McHenry bristled. "First, even Koby said there's no evidence of the existence of these aircraft in space. He's making assumptions. Second, you can't assume that what China may or may not be doing in Mauritania is nefarious. Third, whatever they are doing, it's legal. They're competitors, not adversaries."

"Thanks to you two," Campbell said. "How did you sneak this one past me?"

"That's not fair," Blankenship said.

"I'll tell you what's not fair," Campbell countered. "There are nearly twenty million people in our top five most populated cities—New York, Los Angeles, Chicago, Houston, and Philadelphia or Phoenix, your choice. You've just put them all at risk."

"I would say that obviously the first target of all would be us, right here in D.C.," Bertrand said. "From a timing perspective, I'd say we have less than twenty-four hours. The first launch was nearly two weeks ago, and the fuel burn rate to successfully fire motors and reach a target under guidance points to tomorrow as the day."

"Jesus. What can we do?" Blankenship asked.

"You're supposed to provide me recommendations, not problems, AB," Campbell said. "Goes for all of you."

"When we spoke earlier, Madam President, your comment about General Sinclair and his JSOC team might be a good option," Bertrand said.

"Sinclair is on his way out. He's a liability. He's nowhere to be found and, frankly, an embarrassment to all of us. He's AWOL," Blankenship said.

"Seriously, that guy's toxic. From what I hear about the inspector general investigation, we should be putting him in jail, not relying upon him for anything remotely to do with representing this administration," McHenry said.

Campbell cocked her head and said, "Really? What about representing the American people? I'm thinking he may be our only chance."

26

RELIEF WASHED OVER ME as Zoey struggled against her manacles upon seeing me.

Her captors had tied a rag around her mouth and then circled some tape around the rag and the back of her head, holding the cloth in place. Her wrists were bleeding from vain attempts at breaking free.

The diesel engine roared as the truck crested the hill two hundred meters away. I had seconds to unleash Zoey and at least assume a defensive posture. I grabbed the set of keys I'd secured from the guard and scored on the third key. I had to hold Zoey's bare arm to unlock her other wrist and then pull her up and over the lip of the hole. I flipped her over and used the knife to slice through the cloth and tape, freeing her mouth.

"Are you okay?" I asked.

She pushed herself up and stumbled around the tent, knocking over field chairs, a small wooden desk, milk crates filled with papers, and a fan.

"Dad was right. The rest of the plan is in here!" she said. She ran her fingers through her hair, the blood from her wrists staining the white T-shirt someone had put on her. She still wore the cargo pants I figured she was wearing when she was captured.

"Zoey, we've got thirty seconds," I said.

Her eyes were wide, hair matted, and cheeks salt-stained, and teeth bared.

"It's here! I heard them. The Chinese. Just like we discussed!"

"I know, Zoey. But none of this is going to do us any good if we're dead."

She picked up an external drive from a milk crate.

"This," she said and pocketed it. "Give me a weapon."

I handed her the pistol when Josef came barreling into the tent. He stood there hulking and menacing, so I shot him in the chest, which didn't seem to bother him as he continued to power toward me. Zoey fired until her magazine was empty, and the pistol receiver locked to the rear. Josef's head was a mangled mess as he fell to the floor at my feet. I removed a pistol and phone from his holster and pocket as machine-gun fire began zipping through the tent flaps. Tossing the pistol to Zoey, I shouted, "Down!" and rolled beneath one of the flaps so that I came up behind the truck that spun to a halt in front of the tent.

The truck headlights bounced wildly as Josef's doppelgänger leaped from the driver's side, pistol drawn. I fired the AK-47 in single shots, winging him, which caused him to turn and spray unaimed pistol fire in my direction. The machine gun on the ridge behind us continued to sing and spit lead into the tent. I was concerned about Zoey but had a new concern with my AK trigger-locking, empty of ammunition.

Sanson must have come from the opposite direction because he stood in front of the headlights at a distance so that he was barely visible, like an apparition wafting in and out of the dusty haze. His foot was elevated, and only then did I notice that his boot was on Zoey's back and his saber was hanging loosely in his hand.

"Like father, like daughter, Sinclair?"

How did he know my name?

"First you chase me in Afghanistan. Now you chase me here. What I didn't finish there, I will finish now. You are outnumbered and surrounded by my men and forces beyond your comprehension that will fundamentally alter the world order . . . and make me a rich man, by the way. There was nothing you could do to stop it, but I give you credit for trying."

He reached down and grabbed the hair on the back of Zoey's head and held her up like a trophy. For a brief moment, the way the light was cast, I thought it was her severed head. My blood began to rush. Then I saw her legs scramble beneath her, trying to stand. He doubled her over a small boulder to his left and raised the saber above his head.

I shouted, "No!" and raced toward him, but the doppelgänger had recovered and inched forward, tripping me. I had the knife I had lifted off the first guard in my hand, plunging it into the doppelgänger's heart as a shot sang through the night. The bullet cracked above my head.

Sanson sounded with "Oomph."

As I stood, Sanson was twenty meters away standing straight up, staring in the distance, perhaps wondering what could have put that blossoming red splotch on his shirt. He was shot and dazed, but no follow-on shot came until it was too late. Sanson clutched his saber and backed away into the darkness, out of the range of the piercing headlights.

I scrambled to Zoey, who was still alive. She had scampered off the boulder and was running toward Sanson, who had completely disappeared from sight.

"This way, Zoey!" I said, grabbing her arm.

"I want to kill you, motherfucker!" she yelled in

Sanson's direction. Another shot snapped overhead. I checked Zoey and myself to make sure neither of us were shot. Pulling her to the truck, I shoved her through the open driver's door, leaped over the doppelgänger, and slammed the truck into gear, driving in the general direction of the railroad tracks.

The headlights bounced wildly as we navigated ruts and wadis. On two occasions, we almost tipped over after narrowly missing sharp drop-offs. The headlights would soon become a hindrance, a clue as to where we were. We were maybe a mile north of the excavation site when we bottomed out and nearly tipped over. I pressed the accelerator but got no traction in return. Shutting off the headlights and engine, I placed my hand on Zoey's shoulder.

"Let's go," I said, opening the door. Stepping from the truck, I saw that we were precariously situated in a field of three-foot-high brown boulders. I had managed to get the truck stuck on two of them.

"Not without me," Evelyn Champollion said, climbing over the back of the pickup truck. "Where the hell did you learn to drive, General?"

I lifted the pistol, surprised by her appearance and unsure of her allegiance. She was silhouetted against the brilliant stars swirling behind her.

"Please," she said. "You suspected I was some type of foreign intel operative the minute you met me, just as I knew you are General Garrett Sinclair, JSOC commander. Who do you think shot Sanson back there?"

"I guess there's no time to debate the issue," I said, moving toward her. I patted her down, checking for weapons, and found a pistol and knife, which I gave to Zoey. There was no fat on this woman. She was muscled and quick, flinching at my touch.

"Disarming a helpless woman in the desert, General?"

"I'm just making this up as I go. I've gone from commanding an army to being in charge of myself. I'd rather command an army."

We slid into the desert, running north. We had a long night to blend into the Sahara, and a long day with no water, food, or shelter facing us if we were able to evade what would surely be a manhunt for us.

After a minute, aimless machine-gun fire sang across the desert floor again. We stumbled and rolled and picked ourselves up and continued running until twenty minutes had passed. Based upon the terrain and the speed with which we had moved, I guessed we had ambled two miles mostly in a northern direction. I found a wadi that ran perpendicular to our path and took that west for another mile.

An airplane buzzed low to the south, probably Sanson in his Sherpa with people hanging outside wearing goggles. I found a deep notch in the wadi, checked it for snakes and scorpions, and, finding none, burrowed deep into its wall to let the plane finish its cloverleaf search pattern.

Breathing hard, Zoey whispered in a hoarse voice, "Damn, General. You can hang."

"He's not all that, Zoey," Champollion said.

I was sucking in the oxygen myself and had been mostly concerned about Zoey being able to keep up but realized my concerns were misplaced. Champollion, too, had bounded along like an Olympic athlete. She paced outside the depression for a minute with her hands over her head, fingers laced on top like a runner finishing a race.

"Both of you just try to keep up," I said.

Zoey bumped a shoulder into me and whispered, "It worked."

"It's working."

"Yeah, but I got in. Just like we planned. We found it."

"You shouldn't have left without telling me," I said.

"You would have stopped me," she said.

"Yes. I would have."

"Just like I said—"

"It's all about the geometry," I said.

She nodded. "Just like Dad wrote in his notes. A dummy site next to the actual site. Just needed to find one."

Sly had intercepted notes of Sanson talking with Gambeau and General Liang about his expedition. According to the editorial comments on the flash drive, Liang liked the concept of misdirection, using the dig site as a ruse to what they had planned in the desert.

"Are you okay?" It was such a loaded question that I wasn't sure how she was going to answer.

"I'm fine. They beat me some. That's it. I was supposed to spend time with Sanson tonight, but I think they got distracted with you."

"Spend time? He's bad news. Did he . . . Are you okay?"

"He's the one who came and got me from Chinguetti. This isn't an entirely professional operation here. I wanted more time with him. His handlers are rookies. I doubt the Chinese are the same."

"More time?" I was treading gingerly about my main concern whether she had been assaulted.

"He killed my father. I wanted to at least spit in his face."

"Maybe you'll have that chance. We're not done with him, I'm afraid."

"The Chinese are using him. The entire operation is to act as a cover for all the Chinese activity. Satellites see stuff happening, but it can all be passed off as an archeological dig until they execute the operation."

Champollion crawled into our redoubt and said, "I know more secrets than both of you."

"No doubt. I look forward to hearing them," I said. "Once we're safe."

"Safe? In the Sahara?" she quipped.

The plane continued to buzz. We continued to press ourselves into the wadi wall. I passed Zoey the last of my water. She pulled on the nozzle until she was sucking air.

"Don't mind me. I'm a camel," Champollion said.

Her levity didn't match my concern for Zoey, and I snapped a sharp look at her in the darkness. She held up her hands in a surrender pose.

"Have you eaten in the last two days?" I asked Zoey.

"Nothing. Water, and not much of that," she said. "Freezing."

The temperature had dropped significantly from 120 to 60 degrees. She was shivering uncontrollably. Removing my layers of clothes, I gave her the outer garment, which would serve as a blanket for her. I had considered ditching the outfit after finding her but knew the extremes would require some protection from the elements at both day and night.

After thirty minutes, we moved into the wadi and continued west and then hooked north again. My internal clock told me it was 2:00 a.m., a few hours since we had evaded Sanson and his bunch. We found another concave depression that would keep us out of direct line of sight. Zoey and I huddled to keep warm. Champollion wrapped herself in a sarong and lay down next to us before closing her eyes.

Mist escaped Zoey's mouth as she said, "Where are the others?"

Rangers always established an objective rally point to do last-minute checks prior to a mission and on which to collapse after the operation. Prior to mission launch, we had chosen a piece of land on the eyebrow of the Eye of Africa that would be easily recognizable by aircraft, satellites, and ground-mounted personnel, while at the same time providing ample cover and concealment.

I told Zoey that we were calling the rock escarpment and outcropping above the ridgeline north of the Eye "the Mole."

"General? Are they there? At the Mole?" she asked through chattering teeth.

"Zoey, I'm not sure where any of them are. I can only trust that they will be there sometime today."

She huddled against me, shivering, and nodded.

"Hope they're okay," she said. "Hope the Chinese don't get any helicopters over us."

Zoey was normally a logical thinker, but I could see that she was having colliding thoughts. Lack of sleep and whatever trauma she experienced living in a hole for two days, not to mention what she might have experienced at the hands of Sanson.

"We need to wash your wrists and get some antibiotics in you," I said. My paternal instincts kicked in, but I had to view Zoey as another operator, which she was. This mission originated with her recommendation—no, *insistence*—that she be able to pursue what her father believed he had found.

I recalled our conversation that first night after the ramp ceremony and my return from the Pentagon ambush with Blankenship, Luckey, and the inspector general. Zoey had met me at Pope Field, and we had driven to her father's house.

"This was his third trip, General. He uncovered the Chinese plan," she said.

We were sitting in the basement. Zoey was holding a stack of papers she had printed out from her father's external hard drive. It was just the two of us. We were seated at the poker table.

"I've read his report. I gave it to the president."

"That and five bucks gets me a plain Starbucks," she said.

"I know. Which is why we have to do this ourselves. We have to thread the needle here."

"Ourselves? With no official support?"

"If the secretary of defense and secretary of state are involved with China in helping them build a hypersonic weapons guidance system in the Sahara, then there is no way we can run this up the flagpole."

"Well, they're definitely involved," she said. "He had Blankenship's and McHenry's investment accounts. They're on the take with China Construction, TikTok, Huawei, and a few others."

"Belt and road, influence operations, and communications intercepts."

"General gets a star."

"It's got to be about more than portfolios, though," I said. "We need to figure that part out. That's what your dad was trying to nail down before bringing me into it."

"That's why you get paid the big bucks. To figure that stuff out. What about your friend Madam President?" she asked. "Can she help?"

"Only by not telling me no," I said.

"Sahara Desert. No visible means of support. Not even a crazy medical worker like me would take that on."

"That's why you're not going to be involved."

"I wasn't being serious. I'm the perfect cover," she said.

"How so?"

"I'm rightfully distraught over the death of my father, which is one thousand percent true. I'm a little bit crazy, as the whole Afghanistan Tubman mission revealed. I've got an independent streak in me. And now I'm officially an agent of the government. Not only can you not prevent me from going, but you also need me to go. I'm how you find these guys. Dad's maps are good, but he says right here that the nuclear site is disguised as something else. We have to find it. You can search with satellites for days and never find anything. It's like the ocean. Plus, I'd like to have a shot at that guy."

I nodded and said, "That's what worries me, but I'll think about it."

"Yes, you will. I don't have it all. He has more, but I don't know where it is. You'll have to find it."

"We will find it," I said, holding up my hand.

"Okay, you're in charge," she said.

"If we're going to do this," I said, "you've got to work with me here. Don't go rogue."

She looked away and avoided my comment. Then she looked down at the floor and around the room before placing her head in her hands. "I can't believe he's gone."

"Me neither, Zoey."

"GENERAL?" ZOEY SAID, nudging me with her shoulder.

Apparently, I had dozed. The moon was hanging low in the west, casting a pale light across our cavernous hideout. My mental clock told me it was maybe 5:00 a.m. local. Zoey was shivering next to me. Champollion was on the opposite side of her.

"Zoey. I'm sorry. I fell asleep."

"I let you sleep," she said. "I might have nodded off, too. But Evelyn and I have been having a chat."

Champollion nodded and said, "I see why you came for her. She's special."

"I think we need a conversation about what we do with you," I said to Champollion.

She held up a pistol and knife, which she or Zoey must have retrieved off me during my slumber. "We just had one about what to do with you," Champollion said, smiling.

"What's your mission here?" I asked, looking at Zoey, who shrugged as if she had no idea how the French-woman had lifted weapons off her and me.

"I'm a simple archeologist interested in the history of the universe," she said.

"So, DGSE?" I replied, referring to the French equivalent of the CIA.

She smiled and nodded. "I can neither confirm nor deny, but let's just say that our interests overlap."

"You're after Sanson?" I asked.

"Not directly, no," she replied. "Sanson is a cog, an important one, but still just a widget in the operation. The Dakhla Accords, as they are being called, are a ruse. All the machinations of Big Tech—your government, my government, and others, to be sure—are leading up to a naked attempt by some to actualize globalism. To collocate power in one organizational entity by providing China the opportunity to compete globally militarily and by intentionally reducing the influence of the United States, which many in your government see as a good thing."

"That's a little further than I'd suspected," I said.

"Did you really think that everything happening with viruses, Afghanistan, terrorist attacks, social spending, and so on was random?"

"I focus on killing bad guys," I said.

"You going to try to sell me a bridge, too?" she chuckled. "You're Garrett Sinclair III, the son of Garrett Sinclair II, who was the son of Garrett Sinclair I, all famous Army Rangers and generals. Your grandfather climbed Pointe du Hoc as a Ranger colonel. Your father led an army division in Desert Storm. And here you are, an army of one with two women in the Sahara. You're the Tom Brady of army generals. The Kimi Räikkönen. The Kazuyoshi Miura."

"I'm not sure what I've got in common with an American football quarterback, a Finnish Formula One driver, and a Japanese soccer forward."

"You're fifty years old. Still in the game. You prefer the physical grind over the comforts of an office. You're in the arena, not in the cheap seats, where most generals are. You're an operator."

I said nothing.

"And arguably, yours is the most important mission of them all. Your president has parlayed her friendship with you into using you as a front man, leveraging your inclination to roll your own, as some say, to keep someone between her and the problem as the situation develops."

That Champollion so accurately described my affiliation with President Campbell was unnerving. I never much talked about my relationship with my grandfather or father, either. They were good relationships until they weren't. The men in the Sinclair family were a competitive bunch, and when my grandfather passed several years ago, so did a tangible part of our family heritage. My grandfather was the epitome of a soldier, rough-hewn and straightforward. Some say he lacked a sense of humor, but I always found his dry wit and sardonic view of life fitting with my own personality and style.

"It's a lot of weight to carry on the family name, Garrett. Your sister, Kat, is off flitting about somewhere in the name of do-goodery, but we all know that she is running from the premium-grade masculinity that is all things Sinclair. The world has no room for a female Sinclair as much as it needs you to be successful here. Times don't define the man. The man defines the times. And more often than not, the woman, too. You are not here by accident, my friend."

"I made decisions that put me and my team here," I said. I knew, though, that she was right.

"Who fed Sly Morgan the information?"

"Sly was good. One of the best," I said.

"I agree, and it's obvious that Zoey got all his best characteristics, but still, *that* good? So good that he had full dossiers? The insights on your secretaries of defense and state defecting to the People's Corporate Alliance?"

"That's an oxymoron if I ever heard one. Sounds very Karl Marx. I thought it was the CUSP? The China-U.S. Partnership."

"Same thing, different words. China changed that to make it more appealing to the West. If anyone bothered to look at the Dakhla Accords, they would see an obscure reference to the People's Corporate Alliance in connection with China. That document Gambeau, Blankenship, McHenry, and others signed is a blank check for China to do as they please worldwide, but especially here. CUSP for the West but PCA for the Chinese."

"Who else is in this?" I asked.

"Who else? France, Russia, China, the United States, some others. North Korea," she replied.

"Why North Korea?"

"Every family needs a black sheep. The PCA, or CUSP, will do by proxy through North Korea what they don't want attributed to themselves, much as Iran uses the Shia militias in Iraq, Hezbollah in Lebanon, and the Houthis in Yemen."

I paused. The intel had seemed a little too perfect, but rarely did we get something so tangible and actionable. We consumed the intelligence that in retrospect had been spoon-fed to us. Usually, these kinds of leads were synthetic and misdirection, but here, Champollion had apparently been involved in ensuring the intelligence got to me specifically. She couldn't risk that it would go to the U.S. government, though she had gambled on my relationship with the president. She couldn't be sure that Campbell would support me, but she could reasonably assume that Campbell would give me the rope to explore the situation, which was precisely what she was doing.

"How are the Dakhla Accords involved?" I asked.

"Just cover for a meeting, basically. The Chinese never recognized the Moroccan Southern Province. So, in their view, it's still this ungoverned land of Western Sahara. The Mauritanian government is a shit show. The Polisario has been beating the war drum. Nobody cares. It's West Africa and the Sahara Desert, by God. Who gives a shit what happens here? And I mean that in the most sarcastic and ironic way possible. And why worry about terrorists in ungoverned spaces when we have nations and corporations using them to create an alternate world order?"

"Who was in the meeting?" I asked.

"The principals from the member nations."

I felt a vibration in the ground, like an earthquake.

"Wait, hear that?" Zoey said, placing her hands against our chests like a mother protecting a child in the front seat as she brakes.

A train rumbled along the ground less than a few hundred meters away. The ground shook with violence. Dirt spilled on our faces. The train brakes screeched loud and piercing. Helicopters buzzed in the near distance, swarming around the train, maybe as security for the cargo or in pursuit of us. Surely Sanson had passed the word that we had escaped.

"We'd better move to the next phase of the plan," I said. "We'll continue this conversation when and if necessary."

"I just thought you should know the full picture because, you know, the weight of the free world rests on your shoulders." She gave me that flicker of a smile with an upturned lip and slight crow's-feet around the edges of her intelligent eyes. She wore her age, whatever it might be, well.

"So, I'm standing at the plate with a full count, bases loaded, and we are down by three runs in game seven of the World Series?"

"I prefer cricket, but essentially, yes, and I'm glad to see you have your grandfather's trenchant wit," she said.

I was uncertain how she might have known my grandfather, but she was French, and as she mentioned, my grandfather had climbed the cliffs of Normandy and points beyond in World War II.

"I see the question in your eyes. He saved my grandmother in Cherbourg where the second Ranger battalion moved after Pointe du Hoc. But that train is getting louder, and we have business to conduct. I will save the rest for another time."

Zoey looked at Champollion, then at me, and rolled her eyes before saying, "I think the actual operation is a few miles away. Based on Dad's maps, he thought it was due north of the Eye. They had four locations. Three fake ones and one real one. That's why all the activity. They're trying to keep us guessing to buy time."

"What is the Chinese play with the hypersonic missiles in space right now? Blackmail the countries?"

"It's a simple demonstration of power and unity. Everyone who signed the protocols in Dakhla knows about this and signed on," Champollion said.

I nodded, refocusing on the mission and thinking about my scattered troops. Champollion's easy mannerisms and soft voice were comforting in the unsteady seas in which we found ourselves. When pressing forward on a well-developed plan, there is a level of reassurance that coincides with every step. When following instincts and the traces of a few connected ideas, as we were here, the mind searches for affirmation and reassurance. Champollion was providing a level of confidence that I hadn't felt until now. In retrospect, I probably should have thought more deeply about how she had come to be by our side in the middle of this mission.

We had deliberately separated to build in redundancy to our mission and to accomplish several critical tasks at once.

"I'm just concerned about the rest of the team and how we go from here," I said.

"They're your team, General. They're the best. They're fine, and we will be fine," Zoey said.

"I agree," Champollion said.

Zoey's courage and strength were refreshing, especially after a season of loss. While I had lost my best male friend in Sly Morgan and my best female friend in my wife, Melissa, Zoey had lost her father. The grief was palpable, but she found this mission as a way to honor him and to channel the heartache into something meaningful. After all, he had started this mission with his reconnaissance in Africa. What he had uncovered was an unbelievable collusion between the highest levels of the U.S. government with the Chinese Communist Party to provide them partnership status in Africa that would cement their foreign policy reach into the Western Hemisphere. It was a mind-numbingly stupid move that allowed China access to the one thing they needed. They had every resource they could possibly require. A burgeoning economy. A billion people. Access to every rare earth element in their own backyard. Nuclear weapons of all varieties. Now, Champollion had added a new layer onto the scheme by indicating it went well beyond a simple U.S.-China bilateral scenario.

But still it came down to China with their massive economy and their need for American support and acquiescence in the Western Hemisphere. It seemed like they had navigated that hurdle.

The Dakhla Accords could provide China the forward presence to hold the world hostage by being able to attack with nuclear weapons, against which no nation was capable of defending.

And Sly Morgan, spoon-fed or not, had uncovered this on his first reconnaissance, confirmed it on his second, and was killed on our overlapping mission in the area on his third mission. In combat units, our service is all about those on our left and right flanks. Sly had wanted to live, for sure, but if he had to die in combat, he wanted it to be for a cause much more significant than any one life. I think we all felt that way, and the least I could do was submit a piece of paper to my chain of command telling them my plan without telling them my plan.

I just hoped we weren't too late.

27

THE FIRST NEWS ARTICLE was jarring, written by a twenty-two-year-old operative from the online periodical *Maxios*. The ensuing hundreds of articles spun off this one seed, all seemingly choreographed and blasted across the universe without verification or follow-up. It even included a rare photograph of me, bearded, long hair, camouflaged face, amid my troops on a remote Syrian hilltop after a completed mission.

Special Forces General Accused of Murdering Secretary of State Gone AWOL, Hid Gold Find, Anonymous Source Says

General Garrett Sinclair has lived a shadowy life filled with misdeeds and misappropriation of government equipment, according to a soon-to-be-released Department of Defense Inspector General report. Imminently, he stands to be accused of murder of the nation's top diplomat and illegal pirating of Mauritanian gold.

Amid these allegations, Sinclair has now gone AWOL.

The senior commando in the military, Sinclair

has a history of xenophobia centered on his heralded rival Dariush Parizad, the Iranian boxing icon who championed the Persian people in his every deed. Sinclair falsely claimed that Parizad had entered and prepared to attack the United States, despite there being no evidence that Parizad was ever in the country. Fact-checkers report that the beloved Iranian, nicknamed the "Lion of Tabas" by the Ayatollah Khomeini, had not entered the country at any air, sea, or land checkpoint and that the likelihood of Parizad's presence on inauguration day in our nation's capital is close to zero.

Conversely, sources place Sinclair at the crime scene where revered secretary of state Kyle Estes was found murdered. Witnesses also positively identified Sinclair at multiple crime scenes preceding President Campbell's inauguration, lending credibility to some reports that it was Sinclair, not Parizad, who planned to attack the inauguration. The much-reported-upon and video-recorded scene of Sinclair leaping from a helicopter that he had ordered to violate capital airspace to capture a drone inbound to the Capitol steps now, in retrospect, appears mischaracterized. It is equally likely, according to these sources, that Sinclair was attempting to escort the drones into the inauguration and, when the United States Air Force damaged the drones, destroy the remaining bits of evidence of his plan to interdict the peaceful transition of power.

This mounting evidence perhaps led Sinclair to go into hiding, a specialty of the mysterious soldier.

The article was run in McClatchy, *The Washington Post, The New York Times,* HuffPost, and myriad other online and print outlets. It seemed obvious that Willard Ringley or someone in the Department of Defense Inspector General's office had leaked the investigation arc and the media had created its own salacious narrative. All the major news networks and cable outlets carried the story until it reached a crescendo within twenty-four hours.

President Campbell sat in the Oval Office, staring at the ceiling, looking directly into one of the installed cameras of the Alexa monitoring system until Secretary of Defense Blankenship walked into the room and took a seat opposite her on the sofa.

"What is this fresh hell of media about Garrett?" Campbell asked. "Who's leaking from your inspector general?"

"General Sinclair has been the subject of an inspector general investigation since the Parizad incident. That is well known, Madam President," Blankenship said. She was dressed in a navy pantsuit with a crème-colored blouse beneath the jacket. Her hair was pulled back into a ponytail, and she appeared spry.

"Fuck with me," Campbell said. "I put you in that job over ten other people because I thought you would serve the people, not yourself."

"Ma'am? How am I not serving the people? There's nothing untrue in the media. It's unfortunate that it got out, but we can't unring that bell, can we? What would you like for me to do?" Her voice was dispassionate and unbothered.

"He's on a classified mission beyond anything this country has ever known, and you go out and play fucking politics with this man's life? His team's life? Our nation's security?" Campbell was shouting.

"Madam President, I'm not playing politics with anyone. I understand that you are close with General

Sinclair, but I've done nothing of the sort. We have leaks all the time. People right outside that door," she said, pointing at the anteroom to the Oval Office, "leak all the time. I know you're feeling this one more sharply than others because of your personal connection, however deep that might go," Blankenship said.

Campbell snapped her eyes onto Blankenship's face and said, "What are you implying?"

"I'm not implying anything, ma'am. I am simply the messenger here. I have no idea what your relationship with Sinclair is, nor can I stop the media from speculating. I know that you two got closer after the death of his wife, and there's a rumor that she took a secret to the grave. You know how information management is today. It's impossible." She shrugged, and perhaps the slight upturn of her upper lip was a smile.

"His team is out there to stop the Chinese from being able to direct hypersonic nuclear missiles onto the United States. A threat that you made possible with McHenry and your stupid Dakhla Accords!"

"Madam President, you should have looped me into the mission. I could have resourced him."

Campbell's eyes remained fixed on Blankenship's impassive face.

"You'd rather see this country burn and our soldiers die?"

"I know you don't believe that, Kim. I'm a patriot. I don't believe that China is doing anything more than testing some new technology with partner nations."

"They have five hypersonic vessels in the air."

"I've spoken with my counterpart there. They've assured me we have no concerns."

"They're not a partner nation. They're an adversary."

"Not according to the Dakhla Accords," Blankenship said.

"What have you done?"

"We are advancing U.S. vital interests, ma'am. It would be nice, but not necessary, if you were on board."

"How does allying with China and Russia do anything but give away our state secrets?"

"The idea of the nation-state is passé. We have no borders. We welcome all comers. It's an international economy. The Great Reset is about the world, not just America. We are resetting the global economy. We thought you were on board."

"This will never work. I appointed you to this position."

"And the Senate confirmed me. I'm doing my job. If you feel it's not consistent with your vision, fire me."

"You'd rather put us at risk, have our soldiers killed, than be proven wrong?"

"That's something that someone should have thought about prior to authorizing a rogue mission that kept me out of the loop."

"And what makes you sure of that?" Campbell asked.

"We have the best intelligence apparatus in the world. We can see and hear anything if we wish," she said.

"And what have you seen and heard?"

"We're vetting that information now for your PDB," she said, referring to the President's Daily Brief.

"So, I have a cabinet member hiding information from me and undermining national security by colluding with enemies. What does China have on you, AB?"

"The national defense strategy calls China an adversary, not an enemy, which is an important distinction," Blankenship said.

"Perhaps legally."

"Does anything else really matter?" Blankenship waved her index finger between herself and Campbell. "All that matters is how we leave this place. China is the future. Give a little to get a little. They want a port? Who are we to stop them, and what difference does it make if we give it to them now or ten years from now?" She shrugged.

Campbell said nothing.

"Now this isn't a threat at all—I'm just free-associating here—but if you think that Sinclair piece was bad, imagine your name substituted for his with far worse allegations. We're all just a hairsbreadth away from exposure by these morons."

"Out. Now," Campbell said, pointing at the door.

"Have it your way. I can help your man or not. It's up to you. Just text me," Blankenship said. She got up slowly and didn't look back as she smiled all the way to the door.

Campbell put her head in her hands and then retrieved a cell phone from the Resolute desk drawer. She punched a digit on the phone, held it to her ear, and said, "Garrett!"

28

THE TRAINS CAME AND went with accelerating speed. Zoey was still shivering beneath the outer garment I had provided her, and I was chilled, as well. The sun was still about an hour from rising. Constellations swirled in the outer reaches of the galaxies above us.

"Zoey," I said, nudging her shoulder. Her head lolled to the side, and for a moment, I thought that perhaps she was dead. We needed water and food, and the only path to those necessities was to the linkup location we had selected at the Mole.

My presidential burner buzzed in my pocket. I scrambled to retrieve it from beneath the outer garment. My hand got tangled, but I was able to receive the call before it went to voice mail.

"Yes," I said. It was more of a hiss between attempting to keep my voice low and the fumbling of the phone.

"Garrett!" President Campbell screamed in a low voice.

"I'm here."

"Status?"

"Could use some help," I said.

"Understand. I'm in my own predicament here. I'll do my best," she said.

"All our nation can ask," I said.

"Stay safe."

"Roger that."

She hung up, and I followed suit before snapping the phone in half, removing the SIM card, and bending that back and forth until it, too, snapped. I removed the battery and tossed the pieces in opposite directions.

"Presidential burner, General?" Zoey asked. She was offering me a weak smile behind distant eyes, which reminded me I needed to move her to the linkup point prior to sunrise, and we had scant margin for error.

"It can't be good if she's calling you," Champollion said.

"Nor can it be good if we're still stranded in the Sahara, Evelyn. We need to move." Then to Zoey, I asked, "Can you stand?"

"I feel okay. Weak, but okay," she said. She stood, using her left hand on my shoulder to steady herself. The three of us began climbing out of the wadi and onto the desert floor.

I used the night vision goggles I had taken from Zoey's guard. As we navigated across the desert along a northeasterly azimuth, I stumbled and hallucinated, pointing out trees and houses that I knew weren't there, but somehow appeared in my vision.

"You're tripping, General," Zoey said.

"I know. Little sleep," I said. The mind dredges up some of the oddest images from its reaches when it is deprived of rhythmic rest. Layer dehydration into the mix and the combination is akin to what I imagined mushrooms or LSD *would* produce. "Just tell me we're not in a subdivision with two-story homes right now."

"I think that's a few blocks away," she said. By now, she had a hand on my shoulder, steadying herself as we walked. Her grip was firm and felt like a fixture on my body. I continued to see cars zipping past us, people walking along the sidewalk, and kids on spider-handlebar bicycles with gloves stacked on baseball bats slung over shoulders. These were scenes from my child-hood, no doubt, which was a perfectly normal experi-ence. My mind reeled. I saw my father in his olive army fatigues leaving for combat in Vietnam, his duffel bag slung over his shoulder. My mother and grandmother stood stoic as his plane vanished into the sky. Then the matriarchs were sitting around a coffee table, passing cups of steaming tea and chatting aimlessly to deflect the worry resident within all of the ladies.

More images popped into my mind like fireworks ex-ploding randomly in the sky.

My sister, Katherine—Kat for short—was smiling with my West Point black-and-gold duffel slung over her shoulder on her way out the door to pursue an as-sortment of do-good nonprofits around the developing world.

Random thoughts accompanied the random images.

Same mission, different venue, she would tell me. We were close until we weren't. The riptide of time pulls you away from the shore, where everything you wish for awaits until you tire from the struggle or escape too far out to sea where you lack the energy to get back to where you need to be.

I taught Kat to play baseball. She was a decent sec-ond baseman to the point where she made the boys Little League teams, batting in the number two hole. Her great hand-eye coordination gave her a quick bat and fast hands. She had a flawless double-play turn. However, back in the day when Title IX was paving the way, the societal pressures levered by the matriarchs in my family tugged her in an opposite direction. The kid was getting pulled out to sea in a riptide not of her choosing. So she made a hard break to get away from it all.

"General?"

At first, I thought it was Kat because I saw her standing in front of me on the street corner up the road from our house, baseball hat cocked back on her head, Louisville Slugger over her shoulder, crooked grin, and sharp blue eyes.

But it was Zoey, who again said, "General?"

"What?" I mumbled.

"The sun is coming up," she whispered. "That hilltop over there has someone on it."

"It's a sentry," Champollion said. She held small, collapsible field binoculars to her eyes.

Zoey pointed in the distance. A flashlight appeared and disappeared every few seconds. I pulled from the water nozzle and got rubber-tasting air.

"Let's go," I said. Either it was our team or a Chinese ambush. By now, I could accept either fate. It was the in-between that was unbearable. I was done with the middle ground, the half measures, the platitudes. Either we fight to win, or we don't fight.

We trudged for another twenty minutes as the sun poked above the horizon, a distant flaming orange ball with shimmering waves of heat bouncing off the ground. We arrived at the base of the hill, where I drew my weapon on the man standing in front of me.

"General!"

Zoey's voice was shrill, but it didn't stop me from pulling the trigger, which didn't budge. The safety was engaged, and Hobart snatched the pistol from my hand before I was able to thumb the safety off.

"He's delusional," Hobart said. In retrospect, I admired his professionalism in disarming me before allowing himself to feel the emotion of seeing Zoey alive again. They lifted me and carried me to a small cave where they had established the rally point. Van Dreeves hooked an IV up to my arm, and then they did a full medical check on Zoey, providing her with an IV, as well. I had vague images of Hobart pacing, running his hands through his wavy black hair. His face got close to mine once, and he said, "How could you?!"

But I couldn't be sure if that was Hobart or my own conscience. A couple of hours later, I awoke to conversation in hushed tones.

"He's awake," a female voice said. McCool? I turned my head, and Lieutenant Colonel Sally McCool was kneeling over a map, using an outstretched finger to trace a path on the acetate. Zoey was awake and huddled with a blanket around her shoulders, watching McCool. Hobart and Van Dreeves were opposite her, staring at the map, which I assumed contained the plan we had sketched out for stopping the Chinese nuclear attack. The balled-up mass beneath blankets I took to be Evelyn Champollion.

"Where's the helicopter?" I asked.

She smiled. "Good to see you, too, General."

"Right. Glad you're safe, Sally."

"You know that old saying, 'No single-ship missions'? Well, we might have to do one of those with a single pilot, as well. Jorge took the Beast back to Dakhla with Wang and Black."

"Comms?" I asked.

"Minimal, but some. We need to talk about that presidential burner you carry. If she knows where you are, there's a good chance the Dakhla team will know soon."

"Carried," I said. "I snapped it and tossed it a while back. Is anyone else here?"

"Farouk," she said. "That's how we got here. He met us at the linkup point with yet another stolen truck, and we moved at night to this location. He's behind his sniper rifle scanning on the ridge. He saw you and Zoey and the lady coming from two miles out."

I nodded. McCool, Hobart, Van Dreeves, Zoey, and Farouk. Six of us to accomplish this mission. Having my team surround me like this was comforting. The world and especially combat can be an incredibly lonely place. Command makes it more isolating. I hid the emotions that were raging through me, from the hallucinations to rescuing Zoey to linking up with my team in preparation for the penultimate mission.

"What happened?" McCool asked.

"Might have been some residual Demon Rain," I said, referring to the Iranian mind control drug that Parizad had injected me with via an arrow slung by a crossbow last year. I had experienced serious hallucinations days after the injection but we had still managed to prevent attacks on the country. Perhaps the dehydration had triggered something to reinvigorate the latent chemicals in my system. Or maybe three days without sleep was never a good idea.

"You're looking mighty native, sir," Van Dreeves said. His comment got a chuckle from the group. We could always rely upon Van Dreeves to provide a moment of needed levity. I was sure he knew that his best friend, Hobart, was upset with me for endangering Zoey, but he was able to effortlessly keep us above the surface and focused on the task at hand.

Each of the men were sporting several days' growth, so I shot back, "From the looks of you all, we've got our own *shura* here."

"Definite *shura,*" Van Dreeves said. "Good to have you back, boss. We met your stray. She's interesting."

"Good to be back. Ms. Champollion—or shall we call her Agent Champollion?—has provided some interesting theories about what Sly found—or, in her version of the story, what Sly was given. This may be some giant corporate global takeover, but right now the immediate threat, according to her, is the five hypersonic missiles in space. Once the Chinese get that laser built, they can guide them wherever."

"To be clear," Champollion said, "they can release them now and they'll land one county over from their target, which will still have an impact. We have to take over the control system and guide them away from the targets."

"Welcome, my lady," Van Dreeves said.

Champollion rolled her eyes.

"Give me a hard one," I said.

"No one said this was easy, Garrett," she replied.

My team fell silent, watching us spar, until I said, "So, let's go over what we know and what we don't know."

"I couldn't fly over the build site," McCool said. "Lit up every air defense system in the Sahara, but I was able to drop these boxes of drones, water, medical supplies, ammo, and comms equipment."

She pointed at stacks of green containers pushed into the back of the cave. We appeared no different from the many Taliban or Al Qaeda denizens that holed up in caves surrounded by their means of war. We looked every bit as unruly and rugged.

"Good job," I said.

She and Van Dreeves high-fived. "A 'good job' from the boss. Woot."

"That's the last one of those for a while," I said. "Walk me through the last day."

She made a fat, pouty lip and continued, "We offset several miles away. We created enough of a distraction that the Chinese have taken about half their force and placed them about twenty miles away near their helicopter that was shot down. Polisario, we think. Doesn't matter, it helped us. Linked up with Randy and Joe, and then Farouk met us with the truck. Jorge flew back to Dakhla, and we infiltrated with Farouk and off-loaded the gear from the Beast. Farouk and Joe drove the truck a couple of miles away, stuck it in a wadi, and returned. We've spent a night here with the drones flying around the base and up the rail. There is more infantry guarding the rail. Here at the GLINTS location, they have everything from dozers to full-up construction teams with a microgrid out here. Solar panels appear to have been here for weeks or months. Containers filled with batteries for energy storage. We're assuming all of that is to push the laser system. There's a command center built into the wadi that seems to be a good target for us. It's only a couple of miles from Sanson's dig sites, so those are a ruse."

"Yeah. What's up with Sanson and that whole gig?" I asked.

"He's a no-shit explorer, but," McCool said, "he's also on the Chinese dole. Gambeau is working with McHenry and Blankenship on these Dakhla Accords."

"Please explain," I said, removing the IV from my arm and taking a sip from my refreshed CamelBak.

McCool rolled her eyes at me and continued, "We're still piecing it all together. Your new friend might be able to help."

"My name is Evelyn, child," Champollion said.

McCool grinned. "Yes, ma'am. Anyway, Farouk is Moroccan intel. He was inside the ribbon cutting in Mauritania as a bodyguard for a special envoy for the king of Morocco. Understands French, English, and Arabic. All the hotels were bugged by the Chinese prior to the meeting. Farouk's team hacked into the feed and made themselves privy to the intel. Because our previous administration didn't object to Morocco annexing the Southern Province, Campbell's administration has decided to undo that, which is a big deal. At least on the surface. The Chinese have used that as a wedge issue to say they can come in and stabilize the region in exchange for freedom to do as they please in Mauritania and Morocco."

"And Morocco? Our most important partner on the African continent?" I asked.

"Yes. Hence Farouk's involvement. He's here with full permission of the king."

I nodded. "To summarize. Our secretaries of defense and state cut a deal with China and Big Tech—which, on the surface, seems like an awesome thing because of jobs and stability for the region but ultimately is a ruse to buy time and give some reason for their activity in the desert. Sanson's mission was to serve as a ruse for Chinese activity out here. Someone by chance sees this on satellite, Gambeau intervenes and says, 'Hey, that's our archeological mission.' But the actual purpose is to build a terminal guidance system for the hypersonic vehicles to improve the accuracy of their hypersonic glide planes that are nuked up," I said.

"Bingo. The general gets a star," McCool said.

"He's already got three," Van Dreeves quipped.

"Be lucky to keep those," I said. "Now focus."

She turned to Zoey, who was now huddled into Hobart's side, resting her head on his shoulder. I was glad to see it. We had no idea if we would live tomorrow, and there was no reason for them not to soak up every minute they could. The pained look on Hobart's face spoke of the danger the next twenty-four hours would bring.

"Command Sergeant Major Morgan and Farouk went over all this intelligence in Dakhla on his visit a few months ago. His only problem? Sanson had been at the meeting also. Sergeant major got too close, was followed, and they found his notes. Farouk had departed to debrief the king, and Sly went in for one last mission. He and Sanson had a scuffle. Sanson's a big man, and if it weren't for Jake, he might have been killed two months ago."

"Jake Mahegan?" I asked.

"Do you know any other Jakes? He was on contract in Dakhla doing a security gig for the State Department. He spots Sly coming back from the consulate with three huge guys following him. One was Sanson, and the others were two brutes that look like Sanson."

"I saw them at the excavation site," I said.

"Makes sense. Anyway, Sly copied the Chinese plans. That's what was on his external drive. He photographed everything, and we printed it out." McCool waved her hand across the pictures arranged on the floor of the cave. There was enough sunlight seeping around the edges of the opening so that we could see. Van Dreeves had hung a battery-powered mechanic's work light from a piton he had driven into the ceiling of the cave, which provided decent lighting.

"Dad did good," Zoey whispered. Hobart pulled her tighter to him as if to protect her from what was to come.

"Always," I said.

"As we've already said, the excavation site is part real but mostly gives Sanson the ability to run between the terminal guidance construction site; Dakhla, where he coordinates with the Chinese fishing fleet; and the French consulate, where he updates Gambeau. Farouk has all of this on audio recordings for the king."

"So, why would Blankenship and McHenry be so brazen about supporting China?" I asked.

"Remember, they were high-paid consultants for several years. Once the media laid off China because of prior U.S. political connections, it was open season. McHenry and Blankenship own tens of millions in stock in Chinese Communist Party construction companies, telecom companies, and technology companies. As far as we know, China told them this is just a legit construction job in the desert and that their portfolios would benefit hugely. That's best case. Worst case? They know about all of this," McCool explained.

"In which case, we're screwed. Not only will we not get any support, but they'll come after us and actively deny our efforts to stop the Chinese plan. Maybe with U.S. or allied forces."

"Yes, sir, and with the help of the biggest technology companies in the world who all benefit from an ascendant China," McCool said. "If they're crooked enough to get this far, they'll go all the way to avoid any exposure. Total empire."

"Any idea of their targets on these hypersonic nukes floating around out there?"

"Sly's research showed Washington, D.C., of course—"

"Well, we're not opposed to that," Van Dreeves said.

"Of course not, but they also have New York City, Chicago, Paris, and London."

"No joy from the French or British militaries on this?" I asked.

"Too sensitive to tell them. As far as we know, the only people that know the true reason we're here are us and the president. Not even Jorge and my crew know the truth."

I nodded, thinking. Why did everything always come down to money? Political infighting had left American society so stripped of its constitutional moorings that maybe self-preservation was the only thing that mattered to most people anymore. Basic math tells us that if we continually divide, we end up with smaller and smaller subunits until we're nothing more than millions of shards of shattered glass on the floor. That was essentially where we were. Every person for themselves. Not so much survival of the fittest but survival of those with access to power, which ultimately came down to politics. I wondered what President Campbell thought of this pervasive societal ill. She was no stranger to controversy or political self-preservation, and I liked to think she believed in the country and the future we all wanted for her citizens, though that was a naive concept with today's evolving definitions of nationalism, freedom, and self-determination.

The world had gone mad.

As if to prove the point, Van Dreeves said, "Boss?"

He held out a small, ruggedized tablet he had connected to a virtual private network that communicated with our secure low-earth-orbit satellite.

On the screen was the headline:

SPECIAL FORCES GENERAL ACCUSED OF MURDERING SECRETARY OF STATE GONE AWOL, HID GOLD FIND, ANONYMOUS SOURCE SAYS

"They've made their play," I said, realizing that their goal was to get my picture out there and to sever what little support we had remaining.

We fell silent as helicopters buzzed past the cave mouth.

29

MALIK WATCHED SANSON SHOUT like a madman and emit a high-pitched wail.

"Garrett Sinclair rescued Zoey Morgan again?!"

Sanson began swooshing his saber through the air like a martial artist practicing lunges and thrusts. His arm was bleeding. A red stain was a starburst on his left sleeve.

Malik stepped back and dodged the slicing blade, tripping over a rock and rolling away as if he were the target.

"Her stupid, dead father started it all, Malik!" he shouted. His voice rang across the desert floor. "He was there in Dakhla spying on his own people. And on me and the Chinese, of course. We had been so careful. Gambeau had bought off the Moroccans. The Americans were useful idiots. That was it. It was simple."

Malik's thought was that Sanson would only tell him this information if he was going to kill him later. That was the only way this could work. Malik's job was to run the caravan and the dig sites, but how difficult was that to do? He possessed no real talents beyond having a host of connections and being able to take command of the crew. He ran a tight ship, and the dig was producing gold.

Sanson was a whirling dervish, spinning wildly and slashing with his toy.

"You have the gold, Sanson. You have your mission here," Malik said, figuring it would be good to remind him.

The saber cut through the air again, close to his face.

"That's right! I have the gold," Sanson said.

"You have the gold," Malik reaffirmed. "And you have the history."

The blade was high above Sanson's head as he slowed his spin. Sanson stared at Malik.

"I have the history," he said.

"You have the history of this," Malik said, waving his arm across the dark desert. "The Eye of Africa is yours for eternity."

"Eternity," Sanson said. He lowered the sword.

"We should rest. I'm told they found more gold," Malik said.

"Rest," Sanson replied. His eyes stared into the distance.

"Let's go back to the tent," Malik said. "I must wash your wound."

Sanson looked at his left sleeve, as if noticing for the first time that he had been shot. They walked to Sanson's tent where Malik washed and bandaged the glancing blow that had backed him away from killing Zoey Morgan.

"We must stop them," Sanson said. "They know about this location and will return."

This was a point that Malik didn't want to debate. "Yes. We can move. How does your arm feel?"

"It's fine. How did the American general get into our base camp?"

Malik swallowed, unsure. He packed the medical supplies away, then said, "He arrived in a truck that had been stolen from Amina and Binth al Asman. Perhaps he used the GPS."

"How did you get your injuries, Malik?"

"I was involved in an accident yesterday. I will be fine."

But nothing was fine. Sanson was suspicious. He nodded, which was worse than him asking a follow-up question.

"We will find more gold. We will discover Atlantis. And we will complete my mission for Gambeau. If you want to live, Malik, you will help me. I've never threatened you before. I've come to like you and depend on you, but do not mistake my affection for weakness. You will do as I say and be loyal. Understand?"

"Anything, Sanson."

"'Anything' is right."

They went back to the tent, where Sanson lifted a phone to his ear and said, "Gambeau." Then he walked into the darkness where Malik could not hear him.

30

"TWO BOGIES AT SIX o'clock," Farouk said.

His voice crackled over Van Dreeves's tablet. We stared at the device, waiting for the follow-up report. We were skilled in the art of tactical patience, knowing not to fill the vulnerable airwaves with unnecessary chatter. If he had a follow-up report, he would provide it. Which he did.

"Charlie Mike," he whispered.

Continue the mission. Van Dreeves pressed the Transmit button on the microphone to signal that his report was received.

"We're not dropping a JDAM or JSOC on this because there are suspicions that in addition to the secretaries of state and defense, the chairman of the Joint Chiefs and the SOCOM commander are compromised by the Chinese government as well," I said. "What Sly uncovered showed that maybe General Luckey and the chairman were in on the Dakhla Accords."

"Which means it's just us," McCool said. It was a statement, not a question.

"It's always been just us," I said. "Even when it seemed we had the entire nation behind us. Nobody has been doing what we're doing. Look around. Do you see anyone new or different from the last times we've been in combat?"

"Zoey," McCool said, nodding at Sly's daughter, who was sleeping on Hobart's chest now. "Farouk."

"Zoey was running Operation Tubman to get amcits and women out of Afghanistan," I said.

"I know. She's a great addition. We just need to make sure everyone knows their roles and responsibilities. Nothing easy about this mission. We've employed enough misdirection to get to this point. If Blankenship and McHenry are behind the media leaks, you know the Chinese have been warned. Their reconnaissance is going to increase. Those helicopters are searching for us, most likely. If Big Tech is involved, they've got facial recognition for all of us. We're dancing on the head of a pin here."

"Boss?" Hobart said, speaking for the first time this morning.

"Yes, Joe?"

"I've got a bad feeling about this. There's at least a battalion of Chinese infantry roaming around out here undeterred. They've got attack helicopters. They've got our government in the bag. They've got the best technology in the world. Look at us. We're good and we will win and succeed, but at what cost?"

Hobart was not known for long, extemporaneous speeches, and seven sentences was a significant oration for him. Perhaps it was the presence of Zoey, the woman he loved, that gave rise to his first-ever stated concerns about a mission. Certainly, he had opined on the tactical execution points important to succeed on previous operations, but never had he in general debated the overall purpose or efficacy of executing a task. He opened his palm and slowly swung his arm around the cave. Three men, three women, all in varying degrees of preparedness and disarray. Zoey huddled with him. He looked as drawn and worried as I'd ever seen. McCool was doing her best to remain focused on execution, but away from the Beast, I was sure she felt hamstrung. Like a quarterback playing wide receiver, she could still score, but she had to use other skills. Van Dreeves, ever the optimist and chatterbox, was focused. He was poring over the maps and imagery at one moment, and the next he was looking each team member in the eyes, assessing their status. Then there was the enigma that was Champollion. In the soft, filtered light leaking into the cave, she was a beautiful woman. She removed her Australian bush hat and ran a hand through her dusty brown hair. Her blue eyes reflected a quick intelligence with their penetrating gaze and associated nods and hand gestures.

"I hear you," I said. "The president has trusted us to follow through on this. Given everything they're coming after me with, this could be our last mission together. I feel about each of you the same way I feel about my children, about Melissa. You're family. That's why I asked if everyone was in when we were in Dakhla."

"Wait," McCool protested. "What do you mean by this is our last mission?"

"As you know, I'm under inspector general investigation. There may be criminal referrals. My stock is down, and I can't continue to lead Dagger and JSOC beyond this mission. You saw the news articles. They're gunning for me. Making me an enemy of the state. After this, there will be no future for me regardless of what happens. It has been a long time coming. I'm not sorry for anything that happened—we've had a good run—but there is no future with me. I'm not going to be promoted. I'll be lucky to keep the rank I have. People think I'm a cowboy for being out front with all of you instead of eating grapes and fanning myself in HQ."

"You're the only one with the balls to be here, boss," Hobart said. "I wasn't trying to start some debate. It's just . . . things are more in focus for me right now."

"I know, Joe. And I know this is your way of telling us openly about Zoey and you, something, by the way, we've all known for the last year."

"Yeah, congrats, bro," Van Dreeves said.

"Shall we discuss you and Sally, Randy?"

Van Dreeves flashed that surfer-boy grin and said, "We ain't hiding shit, boss."

McCool rolled her eyes. "What is this, Peyton Place or an objective rally point?"

"Just don't expect me to snuggle with Farouk," I said, which prompted a rare moment of levity that we all needed, but they did cast a quick glance at Champollion. I did love these people. They were who I had chosen to navigate life with, in addition to my family. I couldn't have asked for a better team. Life is about chances and choices, and every step of the way when I had the chance to add one of these people to my inner circle, I made the choice to do so. They were good decisions.

"General finally gets a sense of humor," McCool said.

"He's a funny guy," Zoey said. She had woken up at the laughter and straightened up while still pressing up against Hobart.

"Joe, I hear you. We could ask ourselves, especially after Afghanistan, is this, or anything worth it? So, let's have that conversation. We can't move until nighttime, anyway. China has five hypersonic nuclear vehicles in orbit right now burning very little fuel. They're being used as a blackmail tool against our government. Either give them what they want—ports on the west coast of Africa, infrastructure deals in the United States, access to our national security apparatus—or they launch the vessels onto targets in the U.S. and Europe. Nothing is stopping them from putting more in orbit. The only thing stopping them from attacking is that they haven't built this laser yet that can range the low-earth-orbit satellites and, using mirrors, reflect the beam to guide the nuke to a specific target. It does them some, but not much, good to miss by thirty miles or so. Politicians won't much care unless they feel personally threatened."

Everyone was nodding, paying rapt attention. More helicopters buzzed in the distance. McCool had passed around some combat rations, which were being opened and consumed. I took another pull of water.

"Our objective is to disable the GLINTS, what Sly referenced as a global intermediate nuclear targeting station, and destroy the Chinese capabilities here in the desert."

"Can't they just reconstitute that capability elsewhere, if they don't already have a backup system yet, especially if what Farouk and Evelyn say is true about Big Tech being involved?" Van Dreeves asked. Hobart nodded.

"They can and they could, but we have no intelligence that indicates any such plan or capability. Sly's research shows that this part of the Sahara, the Eye of Africa, uniquely positions China to attack the Western Hemisphere. They put these hypersonic missiles in orbit because someone—probably Blankenship or McHenry—told them that President Campbell was not going to cave to Chinese pressure on trade, Taiwan, Hong Kong, North Korea, West Africa, or any of the other areas they're pressing on internationally. The Chinese probably don't trust the tech moguls enough yet to rely upon them for any substantial backup. It could be a case of self-imposed prisoner's dilemma—no one knows what the other is going to say, so they're holding back. China is driving the change through action, which is their strong suit. Diplomacy has never been their thing."

"So, what we're doing has a chance of keeping us safe. Keeping our families together. Protecting us from Chinese intervention in our way of life," Hobart said. A statement, not a question. He'd seen the full circle of logic. The threats we were facing on a tactical micro level, which could include some of us not returning to enjoy the freedoms we secure, were necessary to have something to return to. Zoey's presence highlighted to him, and all of us, the very real trade-offs and sacrifices we made in pursuit of higher ideals. It wasn't often that there was a tangible reminder of both sides of the dilemma directly in front of us. Should we risk everything we have? If we don't, will we have anything worth living for? To most people, freedom is an abstract concept until, like oxygen, you don't have it anymore; when you can't breathe, you crave it. We had been fighting for freedom for so many years and even we had to remind ourselves of its shelf life and what could happen if it were to vanish from our society.

"We all good?" I asked. "Look me in the eyes, team."

I locked eyes with Van Dreeves, who nodded and flashed me a thumbs-up. Zoey vigorously nodded. Hobart nodded once, keeping his gaze locked with mine. He had simmered some, but not much. McCool looked at me and said, "We're all good, boss. Talking sometimes helps."

I met Evelyn Champollion's gaze, and I saw something there I didn't recognize at first. Her countenance had changed from pensive to sympathetic. Her eyes opened wider, receiving and giving at once. Her cheeks had softened. The longer I stared at her, the flusher her face became. She crossed her arms in a defensive pose and dropped her chin, breaking her gaze. I turned to my team, who were all alternatively staring at me and Champollion, like a tennis match.

"It does. I agree. Now let's go over the plan. We execute tonight," I said.

31

PRESIDENT CAMPBELL SAT IN Air Force One on the ramp of Joint Base Andrews in Maryland. A sleet storm arrived more quickly than expected, so she was jotting thoughts on a piece of White House stationery and looking pensively out the porthole window. The Alexa camera caught a flattering image of her in repose, hand tucked under her chin as she contemplated the weight of her decisions made and to be made. Her blond hair was tucked behind her ears dotted with simple diamond earrings. A matching necklace hung atop a modest light blue blouse. Her blazer hung over the chair next to her.

"Madam President, Director Bertrand is here to see you," her assistant announced by leaning her head in the cabin.

Campbell nodded, and Bertrand entered the small office. He was wearing a navy suit with pinstripes over a white shirt and teal Hermès tie.

"Madam President, are we going somewhere or just camping on the runway?"

She smiled with her lips pressed together, almost a grimace. "Let's chat, shall we?"

"I work for you," he said.

"What is your honest assessment of the Chinese hypersonic missiles? Is it a bluff, or is it real?"

"The missiles are real. Their intent is difficult to ascertain. My deputy is speaking with my counterpart's deputy in China. Apparently, the first one reenters the atmosphere to strike an unnamed target tonight if we don't acquiesce to certain demands. My own back-channel sources tell me that what they're asking for is access to quantum computing codes, which of course is the key to quantum communications. If they lock down that edge, they'll be able to hack anything anywhere—our nuclear codes or your email and everything in between while having the securest network ever. We have the edge now, but they're not far behind."

"We hand over the quantum codes, and they do what, dump the nukes in the ocean?"

"We can't hand over the codes, ma'am," Bertrand said.

"I know that, Koby. I'm speaking hypothetically. I'm trying to understand their endgame."

"Their endgame is total domination, and they're prepared to deliver total violence to achieve total empire. They have more of these hypersonic weapons. Dozens that they can launch from any number of locations around China. They could release these now on the country and may very well with the understanding that the accuracy matters less than the demonstration of capability. This is not something we can do or defend against. It's a new era in game theory. Hypersonic capability changes the calculus."

"Why would my secretaries of defense and state be involved in establishing the Dakhla Accords to help China?"

"Maybe they didn't originally see it that way? You have many members of your team that don't believe in the concept of America anymore. To them, borders are irrelevant. Globalization is the way ahead. There's some talk of a global corporate governance structure taking shape with China and the usual cast of characters. Like Bilderberg, but different, more controlling. The sketches we've seen from what Sinclair turned over to you are plans for a massive, controlled ecosystem in the Mauritanian and Moroccan governments run by a microgrid with a new United Nations–like entity developed in Dakhla called the Tongzhi or Tongyi. They've used both. One means 'unity' and the other means 'domination.' Our analysts have seen documents using both. Perhaps, generously speaking, your cabinet officials saw the one that said unity and have bought into that."

"And you?"

"If we don't turn over our quantum supercomputing materials by midnight, they say they'll launch a hypersonic missile every day until we do."

"Jesus. We seriously have two options? Turn over our most classified technology or get nuked until we do?"

"Well, you do have a suboptimal course of action," Bertrand said. "Which is to see if Sinclair can get in there and disrupt this thing until we catch up with our own technology to reestablish mutual assured destruction."

"Our current array of nukes can destroy China, right?"

"Yes, but our focus has been on destroying their nuclear launch sites to deny them the ability to launch ICBMs at us. They've got at least twenty more of these hypersonic missiles staged on rockets and ready to take off. I think some on your team are trying to lead you to see the benefits of Tongzhi or Tongyi, whichever it is. We're in a new era where people feel empowered by their own information control and access. Government structures are far less important other than as a means to power and control. There are no more ramifications for breaking the law, committing treason as it were. We're in a post-legal environment. Some call it post-truth. Whatever it is, it's not a republic, and it's not democratic."

Bertrand was leaning back in his chair, waxing philosophic with the president, who seemed to be listening intently.

"You're certainly motivational, Koby," Campbell said. She offered the same thin smile she had begun the conversation with. "If I try to exercise my authority through my cabinet, they could very well leave Garrett hanging out to dry . . . and to die. Him and his team."

"They may very well meet that fate no matter what you do, ma'am, but since everyone is rolling their own, you have to ask yourself what you can live with. If you still believe in the America that existed in your childhood and want to steer us toward a future that is at least tethered to that concept, then give Sinclair resources. If you see a future with Chinese unity or domination as the key, then get him out of there. Let him live to fight another day. What we've authorized him to do is highly irregular and dangerous. I can tell you this, though: the American spirit is anathema to China and communism. That's why I believe the virus was the first wave. Maybe intentional or unintentional. It doesn't matter. Socialists here used the opportunity to get the Great Reset in motion. It's happening as we speak. China sees this, and they are the master of opportunity. They've got a huge opportunity in front of them, which they are exploiting."

"My childhood, Koby, was spent catching fireflies and sand crabs at Figure Eight Island in North Carolina. It was magical, but it will still be there no matter what

I do. My parents had a decent income and could afford us vacationing on a private island with its own gated access. My concerns are for the middle class, always have been. What happens to our country if we give in to the brainwashing, the cult that is being developed where we are targeting people just because they think differently from the government? Parents expressing frustration at the school board is about as timeless and American as it gets. America was born out of revolution and resistance to tyranny, and here we are advocating for the very oppression we claim to oppose not only on a local but also on a global scale?"

Bertrand shrugged. "It sounds like you've figured out where you stand. The question is can you succeed—can *we* succeed—in stopping the Chinese and, by the way, the French, who are every bit involved in this present scenario as the Chinese are? They're the ones running interference with Morocco and Mauritania. They've got Henri Sanson on the ground. Our intel shows that Command Sergeant Major Morgan discovered the Rosetta stone to their plan during the Dakhla meeting where McHenry, Blankenship, the Mauritanians, the French, the Moroccans, and the Chinese all signed the Dakhla Accords."

"Did we know he was there? Sylvester Morgan?" Campbell sipped from a cup of coffee she had left untouched for fifteen minutes.

"Before he was killed, he was there twice. He found a treasure of information that has led to all my deductions here. He found documents tying Blankenship and McHenry to major deals with the biggest tech firms and the Chinese Communist Party. I'm an old intel analyst, and I've given this to no one."

"He was decapitated, you know," Campbell said.

"Yes. The Sanson family business was execution by

the blade. Perhaps it's genetic with him, but he also had good reason, in his view, to kill Command Sergeant Major Morgan."

"Why is that?"

"Defense Minister Gambeau is allied with the Chinese just as are McHenry and Blankenship. Sanson is paid handsomely by both Gambeau and the Chinese government to ensure the project succeeds. Morgan was a threat to all that."

"He's not an explorer? He's a defense contractor?" Campbell said.

"Exactly."

"No one else in DNI knows about this?"

"No, ma'am," he said, shaking his head.

She looked out the porthole window again.

"Thank you, Koby, that will be all."

Bertrand nodded, gathered his papers, and left as Campbell reached for a cell phone again, punched a number, and slammed it into the seat cushion after it presumably went to voice mail.

On the television in her office, CNN showed images of a mushroom cloud over a vast suburban area.

UNKNOWN EXPLOSION DECIMATES DULLES AIRPORT AND LOUDOUN COUNTY SUBURBS

The first of the Chinese hypersonic missiles had impacted in Virginia, no doubt a warning shot.

"BOSS, IT'S STARTED," Van Dreeves said as he held the tablet for all to see.

32

"ONE DOWN, FOUR TO go," Hobart said.

We were all numb for a minute, speechless.

Van Dreeves broke the silence when he said, "Feed from Air Force One indicates we have six hours to shut this thing down."

There was no time to waste on eloquent sermons, but I had to acknowledge the enormity of what had just happened.

"Team, this is unprecedented. Thousands of our countrymen have already perished, and thousands more will. 9/11 was a rogue band of terrorists that found a seam and exploited it. This nuclear strike by China is the start of a global war. Their intentions are clear—to force the United States into a global regime or risk at least four more nuclear strikes. Whether our leadership has the wherewithal to strike back, to escalate this into an all-out nuclear Armageddon, I don't know. None of us knows. But what we can do is our part, as we have always done, to protect our nation and our countrymen."

"Well put, boss," Van Dreeves said. Everyone else nodded.

"Okay, let's move," I said.

We departed the cave on the Mole with Hobart and Van Dreeves heading north off the backside of the terrain feature and McCool and me walking a few meters to Farouk's position. We had fully refreshed batteries for our communications systems and IVAS night vision devices.

We were prepared to begin infiltration into the Chinese laser station nearing completion. The sun began sliding beneath the horizon somewhere over Dakhla two hundred miles to the west.

I knelt next to Farouk and said, "Doing okay?"

"Am always okay. Better than that guy." He eyed a dead, decapitated horned viper ten feet away.

"Sanson in the making," I said.

"Bitch tried to bite me."

"Where there's one, there's more."

"Maybe, but usually with these guys, they're territorial. But you're right, this place is ripe terrain for the vipers. There's water on the east side."

He looked down and continued observing from behind the powerful scope atop his sniper rifle.

"Thank you for everything you've done," I said.

"Joe told me about the mission. It's important to my people, too."

"To everyone. This is the new fascism. If China and Big Tech get control, the world will be one giant techno military-industrial complex, and the people will be its subjects."

He nodded.

"Can you do what we're talking about?" I asked.

"It's a bit crazy, but it might work," he said. "It has to work."

To my right, Hobart and Van Dreeves wound down the trail to the bottom of this terrain feature. We were maybe one hundred meters above the desert floor. I watched as they moved stealthily to the southeast. Zoey knelt next to me and placed her hand on my shoulder.

"I feel better. I'm ready to do my part," she said.

"You've done your part. You found Sanson. Sanson led us to the rail. The rail led us to the operation. You've got the external drive that shows the dummy sites. Your only mission is to get home safely with the rest of us. Stay here with Farouk, and we will rally after the mission."

"So boring," she whispered. I imagined that Hobart had forbade her from going forward to the objective area and she was seeking my permission to do so. The reality was that neither of us could stop her.

McCool had taken up a position on my left. We were all hovering over Farouk, because he had staked out the perfect parapet from which to watch Hobart and Van Dreeves's ingress. There were six of us, not including Champollion. They were the very best people I knew. As Van Dreeves and Hobart disappeared into the enveloping darkness, I wondered at the time if I would ever see them again. I didn't recall ever having that thought and was surprised that it had crept into my mind. From where, I didn't know.

The presence of my goddaughter and my most trusted pilot on either side of me comforted me as I watched two men I considered sons snake their way into a deep ravine that would lead to the Chinese terminal guidance construction site. Somewhere in the distance, a camel sounded off with its distinctive bark.

"You ready?" I said, looking at McCool.

"You know the answer to that, General," she said.

I nodded and said to Farouk and Zoey, "No singletons ever anywhere for any reason. I need to hear it from both of you."

Zoey looked at me and then looked away as she had done in Vass after her father's funeral.

"Yes," she muttered unhappily.

"*Oui*," Farouk said. No issues either way for him. I wanted him to make sure Zoey was safe. Our mission was dangerous enough as it was.

"Shoot the video feed from the drones into my IVAS," I directed Farouk.

"Just don't go underground. The network gets weaker."

I nodded and turned to find Champollion's lean figure standing behind me.

"You favor your grandfather. He was a good man. He led the Second Ranger Battalion against all odds during the D-day invasion. While I don't necessarily agree with your tactics here—you're a general, by God—I do support the concept of doing what must be done, regardless of one's station in life."

"As you are doing," I said. "Instead of a comfortable life living off your family's fortunes from interpreting the Rosetta stone and ancient Egyptian hieroglyphics, you joined the DGSE at a young age and lived parallel lives in French social circles as well as dueling it out on the front lines of French intelligence, be that what it is."

"Ouch," she said. "Don't forget I'm an expert at Chinese characters, also."

"You explained your DGSE missions as absences due to grand Egyptian excavations and conferences. Because Henri Champollion, your great-great-something-or-other interpreted the Egyptian artifacts, you are a cult hero in Egypt and North Africa."

"Someone has been doing their homework," she said.

Van Dreeves had downloaded a classified biography we maintained in our JSOC database within our virtual private network, to which we maintained access until General Luckey remembered we had our own network and satellite. We maintained hundreds of names germane to North African operations so we could more rapidly exploit intelligence and identify friend or foe. Evelyn Champollion had been decorated four times with the French Cross for gallantry in Afghanistan, Iraq, Senegal, and Morocco. She was heralded for bringing hostages home, stopping terrorist attacks, and helping French citizens safely escape during the Afghanistan exodus.

"Your reputation is a good one, madam. I trust you to stay here with my goddaughter and Farouk so that we may all rendezvous in twelve hours and return to a securer future than one that includes the Chinese military directing lasers off satellite mirrors to guide nuclear hypersonic weapons to precise locations."

"If you can stop that, General, I suspect there's nothing you can't do," she said. She nodded at me, her eyes glistening in the sunset. I was curious what she hadn't told me about my grandfather. He had been secretive about his World War II battles, having lost over 90 percent of his men from D-day to Cherbourg, but I had found a journal he'd kept in combat after we had buried him in Arlington and cleaned up his Fayetteville home. I read through his musings, some laced with wry humor but most expressing concern for his troops. *Johnny Jackson got winged by a Kraut today . . . Looks like he'll be okay . . . One of nineteen left after climbing the cliff . . . Harlan Ziegler came back from a farm with two chickens . . . We ate well tonight, though stray arty hit, and one of them got away before we could butcher it . . . Met the nicest people in Cherbourg on a risky mission . . . I miss home, but this is my new family . . . I'm losing so many men, a part of me feels like I should be next . . . We're down to just nine men, and we have big*

*missions coming up . . . I imagine we'll all be gone by
the time this is over.*

He often wondered why he had survived and others
had not been so lucky. By the time he had returned from
Germany, he had five men left from his original fifty.
If my grandfather could lead five men across Europe to
do his part in saving the world from Nazi Germany and
Imperial Japan, then I could certainly lead my crew of
seven here to a very specific objective to accomplish
a mission of similar import. It was a testament to the
power of technology that China could achieve essentially the same effect today with its emerging systems
and a couple of infantry battalions as it took Germany
four years and millions of troops to achieve.

"Stay here with my team. You'll be safe with them,"
I said.

She nodded again, and I turned to McCool and said,
"Let's go."

I led McCool off the backside of the Mole and moved
to the west and then south, angling toward the railroad.
Chinese attack helicopters buzzed in the distance. The
train rumbled along the tracks, its frequency every
hour ferrying supplies to the construction site. Darkness enveloped us quickly. Soon, the night chill filtered
in, cooling us as we walked. The desert air carried the
faint smell of eucalyptus and diesel fumes wafting in
from the Chinese build location.

As instructed, Farouk connected the drone video feed
to my IVAS so that I could see Van Dreeves and Hobart infiltrate. Our drones had shown us a potential ingress location along a small wadi that curved in from
the southwest. The basic outline for the plan was for
Van Dreeves and Hobart to work their way in from the
northeast and set up a support-by-fire position. They
would guide us into location to engage the Chinese

infantry that was digging fighting positions along the rail, road, and major wadi ingress/egress locations.

We would make contact as they watched, and then we would support by fire as they moved with the entire base focused on the southern flank. Van Dreeves was the communications expert, and Hobart was the demolition expert. Van Dreeves carried the tools necessary to take control of the laser guidance system while Hobart carried the C4 explosives to destroy it. Having both options were necessary because we weren't certain about the total system design and where the limited resources we had available might need to be placed to achieve maximum effect and defeat the laser capabilities. We had discussed the pros and cons of destroying the optical system versus the command-and-control nerve center. Sly's captured photographs and blueprints showed a complex system with lots of artificial intelligence powering the brains. If we destroyed the lasers, assuming that was possible, would the missiles simply fly to their last computed target, or would they veer wildly off course? The same held true for the command center. If the lasers still worked, would it matter that the brain wasn't communicating to the missiles anymore?

The guidance system involved the ground-based laser and the satellites the laser would reflect off to "paint" the target, whether it be Washington, D.C., or a nuclear power facility, much the same way I had "lased" targets many times behind enemy lines in Desert Storm or other more classified operations as a young officer prowling around the enemy's terrain. Lasers are nothing more than directed energy. A few years ago, the U.S. Army briefed me and some other members of my JSOC team on their plans to field its Tactical High Power Operational Responder, with the sexy acronym THOR. It was basically a giant laser about the size of a shipping container. Because of dwindling budgets and lack of defense industry focus, China was already light-years ahead of the U.S. military in directed energy, and now what they were doing was coupling two highly advanced technologies—hypersonic missiles and directed energy—to reset the global balance of power. They didn't need some giant war crossing the continents. They were smarter than that.

Their plan was to sow political division in the United States and Western world in general. Exploit that division through social media to ossify the rifts. Continue a major media campaign to portray China as sympathetic to Western social issues. Co-opt senior officials before they became senior officials, which required years of cultivation. McHenry and Blankenship were consulting to TikTok, China Construction, and Tencent before people understood what those companies did. Now, with their riches stashed away somewhere safe, the two secretaries could further their influence consolidation through this new China-U.S. Partnership—CUSP. China's final play was to compel the world to sign on to the second phase of the Dakhla Accords, supplanting the United Nations and re-creating it on the Dakhla Peninsula.

Who could argue with dumping billions of dollars into a disputed territory on a forgotten and beleaguered continent to notionally usher in a new era of world harmony?

They only needed a faux Chinese fishing fleet, two battalions of infantry, hypersonic nuclear weapons, cutting-edge directed energy, and a crazy French executioner to enforce the new peace. I had encountered a vast array of asymmetric threats in my career, but never anything as varied or universal as this combination.

After two hours of infiltration, slow and methodical,

McCool and I approached our objective rally point, where the plan was for us to watch and listen.

The sky was black, fueled by billions of stars and a sliver of a waxing moon. We were maybe a couple of hundred meters south of the rail terminus, around which there was a beehive of activity. Trucks spit diesel in the air, ferrying supplies delivered by the train and off-loaded by forklifts. Engines whined and roared. Men shouted and ran the length of the railcars, waving their hands.

They were clearly rushing to complete the job. We had no indication how close they were to being completed. All we had were the intercepts from Air Force One that China intended to begin to execute their mission tonight and the drone video feed piping into my IVAS. The augmented reality devices showed a world in front of us that appeared to be closer to the end than the beginning. Men were scurrying with purpose between containers, under deadline. Some were carrying weapons, others not. The drone feed showed five large weapon systems, large satellite dishes, and bulbous nodules moving slowly upward at varying speeds. Once locked into place, the dishes were all aimed into the western night sky. Two adjacent containers had the tops opened, like a sports coliseum, exposing the high-tech devices.

To our right, other containers were stacked three high in a bulldozed firebase of sorts. A D10 dozer sat at the opening, its blade resting on the ground like an open jaw. The upturned dirt and sand had not been completed, as if the Chinese were rushing everything—the train, the trucks, the construction, the launch of the hypersonic weapons, and now the final touch with the directed energy.

Why would they launch the missiles prior to having

the accuracy issue resolved? It occurred to me that two years ago the Chinese launched several hypersonic missiles and dumped them in the ocean. No one knew that they were in space, orbiting the atmosphere. The world learned because China announced its seventy-seventh and seventy-ninth missile launches, leaving the world to wonder what happened on the seventy-eighth. They had tested a hypersonic missile, China claimed then, surprising the world, though the announcement was mostly lost in the silence of today's incurious media operatives. Or, worse, many media outlets cast doubt on China's proclamation, perhaps deliberately sowing the seeds of doubt that they had even accomplished the test.

Now we knew the answer to that, and the threat was every bit as large, if not larger, than the nuclear arms race borne out of World War II. This technological development was an exponential escalation in the ability to strike first and maintain redundancy.

It was only a few months since America officially abandoned its first-use policy on nuclear weapons. President Campbell had made a controversial decision that was mostly pushed upon her by her base seeking to concede on the nuclear issue to gain concessions on transparency with Russia and China. China had finally agreed to join the Open Skies and Intermediate-Range Nuclear Forces Treaties. Was this a strategic diplomatic move they never intended to fulfill? For years, some members of the defense establishment had argued that these treaties were meaningless without China's membership. China, for their part, had argued that once they caught up with the United States and Russia, they would be happy to join.

And now they had joined. Did that mean they had met their goal of parity? Agree to join the treaties that are now made obsolete by their latest advancements?

With the technology proven, Chinese leadership saw

the opportunity to alter the global balance of power. While most recognized the window of opportunity by the sound of its closing, China was prepared for the success of their persistent belt and road strategy; decades-long recruitment efforts; advances in missile technology; theft of U.S. secrets; development of nuclear missiles harbored within space shuttle–like hypersonic missiles; media manipulation; and divisive rhetoric that had turned the West against itself.

It all made sense now.

"There," McCool said. She was lying next to me, shoulder to shoulder, looking through her goggles, also. "The wadi gets us to within fifty feet or so. No protection. The infantry is focused on off-loading the trains and managing the chaos."

"Dagger Four, Dagger Six," I said.

"Four. Go," Van Dreeves said.

"Blue," I said. "Moving to red."

"Roger."

Blue was the code word that we were in the objective rally point and had conducted our reconnaissance. *Red* was the assault-by-fire position that we were to hold prior to Hobart and Van Dreeves moving to disable the laser.

We moved quietly off the lip of the wadi and into its depths, which was over our heads. We lost sight of the activity above us but could hear the frenetic pace continue. As we approached a bend in the gully, the smell of tobacco smoke trickled through the air. I halted McCool, who nodded that she understood. Through my IVAS, I scouted around the bend using the adaptor on my M4 carbine. There were two Chinese soldiers sitting with their backs to either side of the wadi. They were relaxed, probably on their millionth guard duty with no action. They weren't completely off guard, either, though, as they scanned left and right. One pulled on a cigarette, which was visible in the IVAS.

I spread two fingers above my shoulder for McCool to see and then pointed at my shoulder and to the left, indicating the left-side target was mine. I repeated the process and assigned the right-side target to her. The IVAS provided enough definition to see that the two Chinese soldiers had their night vision goggles propped atop their helmets, probably weary from staring through the devices for too long.

As we moved, their heads turned to the right, away from us, acknowledging two more soldiers scrambling down the ravine, most likely their relief from guard duty or, worst case for us, reinforcements as they prepared to execute.

We engaged the near targets first. Our silenced weapons ratcheted and echoed along the dry riverbed. The two infantrymen fell at their stations, McCool moving swiftly past me and taking a knee to engage the more distant targets from maybe fifty meters away.

They were alerted and already assuming firing positions, which was not good for us in either the tactical or strategic sense. I assumed their weapons were not silenced and that any gunfire would be like an alarm inside the entire base camp, potentially disrupting our entire mission. McCool snapped off two quick shots as I raised my weapon and scanned. There was one soldier lying prone and another crawling, lifting his rifle. I fired two rounds, and the soldier stopped where he was.

The smell of gunpowder filled the air. It was comforting and exhilarating at the same time. McCool jogged forward while I knelt next to the first two dead bodies. A Chinese infantry battalion had about three hundred soldiers. Maybe one hundred were fighting the

Polisario on the desert floor where we had seen them. Maybe another hundred were working the rail line from the shore to the laser terminal location, which left another hundred for guard duty. Covering the massive terrain, they probably had twenty guard posts manned by two soldiers each, which meant there were two shifts with a quick reaction force of twenty.

That calculus, if accurate, would mean that we had chosen either the worst possible time to attack because of maximum deployment of soldiers during shift change, or the best possible time to infiltrate because they were focused on the internal rotation and not the external threat that had not materialized in the weeks they had been deployed in Mauritania. As it turned out, we had eliminated four guards and potentially pierced a hole in the perimeter. Our mission, though, was to hold this spot and allow for Hobart and Van Dreeves to likewise get inside and do their job of neutralizing the container farm that comprised the laser.

To that end, I said, "Red secure."

Hobart came back with, "Roger. Green."

Green was the code for their successful penetration in the north. I never allowed emotions to filter into my mission execution, because they always clouded judgment, but I did feel this uncontrollable sense of satisfaction that we had made it this far. Like any large goal in life, partial achievement was not a harbinger of total success, but it was a milestone on the path. Like the stock market caveat that companies used, *past performance is not an indicator of future success.* We had made it this far and things were looking decent.

Until they weren't.

As McCool approached, she knelt next to me and showed me a handheld radio that was squawking with Mandarin language being barked in urgent tones.

"I think they're supposed to check in once shift change is complete," she said. "But I don't speak Chinese."

"Me neither, but I know someone who does." Then, "Base, prepare to listen," I said in French.

"Base, go," Farouk said.

I held the radio to my throat microphone and pressed to transmit. After a full minute of the Chinese voice barking repetitive instructions, Champollion's voice said into our earpieces, "That's a commander of some type. He's asking for the guards at checkpoint seventeen to report in. If you can fake a guttural accent, say, 'Shíqī gè ānquán.' If you can't fake that well enough, you'll have a quick reaction force coming to your location in a couple of minutes. He's alerted them."

I repeated the phrase to her a few times until she said, "Not excellent, but good enough."

"We have to do the same thing?" Hobart asked.

"He's only asking for seventeen, so maybe you got there after the change," Champollion said.

"Roger," Hobart said.

I looked at McCool and nodded. Holding the radio to my mouth, I said what sounded like "Sheeky gee ankwan." After a long pause, the commander's voice came back and said, "Chóngfù." I held the throat mike open so Champollion could interpret.

"He's asking you to say again," she said.

I repeated the phrase and waited.

The commander came back with another phrase.

"He's scolding you for being late and told you to check in again in fifteen minutes. Say, 'Shì de zhihui guān,' which means, 'Yes, Commander.'"

I repeated the phrase she had given me, "She dee zee-wha gan," and the commander replied.

"He called you an idiot."

"No argument there," I said and refocused on the mission.

"Boss," McCool said. "You need to see this."

I looked over the lip of the ravine where we were positioned. Portable stadium lights cast a bright glow onto the entire area that was probably four football fields in length in width. We were maybe one hundred meters from the laser container farm, which was Hobart and Van Dreeves's objective. The lights shone mostly into the center of the containers but also lit the path from there to the railhead, which was to the northwest. Soldiers scurried back and forth along the road connecting the containers to the rail. A chill settled over the night. The galaxies above were lost in the bright artificial ambient light.

"What do you want me to focus on?" I asked.

"Not up there," she said. "Here." She pointed to a dark hole in the side of the ravine, which was maybe twenty meters deep. The cave mouth was at the base of the ravine and looked as though it oriented north, but there was no telling how deep it might go or in what direction.

"I'm going to check it out," she said.

"No singleton missions," I replied.

"I'm just going to shine my flashlight in there. It could be a path in or out."

"We could push a drone in there," I said.

"Keep the drone over the objective," she said. "I'll just be a minute."

I nodded and watched her slowly slide down the incline of the ravine, shale crumbling beneath her. At the bottom, she stepped into the cave mouth and turned on her flashlight. Disappearing into the darkness, I knew that I should have never let her be more than a few yards from my side other than for actions on the objective.

We had just experienced the guard shift change and two separate target sets.

"Gold," Hobart said, which was the code word for being in a secure area in proximity to the laser container farm. Maybe they had holed up in an empty container. Maybe they were inside the precise area they needed to be. I didn't know, but I did trust them more than I trusted any soldier with whom I've had the privilege to serve. If they said they were in position, that meant for the moment, they didn't need any distraction.

"Roger," I said to ensure they knew I had heard their report.

The Chinese infantry running up and down the road had slowed, and I saw why. They had formed a cordon around a long, straight road that served as a runway for Sanson's Sherpa airplane. A transport helicopter spun up its blades next to two attack helicopters. Sanson deplaned from his Sherpa, and a group from his plane boarded the helicopters while another small group stepped into the Chinese cargo vehicles. It was impossible to tell who had entered which means of transportation.

The helicopters headed north, toward the Mole, where Zoey, Farouk, and Champollion were positioned.

33

PRESIDENT CAMPBELL GAVE SECRETARY of Defense Blankenship a sharp look as she stumbled into Air Force One's presidential office after almost missing the flight.

Blankenship was wearing a blue Department of Defense winter jacket with her name inscribed on the left breast, a tan baseball hat with the DoD emblem stitched on the front, and blue jeans over leather chukkas.

"What took you so long?" Campbell snapped. "The radiation field is growing fast."

"The weather is terrible," Blankenship said. To emphasize her point, sleet poured against the fuselage of the aircraft as it lumbered higher.

"Directly outside of this window, I saw you in your car on the tarmac calmly talking to someone on the phone for about five minutes. Do you make it a habit to keep everyone waiting on you?"

"Madam President, we've just had a nuclear strike on our homeland. I was attempting to coordinate our response." Blankenship's voice was shaky. Nervous.

"We have excellent communications on this aircraft. I'd like to know specifically who you were talking to. Shall I have the communications team look up the records?"

Blankenship began to take a seat when Campbell said, "I didn't invite you to sit down, Secretary."

She stopped and raised herself back up, stiffened, and said, "I was speaking with my deputy, who is headed to Raven Rock."

Campbell gave her a wary eye and said, "I'll confirm that if we live. Have you been talking with your Chinese 'friends'? The ones you said we had no concern over?"

Blankenship looked away and muttered, "I didn't . . . I couldn't . . . I'm sorry, it's not what you think. I would never want this to happen. Our diplomatic efforts were intended to bring harmony, not conflict."

"Well, it's looking a lot like conflict to me. I want your resignation at the end of this fiasco. The only reason I invited you on this airplane was to rub your nose in the big shit pile you created and potentially have you talk to whoever you've been talking to in China. Now give me all your communications gear, and go get the others to bring them in here. You're going to tell us everything you know about the Chinese intentions. Duane, please escort her."

Duane was Campbell's personal bodyguard. He stood six foot seven and could bench-press four hundred pounds. His movements were lumbering and awkward within the relatively confined spaces of the airplane.

As Duane and Campbell watched, Blankenship unloaded an iPad, two cell phones, and a Dell laptop onto the conference table. Duane rummaged through her purse and then checked her coat pockets.

"Watch it," Blankenship said.

"File an EO complaint," Campbell snapped.

"She's clean," Duane said.

Campbell nodded. Blankenship left with Duane in tow and returned with the nexus of the national command authority. While some had recommended relocating to Raven Rock, the hardened bunker compound in Pennsylvania, Campbell wanted to get in the air. Since a previous administration had opened Raven Rock to public tours and used a website to promote it, the enemy could easily target the alternate command post. Not knowing the penetration capabilities of hypersonic missiles flying at Mach five with a nuclear weapon on board, Campbell had accepted the recommendation to get airborne with a couple of refueling tankers.

Blankenship returned with Bertrand, Chairman of the Joint Chiefs Rolfing, National Security Advisor Benito Kidman, and Chief of Staff Quad Jordan. They huddled in the office as the behemoth aircraft powered through the low-pressure system engulfing the East Coast. Bertrand was small and diminutive sitting next to the large General Rolfing, whose hands rested on the top of the desk as if in prayer, which might have been the case given the gravity of the situation. Quad and Kidman sat behind Campbell in the small conference room.

"Where's Bryn?" Campbell asked.

"She's in Dakhla, Morocco, trying to defuse the situation diplomatically, Madam President," Blankenship said. Her voice was sheepish. "I was supposed to join her today per your directions."

Campbell and Blankenship eyed each other coolly.

"Things have been happening so fast," Blankenship said. "I'm sure she has tried to reach you."

Campbell looked at Bertrand and said, "Even though the detonation was thirty miles west of the capital, who is to say that the capital wasn't the intended target? Or that a second hypersonic missile isn't already inbound or planned? Or Joint Base Andrews?"

"Yes, ma'am," Bertrand said.

"But first, I have two questions. What are the initial casualties, and do we have any capability to track these missiles?"

"Too soon for casualty counts, but it's . . . bad," Bertrand said. "I've got communications with DHS and FEMA. Most are moving to Raven Rock. Regarding the missiles, the remaining four are in outer space right now, circling the globe like the space shuttle. It's a speck of hardware in an endless void. So, no," he said.

"Can't we find their communications link? Cut that?"

"Maybe," Bertrand said. "But I wouldn't count on it. Chinese advances in quantum computing, much of which was stolen from us or handed to them by us over the past two years, have hardened their pipes, making it nearly impossible to penetrate their communications infrastructure. That's their gambit."

"Yet they can hack our stuff routinely?" Campbell said.

"Yes, ma'am. China has been preparing for this. We have . . . been unable to get out of our own way."

"Ma'am, the Chinese have seventeen missile silos that have opened with rockets firing for launch, according to the commander of the Defense Intelligence Agency," General Rolfing said. His voice was baritone, packed with gravel.

"So how do we know this but not where the hypersonic missiles are?"

"We knew they launched like any other space launch, but once in space, we have no way to track them," Bertrand said.

"What is the intent of the Chinese with these missiles?" Campbell asked, her voice strained. She might have been wondering if this was it, the nuclear holocaust that so many had predicted and feared during the Cold War with Russia.

"We have no way of telling until the rockets leave the tubes and see whether the arcs are parabolic, which would indicate a traditional intercontinental ballistic missile, or vertical, which would indicate a hypersonic launch into the atmosphere, like the space shuttle, where the missile will orbit until the Chinese are confident in their targeting accuracy," Bertrand said.

"Why launch this many if they're not confident?" Campbell asked.

"Indeed," Bertrand said.

"Options?"

"If the DNI believes the Chinese capabilities are in place, then our only option is to launch a counterstrike," General Rolfing said. "I've placed the nuclear triad on our highest mission-readiness status. Missile teams are in their silos. The submarines are in position in the Pacific. The bombers based in Guam are scrambling, as are the strategic forces globally."

"I think diplomacy still has a path," Blankenship said.

"Diplomacy? With one nuke detonated near our nation's capital and four circling the globe with another seventeen in the air? How do you propose we negotiate our way out of this?" Campbell asked.

"We can reach out to President Shin and talk to him," Blankenship said. "The Chinese conduct open-port missile-launch tests all the time. There's no guarantee that those open silos are going to launch weapons."

"The fact remains, Angela, that they have already struck the United States. We are in an airplane because it is not safe to be with the citizens who elected me and who depend upon us for security. The *one* thing we can't fuck up, we seem to be fucking up," she said, holding a single index finger up above the lacquered wooden table. Sunlight splashed into the office as the airplane broke through the dark, sleet-ridden layers of cloud.

"We have about thirty seconds after launch to make a decision," General Rolfing said.

"Our interceptors?" Campbell asked.

"Useless against hypersonic missiles. Useful but not perfect against ballistic missiles," Bertrand said. "The new versions of the Chinese DF-41 solid-fuel rocket can range just about anywhere in the United States. The hypersonic glide vessels are for stealth and strategic surprise. It makes sense they would then follow with ICBMs once contact has been initiated. They want us to know they're ready to fight back. They have over one hundred new missile silos in the desert in between Mongolia and Kyrgyzstan. If that's what they launch, we will be able to track and know precise targets after a minute of flight time based upon algorithmic interpretations," Bertrand said.

An aide stuck his head in the office and said, "Madam President, President Shin is calling for you."

Campbell looked around the room, making eye contact with everyone, then looked back at the aide and said, "Patch him through."

The aide pressed a button on the secure starfish phone sitting in the middle of the desk. The airplane banked in the sky, causing the sunlight from the porthole window to move slowly across the tabletop, rotating from west to east.

"President Campbell," President Shin said. Shin was a lifetime Communist Party official, a member of the Yue Fei Loyalist Society, and a lifelong operative within the Central Military Commission, beginning as an officer in special forces and transitioning to his civilian leadership roles. A dedicated communist, Shin believed the manifest destiny of China was to impose global domination on the world to enrich and better the Chinese people. The Chinese strategy was one of strategic patience, allowing the United States to expend resources on its domestic divisions.

"Madam President," Shin said. While this team had spoken with Shin before on a previous presidential call, they had no actual way of confirming it was Shin.

"President Shin. You've started World War III," Campbell said. Sitting across from Campbell, Blankenship shook her head either in dismay at the bellicose words or as a signal to Campbell to tone it down.

"We've done no such thing. I was calling you to say that whatever happened in Virginia was an accident. We are merely testing capabilities, and one got away from us. We have no malicious intent," Shin said.

"You really expect me to believe that you lost control of one of your missiles that violates our agreements, and it just happened to land thirty miles from our capital?"

"I can't make you believe the truth if you do not want to see it. We have no agreements on hypersonic missiles. We have reached out to your government many times to discuss these matters, but with no success."

"What do you want?"

"I am not accustomed to such harsh language, Madam President. I prefer to speak in friendlier terms."

"You've nuked our country. What is stopping us from a retaliatory strike?"

Shin said nothing for a moment and then replied, "I'm assuming that's a rhetorical question."

"Actually, it's not."

"Then only you know the answer to that. I'm sure your intelligence apparatus has provided you the information that we have other missiles prepared should you do so. We are prepared for a nuclear war. The damage you inflict on my people will only enrage them for all-out conflict. Total violence. We will stop at nothing should you strike our homeland intentionally."

"I don't like your threats, especially after you've already attacked us," Campbell said.

"As I mentioned, that was not an intentional strike. It was an accident. The media is already reporting it as such. We have issued a statement and express our deepest regrets at any loss of life. We are prepared to make those families whole. It seems someone in your defense establishment disrupted the flight of our vessel and caused it to land in your Virginia region."

Campbell didn't respond for a full minute. The phone connection crackled with static, no doubt recorded by Chinese and American intelligence agencies. Kidman leaned across her and scribbled a number on the notepad in front of her.

"We have over three thousand dead, President Shin. You are responsible for these deaths," Campbell said.

"I accept full responsibility even though Americans meddled with our system. As I said, I will make their families whole. I do not want more bloodshed."

"Surely you cannot believe that you can simply attack us and then pretend it was an accident and we all agree that it is fine," Campbell said.

"I see no other option. We can discuss economic renumeration or other ways to offset the loss and humiliation on the world stage," Shin said.

"What are you prepared to give in exchange for us to not retaliate?" Campbell asked. Bertrand snapped his head up from his note-taking and glared at the president.

"That is the wrong question. The proper question is what you are prepared to deliver in order to avoid conflict. We have a large supply of weapons prepared to release and to launch. While you have been focused on internal divisions, we have thought this through and will stand firm in our resolve to create a peaceful international order. The United Nations is archaic and U.S.-centric. Our proposal is a fair one. We build the structure in Dakhla, Morocco. Common ground in a disputed province on a neglected piece of the world. Sign phase two of the Dakhla Accords and everything will be okay. It will signal your intent for peace."

"Blackmail? I expected more. We will not subjugate ourselves to any international order," Campbell said. "And you're not getting anything from us."

"This is a new alliance between China and the United States, the CUSP, where we combine our collective resources and govern in a united fashion. Our economies are closely linked. All the infrastructure is already in place. Why should we be competitors when we can be teammates and lead the world? We can do a lot of good, too, for the people your country pretends to care about. The downtrodden, the poor, the immigrants, the environment. All of that is on the agenda if you peacefully join forces with us."

"This is what I was talking about, Madam President," Blankenship said. "As part of the Dakhla Accords, we discussed these types of partnerships to further our social agendas and strengthen transparency on the international level. Phase two would solidify those commitments."

"Your secretary of defense is a wise woman, President Campbell. You should listen to her," Shen said.

"President Shin, if you are offering transparency, then advise me of your intentions with the other four missiles in orbit and your ballistic missiles that are smoking in their holes right now," Campbell said.

"As I've stated, I need you to sign on to the China-U.S.

Partnership and delivery of your quantum codes, which provide us the transparency into your systems to ensure you are complying with the terms of the agreement. It's like blockchain. Perfect transparency. I believe one of your presidents used the phrase *trust, but verify,*" Shin said.

"Absolutely not," Campbell said.

"Very well, then. I will not beg. I suggest you think about the concept of the prisoner's dilemma. Which one of us is bluffing? Which one of us is defecting?" Shin replied.

"You've already defected," Campbell said. "Withdraw your weapons, and then we will negotiate."

"I have no weapons deployed. We are conducting tests as you do with your many space launches. Mistakes happen, and I would hate to see more mistakes occur," Shin said.

"It won't be a mistake when we unleash our nuclear arsenal on your country," Campbell said.

"I suspect that my country has more appetite for casualties than yours. Our mistake with the virus indicated such. Now we have a mistake with a nuclear weapon. You should check your media reports."

Campbell turned to Bertrand, who began typing on his tablet.

"'America interferes in Chinese missile test, causing nuclear explosion in Northern Virginia,'" Bertrand read from the screen. "Holy shit, the media is already blaming us." He continued reading. "'President Campbell directed interference in China's peaceful missile tests while Secretary of Defense Blankenship has wisely encouraged restraint and transparency through phase two of the highly ambitious Dakhla Accords.'"

"Like I said, it was an accident. I don't blame America solely. Your General Sinclair has been disrupting things, and so perhaps he is rightfully to blame," Shin said. "And it does seem there are dozens of other articles and reports about to confirm that the United States cut the link to our missile test at your request and against Secretary Blankenship's wishes, and there was no way to determine where it might land. Again, my apologies. We are providing a statement that we will make the people whole no matter what you choose to do about the situation."

"The problem is that half the country will believe this Chinese misinformation, and the media monster just feeds it to them," Campbell said. "It's what happens when you build Frankenstein's monster. He eventually turns on you."

"Perhaps the beast has been better cared for somewhere else," Shin said.

Campbell looked at Blankenship and said, "Secretary Blankenship, do you have anything you'd like to say to President Shin?"

Blankenship looked at Campbell and then the phone.

"President Shin, as President Campbell said, we seek a reasonable peace. We'd like you to cease testing of all weapons of mass destruction, and then we can talk."

"I am trying to be reasonable by offering a compromise," Shin said.

"President Shin," Campbell said. "Withdraw your weapons, and only then can we talk."

"I'm sorry you've made this decision," Shin said. "The world will suffer."

The phone line went dead. Everyone was silent for a full minute until Bertrand interrupted the silence with, "Over three thousand dead. Radiation field is growing with the wind blowing from the northwest, directly into Fairfax County."

"That will be all, except for you, Koby," Campbell said.

Once everyone had left, Bertrand closed the door and said, "Jesus Christ, what a shit show."

"Do we have a status on Garrett?"

"Yes, they're in trouble. The base station reported that someone has hacked their positions."

"Hacked their positions?"

"I've got a trace on where the hack came from. Looks like DIA, who reports to Blankenship."

"The call she made from the tarmac," Campbell said.

"Maybe."

"Have the Secret Service arrest her. I've got all her communications devices here," she said, pointing at the desk. "Have your people scour them."

"Yes, ma'am."

"Tell me they still have a chance."

"It's Garrett Sinclair. He always has a chance," Bertrand said.

Campbell looked out the window, a bright square of sunlight cutting across her face.

"We've put him in an impossible position, but yes, if anyone can do it, he can. He must."

She picked up the burner cell phone and looked at it as if willing it to ring. No doubt she was trapped in the dilemma of saving herself, saving her country, and saving me. Obviously frustrated, she tossed the phone against the wall and shoved her head into her hands.

34

AS THE HELICOPTER ARMADA headed north toward the Mole, I waited another fifteen minutes to support Hobart and Van Dreeves when I realized it had been almost twenty minutes since McCool had entered the tunnel just meters away from my position.

I was torn between continuing to provide observation to my two best operators and removing myself from that role to search for McCool. She was more than capable, and I convinced myself to give her a few more minutes before attempting to locate her. As it was, I was scanning in three directions now, intermittently watching the drone video on my IVAS and the container farm and dark cave mouth through my IVAS. The cave mouth was ninety degrees to my right.

"Bogies inbound Mole," I said on our secure radio network.

"Roger," Farouk said.

A few minutes later, the sound of gunfire erupted north of the container farm and likely near the Mole. Farouk confirmed this suspicion when he radioed and said, "Taking fire."

"Roger. Sitrep when possible."

Zoey had endangered her life to help us find Sanson

and had led us to the Chinese operation her father had discovered at the Dakhla Accords signing. Now, she was in jeopardy again, as well as Farouk and Champollion.

The activity at the Mole seemed to energize the infantry at the objective area. With one company displaced in combat against the Polisario near our original hide site north of Chinguetti over fifty miles away to secure the railroad and major road arteries, and the bulk of the force focused externally to the north on the Mole, our window was now. Meanwhile, muffled sounds seeped from the cave mouth like a mattress falling on the floor several times in a row. *Thud, thud, thud.* But it was difficult to discern whether the sounds truly came from the cave or were echoes from the active combat at the Mole.

"Infantry on the ground," Farouk said. In the background of Farouk's transmission, the sound of machine-gun fire and rocket explosions popped in stereo with what I was hearing from my location.

"Dagger Six?" McCool croaked into the radio.

"Dagger Six here, go," I said.

A long pause ensued. McCool's voice was not her typical cool and confident timbre. Rather, she sounded weak, maybe wounded. As was typical in combat scenarios, especially special operations where teams were flat and everyone had multiple duties, everything seemed to be happening at once, pushing the limits of decision-making efficacy.

I thought about the lost platoon at Ia Drang Valley in Vietnam and how Hal Moore's situation had complicated significantly when a rogue platoon leader took his thirty men into the bush, away from the landing zone, and got trapped by hundreds of Viet Cong, who killed the great majority of the outfit.

Was Sally McCool going to be the Lost Platoon of the battle of the Eye of Africa?

"Dagger Six?" McCool's voice was now a whisper, as if she was having a hard time pressing the detent on her throat microphone.

"Hang tight," I said and began sliding into the ravine.

"No . . . ," she said, but her voice trailed off at the end and was unintelligible.

As I reached the bottom and faced the cave mouth, Farouk said, "Charlie Quebec Charlie."

Close-quarters combat.

Rifle fire sounded off in the background of his brief transmission. The same sounds ricocheted across the desert floor moments later. The mission was still holding steady, though, if Hobart and Van Dreeves could execute their tasks.

Mission versus men. The age-old dilemma.

There was nothing I could immediately affect, other than exploring what had happened to McCool. While my task was to provide support to Hobart and Van Dreeves, I made a razor-thin call to abandon that duty to recover, if possible, one-seventh of our team. I didn't leave my station easily but was compelled to do so in part because I thought I could quickly recover her and reestablish our position without interrupting the overall mission. If our command headquarters at the Mole had been discovered, as was clearly the case, then we would need every able body to fight our way out of the Sahara.

My IVAS provided a significant improvement over previous night vision goggles, and thankfully, our prepositioned resupply drop had gone unmolested and was available to us as we recovered on the Mole. Like a video game, the terrain in front of me was highlighted in three dimensions and transposed colors that provided relief and detail, all powered by the thin battery pack in the head harness strap. The cave was maybe ten feet high, sometimes higher, and twenty feet wide. It had a surprisingly consistent symmetrical shape the deeper I walked.

Perhaps it was a man-made tunnel. Maybe even from thousands of years ago. The Incas and Mayans had constructed elaborate tunnels and pyramids, as had the Egyptians centuries before. Maybe reports of some of these tunnels were what led Plato to believe that this was Atlantis. Who knew?

I was over a hundred meters into the cave when my IVAS alerted on movement. McCool was slumped against the wall on my right, her head lolled to the left. A dark stain appeared on the upper-left side of her torso near her shoulder.

"Dagger Six," she whispered. "Careful . . ."

I felt the presence behind me perhaps a nanosecond early, giving me time to roll to my right and miss the arcing blade that was swinging toward me.

"Sinclair," Sanson said, his saber sparking off the wall of the tunnel.

I had only been in the cave for ten minutes, which I didn't think was enough time for him to get to the Mole and do whatever he intended and then get into this cave unless he had never gone to the Mole. It was entirely possible that he had sent someone else to the Mole and focused on us. But how? Intercept our brief communications? Tap into the drone feed? With Big Tech as part of the CUSP team, all of that was entirely possible. Had someone given away our position? One thing was for certain—there was another exit point than the one I had gained entry through.

I recognized Sanson's voice before I saw him. Rolling to the ground to avoid the blade had dislodged the secure fit of my IVAS goggles. He was a distorted image moving toward me. Reaching for my Beretta, I rolled again and avoided a second sweeping arc of the blade. Cool air brushed across my face in the backwash of his lunge.

I snapped off two quick rounds in his direction, placing myself between McCool and Sanson. He dove behind the bend in the tunnel as I scrambled toward McCool. I saw Malik huddled in the corner.

"Please do not kill me!" he cried. "I can help you!" His breathing was labored. He was bleeding. Dark stains blossomed on his upper-left shoulder and left thigh.

Next to McCool was a big man, one of Sanson's henchmen, no doubt. He was dead by McCool's pistol. It was obvious to me that McCool had disrupted their attempt to flank us. I removed a zip tie from my outer tactical vest and ratcheted it across Malik's wrists. Ripping a sheet of cloth from his clothing, I tied it around his mouth, gagging him to render him mute. All the while, I had an eye on the opposite side, where Sanson had fled. Pushing Malik deeper into the cave, I said in French, "Stay here if you want to live."

Returning to McCool, I inspected her wound quickly. Sanson's saber had slashed across her chest. Her uniform was covered in blood. I lifted her and carried her fifty meters deeper into the tunnel, kicking Malik as I passed him, saying, "Follow us."

Cradling McCool, I reached the opening of the tunnel, which had a makeshift staircase sloping upward toward the bright lights. I laid McCool on the base and climbed the stairs until I could see.

Two things happened.

Sanson was running across the compound from the opposite direction, where McCool and I had originally been, and the video feed from the drone did not reappear in my IVAS goggles. I didn't know if that meant the goggles were having a hard time reconnecting to the virtual network or if the base station at the Mole had been overrun.

I returned to McCool's location and pulled her back into the tunnel, where I inspected her wound.

"Sally, talk to me," I said, feeding her the water tube stowed on the shoulder of her tactical vest. She swallowed and then choked, spitting water out, but then pulled at the tube again.

"Shoulder hurts," she said.

The bloodstain that had blotted her uniform continued to spread. I needed to stop the bleeding. I retrieved an IV from her first aid pouch and punched it in her arm.

"Here, hold this," I said to Malik. "Make yourself useful."

I used my collapsible knife to cut open the sleeve from her elbow to her shoulder and then cut open the rest of the uniform. She had a deep gash running from her abdomen to her shoulder.

I used her first aid kit to pour some Betadine on the wound. She yelped and grabbed my arm with both hands.

"Boss, shit," she said.

Another inch to the left and her heart would have been pierced. As it was, the blade appeared to nick an artery somewhere.

I swabbed the wound, blood continuing to seep. With every swipe of the gauze, a new crimson river would bubble up. I lifted her and wrapped gauze completely around her body.

"Boss, it's okay," she said. "I'm going to die."

"No, you're not, Sally."

I noticed Malik had looked away and was crying.

"Hang tight, Sally," I said.

"Tell Randy I love him. I love all of you," she said.

"You can tell him. Tell all of us," I said, refusing to let her certainty penetrate my wishful thinking.

I placed my hands on her shoulders and looked into her eyes. They were weak. Her hair was matted, her forehead streaked with blood. I used her CamelBak to dampen a cloth and wipe the blood from her eyelids and the bridge of her nose. She glanced up at me.

"You're going to be okay, Sally," I said.

She smiled and shook her head.

"Thanks, boss." Her voice was a whisper.

"Drink water," I said.

"The others?" she asked. Classic McCool, always concerned about the team over herself.

"Everyone is doing their part."

Though I was unsure. I had no communications from the team at the Mole and had not heard from Hobart and Van Dreeves. Our operational maxim had always been to aim for the best to occur but to plan for the worst to happen. In the absence of information, I did not assume that everything had gone wrong. Such a mind-set bred failure and manifestation of the negative outcome. It was a fine line, though, because you had to fully understand and appreciate the possible bad results and plan to prevent them without spiraling down the rabbit hole of doom. I always told my team that much of success was in preventing failure. What were the critical points of failure, and how do we prevent them from becoming reality?

For the battle of the Eye of Africa, we had determined that success depended on destroying the ability to guide the aircraft into precise targets. If we were noticed beforehand, we might fail. If we didn't succeed on the first attempt, we might fail. We then built a plan around surprise and redundancy, which resulted in our concept of multiple ingress routes and smaller teams, all of which could execute the mission.

Malik was scratching at the sand with his feet, trying to say something. Some shadows appeared at the mouth of the entrance to the tunnel as the stadium lights were blocked. I handed McCool a pistol and a knife, saying, "If I go down, defend yourself. Give Joe and Randy a chance to finish the mission."

She nodded, her eyes glancing around. She was not okay, but the tactical situation demanded that we all reach deep down to that place where quitting was not an option. The survival instinct had to be unleashed to tap into the Herculean mental strength of this woman. Though wounded, I knew that she was a warrior and could rally when she needed. Having been on the brink of succumbing to poison and gunshot wounds, I understood where McCool was mentally and physically. She was weak. The body led the mind, and if the mind didn't rear up and stop the slide, she would circle the drain. I couldn't have that.

She placed a weak hand on my shoulder and licked her lips. "You're Garrett Sinclair. You'll live forever," she whispered.

"Sally, I need you to rally here."

She nodded and whispered, "Rally. Yes."

Her eyes started to close when the footsteps behind me became louder. I spun around and laid my body in front of McCool's to protect her and assume a low defensive position. Snapping my IVAS into place, I sighted on the first two to turn the corner and fired from twenty meters away as they scanned. The two infantrymen were wearing night vision goggles and dropped quickly. To their right were two others spinning in the opposite direction to clear the tunnel to the west. I shot them in their backs.

A grenade came spinning toward me like a ground ball at shortstop. I did the only thing I knew to do, which was to field it and toss it back as if I were gunning down a batter at first base. As the grenade landed, it exploded in the middle of ten infantrymen who were attempting to overwhelm our position. Some continued, and I plinked away with my rifle. I felt something on my back, followed by loud explosions.

McCool was firing her pistol. We were Randy Shughart and Gary Gordon in Mogadishu. Hal Moore and Joe Galloway in the Ia Drang Valley. McCool had summoned their spirits and joined the fight. Her firepower came at a crucial time when another five soldiers barreled through the opening, and we knocked them all down. Bodies were stacked two deep at the bend in the cave.

A series of loud explosions disrupted the flow of infantrymen pouring into the tunnel. I used the brief pause as an opportunity to gather up McCool and Malik to move deeper into the tunnel and, best case, seek another outlet or, worst case, defend against a double envelopment. Whatever commotion had occurred near the directed-energy lasers had served to give us an opportunity to change magazines, reposition, hydrate, and prepare for a second wave. If we killed or wounded twenty-five at the bend in the tunnel, that would be the entire rapid reaction force. Would they pull soldiers from their outer perimeter to collapse on the interior and eliminate the threat, or would they fear a perhaps larger threat from the outside? They had plenty of soldiers to reposition, though many were out of position.

The tunnel remained consistently high and wide, barely enough room to stand and plenty of room for two of us to walk abreast into the depths. Underground navigation is always problematic because you can't rely upon terrain features or celestial navigation aids available to assist in course corrections. The compass inside my IVAS was GPS powered and therefore useless. I carried an old-school magnetic compass in my outer tactical vest, and it indicated we were headed on a seventy-one-degree azimuth, or northeast. My calculus put the center of the Chinese operation to the north of our position. After continuing to walk, the compass showed us bending back to the northwest and then west. The air was stale with a thick, musky scent, which told me water was somewhere nearby or had been. At night, there was a chill in here, a stale dampness that seemed permanent.

Mercifully, a dim light snuck through a break in the tunnel maybe thirty meters ahead. I carried McCool while Malik shuffled behind me. She was faltering, heavy in my arms. Her mental and physical toughness were in the top 1 percent of operators I had ever seen. I simply expected her to rally.

A dilapidated stairwell led to the desert surface. I left Malik in the tunnel while I pulled McCool up to ground level, thinking that some fresh air might help her. A few meters from the opening was a low stone fence, maybe a meter high, that seemed to arc forever in both directions. We were a half mile from the stadium lights and the GLINTS directed-energy systems that would guide the hypersonic missiles to precise locations on earth.

"Take a deep breath and drink water, Sally," I said, looking at her face. In the dim starlight, she was drawn and pale. Her eyes weak, half-lidded. She had lost a lot of blood. I stuck my IV in her arm to replace the one her body had already consumed. We were maybe a mile and a half from the Mole. We had blood reserves there. We could make it if Sally could hang on.

"Dagger Four, this is Dagger Six."

No response. I repeated the call multiple times until I said, "Any station, this is Dagger Six."

The next voice sent a chill through my spine.

"Sinclair, c'est Sanson. J'ai ton équipe, et ma lame est tranchante." This is Sanson. I have your team, and my sword is sharp.

McCool's eyes flickered. Was she dying? My team was in the hands of Sanson? Was that why he had given up immediate pursuit of us? Because Hobart, Van Dreeves, and the others had been captured?

There was only one way my entire team might have been compromised: someone gave them our location. In the distance, helicopter blades chopped against the sky. At one point in my life, I would have been encouraged by that sound, because it most likely would have been Sally McCool and her team sweeping in once again to save our asses. But now, I had McCool in my arms, her body losing strength by the second. There was no way she was piloting anything now or perhaps in the future.

Spread out and not in position to support my team on the objective, I thought of the piece of land in Vass, North Carolina. Would we all make it back to that location and reunite in the aftermath? Given the carnage that I had seen throughout my career, my daughter, Reagan, had challenged my religious faith, which had been a bedrock of my marriage to Melissa and our parenting of Reagan and Brad.

Combat and its horrors either convinced you that there was a God or that it was impossible for him to exist. The valiant often assault evil's gate and die in the process. I was steadfast that God would be there for me and my gallant team, even if this was our last tilting at the windmill of higher purpose.

We had answered our calling. I prayed quietly as

McCool's grip simultaneously tightened around my waist and loosened as she lost her will to live. A finer soldier I've never known.

There, on the desert floor in the vastness of the Sahara, Sally McCool's spirit drifted skyward to join the stars, that collection of so many noble souls.

I dropped my chin and cradled her limp body to my chest, wanting to shout to the heavens but lacking the resolve to do so.

I simply cradled her head in my hands and whispered, "Why?"

35

PRESIDENT CAMPBELL STUDIED HER iPad for a long time, reviewing documents and news articles that had been released in the wake of the nuclear weapon "mishap" that had killed and injured over three thousand Americans in Northern Virginia.

The media race was quick to position China as the victim of an innocent mistake by an aggressive administration attempting to penetrate China's mostly peaceful nuclear weapons development program. A few random articles highlighted China's well-documented strategic plan that called for information warfare, followed by biological warfare, followed by nuclear warfare to achieve its strategic aims. Success being achieved in the first two stages had laid the groundwork for the nuclear phase.

One article seemed to catch Campbell's eye.

China-U.S.-French Triumvirate in Western Sahara to Discuss Nuclear Mishap

Dakhla, Morocco (Associated Press): Sources close to the signing of the Dakhla Accords phase 1 have indicated that a phase 2 signing could occur within the next 24 hours, which would put in place controls to prevent the type of nuclear accident that occurred in Loudoun County, Virginia, today.

The belief is that the United States, led by the courageous duo of Secretary of State Bryn McHenry and Secretary of Defense Angela Blankenship, had convinced China not to react aggressively to U.S. manipulation of Chinese communications signals that are believed to have caused the mishap in rural Virginia.

Unnamed sources confirm that there is a meeting in Dakhla in the next 24 hours, and given the crisis in the United States, Secretary McHenry will represent the United States at the table for the signing of phase 2 of the Dakhla Accords. Specified in this round of talks are controls that provide transparency on testing and experimentation of all weapons, compelling signatories to the random inspections of CUSP personnel.

"We're almost realizing a safer world," McHenry said after landing in Dakhla today. "In the aftermath of the horrific accident in Virginia, we must rapidly come together and agree on the path forward. There should be no more innocent loss of life."

Sources say that China has more hypersonic missile tests in the air and that American intervention in one could impact them all. Chinese scientists are working around the clock to prevent other accidents but cannot guarantee complete avoidance. The United States Senate has taken the phase 1 and 2 treaties into conference to discuss possible rapid approval. The Senate requires two-thirds majority to approve any treaty. Given these politically contentious times, such a margin would not seem likely, but given the grave stakes at hand, some see a path. An unnamed Senate Armed Services Committee staffer said, "Our concern is that without approval of the treaty, we will see more nuclear weapons impacting the United States and elsewhere."

Some in conservative media have falsely claimed without evidence that the nuclear incident was intentional. With the high stakes at hand, many Americans are wondering where President Campbell is and why she hasn't addressed the nation. While this may be the biggest challenge of her presidency outside of the Parizad incident, global citizens do believe she got a couple of things right, however: hiring McHenry and Blankenship.

Campbell leaned back in her chair and summoned Bertrand. The plane entered a left turn, causing Bertrand to stumble forward when he arrived.

"Pardon me, Madam President," he said, steadying himself on the desk.

"Have a seat. Talk to me," Campbell said, opening her palm toward the facing chair.

"I'm playing catch-up myself."

"Not like you," Campbell said. "Have you seen this?" She slid a piece of paper across the table to him. On it contained a wiring diagram of an organization intended to replace the United Nations. "I thought this was fantasy when I first saw it, but now I'm not so sure."

"Where did you get this?"

"That's not important," she said.

"Your secretary of state and secretary of defense are listed as leaders in a Chinese-U.S. Partnership?"

"That's what it says. Might explain their insubordination."

"And it seems they have taken steps to lock us into a treaty that you don't want."

"Well, they can't do that."

"If the Senate approves it, they can, but they need two-thirds majority."

"*I* didn't even approve it!" Campbell snapped.

"The Constitution just speaks to the executive branch, not the president. Certainly, you're in charge of the executive branch, but McHenry and Blankenship are in the executive branch as well and are authorized to present treaties to the Senate."

"They're presenting this as a path out of nuclear attack from China. That may get two-thirds. They drop a nuke a day until it's approved."

"I hadn't considered that, but the fact that the Senate leader has the treaty and it's actively being discussed on the floor would indicate you may have a point."

"It's a narrow eye of the needle they have to thread, though," Campbell said. "Drop more, and it becomes evident they're blackmailing us. Don't drop more, and they may not apply enough pressure to get two-thirds."

"True."

She turned to her note-taker and said, "Get me Senator Davenport on the phone, please."

As they were waiting, Campbell turned up the volume on the television, where a reporter, clad in full hazmat gear, was speaking into a microphone from a King Air that was circling north of the blast field over the northern reaches of the Potomac River. The camera panned out and then zoomed in on a subdivision where the houses were flattened to sticks and concrete blocks, like a beach town in the direct path of a hurricane.

"We see a Hiroshima-like impact. Houses are leveled.

Barns. Buildings. Trees. Everything is destroyed. We are two miles in the sky using a high-powered zoom lens called a Digipower 99, so we're getting incredibly clear images from the blast zone while protecting ourselves and remaining upwind of the radiation cloud. There is some risk, but our job is to bring you the information in real time. You can see there are several fires spreading through where neighborhoods once were. Gas lines have burst. Electrical lines are down and still live. What looks like bodies, and I'm sorry to say this on live television, but I think we're in unprecedented times here. What looks like bodies are spread out along the yards and roads, as if they were seeking help and just somehow stopped and fell where they were. A school bus is on fire at a street corner and . . ." The reporter's voice cracked. "And there are children inside still alive, I think. I see movement. Oh my God, the bus just burst into flames."

Campbell hit the Mute button.

"Dear God," she whispered, her hands in her face.

A minute later, a rough male voice came through the starfish phone. "Madam President."

Scott Davenport was the senior senator from Connecticut. Though from the same party as Campbell, the two did not typically agree. Davenport was a hawk on defense issues, almost a neocon, and a wild social spender. Campbell preferred restraint on defense issues while still maintaining a strong military and was much more centrist on the traditional social issues.

"You can't be seriously considering this treaty," Campbell said.

"Your secretaries of state and defense hand-delivered it. We thought you approved. And now that it has been officially read into the record, we must resolve it one way or the other. What is your preference?"

"I can't believe you have to ask me that. You want us to be extorted into signing on to a globalist agenda that puts China in charge?"

"So you'd prefer for nukes to drop from the sky every day?"

"I'd prefer that we hand China their ass!" she snapped.

"Madam President, I stepped off the floor of the Senate to take your call. We are in the middle of a serious debate about the Dakhla Accords, a treaty *your* administration sent to us. We take our advice and consent duties seriously, and so the treaty will get a proper vetting, as your administration requested."

"Scott, Bryn and AB have gotten in front of their skis on this. Can't we just pull it back?"

"Do we have a plan for engaging China? I'm thinking signing some deal with them to get them to back off the nukes might be a good thing. We can always negotiate afterward."

"If you approve both phases of the Dakhla Accords, you'll be signing the United States on to an agreement with China that they have full access to our quantum computing codes and our nuclear secrets—"

"And we will have access to theirs."

"Do you think that ever works in our favor?"

Loud conversations could be heard in the background from where Senator Davenport was speaking.

"Madam President, I have your wishes—not to approve the treaty you sent to us. I will convey that to the caucus and to the floor."

Campbell hung up and looked at Bertrand. "Any word from Garrett?"

Bertrand shook his head. "It doesn't look good, though. French DGSE is reporting gunfire from the GLINTS location. Evidently, they have someone on the ground."

"Our options are to get into a major nuclear war with China or to shut down their targeting capability. We know where it is now, right? They've located it. Can't we just get a bomber up and turn that part of the desert into glass?"

Bertrand nodded slowly and said, "Yes, ma'am. Absolutely. You know such an action will kill your friend and his soldiers."

Campbell looked at him for a full minute without speaking, no doubt considering the ramifications of such an action. The engines whined in the background, droning along.

"'The tree of liberty must be refreshed from time to time with the blood of patriots and tyrants,'" she said, quoting Thomas Jefferson, one of her political guideposts. "Get the chairman in here, but not Blankenship."

A minute later, General Rolfing appeared. He was carrying his olive dress coat in his hand and slinging an arm through an arm hole, saying, "Yes, ma'am."

"General, I need you to attack with bombers that can destroy high-powered laser equipment at the location that Bertrand gives you."

Rolfing nodded warily and looked at Bertrand.

"It's the directed-energy site that provides terminal guidance to the hypersonic missiles to increase their accuracy. We discussed this a few minutes ago. We know its precise location now."

"And how do we know that?"

"We have intelligence sources, General."

"Sinclair?"

Both Campbell and Bertrand said nothing.

"Okay, then. If Sinclair is involved, it's got to be big-time, and it's got to be accurate. What's his location now?" Rolfing asked.

"He's in the proximity of the objective, as is his team," Bertrand said.

"Is he calling in this broken arrow mission?" A broken arrow mission was a call to bomb one's own position because the enemy was, in most cases, overrunning the location.

Campbell said, "General Sinclair is aware of the risks associated with his mission."

"You know, ma'am, I've known Garrett a long time, even though I'm a marine. We've been on the same hilltops fighting the same enemies. If you order me to bomb the location in the name of national security, I'll do as instructed. But know this: Garrett Sinclair, despite his current troubles, is a great American."

"That he is, General. I appreciate your remarks. I venture to guess I've known Garrett a few years longer than you. We drank beer together as teenagers in Raleigh rathskellers. He married my best friend. We all stayed many times at my family beach house on the North Carolina coast. I don't make this decision lightly, and just imagine the import of my making this decision if I'm willing to kill a man I have loved as a friend for four decades."

Rolfing nodded. "Understood. No disrespect. Tough times right now, and I appreciate the background."

"Now, please execute within the hour. We may have less than that."

"General," Bertrand said. "We've got indications that the Chinese have launched fighter jets from their airfield in Djibouti. There's a tanker circling somewhere up there. I think they're running protective cover for the operation tonight; assuming we'll find out sooner or later."

"We can scramble to have something on station in

the next three hours. Secretary Blankenship previously forbade me from putting any aircraft over Mauritania."

"She's relieved. You report directly to me. Execute," Campbell said.

Rolfing departed as Bertrand stared at his tablet sitting on the table.

"We've got something here," Bertrand said. He spun the tablet so that Campbell could see the images.

"Explain," she said, leaning over the table.

He pointed, pinched and pulled, and used a thumb and forefinger to slide the Google Earth image to the center of the display.

"Here's the location where Sinclair is trying to disable the GLINTS. And here's the angle of the laser from fifteen minutes ago. Our analysts computed the angle, shot, and azimuth and ran some algorithms to find space debris and located a field of four Chinese missiles orbiting in space like four space shuttles."

"That's a one-in-a-million find," Campbell said. "But what good does it do us? We have no offensive capability in space."

"If nothing else, it gives us early warning and an ability to scramble jets and put them over the most likely targets, allowing them an opportunity to engage."

"Can they hit something going Mach five?"

"It's a possibility. It's all in the weaponry."

"Okay, let's track those and get everything we've got up providing air cover to the country to neutralize these four. Get the triad focused on China and intercept anything coming in from the north and west. Get tankers in the air and rotate them to keep refueling capability going. I'm assuming the more missiles we shoot at a hypersonic weapon, the better the odds?"

"Theoretically, that makes sense. We are entering

virgin territory here. No one has had to think through these issues."

"So we defend the homeland and continue the attack in Mauritania. We launch a nuclear missile from one of our Pacific-based subs into the outskirts of Beijing. The Chinese understand an eye for an eye. We turn on the full support to Garrett and his team if they survive. Open the pipes and give them a heads-up. They have to be out of there in no less than an hour, probably much sooner."

Campbell was decisive and direct, what she was known for as governor and in business.

"Yes, ma'am."

She looked back at the muted television above her desk.

"And Bertrand, say a prayer for our country."

36

I HAVE YOUR TEAM, and my sword is sharp.

Sanson's words echoed in my mind, haunting me as I held Sally McCool's still body. The grief was immeasurable. I laid her on the ground and knelt, saying a quick prayer. I barely had the energy to lean over her. As I did so, a light breeze brushed my face.

Random gunfire popped near the objective. The stadium lights shone brightly, like a Texas high school football game in the desert. Helicopters chopped in the distance. Drones buzzed overhead, and maybe even a few fighter jets circled. The sounds of the battlefield were close. The air smelled of spent gunpowder. My body was numb from the weary days and nights of this final mission. I had shed the garments that accompanied my nom de guerre and knelt there chilled in my olive cargo pants and black polypropylene long-sleeved T-shirt. My mind was blank as I stared into McCool's face.

I have your team, and my sword is sharp.

I leaned back into the shale. Malik watched me from ten meters away opposite McCool's body. I placed a hand on McCool's warm forehead and slid it across her eyes, closing them. Why had God taken this woman in the prime of her life? A woman who had protected me, defended me, and followed me. She was the epitome of everything right with the United States. Independent, strong, driven, self-sufficient, and brave, McCool was a hero to our country. To lose her now was incalculable.

Melissa's voice crept into my head, saying, "Good wins," as she so frequently did. Though as much as I loved Melissa and kept her memory close, there was no way I could reconcile the concept of good winning anything with the reality of McCool's inert body next to me. I don't remember how long I cradled her face, straightened her uniform, and brushed the matted hair from her eyes. It could have been thirty seconds or ten minutes. It was all I could do to keep my mind from tumbling over the waterfall of despair. Melissa. Sly. Mc-Cool. How many more names? At what cost? Was any of this worth it? Did anyone truly care?

It took every bit of self-discipline to stop the negative thoughts. To prevent my emotions from controlling my actions. I had to regain my composure because we still had a mission to complete. Instead of dwelling on McCool, I tried to think of how we got to this point. We had to have been compromised.

If Van Dreeves had hacked the presidential Alexa system, it was certainly possible for either McHenry's or Blankenship's minions to reverse hack and follow the source. And then provide that to Sanson? Clearly, Sanson was on our virtual private network, which meant he had to have captured at least one of my team or he had been given the information.

I thought of the decades of operations we had conducted. Hobart with his quiet confidence. Van Dreeves and his surfer-boy flair and flashy grin. McCool with her earnest determination. And me, lucky to have been associated with them. It started out like a penny dropped into a cone. My anger grew with each successive rotation until it was cycling faster and faster. My heart was a war drum in my chest. My arms and chest flexed with adrenaline. My eyes focused on the lights a half mile away.

The noise behind me reminded me that Malik was still here. I turned to him, and he cowered, hands bound to his front and gag over his mouth. I grabbed him by his shirt and said, "I'm going to untie you. You watch over her. If I don't come back, your mission is to get her body to the American base in Dakhla. Do you understand?"

Malik nodded weakly.

I grabbed his chin with my trembling hand. "Do you understand?!" I shouted. "Show me you understand!"

He braced and vigorously nodded in affirmation. I removed the gag from his mouth, and he sputtered, "*Je comprends! Je comprends!*"

Using my knife, I cut the ropes around his wrists. I handed him McCool's officer pistol and said, "If you fail, you should use this on yourself instead of facing me."

"*Oui! Je comprends!*"

I checked my rifle and pistol. Put my knife in the sheath. Took a long drag of water from my CamelBak. Wanted to try to communicate with my team but knew I would only be speaking with Sanson.

I started walking, then slowly picked up my pace as the rage fueled my full-on sprint toward the objective area. The land was uneven, riddled with rocks, some of which I leaped over like an Olympic hurdler. I was one with the wind, fueled by the memories of so many missions filled with teamwork, jokes, tough calls, wounds, and death. The sacrifice. It always seemed worth it in the moment. It was only afterward, when we were home again, watching the political back-and-forth, that made us wonder. Could a small percentage of the population continue to protect the American ideal when it was under assault from within? Would there be anything left to defend? None of that mattered. Soldiers fight for each other. We may have been on a mission that the president of the United States had asked me to do, but ultimately, we were there for each other.

And that was all that mattered.

I shouted into the night, my voice floating away like mist. I saw Sanson standing in the middle of the lights. He was holding Joe Hobart by the collar. Randy Van Dreeves was kneeling at Sanson's feet, chin on his chest.

Hobart went to his knees. Both he and Van Dreeves had their hands tied behind their backs. Sanson stepped back and drew his saber. I was close enough to hear the metallic clink of the blade sliding against the scabbard. The Chinese infantry was focused on recovering the bodies from the tunnel nearly a quarter mile to the south. This back entrance to the terminal guidance location was surprisingly undefended.

With the cool desert wind in my face, I thought through what I hadn't seen, which was Zoey, Farouk, and Champollion. Were they dead? Alive? If so, where?

About fifty meters from Sanson, he noticed my movement. I raised my rifle and aimed. He shouted, "Stop! Or I kill them now!"

I continued sprinting. I didn't want to shoot just yet, concerned that an errant shot could kill either Hobart or Van Dreeves. Muzzle flashes to my right front indicated a probable Chinese sniper lying atop one of the containers was firing at me, my speed making for a difficult target.

"Take me!" I shouted. "Let them go and take me!"

Sanson stepped back and drew his sword high. There was a hitch in his movement. Maybe Champollion's gunshot that stopped him from killing Zoey?

I was maybe twenty meters from him now. Hobart and Van Dreeves both rolled away as the blade coursed through the air. Sanson's momentum exposed his right side to me. I ditched my rifle in the direction that Hobart and Van Dreeves had rolled and plowed into Sanson with the full force of a half-mile sprint. While a quick shot to kill Sanson might have worked, it wasn't worth the risk of a stray round to either of my two men. Plus, the intensely personal nature of what he had done to Sly and McCool merited a close encounter with him. Total rage enveloped me. I was a wild animal tearing at the methodical executioner.

Sanson's saber tumbled high into the sky, and for a moment, I was concerned it would stick either Hobart or Van Dreeves. It was close, but Hobart was quick to put the blade to use to cut his ties. Meanwhile, I rolled with Sanson and pulled my knife from its sheath. Sanson punched me in the ribs twice as I lashed at him with the blade. His fists were like wrecking balls, large and forceful. He spun away and stood, keeping a distance as he wiped blood from his eyes and face. My knife had connected with his right cheek, which was oozing a steady stream of blood. Sanson smiled a grisly red-toothed grin.

"Sinclair," he spat, circling with me. Behind me, boots scuffled. Weapons ratcheted. Shots fired. I hoped Van Dreeves or Hobart had found some use for my dropped rifle.

Sanson lunged for me with his big arms and barrel chest embracing me tightly, pinning my arms against my side and rendering the knife nearly useless. I flicked my wrist, angling the knife toward his leg. It caught flesh a couple of times, but that didn't seem to bother Sanson. He was an inch taller than I was and immeasurably more powerful with his slick frame. I was rangy, which made me a good shortstop. He was more of a powerlifter or shot-putter with breathtaking quickness.

Gunfire erupted nearby, causing Sanson to flinch, which gave me time to push away and see that Hobart and Van Dreeves were back-to-back, with Hobart holding the M4 carbine and Van Dreeves with an AK-47 he picked up off the dead Chinese soldier that had just attempted to penetrate their position.

Maybe ten Chinese soldiers had returned from the tunnel and were watching, attempting to determine what was happening. My two soldiers took up firing positions to eliminate that threat.

I needed them to continue their mission, though.

"I've got Sanson," I said.

Sanson was a leering beast ready to rip me to shreds. His neck muscles flared like a cobra hood. His arm and chest muscles rippled beneath his torn, linen shirt. His scabbard belt was cinched tight around his narrow waist. His forearms flexed as he gripped and ungripped his fists.

"You are surrounded by a thousand soldiers, Sinclair. There's no stopping what is happening."

I wasn't in the mood for a lengthy conversation, nor did I believe he was. His purpose now had to be to stall until reinforcements could arrive on the scene. His eyes flicked to the left as Hobart and Van Dreeves walked tactically back-to-back, spinning in every direction to maintain 360-degree situational awareness.

I needed to give Hobart and Van Dreeves the time to

accomplish their mission. As I circled with Sanson like two collegiate wrestlers, my earpiece crackled to life. The static made the words nearly unintelligible.

"Dagger Six?" someone said.

"Go," I whispered while holding Sanson's murderous glower.

"This is Falcon Six. ETA seven minutes."

I racked my mind for the call sign Falcon Six, and when Sanson lunged at me, I remembered it was the moniker for Lieutenant Colonel Jeremy West, the air force special operations pilot that flew everything from C-17 cargo airplanes to MH-60 Black Hawk helicopters.

"Roger. Hot objective."

"Roger. B2 inbound with MOAB. Five minutes ETA."

A MOAB was the "Mother of All Bombs." The closest thing to being a nuclear weapon without actually being a nuclear weapon. We couldn't complete our mission in five minutes, much less get out of the blast radius.

I parried Sanson's lunge using my training and instincts while my mind was elsewhere thinking about Hobart and Van Dreeves, McCool's body, and my team on the Mole, if indeed that was where they still were.

No one would be safe. I tumbled with Sanson, rolling and punching his bleeding arm while avoiding his wrecking-ball fists the best I could. The more I occupied Sanson, the better chance Van Dreeves and Hobart had to finish their task. I was distracted, though. I wondered why President Campbell would order an air strike on a location she knew I inhabited. And why would West be flying into the eye of the bombing target?

Campbell's wink and a nod for me to do this one last mission off the books. Her comment that she couldn't trust anyone but me, and since I was retiring, I should do this heroic gesture to save America from the throes of communism.

Kim Campbell had always played her cards close to her vest, usually to her benefit. This time, however, she may have been a shade too coy.

Sanson was on top of me.

My earpiece burst with Hobart's voice.

"Fire in the hole!"

A series of explosions moved the earth beneath me, dislodging Sanson's death grip on my neck. Successive thunderous booms filled the night. Fire sucked the oxygen out of the air. A moment of suffocation made me wonder if the MOAB hadn't been released. Shrapnel and litter rained down like summer hail, and metal scraps from the containers sang through the air like ninja stars.

I plunged the knife into Sanson's side, penetrating muscle. Sanson yelped, clasped his abdomen, and rolled off me. In the process, I sliced his hand as he attempted to grab my knife. Sanson stumbled away, avoided my arcing blade as I surged toward him. Surprisingly quick for a wounded big man, Sanson ran behind the undamaged containers on the south end of the base camp.

I scrambled to the north where Hobart and Van Dreeves were crawling out from a trench. They surveyed their work, which looked decent to me.

"Four damaged, one still operational," Van Dreeves said.

We dashed toward the bunker that was untouched by the explosives.

"Dud fuse," Hobart said.

"Reset?"

"Out," Hobart replied.

"I'm getting Chinese commands over this radio," Van

Dreeves said. "What was the word Champollion told us to listen for?"

"*Fāshè,*" I said. "Or *lancement* in French."

Van Dreeves held the speaker from the radio to my ear, where a harsh command voice was shouting, "*Fāshè! Fāshè!*"

We stacked against the wall of the container. Van Dreeves used a pair of bolt cutters to snap the lock. Hobart opened the door. Automatic rifle fire spat at us from both sides, pinging against the metal walls. Hobart and Van Dreeves poured fire into the container while I shot the two guards protecting the operator, who I thought we might want to keep alive. A small mound of bodies was stacked fifty meters away where Chinese infantry continued to pour around the corner. Hobart and Van Dreeves had covered positions from which to defend.

"Randy, need you," I said into the throat microphone.

"Roger," he replied.

Hobart adjusted his position to the top of the container, where he could plink in all directions. Van Dreeves knelt next to the terrified Chinese operator, who stared straight ahead at the large monitor. The eighty-inch screen showed a hypersonic glide vehicle being released from orbit and tilting toward the earth's atmosphere. An arcing green line blinked on the map connecting the glide vehicle to a path that terminated in New York City. A straight red line that originated at our location on the map was connected to the nose of the glide vehicle image on the monitor.

I assumed the red line connected the satellite dish and laser sitting above us with the glide vehicle entering the atmosphere. I had no idea whether the glide vehicle would stay on course once guided onto the target

and the laser disappeared. Our only option was to steer
the glide vehicle away from New York City.

Without warning, three other glide vehicles appeared
on the screen behind the lead aircraft in an inverted V,
like fighter jets in attack formation. Did they all follow
the leader? Four nukes headed for New York City? Or
would they disperse to other targets at a certain point?

"Speak English?" Van Dreeves barked at the catatonic operator sitting at the controls.

The baby-faced soldier reached beneath his seat and
retrieved a pistol, and before I could pull the trigger
on my weapon, he stuck the barrel under his chin and
squeezed the trigger.

"I'll take that as a no," Van Dreeves said, blood spatter on his face.

"Figure this thing out. Maybe a minute," I said. "Five
nukes, including the Loudoun County one, just like Sly
said."

Sly had laid out the plan from the files he had retrieved in Dakhla. Senior U.S. officials involved. Five
hypersonic glide vehicles laden with nuclear weapons
to be used as leverage to compel the U.S. to join the
CUSP.

We dumped the operator's body on the floor of the
container, and Van Dreeves sat down. Above, Hobart
continued to fire.

"Still coming," he said. "Hurry up in there."

"This controls the laser," Van Dreeves said after
thirty seconds of playing with the joystick. He turned
it to the right a hair, and the lead aircraft didn't move.

"Is there a manual override? Maybe it's like autopi-
lot?" I asked.

His eyes darted around the dashboard that was as
confusing as any aircraft cockpit. All the writing was

in Chinese characters. A lone toggle switch to the right responded when Van Dreeves reached for it and flipped it up.

Red numbers flashed on the screen.

0:20, 0:19, 0:18 . . .

"No time," I said.

The globe on the monitor spun from a wide field of view to a zoomed panorama of the five boroughs of New York City. The Verrazzano Bridge. The One World Trade Center. The Brooklyn Bridge. The George Washington Bridge. The Empire State Building. The Statue of Liberty. Big orange circles appeared on the screen, flashing around the Financial District, the LaGuardia Airport, Midtown, and Harlem. The glide vehicles had cameras in them, all projecting back a similar series of images.

Four nukes.

New York City top to bottom and left to right. This was an annihilation strike.

Four nukes.

All barreling down on the most populated city in the country. Eight and a half million people. A significant chunk of the cultural and economic center of the country. Theater, television, music, rich, poor, Yankees, Knicks, Wall Street, hedge funds, Central Park, Harlem, Queens.

"Boss," Van Dreeves said. He was in a rhythm now, pushing a dial with one hand and turning the joystick with another.

The lead aircraft started turning slightly. They were moving at Mach five, and there was no such thing as a subtle move. The camera pictures jerked on the monitor, pulled up to where the gothic architecture of West Point blipped by on the screen. Then suddenly Boston's Faneuil Hall, and then nothing but ocean.

The trails on the monitor showed Van Dreeves had maneuvered the glide vehicles in an arc away from the United States across the Atlantic Ocean over Bermuda with its pink hotels and turquoise reefs as they hurtled toward the Chinese fishing fleet off the coast of Mauritania . . . all in a matter of seconds.

The glide vehicles splashed into the ocean and detonated, sending mushroom clouds of water into the sky. Fishing boats flipped into the air, propelled by water jets pushing off the bottom of the ocean.

The monitor switched to an overhead satellite that I presumed was programmed to conduct battle damage assessment for the Chinese high command. That no one in Beijing had been able to override Van Dreeves's last-second diversion was nothing short of amazing.

We looked at each other when Hobart said, "Need help."

With nothing left to do inside the command center, I said, "Coming out."

"Careful to the south. Ten bogies still."

Van Dreeves and I spun out of the container with Hobart providing overhead cover. We killed or wounded enough of them to rejoin on the north side of the command center. Hobart tossed a thermite grenade inside as we scurried through the wreckage of the other satellite laser containers.

"All good?" I asked, looking Hobart in the eyes.

"Think so. Heard the bomber is coming in. We maybe have two minutes to haul ass."

Just then, West said into our earpieces, "Go north of the explosion by one hundred meters. I'm here and taking fire. We have maybe one minute."

I said, "Follow me," to my two men, and we ran toward Malik and McCool, who were right where I'd left them. The Chinese infantry was doing their best to stop us from linking up with West. Van Dreeves picked up McCool, and I heard him saying, "Come on, baby. Come on, baby. Be with us. Be with us." He cradled her like a bride across a threshold, which might have been one day but now was never going to happen.

West was circling the helicopter low in acrobatic fashion to avoid the machine-gun fire that was echoing across the desert floor. Green and red tracers crisscrossed like a light show, some sparking off the Beast's fuselage as West landed it roughly on the shale. When we piled in, there was only Wang and Brown in the helicopter manning the crew hatches while Suarez and West were at the controls. My heart was breaking for Van Dreeves.

"Go, go, go!" West was shouting. "Thirty seconds to TOT."

The time on target of the MOAB was a scant half minute away. We gingerly placed McCool on the floor of the helicopter and then clambered inside. We snapped everyone into safety cables on the floor using mesh special operations rappelling vests. The cargo doors were open so that we could return fire. Malik was huddled in the corner, eyes wide with fear, hands clutching the yellow static line snapped into his vest. Hobart was firing his weapon at the Chinese infantry running toward the helicopter. Van Dreeves cinched two yellow straps over McCool's body and was huddled over her, holding her, praying, and perhaps weeping.

Tracers arced toward the helicopter, which West was flying nap of the earth at max limits.

"Hit," Hobart said. "Bad." He was holding his left shoulder leaning against the command-and-control suite. His eyes were weak, like dimming light bulbs.

"Hang on, Joe," I whispered.

West roared the two T700 engines at max shaft

horsepower as he rocketed forward. He banked north toward the Mole when I shouted, "Get the others at the rally point!"

"They're not there, Garrett," he said solemnly into the headset.

We lurched high into the sky, spinning wildly, as the MOAB detonated beneath and behind us.

37

BY NOW, THE PRESIDENT had a Global Hawk over the Chinese terminal guidance location.

From her vantage point watching the video on the monitor in her Air Force One office, the MOAB appeared to obliterate the entire operation. DNI Bertrand was next to her, eyes glued to the screen. NSA Kidman and CJCS Rolfing were sitting opposite them and watching, as well.

"Assessment? Threat neutralized?" she asked Bertrand.

"Too soon to tell. Looks like it was a direct hit. Our coordinates were good."

"How were we so precise?" Her voice was cool. Asking a question to which she already knew the answer.

"General Sinclair found the Chinese rapid deployment site for the GLINTS. We have been tracking his communications, and therefore we know his location."

"Who knows of our tracking his communications?" She looked at the three cabinet members seated in her office.

Rolfing, Bertrand, and Kidman all raised their hands.

"Blankenship?"

"Yes, ma'am," Rolfing said. "We discussed it."

"Please bring her in here," she said to Kidman. Then she turned to Bertrand and asked, "Where are we, Koby?"

"We are over the Atlantic, ma'am. Safest place to be," he said.

"Where are we going?"

"We have several options. We've refueled in the air twice and may have to a third time. Once we have clarity on the hypersonic targeting system battle damage assessment, we will choose a landing place and head there."

"Casualty counts in Virginia?"

"Approaching ten thousand killed and wounded. Officially now over four thousand dead. Have surpassed 9/11."

"Emergency response?"

"FEMA is on location. It's a radiation field. They've confirmed it was a nuclear device, so everything is infinitely harder. The virus challenged us in protective equipment, and I suspect we'll run into the same challenges here. We talk a good game about preparation, but we rarely are ever prepared for these unthinkable scenarios. DHS turned down a contract for millions of doses of Captura's anti-radiation chelation powder, but thankfully they had some stockpiled."

"Military? Police? Hospitals?"

"National guard is leading the effort with the chembio units. The army is deploying two MASH units. The navy is sending the *Mercy* up the Chesapeake Bay from Norfolk and into the Potomac River to dock at Fort Belvoir to handle overflow and capacity issues. The Virginia emergency management team is on the ground with FEMA. Everything is very preliminary, but given the footprint of this thing, it looks like it was a variant of the JL-3 prototype they are developing for their hypersonic glide vehicle fleet. It ranges up to one megaton. By comparison, Nagasaki was twenty-one kilotons. So, fifty Nagasaki-like effects in one glide vehicle."

"Status of our preparations for retaliatory strike?"

Bertrand paused and then said, "General Rolfing would better answer that."

"Ma'am, we have two boomers in the Pacific ready to launch. Each carries somewhere in the neighborhood of two dozen SLBMs. Our silos are fully manned. Our aircraft are ready. Your directed-strike mission, as you can see, was successful, we believe. We're still doing BDA."

"I want to know if we have any American casualties the minute we get any kind of confirmation. Are we getting boots on the ground? And I want to know the status of the Chinese ICBMs. We need to walk *and* chew gum here."

"I have SEAL Team Six in an airplane right now ready to go if you order it. They work for General Sinclair, anyway. They will be proud to do this mission. My only question, ma'am, is why didn't we start with them instead of sending the general in to do this with a small team?" Rolfing asked.

"Because, General, I obviously couldn't trust my cabinet, and I'm left to wonder if I can trust anyone."

"Yes, ma'am," Rolfing said, looking at Bertrand, who was shaking his head as if to warn off the general from what he might say next.

Kidman stuck his head in the door and said, "We can't find Blankenship on the plane!"

38

THE BEAST LOST CONTROL and was plummeting
to the earth. The shock wave of the MOAB had created
a three-football-field-wide blast zone, violently disrupting the air for at least a mile.

West had done all he could to speed away from the
explosion, but that nagging dilemma of mission and men
refused to overlap sufficiently for any sort of luck to happen. Because the doors were open, we were hanging on
to anything that was secure, our nylon tethers straining
against their anchor points. Even Malik was strapped in
and now flying feet-first out of the cargo bay door as we
spiraled out of control.

The piercing whine indicated that the pitch of the helicopter blades changed. My shoulders were about to
give out as I strained against the stanchion that housed
the command-and-control suite. I caught a glimpse of
West in the cockpit, and his head was thrashing violently as he kept his hands on the controls. Suarez's
helmet was banging against the plexiglass windscreen.
The sense of uncontrolled lift, like a rocket blasting off
with abandon, was overwhelming. Stomach in throat
and then a loss of all equilibrium.

Then, what was a near-flat spin into the skies

suddenly seemed manageable. The sensation of utter reckless abandon, the sheer terror of violently thrashing and falling through the air, was replaced by a consciousness that we were either moments before impact or the machine in which we were hurtling was under some modicum of control.

It was the latter.

"I've got it," West said over the headset.

"Me, too," Suarez said.

"I have the controls," West directed.

"You have the controls," Suarez assented.

The aircraft wobbled and fought against the debris field in the air but seemed to break free of the raging turbulence that was vibrating over the landscape.

"Smooth air," West said.

"Smooth air," Suarez confirmed.

"Status in the back?" West asked.

"Stand by," I muttered.

Van Dreeves was huddled over McCool still. He had snapped his harness in with hers so that if either of them was thrown from the aircraft, they would go together. And if we burned in, he would be side by side with her for eternity.

Hobart was clasped forearm to forearm with Malik, whose only lifeline was my wounded operator, who was hauling in the caravan leader after being slung around like a towed jumper in the turbulence. He was lucky to be alive. Hobart laid Malik's body on the floor next to me. Hobart grimaced as he checked Malik's head wounds. His eyes were open, though, darting around, perhaps wondering where he might be or what was happening.

Wang and Black were strapped into their respective stations, hands on their machine guns, ready to take on whatever may come our way.

"Still here," I replied to West.

"Headed to the Mole for one final check," he said.

We circled north of the MOAB debris field, which in total was a half mile in diameter, maybe more. Dust hung above the desert surface in a thin cloud, like morning fog in San Diego. I laid Hobart down, saying, "Let me check you out."

His eyes were weak. Van Dreeves lifted his head and looked over at us, his face grief-stricken, understanding that this was perhaps the last of us. I slid an IV into Hobart's arm as I used scissors in my aid kit to cut away his shirt. He had taken a 7.62 mm round to his back, directly in the right scapula. The brass was lying against the white bone, having most likely ricocheted to diffuse some of its energy, probably saving Hobart's life. I poured alcohol on the wound and patched it as best I could in the chattering airframe. I pushed gauze into the wound and taped it in place.

Landing on the backside of the Mole, I leaped out and ran into the cave we had used as our rally point. Empty combat ration wrappers and water bottles littered the floor. The burned eucalyptus still smoldered. Shell casings were everywhere.

Farouk, Zoey, and Champollion were nowhere to be found. There had been a fight here. Bloodstains marked the walls of the cave. There were two straight lines in the dirt. Someone had been dragged from the cave. Sanson or his henchmen had been in here and had taken someone.

I followed the tracks out of the cave and down the backside of the ridge. We hadn't spent much time studying the entire terrain feature, which was a mile in circumference, at least. We had inhabited the center and highest peak, but there were other lower peaks that cascaded away on either side.

After counting my pace to two hundred meters, the body of a man I recognized was lying inert on the ground. A second man was moaning, but not long for this world. They were a few of the men who had been sitting off to themselves during Malik's briefing. Security for Sanson. They had attacked the Mole, and Zoey and team had fended them off from this second cave.

Inside this shallow depression was Zoey, who was holding Farouk, rocking him as if he were a baby. She was lost in her thoughts, whispering, "Don't die, don't die, don't die."

"Zoey," I said.

She startled and snatched her pistol with a shaky hand.

"It's me, Garrett Sinclair."

Her eyes were wild. Teeth bared. The gun wobbled. Farouk's head was in her lap, half-missing.

"Fucking animals," she spat.

I knelt next to her and removed the pistol. She was in shock. Farouk was dead. His head was torn apart by a large-caliber bullet or piece of shrapnel. Zoey was sobbing. I took her hand and lifted her away from Farouk's body.

"Jeremy, need some help here," I said. "Send Wang and Black." Then to Zoey, I said, "Evelyn?"

"They took her. The monsters took her."

"How many?" I asked.

"Two dead out there and two others. They put her in a helicopter. Big men."

A minute later, Wang and Black were carrying Farouk's body back to the helicopter while I cradled Zoey in my arms, her head tucked into my shoulder, her body heaving.

We loaded into the Beast and secured everyone to the safety harness. I saw an IV drip set up above Sally

McCool, followed the dripline into her arm, and looked up at Van Dreeves. Finally able to focus on her mortal condition and unable to accept reality, he was frantically pushing on her chest. Checked the IV drip. Felt her for a pulse. Held his head to her ear. As the aircraft took off for Dakhla, Van Dreeves shouted, "No!"

Then he looked at me with mournful eyes, pleading for me to change what had happened. To take us back in time.

But the truth of the matter was that Sally McCool was dead.

39

AFTER A STOP IN Chinguetti and another remote, unnamed airfield for fuel, we landed at the hangar in Dakhla, where everything had started a couple of weeks ago with the mission to retrieve the hostage Stockton. The darkness was beginning to ebb, the slightest hint of gray in the eastern horizon across the gulf toward the mainland of Mauritania.

As we approached, I had used Farouk's radio to call ahead to General Atouk, the Moroccan area commander who had responsibility for the airfield. I gave him the status of my team and requested medical assistance. I still didn't know who I could trust in the U.S. government because Sly's notes didn't end with this action to nuke New York City with hypersonic glide vehicles. The endgame was much more sinister.

We had flown low across the ocean and circled back in from the northwest when Colonel West landed the Beast with a roll in front of the open hangar doors. Once inside, Moroccan soldiers slammed the hangar doors shut. Atouk was standing there waiting for us in his plain green uniform with red epaulets.

When I greeted him, I said, "I'm sorry about Farouk."

"Yes. Me, too. And I am sorry about your pilot," General Farzad Atouk said. He was the commander of the Dakhla Peninsula Moroccan forces and responsible for the airfield we had used many times previously. He was a short man with a round belly, a thick black mustache, and typically a jovial attitude, dampened today only by the sight of my men and his soldier, Farouk. I felt bad for having involved him in our mission, but he had proven to be an invaluable asset.

"Incalculable loss," I said. I was operating on fumes and blocking, blocking, blocking the overwhelming grief.

"He was my best soldier," Atouk said.

"As she was mine," I said.

His eyes cast downward. "It seems we are brothers in loss. I am close to Farouk's family. I gave you my best support. He respected you and your team, and there is something much bigger here."

"What's that?"

"The Chinese. They are at the opposite end of the runway in a hangar with a small force and maybe thirty soldiers, with two trucks. The French have already come into town with a high-level delegation. Lots of cars, lots of soldiers."

"Thanks," I said, though I was not sure what to make of the information. I got to the business at hand and helped to ferry our wounded into the backs of ambulances that were parked inside the hangar nose-first against the wall. Atouk had done us right. Each was like a separate operating room with a doctor and a nurse. Hobart went first. Then Zoey just for observation and to clean up her previous wounds. Then Malik.

A doctor pronounced Farouk dead as he lay in the back of the helicopter and hurried a team over to prepare his body for processing to his family.

Then he fought past Van Dreeves, who was holding

McCool in the corner of the hangar, lightly brushing her hair. The doctor argued with Van Dreeves for a minute and then pronounced McCool dead.

Van Dreeves continued to hold her, lie with her, until he couldn't take it any longer. He walked over to me and stared hard for a few minutes. It was impossible to tell what he was thinking. Tears, mud, and bloodstains streaked his face. He was the most naturally light-hearted person I knew. He acted throughout his life as if there was nothing that could ever go wrong—and, up until this point, nothing major had. He had chosen to love Sally, and their love was unrequited in many ways, especially now.

Perhaps he blamed me for not keeping her alive, but he knew better than that. More likely, he blamed himself, and that was my concern. I stepped toward him and put my arm around his shoulder, pulled him with me until we were outside. The rising sun was peeking over the Sea of Dakhla as we kept walking to the water's edge. We sat down on some rocks and watched the ocean churn. A storm was brewing in the west, and it wouldn't be long before waves were lashing this bulwark.

"She's gone, sir," Van Dreeves said.

"I know, Randy."

I pulled him tight into my side and held his head against my chest. He was a shattered soul. It would have been bad enough if she were just a teammate, but of course she was so much more than that to him.

Zoey's words rang in my mind: *You're in the wrong business, then, General. All sorts of "this" is going to happen and has been happening . . .*

Van Dreeves sobbed and held me tightly. Soldiers become brittle from too much operations tempo. Our psyches become enmeshed with our missions and brothers and sisters in arms. Losing a foxhole buddy was normally enough to send a good soldier to the psych ward. Losing a soul mate and lover was something I had experienced with the death of Melissa less than two years ago. I think Randy understood that. I interpreted his tight grip as an attempt to channel whatever wisdom I had developed from coping with loss. The bad news was it just sucked every day. There was no replacement for true love. You found happiness where you could. The soldier's burden was that they saw the brutality of killing and knew what their buddies and loved ones endured. McCool had suffered. She had hung on, and I had believed she would survive but knew it would be close.

The lack of support from higher headquarters. The need to do this mission off the books very well may have killed her, while at the same time we might all be dead if we had revealed our hand. As it was, cabinet officials had outed us to Gambeau and Sanson, ruining our surprise.

If not for that, we had a chance.

"Jesus," Van Dreeves muttered.

After fifteen minutes, he went limp and lay back against the sand.

"There's nothing that will make it go away, but killing Sanson will make you forget about it for a minute."

Van Dreeves looked at me and nodded. "Let's go," he said.

We had a mission to execute, and despite my own incapacitating grief, I had to rally my troops. With Van Dreeves blocking it out as best he could and my charges tended to, I walked back into the hangar, where Colonel West was lighting up a bent cigarette. He stepped outside, nodded at me, inhaled deeply, exhaled an audible sigh, which maybe it was, and looked at me with intelligent eyes.

"That shit was insane, Garrett," he said. When you've been on enough objectives the following morning to see the sun come up, you lose pretense. I was just Garrett Sinclair, and he was just Jeremy West. Rank didn't matter. Two humans who had survived the impossible. He had saved us, and my team had saved New York City. Another day at the office. But even I had to admit that riding the cresting wave of a MOAB blast radius into the sky and then free-falling until the most talented pilot in the inventory was able to stabilize the machine in the air was, as Jeremy put it, "insane."

"No other word for it," I said.

"Sorry about Sally. She would have been a ten-star general."

"At least that." I grabbed his cigarette and took a long pull. I hadn't smoked a cigar or cigarette in forever, but I needed to punish myself. The hot smoke burned my lungs. I held it and then spit it out in a cough of smoke.

"Jesus, Garrett, this isn't weed."

I shrugged, feeling stupid. We stood in the morning chill, the sun rising above the Sea of Dakhla. I was still thinking about Sally and Randy Van Dreeves. They would have had beautiful, athletic children. That thought brought another wave of crushing guilt.

I was soon distracted by some activity across the runway. A tricolored French flag flew on the hood of one of the black limousines. At the very south of the runway was some minor activity—a few soldiers in olive uniforms milling around—that would not have appeared unusual if Atouk had not informed me of Chinese military on the premises. Beyond the soldiers, on the horizon to the south, was a large, lumbering airplane headed toward the runway.

Jeremy blew out a long puff of smoke, squinted, and

said, "If I weren't high on adrenaline, I would bet a pay-check that plane is Air Force One."

The closer the aircraft came, the more convinced I was that he was correct. Why would the president be landing here? I understood that she had to relocate from Washington, D.C., given the hypersonic glide vehicle threat posed by China. But why land here on the Dakhla Peninsula? Then the rest of Sly's discovery made complete sense.

We walked inside and moved over to a window to watch the presidential aircraft touch down.

"Think she's on it?" he asked me.

"Most likely. It's not like that airplane goes anywhere without her," I said.

The plane lumbered onto the runway, smoke boiling from the rubber tires burning onto the cement. It taxied quickly to the opposite end of the runway, where a convoy of khaki-colored cargo trucks and Chinese WZ-551 fighting vehicles burst from a large hangar similar to ours.

I turned to General Atouk and asked, "Does anyone else know we're here?"

He shook his head. "This is a special operations hangar. No one knows what happens here."

"Keep it that way."

INSIDE THE OFFICE of Air Force One, President Campbell looked at the chairman of the Joint Chiefs of Staff, General Rolfing, and her director of national intelligence, Koby Bertrand. Also seated across from her were her chief of staff, Quad Jordan, and her national security advisor, Benito Kidman.

"Can you give me an update, Koby?"

Instead, Rolfing spoke. "The bomb struck the nerve

center of the Chinese operation to guide the hypersonic glide vehicles into precise targets. As such, the weaponized aircraft struck randomly in the Atlantic Ocean, clear of any U.S. interests."

"But didn't they land in the ocean prior to the bomb landing in the desert?" Campbell asked.

"It's sort of a photo finish. We believe that the operator could hear or feel the MOAB coming in and tried to run," Rolfing said.

"I know what I saw, General," Campbell said. "And I'm unclear why I'm being bullshitted."

"Pardon me, ma'am, but no one is bullshitting you. Given that the country is under attack, it's our belief that we have to manage the situation, which includes managing you."

Campbell snapped her head up and looked out the window. "Where are we landing?" she asked.

"Morocco. Dakhla, to be specific," General Rolfing said.

"Why here?" She looked at Bertrand, who looked away. "We've avoided more nuclear strikes, Koby. I want to go back."

"Ma'am, I'm afraid that's not possible," the chairman said. "It's much too dangerous there."

"And safer here? Where all this began?"

"We've requested negotiations with the Chinese, ma'am," Rolfing said.

"Who is 'we'?"

"Your team, ma'am."

"You made decisions for me?"

"We're making a recommendation to you," he said.

"This is a fait accompli," she said. "Done. You've brought me here under false pretenses."

"Ma'am, that's not the case at all. Both crews need to rest. You have Secretary of State McHenry already here. The rest of your national security team is here. The Secret Service has secured Secretary Blankenship, per your orders. Found her hiding in the luggage compartment below. We have coordinated for lodging at a secure estate nearby."

She looked around the room. "Who isn't in on this?" she asked.

"This is for the best, Madam President," Bertrand said.

"You, too, Koby?"

"This is for the country. It's best this way." Bertrand's glasses slipped down his nose. He pushed them up with his middle finger.

"I should fire you all . . . I will fire you all. You're all fired!" she said. The plane landed and taxied to the hangar, where two black limousines pulled forward. The door opened. The steps drove up to the door. The engines wound down. Military vehicles surrounded the airplane. Soldiers ran back and forth, diligently doing their business.

"Let's go, ma'am. The airplane is a huge target."

"I'm not going anywhere," Campbell said. "You can go."

Two Secret Service beasts appeared at the door. General Rolfing said, "We need to go, ma'am."

"This is a coup, General?"

"I'm as surprised as you are. My job right now is to protect you and make sure this delegation is safe."

"We all agree with the general. The nation is under attack. Landing here on the African continent is seen as a safe space," Chief of Staff Jordan said.

"I don't need a safe space, Quad. I need a platform to speak with the American people."

"You'll have that platform here, ma'am," Rolfing said. "This is the best place for now. For all of us. We've made all the arrangements. You have a full communications suite."

"You're kidnapping the president of the United States?"

"Nothing of the sort, ma'am. You do need to come with us, though."

The two Secret Service hulks came and stood on either side of her. One said, "Let's go, ma'am. This is dangerous. Our duty is to protect you."

With that, she stood. The two agents grasped her arms and guided her into the hallway of Air Force One and began descending the steps into the orange hues of a Moroccan sunrise. She was escorted into the back of a limousine.

As it pulled away with the security detail, two red Chinese flags popped up on the front fenders near the headlights.

40

AS PRESIDENT CAMPBELL, FLANKED by two Secret Service detailees, descended the steps and sped away in a Chinese limo surrounded by Chinese armored vehicles, Atouk provided us a report that Henri Sanson's Sherpa landed twenty miles across the Sea of Dakhla in El Argoub along a straight dirt road.

We were seated in the small office. Hobart was across from me. Zoey was in the chair next to him. Van Dreeves was leaning against the doorjamb, back to us, staring into the hangar in the direction of Sally's body bag.

"He's got a camp here. Knows that this airfield is crawling with French and Chinese soldiers. You disrupted his mission. That's the word from French high command," Atouk said.

"His mission to provide security and cover for the Chinese in the desert?"

"Yes. They're saying he got too carried away with finding the gold and the Atlantis myth." Atouk shrugged his round shoulders and continued, "Me? I think maybe Farouk was that good. Maybe you and your team are that good. As you say, your McCool was the best, also."

"Farouk and McCool were the best. We will honor them, General," I said.

"Honor them with deeds, not words, General. At one time, I was like Farouk. Not as good as he was, but fit and strong." He patted his round belly. "I got weak. Thought rank meant privilege when you make me realize it means just the opposite. Your McCool, no one here was as good as she was, based on what I saw."

I nodded, understanding. One of his best men had been killed. My best soldier had been killed. Grief took on many forms. One form was the guilt that made you wish you were a better leader, believing that perhaps you could have done something to save them. A better plan. A better shot. Anything that would change the mortal outcome.

General Atouk walked to the other side of the hangar, giving me some time to talk to my team. Hobart's arm was in a sling. Van Dreeves was still turned away. Zoey was sullen, almost catatonic.

"We've suffered an incalculable loss with both Sally and Farouk. I'm not a man of many words, so I won't give you many. Sally would want us to finish this mission. Farouk died in defense of his nation, as did Sally. We fight for each other, no one else. We have a president to protect, and only we can get there in time."

"Boss, Randy is hurting bad. Fuck, we all are. But Randy is almost gone," Hobart said. He was bandaged and upright, which was more than I could have hoped for a few hours ago.

"I know. I've talked to Randy." We spoke as if Van Dreeves wasn't right next to us, which I was pretty sure he wasn't. He was with McCool, mentally.

Van Dreeves dropped his head to his chest.

"First Zoey. Now Sally. What were we thinking?" Hobart said, looking away.

It was a tough shot to take from one of my men. I

deserved it, though. I had given Zoey the green light. Better said, I hadn't stopped her when she saw the yellow light. Like when approaching an intersection, she saw it as an opportunity to increase speed as opposed to exercising caution and slowing down. McCool was different. She was a soldier and knew the risks. But still.

"I'm not sure, Joe," I said.

He paused, perhaps surprised at my expression of doubt.

"Boss, we will rally. This is intensely personal right now for all of us. You've got our commitment to making this as right as it can possibly be."

I nodded. That settled it, then. We were back on task.

Atouk returned and said, "My men tell me they have information."

"Where are they taking the president?" I asked.

"There's a compound on the ocean. It's a medieval castle, barely restored except in the living area, which is quite plush. Fit for a king, as they say. And the protection is impenetrable," Atouk said.

He pointed at a close-up satellite image on the wall of our conference room in the hangar. At the tip of the peninsula was a sharp point that rose high into rocky cliffs. Tan boulders with jagged edges guarded the only road into the compound. The castle wall appeared forty feet high. In the image, huge waves crashed against the west and southwest embankments. The winter months were violent with large waves beating against the shoreline. Western Sahara was a centuries-old home to shipwrecks along its coast. The Canary Islands force more water through a narrower passage, increasing the velocity of the aptly named Canary Current, which farther to the south collides with the tropical current shooting north from the Gulf of Guinea.

Point Dakhla was an immovable fixture in the colliding seas.

"Dad was right, you know. About every fucking thing," Zoey said.

"Yes. He was. You did him proud. Took a lot of courage to do what you did," I said.

"It was the only way," she said.

"It was. As hard as it is to believe. The question now is, what do we do?"

"We finish. My dad didn't die for nothing."

"No, Zoey, he didn't. He's already saved millions of lives by preserving that intelligence."

"But we have to finish the job," she said.

"Yes, we must. The question is, though, what is the job? Is the president aware? Not aware? How do we preserve the union and prevent the logical next step of their plan?"

"Randy has the tapes," she said. "He hacked the Alexa system. Joe told me at the Mole. Look at the tapes and we can see."

I nodded and looked at Van Dreeves's back, unsure if he was able to focus on the next mission. He turned and looked at me.

"I've got it," Van Dreeves mumbled.

Van Dreeves's makeshift server farm consisted of a rack with two routers and a bunch of cables that were connected via the virtual private network to the JSOC satellite dish on the back of the hangar. The satellite dish bounced off the private satellite that JSOC leased, and that satellite beamed down to intercept President Campbell's Alexa system meant to record her conversations for historical purposes.

Van Dreeves typed a few strokes into the keyboard, made a few mistakes, reentered, messed it up again, mumbled, "Fuck me," and then finally got it right. He hit Enter, and the monitor jumped to life with an overhead view of President Campbell and her staff on Air Force One.

"You're kidnapping the president of the United States?"

"Nothing of the sort, ma'am. You do need to come with us, though."

Van Dreeves looked at me and said, "This was thirty minutes ago."

I was never clear on whether Campbell suspected that her cabinet had been infected with traitors and intended to record them for posterity or if we just got lucky with Van Dreeves's hack of the system.

Regardless, our mission became clear: save the president of the United States.

"We have to move tonight," I said.

"Boss, Farouk's dead. Sally's dead. Joe is barely alive. Zoey's a basket case from watching Farouk's head get blown off," Van Dreeves snapped.

Anger surrounded his words. He was a man unaccustomed to negative emotions, and I imagined he was struggling with what he was feeling. Sometimes the greatest comics experience the hardest falls when faced with adversity.

"We do what we can," I said. "Good wins."

"Sanson's got Champollion. The cabinet has President Campbell. And there's this," Van Dreeves said. He held up his tablet for me to see.

AWOL General's Fingerprints on Nuke Attack

Washington, D.C. (BREAKING): Unnamed intelligence sources place beleaguered U.S. Army lieutenant general Garrett Sinclair in Mauritania, Africa, at the scene of the Chinese testing facility agreed upon by the Dakhla Accords.

Reports are that Sinclair's intervention in peaceful diplomacy may have resulted in the mishap that has killed and wounded over 10,000 residents of Northern Virginia and surrounding areas. Two sources assert that Chinese officials deterred Sinclair from accidentally launching more nuclear weapons against the United States.

Sought after by the DoD inspector general Willard Ringley for last year's murder of the former secretary of state and his potential involvement in the attacks claimed to be attributed to Dariush Parizad, Sinclair is today a very much wanted man.

"It's becoming clear that there is much more to the story with General Sinclair than meets the eye. We wish he would turn himself in before he does more damage to our national security," Ringley said in what was an uncharacteristic comment from an agency that routinely declines to comment on ongoing investigations.

Potentially responsible for the accident that caused a nuclear missile to leave orbit and strike the United States, Sinclair could be facing serious charges when and if he is found. Sources state that Sinclair and his team may have been present at the peaceful Chinese testing facility located in the Mauritanian desert, where an explosion of unknown origin occurred just hours ago.

China indicated they used this remote area precisely for safety reasons and are saddened by the accident and subsequent loss of life. They promise to make amends and are meeting with U.S. leadership as this story develops.

"How do we get past this bullshit?" Van Dreeves asked. Still angry.

"All this means is that they think I'm dead. Could work to our advantage," I said.

"Here's something about Champollion. I set up an alert on her."

French Aristocrat Feared Missing

Paris (BREAKING): Evelyn Champollion, great-granddaughter of French philologist Jean-François Champollion, is rumored to have been killed in a mishap in the Mauritanian desert as she was researching the Eye of Africa and its possible connections to Plato's Atlantis.

A staunch nationalist, Champollion had fallen out of favor with the current French government as she championed secular culturalism instead of the preferred globalism of many world leaders today.

"The best way to achieve a more peaceful world is to simultaneously herald the rich cultures of all peoples while encouraging them to hang on to their identities fiercely. To abandon heritage is anathema to peaceful advancement," she once famously said at a conference highlighting the benefits of globalism.

Champollion followed in her family's rich tradition of language and cultural understanding and promotion while unfortunately also embroiling herself in politics.

I was left to wonder if Champollion hadn't struck a deal with Sanson to stay alive. She was crafty enough to position herself as someone who could help him decipher whatever remnants were found in the Eye of

Africa. Would Sanson realize that Champollion was the one who shot him? Or could she claim we had abducted her?

The French involvement was still an enigma. Was it that the French were being left out of the mix? Was Gambeau the driver of that equation? Were they hosting the event here in Morocco, evidently against Moroccan government wishes, in this disputed territory that a previous U.S. administration had told the Moroccans it was okay to annex? Because it was not recognized internationally, perhaps this was the perfect venue, and France, with their Moroccan ties, wanted in on the deal.

"Let me know when we have a plan," Van Dreeves said. He looked at Zoey and Hobart, perhaps jealous, or more likely just utterly shattered. "I need some fresh air."

I nodded at Van Dreeves. Hobart and Zoey followed him outside. I used the moment to stare at the map and think about Champollion, Gambeau, and Sanson.

If Gambeau was anything like American political appointees, he was corrupt and self-dealing. Sanson was most likely his spy on the ground for the entire operation. Champollion had used her influence to insert herself into the mix, which Sanson had either tolerated or not known about until the last second. Gambeau might have been double-dealing, as well. Champollion, the good angel, was inside the operation to report out what she saw, while Sanson, the bad angel, was in execute mode to protect the Chinese operation. Or all three could be in it with the Chinese. How did Champollion get away unscathed, if indeed she did?

The thought that continued to cycle through my mind was, because the French military operated in such depth in the Mauritania, Morocco, and Senegal region, the

Chinese would stand no chance of hiding from them. So why not co-opt them?

"Randy," I called out as he was halfway across the hangar. He came back to me, walking lethargically, slowed by the grinding pain and anguish.

"Yes?"

"Before you go, do we have any cell phones?"

"Got a batch of burners in the desk over there," he said, pointing.

"Can you set one up, please?"

He took a few minutes and then handed me a new mobile phone with a fully charged battery.

I recalled the number from memory and sent a text:

New phone

THE MYSTERY OF EVELYN Champollion notwith-
standing, my focus was on rescuing the president of the
United States from what looked like an apparent soft
coup not only by her cabinet but also by China.

Champollion had helped me escape, so there was
that. Was she with Sanson, and was Sanson static in his
position across the gulf?

Van Dreeves came back into the office after thirty
minutes outside.

"Boss, I want to apologize. It's tough—"

"Stop, Randy. You have every right to be mad at me.
As does Joe. We've been on the edge of the razor blade
here. It's my responsibility."

"She died doing what she loved with who she loved
the most," Van Dreeves said. "We should all be so lucky.
She died with purpose."

I nodded. "She did."

"I'm done feeling sorry for myself. Let's pull this
thing together."

"Okay, then. I need a boat and some drones," I said
to Van Dreeves.

"Got the drones. Let me get to work on this boat."

Van Dreeves left. The rest of the day I spent talking

with Hobart, Zoey, Wang, Black, Suarez, and West. McCool's absence was palpable. After he found the boat, Van Dreeves spent a lot of time in McCool's bay, organizing her effects for the eventual trip home; if he didn't make it, he wanted her stuff to be organized. Hobart had repositioned inside Zoey's ambulance, and he held her hand as she sat on the bunk. Wang, Black, Suarez, and West all tended to the Beast, which had taken a beating in the MOAB backblast. West had said it was feasible that the Beast could fly, if necessary but, jokingly, only with a couple of diagonal hexagonal flanges taped to the blades.

He was a funny guy, which was a welcome respite during all the loss and intensity.

The media stories snowballed, and the social media warriors had tried, convicted, and called for my head in less than five hours. Some had even staked out my home in Fayetteville and Brad's and Reagan's separate apartments in Williamsburg and Charlottesville, respectively.

I never felt the need to prove myself to anyone and certainly never believed I would have to prove my innocence to the American people. I had finished a round of chatting with my team and was seated at the desk where we had our makeshift headquarters, when the phone in my cargo pants buzzed.

I looked at the text.

Help

That was clear enough to me.

On the third round of checks on my team, they were chattier and feeling better. All were standing outside of the backs of their ambulances, comparing notes and reviewing the last seventy-two hours.

"Team," I said. "The president of the United States has asked us to help her. She's what I would call a quasi-captive, being held by her own cabinet and the Chinese military. They're trying to strong-arm her into signing phase two of the Dakhla Accords, which importantly cedes certain national authorities. It's all very technical, but the bottom line is that it is the first step toward a globalist world order, which the Dakhla Accords are calling the CUSP."

"Chinese-U.S. Partnership," Zoey muttered.

"That's right, Zoey. I have a plan that allows us to complete the mission despite our limitations. Sanson is across the gulf, rearming and upfitting for the final showdown, whatever he thinks that might be. The president is in the castle on the sea at the southern tip of the peninsula. Only one way in by way of land, and of course, three sides of the castle are protected by the ocean with forty-foot vertical walls. Chinese military and U.S. Secret Service will be guarding the entrance. Boats, I'm sure, will be patrolling the sea despite the rough waters. And there will be layers of security once inside."

"Are you trying to motivate us, boss?" Hobart said.

"Yes, is it working?"

"Well, it's distracting me," Van Dreeves said. "But I don't care if I live or die other than to protect you guys. No offense, General, but right now, it's just us against the world."

I nodded. "That's what Sally said at the Mole. Us against the world. Let's earn it for her."

"Roger that," they said in unison. "For Sally."

"My thoughts are this: Randy and I execute the castle portion of the mission. Joe and Zoey, both of you are winged, so you can stay here and command and control. Zoey, you'll be one hundred percent focused on communicating with the Moroccans, keeping them informed. Jeremy, you and the Beast team will be on standby to extract should everything go to shit, as I expect it to."

"Why I'm here," he said.

"When you're ready, I've drawn the plan on the whiteboard. I want everyone to come in and memorize, and then I'm going to erase it. We can trust no one outside of this circle."

"What about other JSOC units?" Hobart asked.

"The question would be, are they coming to help us or coming to stop us? Because it will be hard to tell, and if we're wrong, it will all be over. They don't have the insight we have or the connections. They're doing what people who have turned are telling them to do. We'll cross that bridge when and if we get to it."

"Let's get some recon out over the objectives and get to work," Van Dreeves said.

My broken and weary team limped and hobbled to their respective desks and positions. Van Dreeves dragged two Raven drones from storage beneath a tarp in the corner of the team room. After thirty minutes, he had them launched and in the air. One circled El Argoub six miles across the gulf. The other began scoping the castle, six miles away to the south.

Van Dreeves sat at a console inside the hangar and flew the drone. Hobart flew the other with one arm in a sling. Van Dreeves found Sanson's airplane and began a slow cloverleaf pattern from there until he found two Zodiac boats bobbing at a pier. Sanson and Champollion were talking, Champollion baring her teeth at him and raising her bound wrists as one of his large bodyguards lifted her into the boat and strapped her in using a couple of round turns around her waist and synching the line through a rubber cleat. Van Dreeves followed the Zodiac as it made the quick trip through the surging swells across the Sea of Dakhla to the castle.

I looked at the feed from the second Raven, which Hobart was flying with the joystick in the office. We used AirMap software to plan the routes but could override them if necessary. Hobart's Raven recorded the violent waves crashing unabated from the Canary Current. He did manage to identify sentries at every guard tower and snipers in the battlements in every cardinal direction.

The drone got close enough to see a group of people on one of the balconies. Huddled together were Secretary of State McHenry, Secretary of Defense Blankenship, Chairman of the Joint Chiefs Rolfing, and National Security Advisor Kidman. They were speaking calmly but with purpose. McHenry seemed to be in charge as she pointed and spoke, then listened, and spoke again. The rest of the group appeared deferential to her. Sanson joined the meeting. There was no sign of Champollion after entering through the castle dock house.

Hobart snapped several screenshots of the meeting and its location in the castle. He then moved his Raven to cover for Van Dreeves as he brought Raven 1 in for recharge. As the field of view switched, Hobart studied the northeast side of the castle where the waters were not as violent.

"Okay, we go in there," I said. Van Dreeves was outside recovering the drone. Zoey helped him while Hobart and I were talking in the office.

"It's just you and Randy, boss. No one else is capable," Hobart said. "Watch out for my brother."

I'll never forget Hobart's sorrowful eyes as he spoke to me. That we had persisted this long as a team, whole and healthy, was a miracle. We knew that we were tempting fate every day we continued. Was this the day everything would come undone? Unravel completely?

"I've always had everyone's back, Joe. You know that. We're all hurting right now. So, yes, it's just me and Randy."

"That's my point. We've lost Sally. Is more risk worth it? Knowing all these people are just double-crossing everyone, looking out for their self-interests?" He pointed at the senior leadership of the government as he spoke.

"I want Sanson. I want every son of a bitch that has turned on our country. If we don't defend it, who will?"

"We will, boss, but Jesus, the entire cabinet? Is there a country left to defend?"

"We do what needs to be done," I said. It was a dilemma, though. What if this was just a routine meeting? What if the president had sanctioned this? What if someone had hijacked her burner? What did the Constitution call for? We had raised our right hands to support and defend the Constitution, not elected or unelected bureaucrats.

We did have a country to defend. People that were counting on us. Van Dreeves downloaded a copy of the castle blueprint onto his tablet, and we studied it for a few minutes. There was a giant ballroom in the middle, with two sets of steps ascending to internal balconies that led to a series of rooms around the perimeter of the castle. President Campbell could be held in any of them if she was being held at all.

This was a perfect mission for SEAL Team Six or Delta Force. I had at my disposal the most elite soldiers in the world but could not risk the orders process to activate them or that their mission wouldn't be subverted by the sedition that was clearly taking place at the highest levels of government. The last thing I wanted was to order my entire JSOC force into action and have to fight against them because some bureaucrat thought they knew what was best for the country.

"They could be held here," I said, pointing at the lines of rooms above the open ballroom, "or here." There were two rooms in the basement area, properly called a dungeon given the age of this castle.

As we watched the monitor, Sanson appeared on the balcony with Defense Minister Gambeau and General Liang dressed in a green uniform. An aide was carrying champagne glasses and two bottles on a tray. His nervous eyes flitted from dignitary to dignitary. He poured glasses, and each person grabbed a flute.

Liang muttered something, and they all raised their glasses, touched the rims, and then drank. They laughed and smiled, chatting with each other, placing hands on shoulders, and took a few selfies with smartphones.

A far cry from the death and destruction in Loudoun County, Virginia, or the Eye of Africa.

McHenry led the team back into the stairwell that fed the crow's nest where they had just toasted. Beneath the crow's nest was a large, extended balcony that overlooked the swirling ocean point.

Some functionaries were setting up lights atop tripods. Someone else was wheeling a television camera onto the balcony. Against the back wall, where the sea was spraying white foam, a blacksmith was hammering pitons into the railing.

Through the glass doors that led to the second-floor landing, Sanson had taken up position behind President Campbell. As they stepped through the open double doors, Sanson's saber sheath bounced against the threshold.

President Campbell's hands were tied behind her back.

42

"WE HAVE TO GO now," I said.

"It's an hour to sunset," Van Dreeves countered.

"By the time we're there, it will be dark."

"Roger, boss."

We moved quickly from the back of the hangar and to the small pier maybe one hundred meters from the building. Scaling down a steep bank, we boarded a Zodiac Hurricane with GPS mounted on top and a .50-caliber machine gun stationed in the center. Two Moroccan Special Forces soldiers were standing on the pier. They were dressed in black cargo pants and black long-sleeve shirts with black outer tactical vests and black balaclavas. One carried an FR-F2 French sniper rifle and the other a Barrett .50-caliber sniper rifle.

I said, "Farouk," and the lead soldier said, "Ahmed."

With bona fides exchanged, we boarded the Zodiac, which quietly and slowly departed the pier as if the Moroccan troops were also urging the sun to set. They took a deliberate wide berth of the shore and entered the Sea of Dakhla about three miles in the middle.

"Farouk was my best friend," the soldier steering the boat said.

"He was a good man. The best," I offered.

"We'll kill for him," he said.

"You most likely will have to."

"I'm Lokmane. This quiet one is Samir."

"Sinclair and Van Dreeves here," I said.

"We know who you are. Farouk told us many stories about both of you and Joe Hobart. We are sorry about Colonel McCool, also."

Van Dreeves looked away. I wondered if he would be able to focus enough. I figured either he would be so fueled by anger at Sanson that he would be motivated to follow through, or his loss would overwhelm him to incapacitation.

As if reading my mind, Van Dreeves said, "Boss, I'm okay. Let's get this done. For Sally."

"For Sally," I said.

A few minutes passed with us drifting in the water when Hobart radioed us. "Joe's up on the net," I said, pointing at my earpiece.

The wind rippled the water, and we continued to drift under minimal power. Once the sun was dipping into the southwestern horizon of the Atlantic Ocean, Lokmane tilted the throttle forward and marginally increased the speed.

The shoreline crept by in the distance. Looming high above the horizon was the castle, right angles and varying elevations jutting upward. Like something out of a horror show, the night completely enveloped the citadel as end-of-evening nautical twilight extinguished all light.

"Now," Lokmane said. "Perfect darkness."

The engine revved some more, still quietly buzzing beneath the ocean's surface. Cool sea mist sprayed our faces as we skipped along the water. We passed a few fishing boats, men pulling in nets beneath spotlights and completely focused on their haul. As we neared the castle, the riptide was strong. The open ocean funneled into the gulf around the point and sucked the water in the center of the channel. Large rocks guarded the shoreline like jagged teeth. Samir lay on the front of the Zodiac, looking through his nightscope. Van Dreeves and I adjusted our refreshed IVAS.

"We will cut the power to the castle when you give the word. We are up on your comms net," Lokmane said.

He slowed the Zodiac to a stall, and we drifted with the rip, which pulled us parallel to the shoreline and then released us from its grip maybe fifty meters from an opening in the rock formation. Lokmane slipped a trolling motor over the bow, and it purred, pulling us silently into a cordoned cove, where Sanson's boat sat empty.

Two coughs from Samir's silenced FA2 sniper rifle dropped two men who were standing on the dock. We had scant time to get to their communications equipment and prevent them from talking if either were wounded. Seconds later, Van Dreeves was scaling the dock while Samir was tying off the line to the pier. Van Dreeves confirmed Samir's shots had killed both men.

"One MSS and one DGSE," Van Dreeves whispered. MSS was the Chinese Ministry of State Security, the rough equivalent to the United States' Secret Service. What we saw on the battlement with the Raven drone meshed with what we were seeing here: Chinese and French teamwork. It was a consistent theme from the very beginning. Sanson and the Chinese were paired in a massive ruse to provide satellite imagery top cover for the rapid installation of the Chinese GLINTS. All the lock's tumblers were falling into place now.

"Thirty minutes, we are gone," Lokmane said.

"Roger that."

After removing the communications devices of the guards, Van Dreeves and I moved into the dark recess of an alcove, which required a scan of a chip card. Van Dreeves had secured both sets of identity markers from the guards and used one card to scan us both into the hallway. The dim red light turned green, and a sharp beep sounded once, followed by the unlocking of the door.

We were in. The air was damp and musty. The contrast from the surging waves and rip currents to the still confines of the castle tunnel was stark.

The stone hallway led to an iron-bar gate that required another keypad entry, which Van Dreeves buzzed us through. The blueprint had shown two large rooms off this hallway, and the first was empty, save a few marketing materials, such as signs and brochures, a few tables, and scattered chairs.

The second room was piled with dead bodies. I watched the hallway as Van Dreeves counted each person.

"Four Secret Service. Bullet wounds to the head. Hands behind the back. A few staffers. Don't recognize any of them. Maybe the chief of staff. Dreads around the bullet hole in his head. He looks familiar. Maybe the DNI, too. All executed. President not here. Champollion not here. Assuming other cabinet members still up top. No clue on president."

"Infinity is missing . . . Infinity is missing . . ."

The earpiece had popped out of one of the dead agent's ears, and a tinny voice kept whispering, "Infinity is missing . . . Infinity is missing . . ."

President Campbell often spoke about her childhood growing up on the exclusive Figure Eight Island just north of Wilmington, North Carolina. As a child, she playfully called it "Infinity Island," because on the map, the landmass looked more like a tilted infinity symbol. *The Washington Post* had referenced this fact in one of many profiles on her, quoting her, "Yes, Infinity Island is my happy place." Upon election to the presidency, the Secret Service had assigned her the call sign Infinity.

The voice was scratchy and removed from the microphone on the sending end of the communication. It was impossible to determine if it was male or female. Was it President Campbell herself? Her bodyguard?

Van Dreeves removed the device and set it up on himself while I did the same with the other dead agent's equipment. I stuffed the earpiece in my pocket so that I could continue to communicate with our throat microphones and earpieces yet have access to the Secret Service system if needed.

Backing out of the kill room, we found a stairway that led up to the ballroom level, where we expected the main force to be. The door at the top required another keypad swipe, and evidently, the security teams had leaned upon two guards at the pier to secure the bottom half of the castle. Van Dreeves swiped the card and slowly pushed the heavy oak and wrought iron door open. It creaked on old hinges and opened to a dark, motionless ballroom, save a rat skittering along the stone floor, searching for scraps.

Checking at every juncture for cameras, we found no obvious signs of fiber optics or security alarms. I was beginning to think this was a baited ambush when a light switched on behind the ballroom. Beyond that large expanse was a balcony that overlooked Point Dakhla with its crashing seas and vicious rip currents.

Two men moved quickly through the balcony doors and into the ballroom. They were husky, shoulders and arms bursting at the seams of their suit coats. More of

Sanson's men, I presumed. Pistols in their hands, the men darted directly toward us, possibly having been alerted after failing a radio check with the pier security force.

We had moved away from the door behind a long dining table with ornate high-backed chairs. A large chandelier hung precariously above the table, suspended from the castle ceiling. Light skidded from beneath the doors on the interior balcony above us and from the exterior balcony to our two o'clock position.

The men spun around, looking upward and in all directions as they moved in a two-person rotating huddle toward the basement door. Van Dreeves nodded at the large iron hinged locking bar and two U-bolts on either side of the jamb. Concerned that dead bodies on the dance floor might become an issue, as soon as the lead man opened the door, I shot the guard facing the ballroom. Van Dreeves raced the ten meters to the slumping man, caught him, fired two silenced shots behind the door, presumably hitting the lead man. He tossed the dead man he was holding into the stairwell and disappeared for thirty seconds. Reappearing, he closed the door and slid the locking bar across the door.

That avenue was secure, and we now had four fewer bodyguards to concern ourselves with.

One of the information gaps we had was knowing who had departed Air Force One and who had remained. We had two dead Secret Service agents and four staffers in the kill room. How many were ordinarily on the detail when you had a plane full of administration types wanting to escape what they knew was coming?

We had to assume that the French and Chinese joint venture had disposed of everyone they didn't need at the beginning of this operation. Who remained? Where was President Campbell? Killing her would simply put the vice president in charge. But in charge of what? A country that had signed a treaty subordinating itself to a global entity?

"Saving Infinity is the mission," I said to Van Dreeves. The others heard my statement, as well.

Hobart said, "Roger. Infinity is the objective. Drones showing activity on middle balcony. Crow's nest empty. Security repositioning."

We raced up the northern staircase that curled from the center of the ballroom to the far edge of the interior balcony. I scaled the marble steps two at a time, my five-decade-old body taking the punishment but not without complaint. Adrenaline fueled me as I spun to the right and fired twice at two Chinese guards who had repositioned from the roof. Hobart's heads-up had made us extra alert to new defenses coming our way. To continue moving and keeping the enemy off guard was the key to sustaining momentum.

Van Dreeves fired twice at two men across the interior landing. I continued searching the long hall to the north. For the first time, the guards fired, and their weapons were not silenced. Loud booms echoed in the cavernous building.

All surprise was lost as we fired and maneuvered our way to the balcony, where stadium lights shone down on a small gaggle in the center of the curving veranda. White foam sprayed upward from the crashing waves. The roar of the sea drowned out many of the shouts. Gunfire rained down on our position. We held our fire as we sought cover behind the interior wall separating the main castle and the balcony.

"Sinclair!"

It was Sanson's voice.

"Sinclair. Show yourself!"

I nodded at Van Dreeves, who remained in place as I slowly stepped into view. President Campbell and

Evelyn Champollion were kneeling with their backs to the stone railing. Seawater sprayed against their faces. Sanson stood behind them, saber in hand. To his right was a security guard with an AK-47, the source of the initial fire from the balcony. To their right were three tech moguls sipping from long-stemmed champagne glasses and chatting with Blankenship, Kidman, Rolfing, and McHenry, all of whom had stopped smiling. The National Command Authority had conspired against the president.

"I want you to watch this with the rest of the world!"

A camera was set up with bright lights shining onto them. To the side was General Liang on the phone, barking something.

"He's negotiating, Garrett! He's telling the Senate to take the deal, or we die!" Champollion shouted. She was drenched. Her hair was matted to her forehead. Her clothes clung to her body. Campbell was also in disarray, struggling against the binds around her wrists.

"Shut up!" Sanson said.

The only person I had not seen was Gambeau. Was he already dead? With the endgame being U.S. subservience to China and an international order, it appeared that the French were the useful idiots to China until the very end.

"Boss," Van Dreeves said.

I felt a presence at my back and turned slightly.

"It's time to drop the weapons. Both of you," Gambeau said.

I turned, and Gambeau plus one Chinese soldier and a French DGSE bodyguard were brandishing pistols at Van Dreeves and me. There was no escape. We were surrounded.

We lowered our weapons to the floor and stepped onto the balcony, which was when all hell broke loose.

43

THE DAGGER TEAM HAD been my heart and soul for so many years. I had led and mentored these men and women, who always demonstrated their initiative and drive without my telling them what to do.

One of my favorite Thomas Wolfe quotes was, "I put the relation of a fine teacher to a student just below the relation of a mother to a son." The investment I had made in the relationships with my team were everything to me. It was why Melissa and I had bought the large plat of land and provided the space for their eternal resting places. They were family.

And family always mattered. Always came to the rescue. It was why we had pursued Zoey into the middle of the Sahara.

We left no one behind or would die trying not to. Because nothing else mattered in life. Family and teammates. The world is a brutal place full of selfish and dishonest charlatans, as we were seeing at this moment, and all we could do was take care of one another. Even if bureaucrats were giving away the country so many had fought so hard to preserve, the best we could do was execute our mission. Even if those bureaucrats were leaking false information about me to the press, dehumanizing me in preparation for a planned fall from grace.

We still had to execute our mission. We still had to take care of one another.

It was all we had.

When West said into my earpiece, and I could hear the Beast's rotor blades chopping in the background as he spoke, "Dagger Six, this is Falcon Six coming in hot in McCool's Beast," I was never prouder of my team. They had rallied.

The sound of the helicopter caused everyone on the balcony to crane their heads upward for the briefest second. From the Beast's cargo bay, Hobart shined a high-intensity searchlight onto the scene as Van Dreeves spun and did a low kick on the French guard nearest him. I stepped to the side and ratcheted an elbow into the nose of the Chinese guard and did a simple armlock to snap his elbow against its joint and catch his pistol before it fell.

I turned and ran toward Campbell and Champollion, who had fallen to the slate floor of the balcony as Sanson's blade whisked over their heads. Fearing the big man could take multiple bullets and still complete his task, I dove headlong into his large body, bracing him against the railing, where a wave crashed and spit salt water in my eyes. Because I was hugging him tightly, he was unable to maneuver his unwieldy saber sufficiently to gain any leverage for a decent blow.

Van Dreeves was busy behind me as Hobart kept the light shining on the balcony. Sanson pounded my back with both fists wrapped around the saber grip. Its guard had a sharp finial that pierced the flesh of my back and dug into my ribs. I continued to bear-hug him and lifted him high off the ground like a wrestler doing a suplex. The stone rail dug into my back as I leaned against it. Rotor wash seemed to push me to the side even though I was holding a 250-pound man in the death grip of my life.

People were shouting words I couldn't understand when Sanson's eyes grew wide. I was lying flat on the two-foot-wide railing now, balanced there like a seesaw with my feet barely touching the balcony floor. Sanson's motion with the saber stopped, as it might propel us over the railing into the rocks and ocean below. Instead, he attempted a deft maneuver to flip the saber in his hand so that it was pointed downward. The prop wash, though, blew the blade a fraction off course from where his hand expected it to be.

The shining tip arced above me, and it nosed downward directly toward my forehead, which I turned at the last second. The executioner scrambled backward and attempted a simple maneuver to push me over the rail, but I was already moving, lunging for the sword, to no avail. Sanson accidentally kicked the damaged blade as he rolled in front of me. I retrieved my Blackhawk knife and popped it open as he swept up with the saber, this time successfully grabbing it.

In my attempt to parry his thrust, I again leaned over the rail and used my left arm to thwart his wrecking-ball fists. His momentum carried him forward into me like a baseball batter taking a home run swing, and we both rolled over the railing.

My only real concern about the eighty-foot fall was not knowing what lay beneath. I was either going to be split open on the rocks or continue the fight in the swirling seas of Dakhla Point. I managed to hang on to my knife as we plunged into the water. Sanson was at least fifty pounds heavier than I was and landed with a cannonball splash that had a secondary explosion of water upward. I entered the water headfirst, not an optimal angle, but quickly righted myself.

The water was black and swirling. It was difficult to tell the difference between human movement and a riptide or swell. The only distinction from the black void were bubbles that swirled in the wake of Sanson's overhead chop with the blade. I was deep enough that the glancing blow didn't strike hard, but it did strike. My left shoulder ached and was bleeding.

The momentum had carried him forward, presenting his upper-left back to me as he attempted to scramble and retrieve the sword that had slipped his grip. Three quick jabs with the knife into his shoulder caused him to reach up with an open right hand. I allowed him to clasp the blade, which he could not see, then raked it deep into his palm. His face contorted painfully as I quickly stabbed him several more times in the neck and torso. The water slowed my movement, but it was the same for him.

He attempted to lift the saber with his left hand, the salt water no doubt stinging his wounded right hand. The movement was cumbersome. I was almost out of oxygen, but I didn't dare lose sight of him. My lungs were aching for air. My brain was shutting down, and he must have noticed, because he dropped his sword and tugged me down with him.

I stabbed at his hands, connected some, and missed some. Kicking my leg free, I thought of Sly Morgan and the pain Zoey would endure throughout her life not having him around. I thought of Farouk and his selfless acts to serve us and his country. And I thought of Colonel Sally McCool, who had given her life for me and our team and who had died at Sanson's blade. She gave me this opportunity to execute this mission and protect our nation.

Sally helped me find one final surge of adrenaline to fuel my move to lace my arm around his torso and drag the knife deep into his neck.

If I could have cut off his head, I would have. As it was, hands were pulling me to the surface, and then I blacked out.

44

FIGURE EIGHT ISLAND IN the spring is probably one of the most peaceful places on earth. Sea oats bent gently with the fresh breeze off the Atlantic Ocean. The large homes were dispersed well enough to provide ample privacy. The gate on the other side of the bridge kept the media at bay, for now.

Jimmy Rawl, a childhood friend of mine from Fayetteville, had done okay in life, allowing him to buy two lots, one on the oceanfront and one on the sound, bisected only by the single road on the island. At the south end, we were alone, save a few Secret Service personnel who blended with the terrain around the house next door.

"That video saved your ass, boss," Hobart said.

"Needed saving," I said.

The cameras had kept rolling during the action, catching me saving the president as well as Van Dreeves then securing and protecting the president, warding off the tech moguls and cabinet members until they entered a seaplane and flew to the airport, escaping in their jets. So far, none of them had been held accountable for even being there, claiming they thought they were participating in a historic deal for world peace.

Hobart was wearing jeans and a T-shirt with his arm in a sling. Zoey was next to him wearing a Duke University sweatshirt and jeans. Van Dreeves was in a 4 mm wet suit holding an urn full of McCool's ashes. Jake Mahegan was also in a wet suit, sitting at the counter, staring out of the window, watching the waves, thinking of Sally and his buddy Van Dreeves, no doubt.

A knock on the door preceded a tall man entering the house and sweeping from left to right and top to bottom.

"Can we hurry this shit up?" Van Dreeves said. "I've got something to do."

"It can wait ten minutes, Randy," I said.

Mahegan nodded, still looking at the ocean and horizon. We could have used him on this mission, and maybe his presence here today meant he was coming back.

"Anyone else in the house?" the Secret Service agent asked.

"No," I said. "Not that I'm aware of, anyway." Which wasn't what he wanted to hear after the events of the last few days.

"Are any of you armed?" he asked.

"All of us, I think," I said. "I'm firing anyone who's not."

"I'm going to need you to hand over your weapons," he said.

There was something in his voice that was the tiniest bit off. Maybe he had rehearsed his line too many times, but I removed my Beretta and aimed it at him.

"I'm thinking that's not such a good idea," I said.

He backed up a step and said, "Protocol."

"Not happening."

"George, get the fuck out of here," President Campbell said.

She walked in with two bodyguards by her side and the enchanting Evelyn Champollion in tow. Both were casually dressed in slacks and sweaters with their hair pulled back in ponytails. Champollion had her Australian breezer hat on.

They sat down, and Campbell said, "First, I can't express how sorry I am about Colonel McCool."

We listened as she continued, "I've had her submitted for a Medal of Honor. I know that is meaningless compared to the loss you've suffered, Randy. And your actions that night. Protecting Evelyn and me. I can't ever express my gratitude. You literally saved our lives." Her eyes stared at Van Dreeves and then dropped to the urn.

"Dagger has served me well as a discreet team. A team I can count on, and count on you I did. I owe all of you, and Sally, my life."

Van Dreeves stared at the floor and pulled the urn a bit closer to his chest.

"I can't ever thank you enough. Garrett, when you provided me everything on the flash drive, I couldn't really believe what I had seen. The depths the cabinet went to overthrow the presidency are hard to believe. We're still digging through the layers of people involved. And, Zoey, the bravery you showed exposing yourself to the dangers you knew you would face, just so Dagger could find Sanson, who would lead you to the Chinese hypersonic targeting location. I'm going to award you the Presidential Medal of Freedom."

"I don't want it," she said. "Give it to my dad."

Campbell paused and nodded. "As you wish. He's more than deserving. His intelligence was the seed that put all of this in motion. Dagger did a great service to our nation."

"We did it for ourselves," I said. "Nothing else. With no support from anyone."

Campbell nodded. "I understand your anger. At me. At the situation. At everything."

"It doesn't matter. Nothing matters other than everyone I care about is right here. Sally's not coming back. She gave her life to you and this nation, but more importantly, she gave it to me and this team."

I was near tears. The emotions were overwhelming. Whatever blocking mechanism I had put in place to help us get through the rest of the mission wasn't strong enough to stop the anguish we were all feeling right now.

Melissa. Sly. Sally. Where did it end?

It was Campbell's turn to look at the floor. She was a politician, but the pilot light of a soul flickered deep in her recesses somewhere.

"You sound like a man at the end of his career, General," Champollion interjected. "I think you're the bravest man I've ever met. It would be a shame for you to leave the service. James Bond never quit, you know."

Her attempt at mild levity during this moment was either awkward or brilliant. We had accomplished so much. Our team was excellent. We needed to move forward with dignity and honor.

"Nobody asked or invited you," I replied. "And frankly, Bond was older."

"And less skilled," Van Dreeves added.

"I'm surprised the Secret Service let you in," I said.

Champollion offered a small smile and a nod.

"She's with me, Garrett. She was DGSE inside the entire thing. She was one of the few senior people that could speak French, Chinese, and English fluently."

"Is that why you dropped a bomb on us?" I asked.

"I didn't know what else to do," she said.

"I could think of a million things other than ordering a MOAB strike," I replied.

Out of the corner of my eyes, I could see my team smirking, trying to maintain their composure. Maybe Champollion had changed the mood, if only mildly.

"Yes, well, you're you, and you're much better at this sort of thing," she said.

"How are your tech buddies and cabinet?" I asked.

"They're either dead or on the run. Evidently, one thought he could stop the madness and got in the way of Sanson's sword. The other two are relocating every day. The media seems to be covering for them enough that it will soon be okay for them to resume their lives. Blankenship and McHenry are holing up in Switzerland, confident the media storm will refocus on the suffering in Virginia. I've spent the last three days with the governor there. It's tragic. Your detainee Malik is in a CIA safe house in North Carolina. And the young lady from the camp, Amina? She's with a host family in Tampa until she figures out what to do."

"Could have been a lot worse," I said.

"Yes. I'm curious what you did with Sanson's body."

"Confirmed he was dead and gave him an Osama bin Laden," Hobart said.

"Very well, we will go with that," Campbell said.

"Is this a 'let me thank the troops' visit or something else?" I asked. Van Dreeves and Mahegan continued to watch the ocean. Zoey and Hobart were focused inward on the conversation.

"I wanted to talk to you about this," she said. She unfolded the piece of paper I had given her a few weeks ago, before all of this happened.

She showed it to me, and I confirmed it was mine.

I will turn myself in to the inspector general after this mission, no questions asked, and go to jail if necessary. My team is innocent in all of this, and my trade is that you give them full immunity in any investigation.

She read it out loud, and my entire team snapped their heads toward me.

Van Dreeves said, "Whiskey Tango Foxtrot, boss."

"Is this still your position?" she asked.

"What's left of my people are safe. It doesn't matter what comes next," I replied.

"You can't do this," Hobart said to the president.

She looked at him with a hawk's stare and said, "I'm the president. I can do whatever I want."

Hobart set his jaw, ready to bark something, but I held up my hands. "She's right," I said.

"Damn right. And that's why I'm tearing this up. I'll give Dagger your next mission after you heal up." She ripped the paper to shreds. "Now walk outside with me, Garrett, please."

After walking into the bathroom and staring at the mirror for a minute, I joined her and Champollion on the beach. Mahegan and Van Dreeves were already paddling out. Van Dreeves had used a bungee cord to secure the urn to his longboard. A spring cold front had whipped through two days ago and kicked up head-high set waves off the island with a mild west breeze to smooth the surface. They were zipping along a rip current in between sets and out beyond the breakers quickly. Zoey and Hobart held hands in the dunes not far away, her head on his shoulder, perhaps feeling lucky, definitely feeling sad.

Hobart nodded at me, pulling me away from Campbell for a moment. He reached into the cargo pocket of his jeans and extracted a sliver of a rock the size of a smartphone. It was gray and worn, like a river rock. I could see etchings on it like someone had used a sharp tool to engrave.

"Is that Greek?" I asked after studying the rock.

"Randy found it in Sally's cargo pants. I think she found it in the tunnel where she was killed. Maybe it was what took her an extra few minutes in the tunnel. Got distracted. Not sure."

"If Sally thought it was important, hang on to it," I said. "And she saved the mission by finding Sanson before he found us."

"Roger that," Hobart replied.

Champollion walked over and looked at it. "This is interesting," she said. "May I take a look?"

I handed her the stone, which she studied for a minute or two without speaking. I lost interest and watched Van Dreeves and Mahegan on their boards, bobbing in the ocean.

"It's a cornerstone," Champollion said. "May I keep it?"

"No. Sally found it. Joe or Randy will keep it."

She handed me the stone back and said, "It's significant. The names of Poseidon's family tree."

"Good," I said. I handed the stone back to Hobart. "You and Randy figure out what to do with this. Always respect Sally's memory."

President Campbell joined us and said, "Collecting rocks now?"

"Something like that," I replied, then changed the topic by asking, "How close was it?" The four hypersonic missiles we had dunked in the ocean had missed their New York City targets by seconds.

"It's still close. The threat hasn't gone away," Champollion said. "It's not safe for me back in France. The world is changing. I'm afraid much larger missions lie in the future. CUSP is still a thing. We avoided this disaster, but we didn't eliminate the threat."

As I'd suspected. I watched Van Dreeves and Mahegan sit in the waves, lines of swells on the horizon maybe a minute or two out. They pulled their boards close together and bowed their heads in prayer. Van Dreeves and Mahegan were both spiritual men with a deep connection to nature. Van Dreeves held the urn high above his head as Mahegan reached out and steadied his body and board in the surf. I bowed my head, as did the others.

Van Dreeves opened and tilted the urn, ashes swirling into the wind, some floating upward into the sky and others falling into the ocean, probably how McCool would have wanted it.

Van Dreeves handed Mahegan the empty urn and then paddled into and popped up on the first set wave with ease. He carved a line on the face as the much larger Mahegan followed on a longboard, low and slow, balancing the urn. Soon, they were a couple of hundred meters up the beach, peeling off the wave.

I loved my team with all my being. And I loved the country that made us who we are. I couldn't say no to a president who was asking me to do my duty, no matter the risk, even if it meant losing Sly and McCool and maybe others to come.

Mahegan had said, "Better to die a warrior than grow old." Sly had asked for that to be on his tombstone.

Sally had died a warrior. So had Sly. There was some comfort in that.

I looked at Zoey, and Hobart nodded. They gave me reluctant smiles, perhaps the best it would ever get in the future. Zoey was no doubt processing losing her father and the fact that she had been the vanguard on this ultra-classified mission to stop China. The mission that led to Sally's ultimate death. There was no taking that back, no matter how much we wished she might have lived.

"Boss?" Hobart said, approaching me. The stiff off-shore wind tousled Zoey's black hair as she followed him, her arm looped through his. "Can I have a minute?"

"Of course," I said. "Madam President. Ms. Champollion. Will you give us a moment?"

The two ladies stepped slowly through the dunes until they were a respectable distance away.

"I just wanted to ask . . ." He fumbled with the words. I had an idea what he might be wishing to discuss. After all the death and destruction we had faced in the last twenty-five years plus, I figured he wanted something to anchor him. Losing Sally delivered a new reality to our doorsteps. When coupled with the perpetual duplicity of senior government officials, we had to ask ourselves if we weren't pawns in some larger scheme. The question was, did we wish to participate in the political dance?

"What is it, Joe?"

"With Sly gone—I mean, he's always with us, but still gone."

"I understand," I said.

"You being Zoey's godfather and all . . ."

This was not what I was expecting. I smiled. "Nothing would make me happier, Joe."

"I need to do this formally. It's important," he said.

I nodded.

"Will you allow me to take Zoey's hand in marriage?"

I looked at Zoey. Her eyes had brightened but with

an expectant eagerness, as if my answer was in question.

"This what you want, Zoey?" I asked.

She nodded rapidly as she wiped away tears and placed a hand on her stomach. "More than anything," she said.

"Joe, you have my blessing . . . as long as . . ."

"What?" he asked.

I looked at Zoey's hand on her stomach, as if protecting something.

Zoey caught my eyes and broke into a big grin, nodding and saying, "Yes, General, I'm pregnant."

"As long as you name the baby Sally if it's a girl and Sylvester if it's a boy, then I approve," I said.

They both laughed. Hobart's eyes misted for the first time I had ever noticed. They hugged and kissed. The sea oats danced in celebration.

"Sally Sylvester Hobart it is," Zoey said. "Syl for short."

I don't know why, but her comment struck an emotional chord within me. That they could find a path forward through love and new life. Maybe *good wins,* after all?

Van Dreeves and Mahegan stepped out of the ocean carrying their boards and Sally's urn. Van Dreeves stopped and watched us. He dropped his head, probably thinking about what life might have been with Sally, raising a family. Mahegan watched his friend, then put an arm around him. Van Dreeves nodded, shook it off, and then walked up to us with a smile.

"This mean what I think it does?" he asked.

"Yes, bro," Hobart said.

"Randy," Zoey said. She stopped short of saying anything else. There was nothing she could say. Instead, she hugged him, and they wept together. Campbell and Champollion watched briefly from an adjacent dune and turned around to walk back to Campbell's house.

Quick movements flashed in my periphery. Black windbreakers with gold letters. Rifles drawn. Coming at us from both sides.

"Hands up! FBI!"

I drew my weapon.

ACKNOWLEDGMENTS

I DEDICATED THIS novel to my parents because they instilled in me a desire, if not an obligation, to serve our country in whatever capacity I could. It is that voice that I think speaks through Garrett Sinclair—an earnest duty to serve.

We lost Dad June 11, 2021, at ninety-one years old, and this is my first book published since his death. My mother left us November 26, 2017, at ninety. The son of Italian immigrants who established a bricklaying business in Detroit in the 1920s, Dad was a high school football coach and thirty-year state delegate in Virginia. Mom was the daughter of a lifelong teacher and a merchant who owned the corner store in Stanardsville, Virginia, where she grew up. The family farm where my parents spent their final years is a mile from Mom's birthplace on Main Street and near where they met while teaching public school in Albemarle County. They were married for sixty-two years until Mom's passing.

On June 11, 2021, I had planned a golf outing with Dad, our first time since COVID struck nearly sixteen months before. He could still swing a club at ninety-one—ever the athlete as his University of Virginia football and baseball records demonstrated. As we began the two-day trek to the farm to see him, we received alarming notices that Dad's health was declining rapidly. We arrived that afternoon, and my sister, as always, was there by Dad's side. My brother and his wife were racing up from Virginia Beach, their home.

Dad held on long enough for us to tell him what a great man he was and how much we loved him. His grip was signature strong, but he left us a couple hours before midnight on his and my mother's sixty-sixth wedding anniversary.

Both career public school educators, my parents were proud of the books I have written, and this acknowledgment is a simple thank-you to two great people. I appreciate the support of my brother, Bob Tata, who dutifully managed Dad's affairs, and my sister, Kendall Tata, who literally improved my parents' quality of life by a million percent in their final years. Before he passed, one of Dad's former high school football players turned journalist did a feature in *The Virginian-Pilot* on him. At the close, Harry Minium quoted Dad as saying, "Enjoy life while you can. And make sure you take care of your children and your wife. Take good care of them. That's all that really matters."

Life really is that simple.

Sinclair gets that. He talks about family and the crushing emotions of loss. His arc is one of a man fighting to protect the people he loves while still attempting to perform his duty. Today's political chasms and information warfare make that task harder than ever, but the missions continue. Duty gives no respite.

I'm most grateful to my editor, Marc Resnick, who has been a dutiful coach, teacher, mentor, and friend. Like the rest of the Macmillan/St. Martin's team, Marc has been extra supportive during a turbulent past five years and encourages me to continue telling these stories. His stellar editorial assistant, Lily Cronig, is always the voice of reason and juggles all the glass balls effortlessly.

My agent, Scott Miller, continues to coach and mentor me, guiding me in the right direction. I'm thankful for the entire team at Trident Media Agency who row hard for all their authors. It was Scott's idea to create Sinclair as a protagonist, a seasoned senior officer that juggles family, command, and controversy, perhaps uniquely so.

Kaitlin Murphy-Knudsen, my writing coach and proofreader, did her usual fabulous job. She knows my characters as well or better than I do and I'm thankful that she does.

My support team of Laura, Snowy, and Bandit (new addition) put up with my crazy hours and multiple drafts, and I appreciate them more than I can say.

Lastly, you, my readers, make it all worthwhile. My goal is to entertain, and while doing so have you care about the men and women who are engaged in the story. To that end, I hope I succeeded with *Total Empire* and that you enjoyed the narrative. I appreciate your support and look forward to delivering you the next Garrett Sinclair saga.

Read on for a sneak peek at Garrett
Sinclair's next adventure in *The Phalanx Code*,
available soon in hardcover from
St. Martin's Press.

1

NEARLY TWO DAYS INTO the D-Day invasion of Normandy Beach, newly promoted Army Ranger Major Garrett "Coop" Sinclair stood atop Pointe du Hoc with the sun setting behind an American flag snapping in the stiff breeze.

Coop's youthful face was smeared with mud and camouflage on top of three days of beard stubble. His tired eyes stared into the horizon of the undulating Normandy Peninsula as a line of German prisoners, hands laced over their Stahlhelm helmets, walked under guard just beyond the casement Coop's Rangers had captured.

Second Ranger Battalion Commander Lieutenant Colonel James Rudder approached with a young Frenchman in tow.

"The 505th paras are having a hard go of it a few miles from here," Rudder said. "This is Marius. He's with a resistance group that was tasked with guiding us, but he says there're some women and children in trouble up the road. Take five men and go see what's happening. Then come back or we'll come to you, whichever makes sense."

The eager-eyed Frenchman was maybe sixteen years old. He was wearing a black beret and gray herringbone coat. His leather shoes looked ill-suited for the task of guiding Rangers through German defenses. When Marius pointed west, a rhombus-shaped black tattoo flashed inside the wrist of his right hand. It was the same insignia turned on its side, like an elongated baseball diamond, that Coop and the other Rangers wore on the sleeve of their uniforms. The Rangers had been briefed they would be linking up with resistance members and that they should look for the Ranger rhombus-shaped tattoos that signaled they were talking to bona fide allies.

"Rapide! Rapide!" the man said.

"Cool it, Frenchy," Coop said, then to Rudder: "Sir, we're barely hanging on here. If I take five of my men things will get even more dicey."

As if to emphasize Coop's point, machine-gun fire chattered nearby, snapping overhead with white arcs of German tracers etching against the muted purple hues of dusk. Waves of Allied troops continued to pour onto Utah and Omaha beaches below Coop's position.

"We've got this, Coop. If we can't save women and children, what's the point? Now get moving," Rudder said.

"Roger that, Colonel," Coop replied. He'd made his protest and now would follow his commander's orders.

Explosions from the naval artillery blanketing the coastline rumbled. The ground shook. Someone yelled, "Incoming!" and Coop grabbed Marius and dove to the ground, shrapnel whizzing like angry hornets.

"Can't show us the way if you're dead," Coop grumbled.

"Je suis pierre-tranchant," Marius said, holding up

his wrist with the tattoo and pointing at the small black rhombus. *"La pierre est tranchant."*

"Rudder said you're good to go, but thanks for that. Yes, the stone is sharp," Coop said in reply to Marius's offering of bona fides. The planning in Titchfield, England, had called for French resistance members to etch a small Ranger rhombus henna tattoo on the inside of their right wrist and use the phrase "The stone is sharp" when linking up with the Rangers. The French liaison suggested this because the Ranger insignia looked like a "sharp stone."

Coop pulled Marius by his trench coat the way a coach tugs a quarterback into a sideline huddle. He eyed his gaggle of twenty men and gathered his five nearest Rangers, who were cleaning their M1 Garand rifles and licking the inside of combat ration cans, commonly known as "c-rats."

"Special mission, men, let's go," he said. They reassembled their weapons and grabbed their gear without complaint. They had survived the climb up Pointe du Hoc and most likely considered themselves invincible or lucky or both. Coop tucked in behind Marius, who hurried them along a trail that kept the assault on Utah Beach to their immediate rear and right flank. Marius's shoes didn't seem to be an impediment as Coop and his men began running to keep up with the worried Frenchman.

"Rapide! Rapide!" Marius whispered over his shoulder, loud enough for the men to hear.

It was the second night of the invasion. Coop and his men had been operating continuously. Artillery rained down. Naval ships bombed the coast without precision. Machine-gun fire chattered. Lead pinged off thousands of landing craft in Seine Bay, which fronted Normandy Beach, sounding like a symphony from hell.

Following a drainage gulley from north to south, Marius led Coop and his team to a small shelter. Stemming from the outbuilding was a worn path to the town. By now, Coop could hear shrieks louder than any artillery explosion or rifle fire. The plaintive cries of women and children became his beacon in the night.

Coop grabbed Marius by the shoulder and said, "We've got it from here."

Marius pointed at a group of German soldiers herding women and children into the basement of a French farmhouse situated on a sloping ridge. The box frame of the house fronted the high ground while the back side offered a generous bottom level dug into the terrain. One of the Germans near the cellar door was holding a jerry can filled with gasoline.

"Follow me, men," Coop said to his Rangers.

Coop and his men charged the German troops, who were shouting, *"Tod durch feurer! Tod durch feurer!"* Death by fire! Death by fire!

Coop fired his M1 Garand rifle until he ran out of ammunition. His teammates provided cover for one another as they took turns charging the Germans. Coop led the assault and stuck his bayonet in the man by the basement door. Another German soldier held the petrol can and a lighter, which he tossed into the doorway leading to the basement just as Coop rammed the butt of his rifle into the man's face.

The flame ignited, burning red and yellow against the angry black sky.

Screams pierced the night as Coop ran into the blazing inferno toward the prisoners inside.

2

I CLOSED MY GRANDFATHER'S World War II combat diary, the ink diffused by tears, the pages covered in dark stains I took to be blood. I ran my finger across the worn cover where he had drawn in pencil the Ranger patch rhombus, a square turned on a point. The pencil had traced and retraced the four sides, as if he had been deep in thought when sketching.

Holding the leather-bound tome in my manacled hands, as if in prayer, I looked up when the guard rattled her baton between the bars of my cell.

"Let's go, Sinclair," Sergeant Robin Calles said. "Going to see the big guy."

I slid the diary beneath my mattress and walked with Calles's baton in my back through the byzantine maze of new and old construction until I was standing in the warden's office, looking through his panoptic window.

The winter sun hung low behind the khaki-colored cornfields, stalks severed and broken; a metaphor for something, I thought. Perhaps the state of the country or even the world. The warden's view looked down upon the prison yard, the razor wire stretching between the guard towers and the bluffs of the Missouri River. The sun's muted, fading hues cast a diminishing glow across the acres of frozen penitentiary land the inmates tended in the spring under the watchful eyes of snipers.

"Inmate Sinclair, why do you think you're still under my charge?" Warden Phillip Smyth asked me.

Smyth was an active-duty full bird colonel. His hair was gelled back Gordon Gekko style. His throwback Army olive-and-tan uniform bulged at all the seams. Tall and thickset, Smyth was a military police officer charged with operating the Fort Leavenworth Disciplinary Barracks, known in the military as "the DB." The DB was a maximum-security prison that held everything from death row inmates who would receive lethal injections to felons who cheated the military supply system by stealing blankets. And then there was me with pending murder charges, among other lesser allegations, to the best of my knowledge. No one had told me. Normally a prisoner was afforded protections of due process but given the atmospherics around my arrest, I'd yet to be charged with a crime.

Smyth stood profile to me, gazing out the same window as if he were posing for a Grant Wood portrait. Instead of the pitchfork of *American Gothic* fame, he held a gnarled and lacquered walking stick in his fleshy right fist, its shiny tip appearing unblemished and pristine. I shifted my gaze from beyond the walls of the prison to Smyth's narrow eyes, which refused to meet mine. His typically arrogant countenance was replaced by something I hadn't seen before. Perhaps, worry?

I had been in this office only once before and that was a year ago when the FBI had delivered me here fresh from an FBI ambush on Figure Eight Island, North Carolina, perhaps baited by the president of the United States herself.

"Warden, I don't know what day it is, much less why I'm in your facility," I replied.

"It's Thursday. President's Day weekend is coming up. A holiday," he said, as if that mattered to me. Finally, he turned and looked at me. "I've been instructed to give you two pieces of information."

He paused, but I said nothing.

"First, your lawyer was found dead yesterday," Smyth said.

My "lawyer" was Charles Green, a family friend of my late grandfather, General Garrett "Coop" Sinclair. Green was a garden-variety attorney who handled everything imaginable in Fayetteville, North Carolina. Before writing a dozen letters to the president and chief of staff of the army about my confinement, to no avail, his most important duty had been handling Coop's estate when my grandfather had passed a few years ago. Coop was a genuine World War II legend, having scaled the cliffs of Pointe du Hoc on D-Day during the Normandy Invasion with the Second Ranger Battalion. Green had smuggled my grandfather's combat diary inside a leather-bound Bible during his one and only visit a year ago.

I shrugged. I had liked Green and knew him mostly from when I was a kid helping Coop work on his cars.

"Our communications department tells me he sent a package for you, which you can have tomorrow," Smyth said.

"Why can't I have it today?" I didn't really care, but I was mildly curious.

He coughed and said, "That's the second piece of information. I've been instructed to release you. Tomorrow, you'll be officially discharged from my facility and the army. The inspector general's office has completed their investigation and made their recommendations to the secretary of defense, who has reported the findings to the president. The president, evidently, showed mercy and granted you a pardon, which allows you to maintain your rank. Your discharge is effective at noon tomorrow. Behave until then and you're free, a retired three-star general. Give me one reason . . . one reason . . . to keep you here, and I will. Understand?"

I stood there motionless. His words were artificial. They didn't resonate. They couldn't be real.

"You're gone tomorrow," Smyth said again. "Discharged. Full pension. Not my choice, but the president is in charge."

I remained motionless and said nothing.

"Sinclair. Do you hear me, inmate Sinclair?"

The volume of his voice cracked the veneer of my protective shield. In prison I felt nothing, believed very little, and said even less.

"One more time, Sinclair. Do you understand me?!"

I didn't respond then, either, but a sense of sorrow washed over me. I'd had nearly a year to contemplate my situation and the likelihood that my career was over, but that didn't make this news any easier to accept. I had never expected a gold watch or farewell party, not even before I'd been secreted to the shadowy confines of the DB. But I had thought this mistake would have been rectified, that they would have cleared my name when I was released. At the very least, I wanted the opportunity to thank my troops and say goodbye to a few friends. Instead, I was being shamefully ushered into the cold winter of Kansas. The finality was incomprehensible.

A year ago, the FBI had swarmed across the sand dunes of Figure Eight Island, North Carolina, and snatched Sergeants Major Joe Hobart, Randy Van Dreeves, and me when we were debriefing the Eye of Africa mission with President Campbell. Somehow my former team member Jake Mahegan had avoided capture. Last I saw, he had a federal agent in a hammerlock as they wrestled on the beach. My money had been on Mahegan, though I had never learned the outcome.

Once a college roommate of my wife and a theoretical friend to me, President Campbell was now trying to salvage what was left of her term and consolidate her political power. Her cabinet had secretly enhanced ties with the Chinese government and some tech moguls, but only she and her team knew their part in the endgame in that relationship. Once someone who had been read on to every special access, code word program in the United States government, I was now just another prisoner and, evidently, a soon-to-be discharged veteran. No charges filed. No trial date set. And now released and retired? I didn't believe what Smyth was saying.

"I'm calling the guards unless you acknowledge that you understand what I just said, inmate Sinclair."

"I do," I said, but I didn't. There was no way it was over, just like that. Either I was being ambushed when I left tomorrow, or I would find an untimely demise this evening in my cell.

"Nothing to say? Your career is over and you're speechless?"

"No farewell party?" I quipped.

Smyth's eyes got distant, and the faintest hint of a smirk turned on his lips.

"I'm sure your peers will think of something," he said. "Golden handcuffs might be fitting, don't you think?"

I caught the flash of a police strobe outside on Route 73, which bordered the military reservation. A gaggle of black-and-white police cars had gathered about a mile away. A spider of intuition crawled along my spine.

I nodded. "Sure. I'd like to notify my kids."

"Tomorrow morning you will be allowed to make

one phone call prior to your departure. In the meantime, Sergeant Calles will escort you to dinner and then back to your cell. And remember, Sinclair, you're still just another inmate doing time while you're in my facility."

"Roger that," I replied.

"Let's go, Sinclair," Sergeant Calles said.

Calles was a big woman with inch-long blond hair on top that was tapered with shears on the sides and back. One day several months ago while working the mail room, I'd overheard her complaining to another guard that she had failed out of the army's challenging Ranger School. Originally from Nebraska, she had chosen military police as her career field, and Fort Leavenworth as her first assignment to be near her home. I respected her straightforward approach to her job and her inmates, but her wanton use of the baton had grown tiresome. In her block, I was just another prisoner, as it should be, though she must have recognized the pressure of housing a three-star general in pretrial confinement.

Prison had not required much of an adjustment for me. I had never taken comfort in the trappings of rank. Having led from the front lines, much to the criticism of some of my peers who saw career progression as a pathway out of danger, I didn't see a wide chasm between a foxhole and a prison cell. Three hots and a cot, as they say. Many had it worse. Who was I to bitch?

With Calles's baton in my back, we departed the command wing of the prison with its big windows full of daylight, shiny floors, and executive furniture. We transitioned back into the dark, depressing catacombs of muted cinder block walls and hydraulic barred doors. I shuffled along until the heavy metal door opened with a hiss and I was standing in the cafeteria line with my fellow inmates.

"General," Private First-Class Johnnie Hooper said. Hooper had been convicted for distributing fentanyl from his barracks room in Fort Hood, Texas.

"Hoop," I replied.

"No talking!" Calles shouted. Her baton plowed into my kidney. I nodded at her as the forty or so prisoners turned and looked at her with hard eyes. I might have been an inmate, but they knew I was an active-duty general. More to the point, I was *their* general. An odd respect emanated from my status and my reputation as a combat warrior.

Not a day went by where there wasn't some rumor about me and my status, especially in relation to the Eye of Africa battle last year. My Dagger team had risked it all to stop China from releasing four or five nuclear hypersonic glide vehicles on the United States and maybe several European cities. The irony was that there had been online traffic, surely fabricated, that implicated my team and me in the Chinese scheme to launch nukes at the United States. The media had portrayed me as the ringleader of the nuclear threat against America. It was preposterous, but the power of the corporate media had half the world believing it to be true. I had transitioned from a shadow warrior leading our nation's finest to support and defend our Constitution, to an infamous prisoner mysteriously held in contravention of that very document.

Because I took no part in social media, I didn't see the volumes of information people told me were being spewed across all the platforms such as Twitter, Facebook, Instagram, billionaire Mitch Drewson's newest app called Shoutter, and LanxPro, tech mogul Aurelius Blanc's app. My fellow inmates tried to keep me up to date with the latest musings about my fate.

A broken man, I was barely interested.

I shuffled forward in the line for food, Calles still at my back. Hooper got his glop, then I held up my tray. With his white hairnet and apron, Private Sam McWhorley looked like a fry cook at McDonald's. Grease-stained white apron. Stringy mustache and beard. Tattoo sleeves on both arms. Hateful sneer on his face. He leaned over and let a long stringy loogie slip between his lips and sucked it back in before it hit the ladle in his hand. He had been a mechanic at Fort Campbell in Kentucky and was here for sexual assault of a fellow soldier. I had been the court-martial convening authority at the time and gave him the maximum punishment. I figured no chow was better than something mixed with his bodily fluids, so I kept shuffling ahead. If there was an inside job to hit me this evening, McWhorley would gladly be the ringleader.

Handing out the sweet tea in plastic cups was Corporal Sonny Jones, a big African American from New Orleans and relatively recent addition to the Disciplinary Barracks population. He put a cup of iced tea on my tray and slid a cheeseburger from who knows where next to it.

"General," he said with a nod. "Hearing news."

"Sonny," I said.

He smiled. A few weeks ago, Jones told me he had posted a long rant about the Eye of Africa battle and how my former Dagger team had saved the country, maybe the world. He said that it was trending on social media and he had used the hashtags #EAB #garrettsinclair #savingamerica.

I sat down and listened to the sounds of chains scraping, men slurping gravy, and guard boots tapping the linoleum floor. The place smelled of decaying meat and disinfectant. I lifted the bun of my cheeseburger after spying a white hair on it. The hair turned out to be a piece of paper with a message:

8 pm tonight. Stay in bed!

I looked at the clock on the wall, which read 7:04 p.m. The clock was circular like we had in Fayetteville Public Schools some forty years ago. It was battery powered and high up on the wall so no one could reach in and use the second hand as a shiv.

In my periphery, I saw McWhorley's hand flash with a kitchen knife. A small group of unfamiliar prisoners gathered maybe twenty meters away near the kitchen entrance. In the opposite direction I noticed Smyth ascend the steps to a small sally port bridge that looked like a church choir balcony. He stared in my direction as the group near the kitchen began walking toward me like a blocking wedge for a kick-off returner on the football field.

I rotated my neck and rolled my shoulders. I ate the cheeseburger and the piece of paper, which went down smoothly with the warm, diluted tea. Was it poisoned? I pushed away from my table and began to stand to confront the aggressors.

"What's that?" Calles demanded. She moved between me and McWhorley's wedge; McWhorley stopped, eyes curious, when Calles inserted herself in the equation. Without her, the battlefield geometry was five to one. After a year of lifting weights, I put my meager prison bank account on me, despite my fifty-two years.

I continued to stand. That was the protocol. If a guard addressed you, standing to pay respects was expected. I was six feet two inches tall, and she was every bit of six feet in her jackboots.

"Cheeseburger, Sergeant," I said. McWhorley's group inched forward, some casting their eyes upward at the bridge where Smyth stood.

"The white thing," she snapped.

"Oh, mayonnaise, I guess. Or maggots. I don't look at it. I just eat it. Like in Ranger school," I said.

Importantly, the inmate chatter claimed that Calles had played college softball at the University of Nebraska. The Ranger School comment was probably unnecessary and resulted in a swing for the fences into my kidneys. I would be pissing blood tonight for sure. Was she the artillery to soften up the target for McWhorley and team?

"You're out of line, Sinclair," she barked in my face. Then she turned to the halted wedge and said through clenched teeth, "Stand down!"

The entire cafeteria had gone silent. The clock ticked loudly. Time froze. McWhorley's wedge was conspicuously motionless, maybe stunned by her intervention.

"Yes, Sergeant," I said.

I was thankful for the interruption, though I wouldn't have minded a good fight right now. Emotionally processing an abrupt halt to a lifetime of service was already challenging, especially from the confines of a maximum-security prison. So, goddamnit, bring it on. Make me a convict and I'll act like one.

As I stood there watching the motionless cafeteria like a narrator walking through a three-dimensional movie freeze-frame, I reverted to my observation training as an army Ranger and special mission unit operator.

McWhorley's knife was a forked garden tool with a wooden handle and tips honed to razor points. The lead man in the attack had a shaved head and tattoos crawling up his neck. He was jacked and the look in his eyes told me he was high on meth. He stood there flexing like a weight lifter who had just bounced a personal best snatch-and-clean on the floor. The two men on either flank of McWhorley were equally muscled. Why they had left the task to the smallest guy in the foursome, McWhorley, was a mystery, but I could guess it was revenge for my sentencing of his rape charge.

I thought of my dead wife, Melissa, and my daughter, Reagan, anger rising again at his crime. Maybe now I could give him an even more proper sentence.

The freeze-frame went from motionless to fast-forward.

The man leading the wedge barreled toward me. Calles attempted to block him but was tossed aside with the flick of the man's left arm. His demonic eyes sparked red with evil. The two flankers protected McWhorley. The thing about fighting someone doped up on amphetamines is that they are all energy and no co-ordination. The army had transitioned to a respectable hand-to-hand combat training regimen about twenty years before in special mission units; we practiced combative techniques almost daily. As the commander, I did "man in the middle" drills where my men would come at me one at a time from a different direction as I stood in the center of the circle they formed.

It was rare that I lost.

My mind roared. *Make me a convict and I'll act like one.*

I let the wedge leader into my personal space, where I immediately clinched him and landed four debilitating knee strikes into his ribs then used his momentum to trip him forward. I spun to find the right-side flanker dueling with Calles, who had rejoined the fray. McWhorley was pushing the left-side flanker with his right hand. I jabbed the left flanker twice as he broke his focus when McWhorley tried to hide behind him. A roundhouse kick snapped his neck to the left, causing him to stand up straight. I used that opening to land two straight kicks to his larynx with my prison boots. As he clasped his neck with both hands, I put the toe of my boot squarely in his crotch. He doubled over, whereupon I laced my fingers and pulled his head down with my hands and drove my knee into his face, breaking his nose, blood spraying everywhere.

With the wedge breaker and flankers preoccupied, McWhorley skittered haplessly toward me with his modified garden tool. As the wiry, skinny meth head and rapist lunged at me, my hand was like a rattlesnake, latching onto his wrist and twisting his arm upward. I did a sweeping back kick, landing him on the table where I had been eating. Drinks and food exploded onto the chairs and floor. I wrapped my hand like a vise around his left fist holding the weapon and slowly arced it toward his face. The two shiny, sharpened prongs were closing with his eyes. His breath smelled like a dead rat in a week-old garbage pail of rotting food. Piss spread on his orange jumpsuit, and I smelled feces.

I was laser focused on his scared pupils flitting about, looking for help. By now the entire cafeteria full of convicts was chanting, "Sinclair! Sinclair! Sinclair!"

As I slowly lowered his resisting fist toward his face, I whispered into the noise, "Come at me, you little bitch? I'm not some fourteen-year-old girl."

Calles shouted, "Sinclair, stand down!" Two guards pulled at me with the weapon scraping McWhorley's cheek. "Stand down! Stand down!"

As two beefy military police prison guards muscled me away from McWhorley, I released his fist that had been resisting. The weapon shot forward and scraped my biceps as the guards held me in place, almost as if they wanted to do the wedge breaker's job and make me a target. Calles intervened and flung

McWhorley up against the wall where two more military police guards secured him and the garden tool.

"Sinclair, you're headed to solitary!" Calles shouted as she pushed me through the crowd.

Smyth bellowed from the bridge, "Sinclair! You couldn't even behave for an hour?" Then, "Sergeant Calles, make sure inmate Sinclair is properly treated in solitary."

"Roger that, sir," she said. Another demonstrative thud with the baton drew a thin-lipped smile from Smyth. Pain rocketed through my back into my shoulder blades and up my spine into the base of my skull.

"You're clearly a danger, Sinclair. I'll be making a report posthaste," Smyth said. There was satisfaction in his voice. I wasn't sure if he wanted me dead or mixed up in a fight so he could try to overturn my release. Ankles chained and wrists handcuffed, I shuffled along with Calles, who was shouting down each corridor, "Solitary coming through!"

We arrived in the solitary wing where a guard I had never seen before opened the door and shoved me in, but not before Calle's baton landed one more blow on my bruised back. She tossed a bottle of Betadine and some gauze on the concrete slab that passed for a bed.

"Get on the bed and don't move other than patching yourself up. Understand?" Calles said.

I nodded.

"I asked you a question, inmate. Do you understand that for the next thirty minutes you are confined to that bed?"

As if solitary wasn't enough, now she wanted me in a specific location in a cell isolated from the rest of the prison.

"Yes, Sergeant," I said as if I was a young lieutenant attending basic training.

The heavy door closed with a metallic clank, the lock snapping with a hydraulic whisper.

I had no wristwatch, phone, or wall clock. The solitary room was simple, but bigger than I expected. It was maybe twenty-five feet wide. A concrete slab on the left was covered with a threadbare blanket and thin feather pillow dotted with the cavity drool of hundreds of previous inmates. There was a concrete divider maybe three feet wide at the head of the bed. A toilet on the right. No lid. No seat. Just a hole.

I sat on the bed, leaned against the cinder block wall, and thought about the note on my cheeseburger.

8 pm tonight. Stay in bed!

The clock in my head told me I had twenty-two minutes to go.

Whatever was supposed to happen at 8:00 p.m., I was in a different location than anyone might expect me to be. It could have been that Smyth preferred I be assassinated here in solitary since the attempt in the dining facility had not panned out. Or it may have been a warning from a friend to protect me from some violent act that was happening at the prison that night. Or it might have been something random, like a gathering to discuss potential informal inmate leadership moves, rule changes, or the latest social media screed about me.

I was breathing rapidly from the exertion and checked myself the way I would do after any airborne or combat operation. Feet, legs, torso, face, neck, skull. Check. Right arm bleeding but not terribly. My back was hurting from Calles's baseball swings, but there was nothing I could do about that. My lungs were burning from the aerobic exercise, but that felt good. Other than my arm and back, I was fine. I picked up the Betadine and checked the laceration. I peeled away the jumpsuit as best I could, revealing two parallel gashes across my right biceps muscle. Blood was seeping. I dabbed at it with the gauze, then poured the purple disinfectant all over my arm. Once the stinging subsided, I poured more, then wrapped my arm in gauze, which quickly soaked up the blood and medicine.

I used my teeth and cuffed hands to tie the gauze, then lay down on the bed, curious why Calles had instructed me to be in that one spot. My primal defenses were on high alert after the fight and Smyth's obvious manipulation. Was there a bomb under the bed? Cage fight with another inmate? What was the play?

A small camera was situated in the top right-hand corner of the cell, its smoky gray globe concealing the actual lens. Was it off or "malfunctioning"? If everything was on the level, I figured I should probably stay where I was unless I wanted more shots to the kidneys.

After twenty minutes of reflection about Sally Mc-Cool, Joe Hobart, and Randy Van Dreeves, the heart of my Dagger team, my head shot up.

Three knocks on the outer wall, not the door, preceded a blast in the far opposite corner of the cell, blowing inward. Smoke and debris ricocheted around the cell, the concrete divider at my head absorbing some of the blast. A hole the size of a car was left in its wake. Alarms sounded. Lights flashed. Sprinklers sprayed.

Through the smoke and haze, Jake Mahegan stepped into the opening wearing night vision goggles and carrying enough weapons for both of us.

He used a set of bolt cutters to snap my ankle chains and handcuffs, handed me a Beretta pistol, and said, "Follow me, boss."